Wilds of Wonder

STOLEN CROWNS
BOOK FOUR

TEE HARLOWE

Introduction

If you'd like access to a free fantasy romance novella, plus exclusive content like bonus scenes, behind-the-scenes looks, and early sneak peeks at character art and cover reveals, then click here to subscribe to my newsletter or visit www.teeharlowe.com.

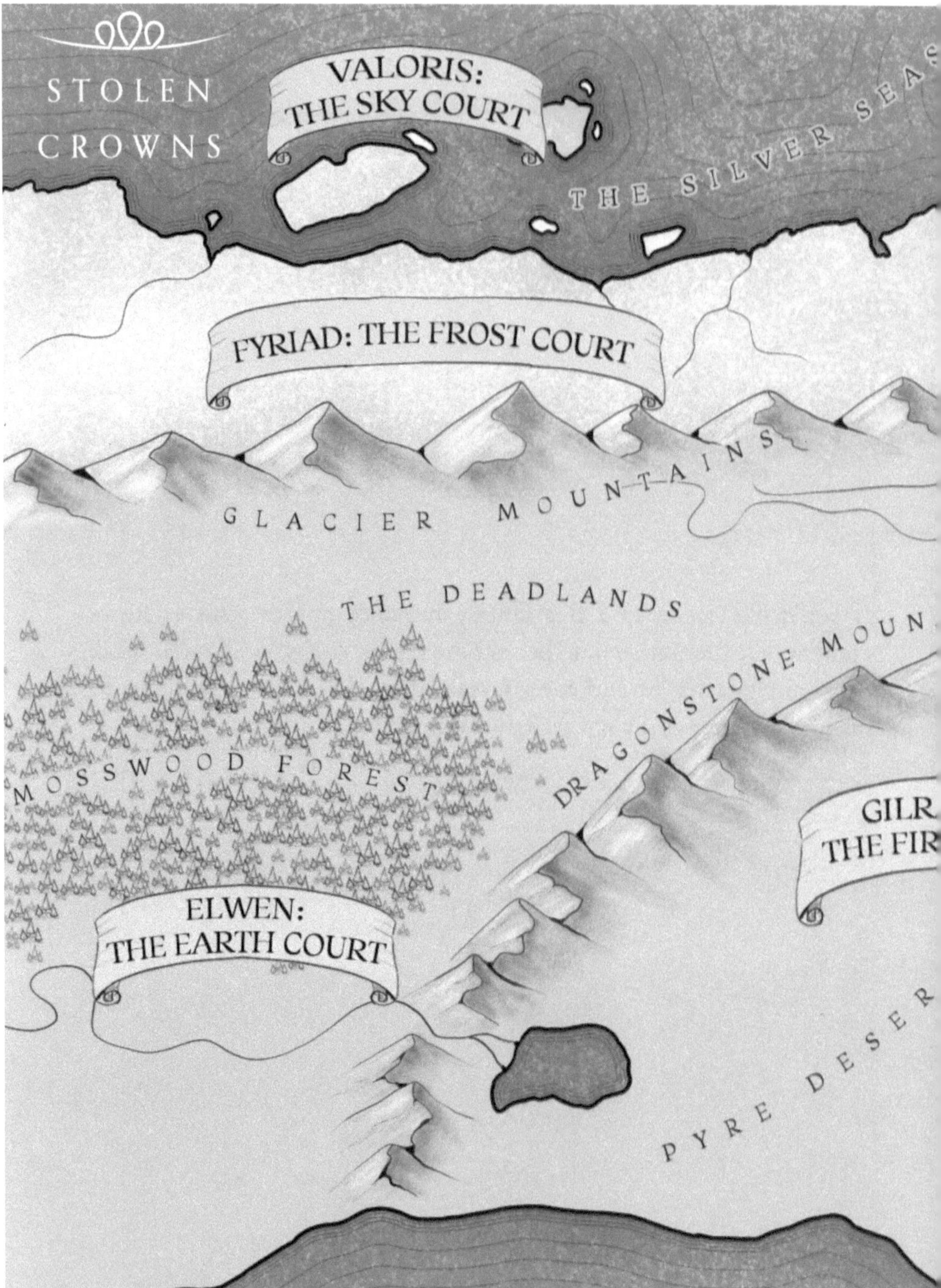

STOLEN CROWNS
VALORIS: THE SKY COURT
THE SILVER SEAS
FYRIAD: THE FROST COURT
GLACIER MOUNTAINS
THE DEADLANDS
DRAGONSTONE MOUN
MOSSWOOD FOREST
ELWEN: THE EARTH COURT
GILR
THE FIR
PYRE DESER

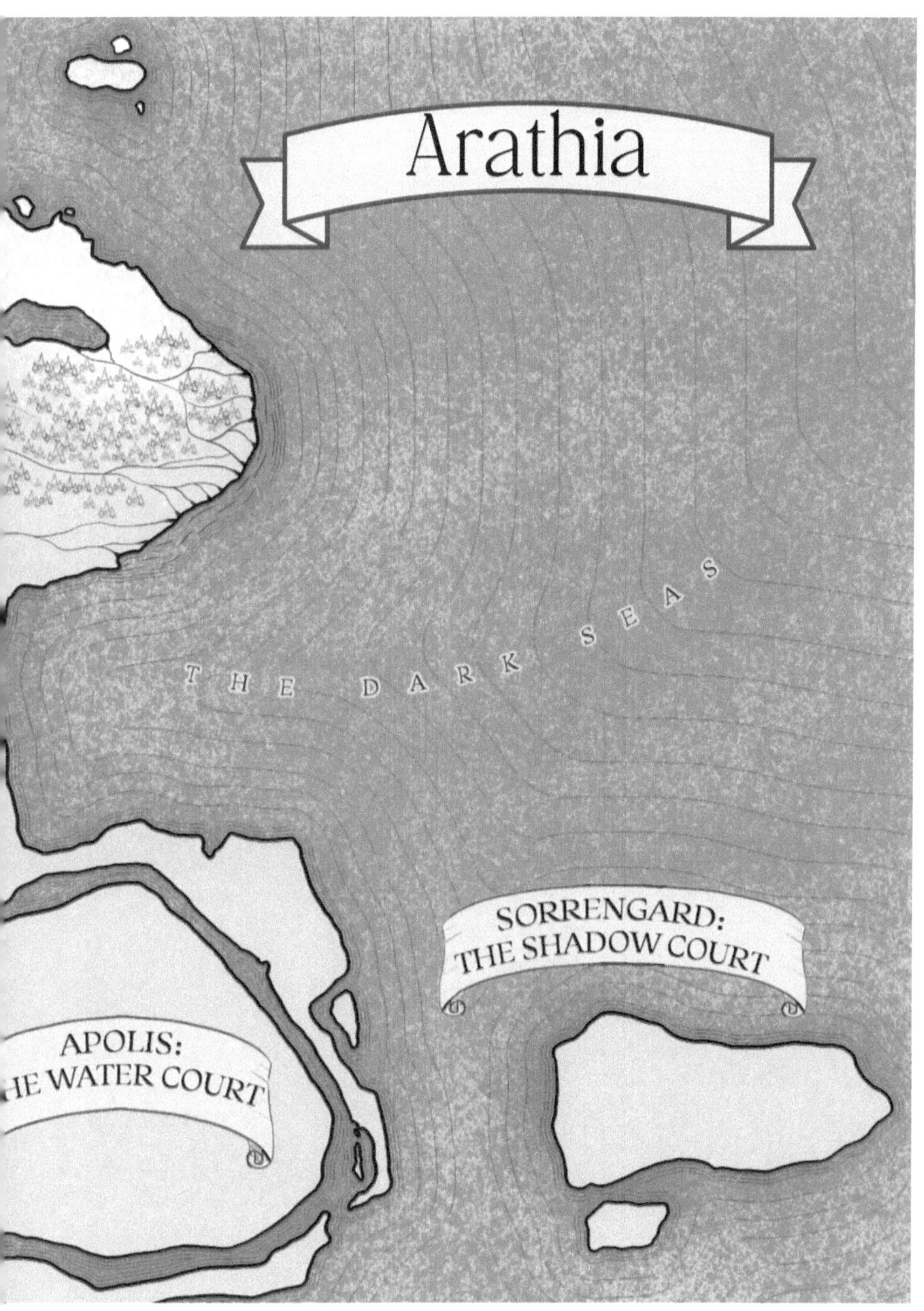

Arathia
THE DARK SEAS
SORRENGARD:
THE SHADOW COURT
APOLIS:
THE WATER COURT

Part One

"Not all who wander are lost."

Chapter One

EMORY

I couldn't stop staring at the woman's ring. It was the last thing I should've been doing. Not here, in the great hall of my home, as the hostess of yet another soiree my husband insisted on throwing for the nobles of the frost court.

The council members, the high priests and priestesses, the other ambassadors, and of course, anyone related to Her Majesty, all stood in the rectangular room. Basically, anyone with money or power. Preferably both.

A warm glow cascaded over the log walls, glowing from sconces attached to the wood with flickering flames. A chandelier made of antler horns hung overhead.

Windows stretched on either side of the room to allow a view of the white-blanketed lands around us. My favorite view in the world. Mountains rose in the distance, peaked with snow, and the royal city of the frost court—Karstad—glowed and flickered with lights in the distance. Meanwhile, thick flakes continued to fall from the night sky.

I breathed out a sigh of relief that I was home after traveling with my husband for the last few months. I hated being in the sky court, so high above the rest of the world on the top of their isles.

I looked at my wingless back and shuddered. I stayed far away from any cliff sides or edges while in Valoris, afraid that one day I'd trip and fall to my death. I glanced at my husband through the crowd of chattering people, his broad beige wings furled behind him as he spoke with one of the council members, clapping the man on the back and laughing about something. He certainly wouldn't save me if I fell. Would likely rejoice over finally being rid of me.

I fiddled with the pearls nestled around my neck. I hated these events. Hated having to smile and laugh and listen to the endless dribble about how the maid folded the towels all wrong or how a dress wasn't properly steamed or how, Spirits forbid, the frost queen was becoming more paranoid, tightening the circle of those she trusted.

Okay, that last fact was actually interesting and something I wondered about.

Fire lit the space behind me as an entertainer my husband had hired stood in the middle of the room. Or, rather, whom I hired. My husband loved throwing parties that were the talk of the town, and as his wife, it was my responsibility to plan it all and make said parties worth talking about. I'd heard of this talented fire elemental who often performed at various events across the six courts, so I'd reached out to see if he might be interested in coming to Fyriad.

He held out his hands, a ring of fire appearing that he spun in circles. It widened bigger and bigger, flames leaping out and smoke curling into the air. A few of our guests clapped their hands in delight while others gasped. He threw his hands up and directed the fiery ring to fly above his head. The heat of it brushed across my face, and I fanned myself.

"Emory, have you heard a word I've said?" the woman in front of me asked, glancing down at the ring I'd fixated on earlier. The gold band shined from her middle finger, black stones surrounding an engraved gray gem with a little tree carved into it.

I shuffled my feet, patting my red silk dress, about to respond when I felt his presence beside me.

"Don't take offense, Elisabeth." My husband stepped up next to me, his wings brushing my arm.

The light glinted off his balding head, and his sunken beady eyes fixed on me. "Always has her head in the clouds, this one."

He didn't say it like it was a compliment, though I generally thought having my head in the clouds sounded far better than down here with him.

His hand gripped my elbow tight. Too tight. A warning. *Do not embarrass me.* Spirits knew I'd done enough of that lately. I shook myself from his grasp and took one step to the left, putting space between us.

A servant brushed past us, carrying a tray full of Fyriad delicacies: spiced eel kabobs, sautéed cod bites, yellow frost berries with honey and cream. Another servant whisked through the crowd with a tray of drinks, and I nabbed a sparkling pink one, taking a deep gulp.

"Apologies." I set my gaze on Elisabeth, her long dark hair tied with a ribbon, no wings on her back, just like me. "I was admiring your ring. It's beautiful."

She looked at it and wrinkled her nose. "A gift from my husband's mother. I feel obligated to wear it, though I think it's rather unsightly."

I almost choked on my drink. Unsightly. She had no idea what she wore. I'd recognized the emblem immediately: it was one of the first rings crafted by the mountain dwellers, a powerful symbol that represented their freedom after they broke off from the earth court and created their own court, tucked into Mosswood Forest and hidden away for years. Rumor had it that the former king of the earth court stole many of their treasures and possessions after the war he led against them. He'd then distributed those stolen treasures across the continent of Arathia to nobles and royalty, no doubt how it came to be with Elisabeth's mother-in-law.

Elisabeth was still frowning at it like she didn't have an amazing piece of history right there on her finger.

"Lord Growley," she said to my husband, a conspiratorial note to her voice, "I think your wife might be hinting that she wants some new jewelry."

I snorted, then cleared my throat as my husband huffed. "She has plenty already. Everything she could want, in fact."

Not even close, but he wouldn't know that. Or care to know.

"If you'll excuse me." He nodded at us. "I see that the Faraways have just arrived."

Two winged elementals stepped through the huge opening of our great hall, big enough to accommodate wings—as was everything in our log cabin.

Elisabeth looked around the bright room, lips pursed. "I don't know how you live in that cave home of yours in the sky court."

Elisabeth and her husband were frost elementals like myself, and while her husband served as ambassador to the water court, they primarily resided here.

"It's an adjustment." Though my husband was from the sky court, as ambassador to the frost court, we spent half our time in his court, and half our time in mine. Every time I had to travel to Valoris, I counted the days until I could come home. I'd done the best I could with our dwelling there. Hanging bright paintings on the walls, throwing plush, colorful rugs across the floors. Installing chandeliers and sconces to make it brighter, more homey. My husband had grumbled about it all when I'd first come to live with him, prattling on about unnecessary expenses.

"Do you miss the frost court when you're away?" she asked.

"We visit often enough," I answered noncommittally. The last thing I needed was it getting back to my husband that I was complaining about the home, this life, he provided for me. Which he liked to constantly remind me of. Although he had no problem complaining about the snow and ice and cold of my home, and I just had to grit my teeth and nod along . . . or suffer his temper.

The door opened, and gasps sounded around the room as a figure stepped inside, black cloak dotted with snow, flurries whirling in after him. A servant shut the door and took his cloak, hanging it on the wall behind him. His umber skin glowed in the warm light, his black hair shorn close to his head, matching black stubble covering his strong jaw.

"Maverick Von Lucas," Elisabeth said in awe. "He never comes to these things."

He straightened, face severe as he sent a cursory look around the room, gaze roaming right past me. I hadn't invited him, which meant . . . my husband marched his way and shook his hand, clapping the famous adventurer on the back. Not just an adventurer. Explorer, historian, scholar. Maverick did it all, and he'd earned many admirers in the process. Along with a coveted position as the frost queen's historical advisor. He took another step into the room, everyone crowding around him to hear about his latest escapade.

"If you'll excuse me," Elisabeth said, brushing past me and joining the crowd of revelers.

"Tell us about how you got that bejeweled goblet," a man called. "I heard you had to outrun a few boulders to escape with it."

Maverick smiled good-naturedly. "And nearly fell into a snake pit in the process."

A few women, including Elisabeth, raised their hands to their mouths in horror while the men chuckled.

My husband raised his hands to shush everyone. "At least let the man get a drink before you barrage him with questions about his latest quests."

My throat grew thick as I hung back. I'd love nothing more than to sit next to Maverick and spend the entire night listening to his adventures. But my husband would never allow it, not when I had duties to perform, like mingling and making him look good.

Calls for my name echoed across the room, some high priest's wife who probably wanted to gossip. I needed to stop staring at Maverick and mingle with others, to represent my husband with a smile on my face. I glanced back at Elisabeth's ring, my fingers twitching as I heard bits and pieces of Maverick's latest conquest: where he barely escaped with his life after diving in the frigid Silver Seas to explore its icy depths. Then he'd had a run-in with the notoriously secretive seafolk. So many adventures. So many treasures. So much history.

My fingers twitched again as Elisabeth's ring glinted in the light. No. No. I could not do that here. My extracurricular activities happened outside the home, in secret. Never so close to my husband, and definitely never in front of so many people.

Maverick's voice rang out from the middle of the crowd. "The golden rope was a challenge. I had to scale a cliff to get it while fighting off dragons. I didn't realize until I got to the top of the damn mountain that they were actually just protecting their eggs—which lay on top of the rope. I got quite a few burns." Through the crowd I could see him rolling up his black sleeves, revealing scar-riddled arms.

"He's so gorgeous," a water court ambassador said as she passed me.

"And he's single," the woman next to the ambassador murmured.

The ambassador waved her hand. "He's always single. Too focused on his work to take a wife."

"Maybe that'll change once he meets me," the other woman said, and they both laughed, weaving their way toward him.

Oh, screw it. I may not ever experience the life Maverick Von Lucas lived. But I could live out my own passions, in my own small way.

I sidled toward Elisabeth, ring sparkling on her finger. If Maverick saw it first, he'd no doubt want it, and he'd get it. The difference was all he'd have to do was ask. Then he'd take it back to the Academy of Scholars & Historians, where it would be forever out of my reach.

The history behind it. The stories it could tell. It would be an amazing addition to my collection. After tonight, Elisabeth might shove it in some drawer, not even caring about the valuable artifact she possessed. It would be lost to time. I swallowed as she turned to whisper with one of the high priestesses of the frost court, whose gown was long and flowing, fabric thin, unlike the rest of the ladies from other courts who wore thick wool dresses, often layered with fur-lined jackets and sturdy boots. Like the priestess, I didn't need to bother with all that, being from the frost court. Ice flowed through my blood.

Someone called for me again, and I caught the sharp look my husband sent me.

Do not embarrass me.

I bit my lip, then he looked away, and I had my opportunity. Before I even knew what I was doing, I stumbled forward, bumping into Elisabeth, muttering some apology, placing one hand on her arm while the other deftly reached to that ring and slipped it right off her finger and into the pocket of my dress.

I spun on my heel and made my way across the room toward the calls for my voice, heart hammering. If I got caught stealing, it wouldn't just be my husband's wrath I'd have to endure. It would be the frost queen's as well.

It was a good thing I'd never been caught, and I had no intentions of starting now.

Chapter Two

Maverick didn't stay long. I suspected he came only to do my husband a favor. Lord Growley regularly donated to the academy where Maverick was a professor—his other coveted position—so he'd likely been forced to make an appearance and keep one of their wealthy donors happy.

I'd frequented the same parties and dinners and balls as him over the years, had thought about formally introducing myself, but in the end, what was there to say? If I was going to speak with Maverick Von Lucas, I wanted to be able to show him who I was, who I wanted to be. I wanted to speak with him about history and his groundbreaking discoveries—my own discoveries.

But I wouldn't be able to do any of that tonight. Not without revealing far too much about myself and my secrets. So instead, I spent the night lurking close enough that I could hear his stories but far enough that I wouldn't catch his attention.

Then he left, and so did my chance of speaking with him.

It was for the best.

Meanwhile, the party droned on. Three exhausting hours of nodding along to inane chatter, smiling as others complimented my red silk dress, the pearls around my neck, laughing at my husband's jokes, most of which were made at my expense.

He stood next to me now, arm wound around my back, fingers digging into my skin. "You'd think for someone who attended the Academy of Ladies, Emory would be a little better at planning these events, but my Emory's mind is so often somewhere else, I'm surprised she even remembered to show up."

Everyone standing around us laughed, though I heard the edge to my husband's words. I'd done something wrong. I wasn't sure what, but I'd no doubt hear about it later. He'd never physically hurt me, probably because he suspected if he dared hit me, I'd fight back. But he didn't need to. His harsh words, his constant displeasure, was enough of a punishment, enough to keep me in line.

Well, mostly. He thought he kept me in line, which was all that really mattered.

He wasn't incorrect about my mind often being somewhere else. Right now, my hand itched to take the ring I'd stolen out of my pocket and study it. To add it to my collection of artifacts and stay up late into the night trying to piece together its history.

"Lord Growley, have you had a chance to speak with the frost queen after that disaster at the conclave?" a woman next to my husband said. I believed she was a council member for the frost court.

My husband glowered, running a hand over his bald head. "Not yet. I have a lot of damage control to do."

He hadn't told me about this. To be fair, he didn't tell me about anything, but this seemed big. The new king of the water court, King Maledonan, had called a conclave. The first conclave in sixty years. He'd claimed he had dire news and all the leaders of the courts must convene to discuss it. Everyone was abuzz about it.

A mysterious power was rising in the shadow court: a shadow king who wanted revenge on all the other courts for banishing the shadow elementals to their little island sixty years ago. This shadow king was wreaking havoc, kidnapping boys, taking their shadows, and the water court wanted to do something about it, wanted all the courts involved to fight this emerging threat before it became something we couldn't handle.

"What happened with the frost queen?" I asked, giving the woman a polite smile while my husband's lip curled.

She flipped her long red hair over her shoulder. "Did you not tell your wife, Lord Growley?" She tsked. "The frost queen stormed out of the conclave. We don't know why yet, just that she left early and refused to listen to anything the other rulers had to say."

What a fool. This shadow king could be a serious threat, and if there was anything I'd learned from studying history, it was that war was inevitable, and those who were in denial were usually on the losing side. We needed to be prepared. I turned to say something, but one of our guests began playing the white piano situated in the corner of the room, and everyone dispersed, gathering around and listening to the melody.

I made to move, but my husband's arm curled tightly around my back, his voice dropping to a low murmur. "You didn't tell me you invited an ambassador from the earth court, nor the sky princess's new captain of the guard."

My brows shot up at that. So that's why he'd made the jab. He was angry I'd invited someone he hadn't approved of. Except . . . I didn't. I didn't even know any ambassadors from the earth court, not well enough to invite them here. And the princess of the sky court . . . I'd only had a few interactions with her.

"You've embarrassed me, wife." His voice cut through me, and I winced. "I didn't even know their names when they arrived. They had to introduce themselves. Driscoll Bayliss and Leoni Andora?"

I stilled. Wait. I did know them. I'd hosted them in our home in the sky court without my husband's knowledge. I'd helped them on a mission that, if my husband found out about, would be the end of me. But that had been months ago.

Now they were here. In my home in the frost court. Blood and frost. I needed to speak with them before they did something stupid, before they said too much, revealed too much, to my husband.

I unwound his arm from my waist. "Apologies, my lord. I met them both in the sky court and invited them here last minute. It slipped my mind to mention it, but I thought you'd be pleased to have an ambassador here from the earth court so you can make a connection with Queen Liliath." I bit my lip. "And the princess of the sky court suggested Leoni come and get acquainted with you. The princess must already have her eye on you as one of her valued ambassadors."

He peered at me with his beady eyes, and my heart hammered. I hoped he'd buy that explanation, that it would soften his temper.

He patted his round belly, then gave a stiff nod and gestured to Leoni and Driscoll, who both stood near the entryway. "Well, go speak to your guests, then. And make sure to apologize for your blunder. I want to make a good impression on Queen Liliath and Princess Poppy, as you well know."

Of course he did. That was all he cared about: his reputation.

I bit back a retort and plastered a smile on my face. "Yes, my lord."

He spun on his heel and strode toward the piano, joining the rest of the party.

I hurried toward Driscoll and Leoni. Driscoll ran a hand over his coiled black hair, snowflakes melting on his desert-hued skin. Leoni barely reached his chest, her pale skin flushed pink, her red-gold hair in the same tight bun it had been the last time I saw her.

"Typically when you come to a party, it's because you've been invited," I said as I approached them, my smile wide and welcoming, the opposite of my words.

Leoni winced while Driscoll just smirked. "At least offer us a drink," he said. "Spirits know I could use some alcohol."

"I'm not offering you a drink," I snapped. "Because you're not staying."

"But we have to talk." Leoni grabbed my hands, and I shushed her, sending a glance behind me to my husband.

I never should've gotten involved with them, never should've helped them and the princess of the sky court on their little mission.

We'd met at the sky court castle a few months ago, I'd mistaken the princess as a commoner. I hadn't told her my secret hobby, of course. But I had told her a lot about my passion for hunting and collecting historical objects. Then I'd gone and saved her life along with Leoni's and Driscoll's.

It had all been so stupid, put me on their radar, and now they were here. Jeopardizing everything.

I felt for the ring in my pocket again, wishing I'd had more self-control, but I never could help myself, not when it came to my obsession.

"Whatever you have to say, it can wait." I sent a cursory glance around the room. "You can't be here right now."

Driscoll raised a finger and summoned one of the servants with a drink tray. He grabbed the drink and threw his head back, downing it in one gulp. "I happen to be an expert in parties." He stretched his head to look behind him. "Honestly, this one's looking a little dull. You might want me around to inject some life into it."

I snatched the empty glass from his hand and set it on a small table against the wall.

"We can talk another time," I gritted out. "Thank you for coming. Now you both need to leave."

"The bone collector has the bolt," Leoni rushed out.

I went completely still.

The bone collector. The bolt.

That was what she'd said.

I couldn't form words. So it was real. The mythical bolt that belonged to one of the Seven Spirits. The one I'd been looking for. I'd been right. It existed.

My shoulders sank.

And now it was in the possession of the bone collector. My nemesis. A friendly nemesis, if I was being honest.

I couldn't imagine how he found it. It stung that he'd gotten to it before I had. That he'd proven himself to be more clever, more adept, just more.

"My dear." The jagged edges of my husband's voice made me wince. "Is everything all right over here?"

"Yes." I tried to keep my tone light. "Just welcoming our guests."

Driscoll stepped forward. "Great party." He winked. "And beautiful home, Lord Growley. Tell me, do you happen to have any more of those smoked eel kabobs?" Driscoll nudged his head toward a nearby man gnawing on one.

A small smile quirked my husband's lips at the compliment.

At least Driscoll was charming. I couldn't say the same for Leoni, who shifted from foot to foot, looking as uncomfortable as I felt. I prayed to the Seven Spirits that my husband hadn't heard any of our conversation about the bolt. About the bone collector, who was well known among the frost queen and her circle. A conversation about him would raise far too many questions with my husband.

"Unfortunately, our guests were just leaving," I said.

"But you just arrived." My husband's brows furrowed. "I hope my wife didn't say something to upset you."

"No," Leoni burst out, and I rolled my eyes at the panic in her voice.

She was going to blow my entire life to pieces if she didn't get it together.

"Are you okay?" My husband peered down at her. "You look rather pale."

Driscoll waved his hand. "Oh, she's lost that golden sheen after spending months away from Apolis. No, we were leaving because we're very tired. We've heard such great things about the parties you throw and decided to come last minute, and let me tell you, it did not disappoint."

My husband's chest puffed out while relief spread across my own tight chest.

"But we just arrived in the frost court and are in need of some sleep. Hopefully next time we can come a little earlier." He nudged my husband. "Get some of those eel kabobs before they run out."

Leoni nodded, eyes shifting to me, and I sent her a glare that hopefully conveyed that she needed to keep her cool . . . or find it. Keeping it would imply she had it, which she most definitely did not.

"Well, it was a pleasure meeting you both. Emory will see you out." My husband nodded to me and walked away.

I blew out a breath at the same time as Leoni sank against the wall.

"What is wrong with you?" I hissed. "Are you two trying to get me in trouble? Coming here and talking about the"—I lowered my voice to a whisper—"the bone collector? Spirit Sky's bolt?"

"Oh, we have other things to talk about as well," Driscoll said, studying his nails like he was bored. "Like the white rabbit."

The name sent sparks of panic shooting through me. That wasn't a name that could ever be uttered in this household. Not a name that could be connected to me in any way. Not when that was the name I was known by for stealing sacred and historical relics and artifacts, much like the bone collector.

I grabbed both their arms. "Out." I shoved them toward the door, glancing over to see my husband distracted by the piano player.

I swung the door open as an icy blast ripped into our home, flakes floating through the air and melting onto the wooden floor.

"Wait," Driscoll said. "I'm sorry, okay? We need your help."

"No." I grabbed their cloaks from hooks along the wall and pushed them into their arms. "I can't help you. I'm not who you think I am."

Driscoll's brows furrowed, and he shivered as another wave of icy wind rippled past him and Leoni.

"But all those things you revealed about yourself to Princess Poppy . . ." Leoni started.

"Was a mistake," I said, thinking back to just a month ago when I'd lost my mind and told Princess Poppy far too much about myself, my interests. This was what I got for meddling. For daring to hope that I could be more than just Lord Growley's wife.

It hit me in that moment, staring at Driscoll and Leoni as snow whisked around them: the truth. I couldn't be more. That was painstakingly obvious now. I had no idea how they thought I could help them with the bone collector, with the bolt, but I couldn't. I couldn't even talk to them about it without risking losing my freedom.

I thought about the ring in my pocket. How stupid I'd been to take it.

"Meet us at the Haverford Inn tomorrow," Leoni whispered quietly. "It's where we're staying. We'll tell you everything." She leaned in. "Where he found the bolt. How he got it."

"Enough," I said, tone resolute. "And good night to you both."

I slammed the door on their crestfallen faces and marched back toward the party, where the fire elemental had summoned a sword of fire that he shoved down his throat to everyone's delight and horror.

I sank against the wall, legs weak after that encounter. They knew my name. My secret name. The ring in my pocket weighed heavier than ever. I hadn't been nearly as careful as I'd thought. If my identity got out, it wouldn't just be my reputation at risk. It would be my life.

I swallowed back the tears gathering and tried to ignore the growing pit in my stomach. It was clear what I had to do, even if it meant giving up the one thing I loved.

Chapter Three

EMORY

Moonlight slashed across my dark bedroom. Outside, snow still fell, the flakes so thick it created a curtain of white. As the dying fire sparked in the hearth, I slipped out of bed and shoved my feet into two white slippers. My husband lay naked in bed, snoring loudly after he'd crawled over my body and shoved himself inside of me, pumping in and out, all while reminding me once again what a failure I was because I hadn't yet given him an heir.

He didn't know it, but I secretly took cassroot every month, an herb that prevented pregnancy. I might have been his wife, but I could not bear his child. Couldn't bring a child into this world in good conscious, not when he'd be the father. It was another little way I could rebel against him.

But I'd taken my rebellion too far lately. I'd been playing at something that I shouldn't have. All my life, I'd been told what I needed to do. I would be a good daughter and find a wealthy, powerful man to marry, just like my mother had. I'd have prestige. I'd make her proud.

But I'd just had to have more.

I padded across the room and quietly clicked open the door, then slipped out. Darkness cascaded across the narrow hallway, but I didn't need light. I knew my home well enough to make my way without it. I'd done this very thing enough times now, but this would be the last time. It had to be.

Driscoll and Leoni showing up tonight was a wake-up call. I might not have liked my life with my husband, but it was the only life I had. The white rabbit, my collection, my passion, it was a lie. Something shrouded in secrecy that I had to do in the middle of the night. It wasn't me. I thought about the bone collector, the last encounter I'd had with him. My heart thumped hard at the memory.

I'd had too many close calls lately, and my husband was growing suspicious about my "outings." It was time to give it all up and say goodbye to the white rabbit for good.

Tears gathered in the corners of my eyes that I brushed away.

I stalked down the wooden stairs at the end of the hallway, which creaked under my feet, then swept through the kitchen, now dark and silent. I opened the door to the cellar, creeping down the stairs.

I felt for the matches that sat on a shelf above my head, then lit the sconce on the wall. A glow flickered over the room. Canned goods, vegetables, and fruits lined the shelves on the wall, and barrels filled the space, brimming with water, ale, and wine. No one came down here, save our cook, and even then, she wouldn't find my hiding spot for my most treasured artifacts.

I squeezed through the barrels and tiptoed to the back of the cellar, slipping a stone block out of the wall. A chest sat there, wooden and carved with seashells and fish. I'd come across it one day when foraging by the icy waters of the Silver Seas and immediately noticed the strange carvings on its sides. After further research about the curious fish with their twisted bodies that looked like ropes twined together, I'd realized the carvings were an ancient species. A species that existed in the Old World when the Seven Spirits still walked among elementals, ruled over them, were adored by them. That had been before they'd destroyed the Old World—and everyone who lived in it—and then disappeared and hadn't been seen since.

I snorted as I slid the box from its hiding place, cradling it gingerly. That was the story we'd been told anyway. That the Seven Spirits had decided to go to Galaysia, the spirit world, and no longer meddle in mortal lives. I had a hunch that there was much more to the story. There always was when it came to history.

This chest, for example. After I found out that it dated back to the Old World, I'd studied it further. I ran my finger over the gold lining the bottom. Gold was a popular stylistic choice in the Old World for those who could afford it, which was very few. But even those who could afford to make a chest with actual gold wouldn't have. They saw something like that as frivolous. Only the spirits owned things made with gold.

Which meant this chest had to have belonged to one of the Seven Spirits. Spirit Water, if I had to guess. I'd come across a priceless treasure chest, right there on the sandy beach of the frigid Silver Seas.

I sank to the floor and opened it to reveal my most treasured artifacts: a shimmering ruby ring, a delicate wine glass, a beautiful blue scarf, a small calcified rabbit foot, an ancient dagger with a stone hilt. Each of these items was special for a different reason: the first one I ever discovered, the first time I'd taken something from the frost castle, the first time I met the bone collector. My breath hitched. Little mementos.

And now I'd have to give them all up.

Tears welled in my eyes once again as I dug the ring I'd stolen out of my nightgown pocket and dropped it into the box. Tonight, I'd be getting rid of it all. Then I'd go to the bunker where I hid the rest of my artifacts, and I'd empty it out. I wouldn't destroy any of it. I couldn't bear to. But I would leave them somewhere they could be discovered.

Once upon a time, I'd hoped that one day I could collect enough artifacts, perhaps do enough research of significance to impress my husband and the Academy of Scholars & Historians. That maybe I could join and become an esteemed historian, advise the queen, like Maverick Von Lucas.

A tear rolled down my cheek.

This was for the best, I reminded myself.

It was nothing more than a dream. My husband would never allow it, and if he ever found out about this, he'd likely turn me in for stealing. It was everyone's duty to take ancient artifacts directly to the frost queen. According to Her Majesty's credence, these artifacts did not belong to those who found them. They belonged to her, belonged to the academy, where they could be catalogued, studied. By real historians. Not those like me who played pretend.

I blew out a shaky breath. I'd take this chest now and be back before my husband awoke, and the white rabbit would officially be no more.

"So it's true," a voice said from behind me.

My blood turned to ice as I straightened.

"You are the white rabbit," my husband growled.

His wings rustled as he stepped closer, and the sour odor of dried sweat filled the air. He always smelled of sweat, especially after he drank, and bile rose in my throat.

I slowly stood, leaving the open chest on the ground behind me. "I don't know what you're talking about." I crossed my arms, and he let out a laugh.

"Oh, Emory." He lifted his hand, and that's when I realized he was holding my white fur cloak. The one that had earned me my nickname. I always kept it hidden in a secret compartment of my wardrobe.

Not as secret as I'd hoped. I'd been such a fool.

"You really thought you could get away with all of this?" He gestured to the chest behind me. "Stealing important historical artifacts and keeping them for yourself? What were you going to do? Sell them and buy passage out of this place? Away from your life? From me? Is that what you want?"

My upper lip curled. "It would be hard for you to know what I want when you never bother to ask. I am more than just your wife, you know."

"Really?" He laughed, the sound cruel. "You attended the Academy of Ladies. Your mother's greatest dream for you was to become my wife."

His words brought back the memories of me begging my mother to send me to any other academy, but she insisted that was not the right path for me. Said I would be better off marrying a rich man who could provide a stable life for me, just like she'd done. So I got to learn what it meant to run a household, throw dinner parties, and make your future husband look good. Learn how to make yourself amenable to your husband, to meet his every need.

I swallowed.

My husband laughed again, no amusement behind the sound. "It was too easy, you know. I've had my suspicions about your identity for a while, especially after the maid found this white cloak in the back of your wardrobe and brought it to me. The staff might like you more, but I pay them to keep an eye on you. Then there's the fact that you prattle on with everyone you meet about this artifact or that new historical finding that's come out of the academy. How you practically drank up every word that came from Maverick Von Lucas's mouth tonight. As if he'd ever care about meeting you."

The words were a punch to my gut.

"So I asked Elisabeth to wear the ring. I told her it was a little game you and I were playing so she wouldn't dig into it. I wondered if you'd take the bait. And you did. Slipped it right off her finger." He nodded toward the chest behind me. "Divorce is allowed in Arathia but frowned upon. Imagine the scandal it would cause, how it would look. Me divorcing my beloved, dutiful wife. But now?" He stepped closer, wings spreading out behind him. "Now I have reason. You are a criminal and will be tried in the frost court, sentenced for your crimes. And me?" He pressed his hands to his chest. "Well, I'll be the grieving husband. In shock over my wife's horrible deception."

"I never thought I could hate you more than I do in this moment," I said. "But maybe this is actually a gift."

His eyes narrowed over his long nose. "What are you talking about?"

"Prison would be preferable to being married to you."

"How dare you." His face turned a bright shade of red.

"It took me until now to realize it. I was so afraid of losing this life, but now that you've found me out. I'm . . ." I paused. "Relieved."

I was scared too. Terrified, actually. But I'd be damned if I admitted that to him. Everything else I'd said was true, though. I could survive prison. I could pay my dues and come out on the other side. But this marriage? I wasn't sure I could survive another day in it. Not with him.

My hands curled into fists. "Instead of trying to trap me, you could've shown interest in something that excited me. You know that I have a passion for history. You could've encouraged it instead of acting like it was some threat."

He took a step forward, the vein in his temple throbbing. "It was a threat. Instead of focusing on being my wife, on supporting me and my career, you were traipsing off playing pretend. You are never going to be a historian, Emory. You will never be anything more than what you are, what you've been raised to be."

His words struck me in the chest. Right in the most tender part of my heart.

"Just so you know," I said, "I've hated every moment of being married to you. Every time you touched me, it made my insides shrivel. Every time you kissed me, it made my stomach twist."

His face was now a dark shade of purple.

"And let's not even get started on the pathetic thing you call sex." He was shaking now, and I wondered if he might actually strike me. "I would just go somewhere else in my mind every time you climbed atop me. Think about my favorite things to make it bearable. Thank the spirits for the cassroot."

He stilled. "What are you talking about?"

"Why do you think I haven't become pregnant after seven long years of marriage?" I laughed. "Because I couldn't stand the thought of having your child."

"You bitch." He lunged at me, his meaty hands wrapping around my throat as his face twisted in rage. I clawed at him, fingers digging into his arms, hands trying to reach for his face, for anything that could loosen his grip. When that didn't work, I kicked out my legs, and he lifted me into the air. My vision blurred, and my throat burned as his hands clenched tighter. Meanwhile wind stirred and wrapped around me, pushing my hands down and binding them to my sides. He was using his sky magic. Stars dotted my vision, terror freezing me.

I was going to die here.

His eyes bulged from his head, veins popping under his bald scalp. My vision started going black, and my lungs clenched in pain just as my husband let out a garbled choking sound.

His hands froze, and I managed to kick at him and get free from his grasp. I fell to the ground, coughing and sputtering. Air rushed into my lungs as I took heaping gasps. My throat burned, skin bruised and sore from where his hands had gripped me tight. What in the spirits below had just happened?

I looked up at my husband to see him clutching his chest, still making that garbled, choking sound.

"Gregory?" I said slowly.

He fell to his knees, face stricken.

"Gregory!" I rushed to him, the fact that he'd just tried to kill me forgotten with this turn of events. I patted at him, looking for any kind of wound or injury, but I didn't see anything. "What hurts?"

Spittle flew from his mouth, eyes now veined with red. A croak escaped his mouth as he fell to the floor with a thud. I watched in horror, the events unfolding in slow motion, his body slamming to the ground, wings shuddering, and one last garbled breath escaping him. Then everything went still and silent.

"Gregory?" I asked, reaching out trembling fingers that I pressed into his neck.

No pulse. Blood and frost. My husband was dead.

Chapter Four

EMORY

I burst out of my house in a panic, carrying my little chest of artifacts, wearing my boots, my nightgown, and my heavy fur cloak I'd had the wherewithal to grab before I fled.

Now I trudged through the snow-covered ground, passing log cabin after log cabin, all lined in neat rows that hedged the cobblestone road where I walked.

I had no idea where to go, what to do. I just knew I couldn't stay in that house with my dead husband. I stopped, looking back and wondering if I'd lost my mind.

Oh, I'd definitely lost my mind, but some part of me still knew that I couldn't go back there. With my husband dead, my mother gone, I'd have nowhere to turn. Women could receive titles, deeds, inheritance from their spouses, but only if it was granted, and my husband had always made it clear he'd only be leaving those things to an heir. One I'd never given him. His cruel words echoed in my head. He was right about my future. I had no formal training, no skills, no money. I didn't know how to be anything but a wife.

Despair swallowed me up. A frigid gale swept past me, fluffs of snow sticking to my skin and hair. I knelt down and opened up the chest, pulling out a scarf that I wrapped around my throat to cover the mottled bruises my husband had inflicted. I shouldn't be wearing this scarf. It was precious and rare, a relic that many say Spirit Sky gifted to a mortal woman he'd fallen in love with. But I also couldn't have these bruises on display and had no other clothes on me since I'd left the house in such a hurry.

I needed to find shelter, or at the very least, I needed to get out of the middle of the road, before any curious eyes might have enough time to wonder what Lord Growley's wife was doing traipsing through a snowstorm in the middle of the night.

The sun peeked over the horizon. Not the middle of the night anymore. Early morning. Even more reason why I needed to come up with a plan.

My heart thumped so hard my chest ached, and I was having trouble getting air through my passageways. What had I been thinking? Why had I run like that? The servants would be waking now, might have already found him. If I came back, it would look suspicious. If I didn't go back, it would look even more suspicious.

I turned halfway, staring at our three-story wood cabin in the distance, frozen with indecision.

I should return. I stared at the familiar wooden front door. The little steps that led up to the porch with the swing I'd sit on during snowstorms. From here I could see through the window of the first floor into the parlor with all my favorite books and couch where I'd sit and read in front of a warm fire. Another window showed the great hall where we'd host parties for all my husband's friends.

I had no choice. I had to go back. There was nothing else for me, no one I could go to.

Driscoll's and Leoni's faces popped into my mind, and I straightened, their visit suddenly rushing back with stark clarity.

The lightning bolt. The bone collector. Their mission. And they wanted my help. They saw me as more than just someone's wife.

My mind began spinning with possibilities. With hope. That lightning bolt was valuable, a relic among the likes of which we'd never seen. The Academy of Scholars & Historians would want to collect it so they could study it, so they could get clues about where the other spirits' weapons might be located.

If I brought that bolt to them, they might take me seriously as a candidate, might even allow me to join the academy. I could finally live my life on my own terms and not someone else's.

If I went after it, I'd also have a chance to see the bone collector again. My heart thumped for a different reason I didn't particularly want to explore.

My feet started moving again. I trudged through the snow toward the town that sat nestled at the top of the road, all the wooden buildings topped with heavy snowfall.

Leoni and Driscoll had told me to meet them there. I would go now. I'd wait for them at the inn all day if that's what it took. My neck pulsed with pain, and I winced, hoping this scarf covered all the bruises.

Despite all the horrible things that had happened, for the first time in a long time, a curious emotion stirred inside of me. An emotion that felt suspiciously like hope.

Chapter Five

EMORY

By the time I made my way into the Haverford Inn, my feet and hands had gone numb, and ice crystals lined my eyelashes. My frost magic made me less susceptible to the cold but not immune. Long exposure and inappropriate clothing for the winter weather still affected frost elementals, just less than it would others. Someone without frost magic might have frostbite and be on their way to losing multiple toes and fingers by now. Neither would happen to me, but I was eager to get out of the cold. Warmth immediately spread through me as I entered the cozy space, full of high-top tables and plush leather chairs and couches. A huge crackling fire burned in the stone hearth. The large square hearth sat in the middle of the room, and I immediately wove toward it.

Two sky elementals sat at a table, wings spread out behind them as they bent their heads together. Other than them and the barkeep, the place was empty. I caught random bits of the elementals' conversation. About the conclave. The frost queen. How she wanted to control the narrative about this shadow king, wanted to investigate more herself before believing the other rulers about his existence. A problem, but not mine to deal with, thankfully.

My gaze wandered to the staircase that led up to the second level, where the rooms were. They were somewhere up there right now, probably still sleeping. I warmed my hands over the fire, melting away the cold still lurking in my bones. I could only stand the heat for a few minutes before it became overbearing and I had to move away. Unsurprisingly, frost elementals weren't big fans of fire.

Color had returned to my hands, and I wiggled my toes in my boots.

"Miss?" a voice said.

I turned to see a man standing there, skin and hair pale, as was common with those from Fyriad. His eyes trailed down my body, and I flushed as I realized what he was seeing: me in my thin, silver nightgown, with only my fur cloak covering me while I held the chest in my arms. I cleared my throat and set the chest down, then tugged the cloak tight over my shoulders.

"Good morning. I'm meeting someone here. Guests, actually. Maybe you could point me in the direction of their room?" He stared at me like he wasn't sure what to do, so I kept talking. I raised my hand over my head. "Tall, skinny man with light brown skin and a penchant for talking nonstop." I lowered my hand down to my shoulders. "Short woman, pale, freckles, wears her hair in a bun and is generally very serious."

He continued to stare. "You're Lord Growley's wife, aren't you? Lady Emory?" He scratched his head.

I inwardly cursed. Of course I'd be recognized. This had been a bad idea. I should've been more covert, at least used the hood of my cloak to cover my head. I might as well have attached a bell to myself that could ring out my presence everywhere I went.

I cleared my throat and raised my chin, adopting the calm, self-assured Lady Emory. "Yes, I am. I'm actually here on my husband's behalf, meeting Driscoll Bayliss, the ambassador of the earth court. My husband wanted me to greet him myself and make his acquaintance."

The man's gaze flicked to my cloak like he could still see the nightgown underneath. My brain scrambled for some explanation about why

I would come here on my husband's behalf wearing nothing but a nightgown.

Unsurprisingly it couldn't because there was absolutely no reason I'd do such a thing unless I was raving mad. Which I was starting to think might be the case.

His eyes widened, and my heart thundered. Oh, spirits below. I hoped he wasn't about to send someone to my house, to fetch my husband. My dead husband.

Surprise hit me when a smile curved the man's lips. "Ah, yes, my lady. I can be discreet about these things." He winked. "I run an inn. These little . . . trysts are very common, and I'm a very good secret keeper. For a price."

My mouth dropped open, and realization flooded me. "Oh, no. That's not why I'm—" I stuttered, not even sure what I could say. He thought I was here to have an affair with Driscoll.

I'd never cheated on my husband. Guilt flared inside of me as an unbidden image of the bone collector flashed in my mind. Laying together side by side on a grassy hill. I banished the thought. I'd never done anything wrong.

I didn't have a whole lot of interest in men, in being controlled by another one, no matter how good the sex might be. I peered at the innkeeper as he stared at me with that knowing look in his eyes and bit the inside of my cheek.

Maybe this wasn't so bad after all. He'd show me to Driscoll's room. He'd give me the alibi I needed. No one would know I was here.

My cheeks flushed red as I stuck out my hand, the pale blue bracelet jangling on it that everyone in Fyriad wore. He lifted my wrist and looked at the number, then nodded. "I'll charge it to your house coffers, and I'll make sure the charge is labeled as food from the market. Just so we don't raise any suspicions."

He wasn't lying. He had done this many times before. Had an entire system worked out.

"Thank you," I said airily. "Much appreciated. Now if you'll show me the way?"

He nodded his head toward the stairs. "Room five. Have a good morning."

My cheeks flushed hotter as I grabbed the chest of artifacts and made my way upstairs and away from prying eyes.

Chapter Six

EMORY

I banged on Driscoll and Leoni's door.

"Go away." Driscoll's groggy voice floated from inside.

"It's me," I whisper-yelled, looking up and down the hallway, hoping I wasn't waking anyone else. If someone saw me, my entire cover could be blown. While Fyriad was one of the bigger courts, Karstad, where we resided often felt like a small village, everyone knowing each other—and each other's business. Once word of my husband's death—and my coinciding disappearance—spread, people would be looking for me, and I needed to be gone before they had a chance to find me.

I knocked again and the door swung open.

"Would you please stop doing that?" Driscoll gritted out, shirtless, his bare chest and lean torso on display.

A tunic flew through the air and hit him in the face.

"Put on a shirt," Leoni said from behind him. "Lady Emory doesn't need to see you half naked."

"You see me half naked all the time," Driscoll shot back.

"Not because I want to," Leoni said with an eye roll as she sat on the edge of her bed, pulling her boots on. "I don't have a choice when we're together night and day, but she, at least, should."

Driscoll turned. "You know, you should be more grateful. I don't just let anybody gaze upon my beautiful bare skin."

"Put. On. The. Shirt," she gritted out.

"Okay, okay." He stretched it overhead while I stood in the doorway, shooting nervous glances down the hall.

"Can I come in?" I asked.

"Oh, right." Driscoll gestured inside.

I stepped in, and he shut the door behind him.

"Excuse shorty, over here. She gets grumpy when she hasn't been fed."

Leoni shot him a look. "That's you."

He stroked his clean-shaven chin. "Oh. Right. She's just generally a grumpy person."

This time, it was a boot that she threw at his head. He ducked and sank down onto his bed.

I stepped further in, setting down the chest, which was growing heavy in my arms. The room was small with just two beds and a fire that made the space feel blazing hot. Two chairs sat in front of the hearth, but I scuttled to the opposite corner of the room, wishing I could open a window and let some of the frosty air in. Just moments ago I'd been freezing, but now that my body was balanced again, I craved the winter elements.

Driscoll gestured to the fire. "Don't you want to sit down?" His gaze bounced between me and the flames. "Oh, right. You're a frosty. Forgot. You all like it abnormally cold." He shuddered.

"A frosty?" I asked.

Leoni finished putting on her other boot. "Ignore him. He likes his nicknames." She looked closer at me, seeing my nightgown, then her gaze trailed up to my neck, where the scarf hid my bruises.

"Your husband let you leave your house?" Driscoll wrinkled his nose, staring at the low cut of my nightgown. "In that?"

"We came to an understanding." I let out a nervous laugh. "Turns out he knew my identity all along, and I just couldn't wait to come see you both."

Driscoll scratched his head. "Huh. Didn't really take your husband to be that understanding. Not after everything you told us about him when we first met."

"Enough about my husband," I said, voice sharper than I'd intended. "I'm here to learn about the bolt. You said the bone collector took it. I need more information if I'm going to track him and find it."

Leoni and Driscoll shot each other looks, some silent conversation happening between them before Driscoll finally gave a nod, and Leoni turned to me. "We're actually the ones who found the bolt. Hidden in Spirit Sky's tower."

I gasped. From all my research, I'd known the bolt had to be hidden somewhere sacred, and I'd even mused that it might be in his tower. The tower he often used to imprison and torture those who angered him. But no one knew the exact location of it. Records never indicated where the tower might be located in the sky court. So I'd never known where to look. But they'd actually found it. Unbelievable.

Leoni shifted on the bed. Sunlight shone through the little window of their room, full and bright and highlighting the gold shimmers in her red hair. "Right after we found it, he came. The bone collector. And then he mentioned a white rabbit who'd also been looking for it. We put the pieces together."

She stared pointedly at the cloak wrapped around my shoulders, the same cloak I'd been wearing when I first met them over a month ago. That alone wouldn't be enough to identify me. Many women wore fur cloaks. But this coupled with everything else I'd revealed about myself? Well, that was damning. Stupid bone collector. I wrung my hands together.

"Does the bone collector know you're Lady Emory? Do you know who he is?"

"No and no," I snapped. We'd always been careful to keep our identities secret from each other—and everyone else.

I swore.

I'd worn that white fur cloak on my outings as the white rabbit to keep myself hidden, but over the years I'd been spotted in it while in a few compromising positions where I'd taken—stolen—valuable items. Before I knew it, my reputation had spread to the frost queen—and she'd dubbed me the white rabbit. I wasn't famous or anything. Most people had no idea who I was. It was mainly the frost queen and anyone who worked for her or worked at the academy.

"We don't want to reveal who you are." Leoni held up her hands. "We just want you to get that bolt. If you do, Princess Poppy of the sky court will pardon you and your crimes as the white rabbit."

I took a step back. That wasn't something I ever expected. "So Princess Poppy is the one who sent you?" I asked, and they nodded.

I bit my lip. "Why does she want the bolt?"

"She doesn't," Leoni said. "She just doesn't want it in the wrong hands." She and Driscoll looked at each other. "Think of the power whoever has it could wield."

I raised a brow. "And you trust me with that power?"

"More than the bone collector," Driscoll muttered. "What do you know about him?"

Much more than I'd ever bargained for. I sighed and looked out the window at the sleepy royal city coming to life. Frost elementals made their way through the snowy streets; carriages with horses bumped along. Others pushed carts full of steaming hot coffee and egg buns, their breaths puffing into the air. Everyone wore boots and thick pants with jackets over their tunics.

I turned back to them. "I don't know much," I admitted, though it tasted like a lie. I didn't know his name or what he looked like underneath that black hood that covered his face. But I knew his movements, knew that he was as passionate about history as me. I knew his best barbs, since he'd slung them at me time and time again. I knew his handwriting. I knew that he thought it was funny when I insulted him. That he was competitive. I felt like I knew his soul, yet I couldn't name hardly any tangible facts about him. "He started appearing years ago in the same places I was. We'd go after the same objects." He'd taken quite a few artifacts right from under my nose, which had infuriated me. "He was always cloaked like I was."

I'd summarized our relationship so neatly, so easily, yet it felt far, far more complicated than I was letting on.

"I have seen him use fire," I said cautiously after noticing the crestfallen looks on Driscoll's and Leoni's faces. "So he's from the fire court, but he must live here because he's always frequenting the same locations as me. He wouldn't be able to do that if he were living in Gilraeth."

The fire court would easily take a month by horseback to travel from Fyriad, and even longer from Valoris, the sky court, where I also had run into the bone collector on a few occasions.

Leoni bit her lip. "We already knew he had fire magic. That's what he used to steal the bolt from us."

"I believe he lives in Fyriad." I began pacing the way I did when my mind started piecing information together. "The majority of our encounters have happened here, so it makes sense."

"Well that's a start." Leoni's blue eyes lit up. "Surely we can find a fire elemental in the frost court. He wouldn't exactly blend in."

"So when do we start?" Driscoll rubbed his hands together.

"There's no we," I said. I worked alone, and that was the way I preferred it. I didn't trust anyone enough to work with them. "You all have done your duty, and you can go back to Princess Poppy and let her know I'll get that bolt. I'll start questioning residents. Discreetly. Finding anything I can about fire elementals who reside here."

Driscoll sent me a pointed look. "And are you going to do the questioning while wearing that?" He gestured to my nightgown, which barely grazed the tops of my boots. "It might serve as a good distraction, but I'd wager it may be a little too distracting to get the information you want."

My cheeks burned and I wrapped my cloak around myself. "Right. I probably need to find something appropriate to wear."

"So go back to your house and get dressed and we'll meet—"

"No," I burst out. Too quickly. Too loudly.

Driscoll and Leoni both stilled.

"We don't have time." I looked away. "And like I said, I don't need your help."

"We've been ordered to help you find it," Leoni said. "A direct order from Princess Poppy. I'm her captain of the guard, and I won't disobey."

Damnit.

"Are you hiding something from us?" Leoni asked as she strapped a belt around her trousers, a sword hanging from it, the steel glinting in the rays of the sun.

"Kinda seems like it," Driscoll mumbled as he shoved on his boots.

Before I could answer, a loud knock banged on the door. "Open up!" a voice yelled, and my stomach hardened to a rock.

Driscoll stood and started walking to the door, but I ran in front of him. "Wait, don't." I flung my arms, blocking his pathway. "Don't open that door."

His brows furrowed. "Why not?"

"You're under arrest for harboring a criminal," the voice yelled, "and are hereby being summoned by the queen of the frost court."

Driscoll's eyes widened while Leoni's face paled, her hand now resting on the hilt of her sword.

"What criminal?" Driscoll yelled. "There's been a mistake. We don't have a criminal in here." He glanced over his shoulder at us with wild eyes.

"Lady Emory Growley," the voice said. "Under arrest for the murder of her husband."

Chapter Seven

EMORY

Driscoll whipped around. "The murder of your husband?" he whispered. "That might've been worth mentioning!"

Leoni held out her hand and water appeared in a ball that hovered over her palm, spinning and forming into handcuffs. "Is that true?" she asked with a deadly calm, all business now. "Because if you murdered your husband, I will have to arrest you. I'm the captain of the guard for the princess of the sky court. I can't aid and abet a criminal."

"Yes, so you've mentioned," I said. "Many times."

"Except your princess also ordered you to find Emory and send her to get the bolt." Driscoll stroked his chin. "That's quite a moral conundrum."

The banging on the door made us all jump again. "If you don't let me in, I will use force!" Ice crackled around the seams of the door, spreading like a web over it.

"I didn't murder my husband," I said quickly, hand going to the scarf and unwrapping it from my neck, revealing the bruises.

Leoni's eyes widened, and sympathy flashed in them.

"I was defending myself and he . . . I think he might have had a heart attack. I didn't do anything to him, though. I swear."

"Except run away after he died?" Driscoll pointed out.

I wrapped the scarf back around my neck. "Okay, smart-ass. Yes, I did do that, but I was scared. In shock. I wasn't thinking clearly. So I came here."

"And brought the frost guards upon us," Leoni hissed, any sympathy I'd seen now gone again as she scowled, the bun on her head making her look even more severe.

"I'm about to break down this door and arrest all three of you!" the guard shouted, the door now a wall of shimmering ice as his magic encapsulated it.

"Just a minute!" Driscoll called. "I'm . . . naked and need to get dressed."

The guard scoffed. "Seriously?"

Driscoll's words must have had some impact because he didn't come barging into the room. Not yet anyway.

"Okay," Driscoll whispered. "We have two options: we either turn her in or we all escape out that window." He pointed at the window behind us.

Leoni groaned.

Driscoll shot me a pitying look. "Like I said, it's a bit of a moral conundrum for her. She really hates to break the rules and has been breaking more of them recently than she'd like, which I think is giving her an identity crisis—"

"Will you shut up?" Leoni massaged her temples.

My heart hammered. If they decided to turn me in, I'd have to fight them and run. Not ideal. It would be much easier if I had their help escaping this situation.

Leoni's eyes rolled upward as she thought through the options.

"I'm coming in on the count of three. I suggest you back away from the door to avoid getting impaled with ice shards!" the guard shouted.

"Leoni," Driscoll urged.

"One!"

The water cuffs still hovered over Leoni's palm as she stared at me.

"Two!"

"I really don't want to be impaled by ice. I don't want to be impaled by anything." Driscoll's smile turned wicked. "Unless it's a big, stiff—"

"Three!"

The door shattered into a million ice shards, all of them flying through the air. Leoni grabbed my arm and wrenched me backward. I shook from her grasp and scooped up my chest as the three of us bolted toward the window. She shoved it open, and without warning, pushed me right through the opening.

My stomach leapt to my throat as I careened through the air, clutching the chest, not enough time to form a plan while my body was in a free fall.

"Why would you just shove her like that?" Driscoll yelled.

"I didn't exactly have a choice," Leoni shouted back. "I figured she'd drop the chest!"

Not on my life. Not when doing so could break it. Although not doing so could break me.

I barreled toward the ground and stared in horror as it came alarmingly close. Something thin snaked around my waist, yanking me right before I made impact.

I peeked one eye open, realizing a vine was holding me. I shot a look above me to see Driscoll commanding the vine, using his earth magic.

I breathed heavy, my pulse still thundering, blood roaring in my ears while my stomach slowly lowered back in place. The guard stuck his head out the window as the vine dropped me the short distance to the ground, Leoni and Driscoll shimmying down behind me.

"Halt!" the guard shouted from above. "In the name of Queen Larissa, ruler of the frost court—"

Leoni grabbed my arm again and yanked me forward as I stared. The guard held out his palm, summoning daggers of ice that he shot directly at us.

Leoni twisted her wrist, a wall of water rising up behind us that the shards hit, making them dissolve.

"Run!" Leoni yelled while I stared shell-shocked, gaze shifting between the wall of water and my new companions, unable to believe this was happening. Everything had fallen apart so quickly.

Leoni let out a frustrated grunt and, for the third time, snatched my arm and pulled me forward.

I stumbled after her while still clutching the chest as passersby stared.

"Don't let them get away!" the guard shouted from somewhere behind us.

He knew my husband was dead. Thought I murdered him. I was in major, major trouble.

I tugged my arm free from Leoni's grasp and pumped my legs.

"Finally." Driscoll dodged a man pushing his wooden cart full of steaming cider. "I was starting to think she didn't know what 'run' meant."

A loud crash sounded behind us, and I turned my head to see Leoni's wall of water tumbling down, drenching anyone in its vicinity, steam rising from the victims' bodies as they lay in the snow. Women and children shrieked and dove out of the way, and the guard's head had disappeared from the window of the inn. I really hoped he was alone. We might be able to dodge him yet.

I whirled in a spin to avoid a man using his magic to clear away the snow on the road. "Sorry!" I yelled behind me, following Driscoll and Leoni as they hurried down the street.

The snow was slushy and wet under the rising sun, and soon the street would be cleared away for the day.

"We need to get off the main road," I called ahead as they continued to run.

"Any suggestions?" Driscoll asked. "Because in case you hadn't noticed, we're not exactly from around here."

Before I could reply, four guards emerged from alleyways into the street in front of us, slowing us to a stop.

"We have to go back," I said, mind racing through our options, any places we could duck into and hide. I spun, cloak whipping behind me, and ran right into the guard who'd been in our window.

His pale blond hair gleamed under the silver helmet all guards in the frost court wore. "Going somewhere?" he asked.

I stumbled back, Leoni and Driscoll now at my side.

"How do I get myself into these messes?" Driscoll whined. "Sure, I'll come to the frost court. No problem. We'll just find Emory and then be on our way." He rolled his eyes. "Spoiler alert: we're never just 'on our way.'"

"Shut up," Leoni said out the side of her mouth.

The guard in front of us stepped closer, ice crackling from his hand and forming a long sword that he raised up and pointed at my neck. The icy tip pushed into my skin.

"I didn't kill my husband," I said.

He reached out, and I was afraid he was going to grab the chest, but instead, he yanked the blue bracelet off my wrist, the one that every citizen of Fyriad had, that we used to buy things. There went all my access to our money.

He shoved the bracelet in his pocket.

"I'm innocent," I insisted.

He cocked a brow. "Really? Because it looks like your husband died and you ran."

I squeezed my eyes shut. Yes, it looked exactly like that. And there were no witnesses to back up my side of the story.

His eyes dipped to the chest I clutched tight to me. "Not only that, but you stole items when you ran. Valuables belonging to your husband?" His lip curled. "Disgusting behavior for a lady of the frost court, for a valued ambassador's wife."

"These are not my husband's," I snapped, tightening my hold on the chest, on my most precious artifacts.

"Can you just let go of that thing?" Driscoll whispered. "We'll get you a new chest. Fill it with new trinkets."

I shot him a glare, stubbornness rising in me. I hadn't done anything wrong. Okay, I had. But I hadn't done what they thought I'd done. And I wouldn't bow down to this man and his intimidation tactics, not like I always had with my husband. Smiling and pretending like everything was okay while I was dying inside.

I raised my chin. "I'm innocent, and I will not go quietly."

Driscoll sighed. "Perfect."

"Well, then there's only one thing left to do." The guard raised his other hand, ice shackles forming that floated toward my hands.

"Sir," Leoni said, stepping forward. "I'm Leoni Andora, captain of the guard for Princess Poppy of the sky court."

The guard paused, the shackles pausing as well, hovering between his outstretched hand and me.

"I just want to say that as a fellow royal guard, I have the utmost respect for you, so please don't take this personally."

His blond brows furrowed. "Take what personally?"

I twisted my head to see the other guards shoot each other unsure looks, and Leoni sighed heavily.

"This," she said right before shoving out her hands, water shooting in a stream straight into the guard's chest. He flew back with force, his ice magic shattering over his body as he hit the ground.

Driscoll's mouth dropped open.

"I just assaulted another guard," Leoni said in a panicked voice, spinning and glancing at Driscoll. "Well, what are you waiting for? Help me!"

He jumped as the other guards closed in around us, and my pulse spiked. I wanted to help them, but . . . I looked down at the chest cradled in my arms. My artifacts. Everything I'd spent years collecting. Still, I couldn't let Leoni and Driscoll do all the work, not when they were risking their lives for me. I crouched to gently set the chest down in the snow when a voice rang out in the now-empty street, everyone peering out from behind the safety of their windows and doors.

"Stop!" A man marched down the street.

Everybody whipped around to look at the man, no one moving as we watched him striding toward us.

My mouth dropped open.

His black boots kicked up tufts of snow behind him, and his long black coat billowed in the wind.

Spirits below. It was him. Maverick Von Lucas. And he was looking directly at me.

Chapter Eight

EMORY

"Oh, great." Driscoll dragged a hand down his face. "Who is this? The executioner, here to cut off our heads with his icy sword right in the middle of the street?"

Maverick stalked forward. Sweat sheened his umber-brown skin, his short black hair cropped close to his head, his copper eyes gleaming with annoyance—and maybe confusion? He frowned at all of us, fists curled at his sides.

Leoni leaned over to Driscoll and whispered out the side of her mouth. "Let's strike now. While they're distracted."

My stomach twisted. They'd hit Maverick in the process. One of the greatest minds of our time.

My companions nodded at each other, pushing out their hands, tendrils of their magic creeping from them.

"Stop!" I yelled, shoving through them right as Maverick stopped in front of the guards. Everyone's eyes turned to me.

"Why would you do that?" Driscoll groaned. "It was the perfect chance to get away."

Maverick's gaze lowered to the chest I still held in my arms, and his brown eyes snapped up, searing into me. He was tall, shoulders broad, and even from under his coat, I could tell he was fit, muscular. He had to be to go on all the adventures he did.

"Sir!" The guards straightened, all of them saluting Maverick.

"What's going on here?" Maverick barked.

"Lady Emory Growley is under arrest," one of the guards said, cowering under Maverick's menacing glare. "She's been summoned to the castle."

"Ugh, I knew it." Driscoll dragged a hand over his tight curls. "He is the executioner, isn't he?"

"No," I said. "This is Maverick Von Lucas. Her Majesty's personal scholar and historian."

Even though we'd attended many events together, even though he'd been in my home just last night, this was the closest I'd ever stood to him. Here he was. Right in front of me . . . while I was on the run from the royal guards. I glanced down and my cheeks burned. And wearing a nightgown, nipples and all on display.

Driscoll gaped at Maverick. "I'm sorry, he's a historian?" He jabbed a thumb at Maverick. "Him? Mr. Hotty McHotterson?"

Leoni sighed. "Here we go."

The guards scratched their chins, and their confused gazes bounced between us all.

"What?" Driscoll threw up his hands as Maverick turned his glare onto him. "I'm just saying what we all must be thinking. This man is a piece of eye candy." Driscoll's eyes widened. "Did you really jump off that pirate ship into the ocean and then use driftwood and the sword to paddle to land?"

The guards stared at Maverick with curious gazes, waiting for an answer, which Maverick didn't provide.

"What are you doing with that chest?" Maverick asked, ignoring everything Driscoll had just said.

I gripped it protectively but answered his question. "It's mine."

"It dates back to the Old World." Maverick pointed to the etchings. "It can't belong to you unless you're telling me you're somehow related to one of the millions of people who died during the Old World Catastrophe."

The event where every single person in the Old World disappeared, and no one knew why. We had theories, of course, many of those theories proposed by Maverick Von Lucas himself. Theories about how it was the Seven Spirits who killed all the people of the Old World, displeased by how they were misusing their magic. I didn't agree with the theory in its entirety, but a lot of it was backed by historical evidence.

"No." This was definitely not how I envisioned meeting my hero. "I'm not claiming to be related to anyone from the Old World. Obviously. I found the chest." I winced. "So it's mine."

Maverick stepped closer, his intense gaze never wavering from mine. "That's against the law, and you know it. Any artifacts found belong to the queen, and the academy by default."

"I didn't know it was a historical artifact." A lie, and from the way Maverick's eyes flashed, it seemed like he knew it.

"Sir, we're under orders by Her Majesty to bring this woman to the castle for questioning," one of the guards said tentatively, the four of them standing with hands hovered over the swords hanging from their belts.

Right. Because my husband was one of her ambassadors. Let's not even get into the fact that she didn't know I was the white rabbit. Yet.

Maverick huffed like the entire situation was an inconvenience to him.

Driscoll shivered. "Can we wrap this up? I'm getting cold." He glanced down. "And I'd rather not lose any important parts to frostbite."

"Hand the chest over, and then you can go to prison, where you clearly belong." Maverick's gaze roamed over me dismissively.

My heart sank. He didn't realize I was a historian, like him. All my hard work would be gone. Just like that. Because I'd been a complete and utter fool. I didn't see any way out of this situation. For me or Leoni and Driscoll. Maybe Princess Poppy would intervene on their behalves. But she wouldn't be able to save me, not when I stood accused of murder. I thought of all the valuables inside this chest that Maverick would discover. All the items I'd so painstakingly found. There were even more in the bunker by my house. Larger items I couldn't fit in my chest that I'd hidden for safekeeping. At least those would be safe.

I glanced down at it, then back up to him as he held out his hand impatiently.

Something about his entire entitled, impatient demeanor made me want to be stubborn. To say no.

One of the guards stretched out their palms, those same ice shackles from before appearing and floating once again toward my hands.

Maverick reached out to grab the chest but stilled, the scarf around my neck catching his attention. Spirits below. I forgot I was wearing this thing. Of course he'd recognize it. His gaze slowly moved up to my face, eyes flashing with a look I couldn't decipher. He stared at me in shock for so long, I started to wonder if I'd broken something in his brain.

"Change of plan. She's coming with me," Maverick said abruptly, turning to the guards.

The ice shackles stopped inches from closing around my wrists.

Driscoll pinched the bridge of his nose. "This is a lot of whiplash for so early in the morning."

Leoni frowned, eyes bouncing from me to Maverick to the guards like she had no idea what to do.

My eyebrows shot up. That wasn't a terrible idea. I'd rather go with him than them. At least I'd have more time to plan an escape. Maverick wasn't a guard. He was a scholar. I could work with that. Plus . . . did this mean I'd actually get to see the inside of the academy?

Probably not what should be on my mind at this moment.

The guards looked at each other uneasily. "That's not what we were told—"

"I'm the queen's historical advisor," Maverick said, voice sharp. "And if I want to bring someone in for questioning because they have priceless historical artifacts, then don't you think Her Majesty would give me that leeway?"

The guard cleared his throat. "I suppose so, sir."

Maverick gave a sharp nod of his head. "Then it's settled. You can escort us to the academy, then escort them to the castle when I'm done questioning them about some of these"—his gaze flicked to the scarf wrapped around my neck—"unusual items."

With that he spun on his heel and strode away, and I had no idea whether to be relieved or terrified. Possibly both.

"Does that mean we're supposed to follow?" Driscoll gestured after him.

The guards grabbed us and shoved us forward. "I guess so," I mumbled as we marched through the snow and straight toward the Academy of Scholars & Historians.

Chapter Nine

MAVERICK

I had to be seeing things. Or I was losing my mind. That was the only explanation for my current situation.

Imagine my surprise when on my morning walk to the academy, I'd seen a random woman running through the streets, snow flying up behind her—and she was in nothing but her nightgown and a white fur cloak. At first, I thought she was running because she'd stolen the chest she was clutching so tightly, and I was going to let the guards handle it. Then I'd gotten a closer glimpse of the chest, of those etchings on it. They depicted the impacious fish, a rare species of flesh-eating fish that existed in the Old World. We had at least two of their skeletons on display in our academy museum, as well as some of their teeth.

I didn't trust the guards to recognize such an important relic, so I had to intervene. My plan had been to seize the chest—until I'd laid eyes on that scarf wrapped around her neck. One thought to have been worn by one of Spirit Sky's lovers. A scarf that I'd thought had been stolen by the white rabbit.

The very same scarf currently wrapped around that woman's neck.

I shot a glance behind me as the guards prodded the woman and her companions forward. The others looked familiar, though I couldn't quite figure out why. The tall, lanky man had produced earth magic, so he was clearly from Elwen, and the pale, short woman had used water magic, which meant she was from Apolis. So what in the bloody fires were they doing here with this woman in the frost court?

The historian in me wanted to piece this together, but the logical part of my brain reminded me that I had far greater problems to worry about. I was leaving soon. Today, in fact. On a long journey that I had barely prepared for. An important journey.

But Lady Emory Growley was wearing a scarf stolen by the white rabbit. I'd never formally met Mrs. Growley, but I'd met her husband many times.

Her husband. Fuck.

It didn't help that she was distractingly gorgeous with her white-blonde hair that reminded me of the palest rays of the sun when they splashed across the snow. Her creamy complexion, pink cheeks, and even pinker lips. Those ice-blue eyes that seared into me.

I shouldn't have interfered with this, but I did, and now I needed to confirm my suspicions that Emory was who I thought she was.

A blast of wind rustled my coat, and I pulled it tighter and summoned my fire magic, letting it flow through my blood and warm me against the chill. If it weren't for the academy, I would never step foot in this court again.

That wasn't true. A faint voice in my head whispered that there was something else keeping me here, but that voice wasn't one I ever allowed myself to listen to.

Ahead, the street led straight to the Academy of Scholars & Historians. A huge grassy expanse opened up in front of the academy, dusted with white. Thick trees shot up in the air, branches sagging with the recent snowfall. Benches lined a walking path that led to the front doors of the academy. It was an impressive building made from crystal that shimmered and reflected the snowy world around us. It rose up with tall, pointed peaks that looked like jagged glass.

Emory and her friends stared at it in awe.

I pushed open the large glass double doors, the winter wind barreling in behind me. Students eyed me, some brave enough to make eye contact but most avoiding my gaze. I glared at a first-year student, and she yelped and swiftly turned to go in the other direction.

Others scurried past, hurrying to their classes. A tall silver clock stood against the back wall, which would ring in a few moments, signaling the start of morning classes. I had an assistant handling the one class I still taught. He'd be taking over my class until I was back from my trip. If I came back.

Two sets of wide staircases wound upward on either side of the room, and I veered to my right, not bothering to look behind me as I marched upward.

The clock struck nine, the bell dinging out its final warning as stragglers raced to their classes and doors began slamming closed. Anyone who didn't make it on time would not be allowed in. We didn't tolerate tardiness at the academy. The final door closed, the last patter of footsteps fading away.

All at once, everything fell quiet. Students in their classes, professors now lecturing. All was right. I let out a breath of relief as I turned to the right and walked down a hallway lined with doors, then stopped at the one on the left with my name printed across the glass: Maverick Von Lucas, Master Historian.

I dug into my coat pocket and pulled out the key, sticking it into the lock and opening the door. The guards stopped behind me with their three prisoners.

"You can wait outside," I said to them. "While I ask a few questions of our guests."

My gaze landed on Emory. Time to find out if she was the white rabbit. Because if she was, I was about to do something very, very stupid.

Chapter Ten

I grunted as I lifted another heavy rock from the pile sitting outside the cave. Of all my dumb ideas, this one was truly the dumbest. I'd read about an avalanche of rocks that had happened nearly a thousand years ago, killing multiple sky elementals from the Old World, and I just couldn't help myself. Actual evidence of the Old World Catastrophe—otherwise known as the end of the Old World. If I found bones, let alone something amazing like a journal or clothing or jewelry, it would be a huge discovery. I lifted my lantern higher, trying to angle it just right so that I could see the progress I'd made.

Very little, as it would turn out. There was no way I'd be able to get through these rocks in one night. It would take multiple visits, likely over a series of months. I lifted another heavy rock and threw it.

The wind whistled around me, chilly and refreshing. I lifted my face. Thankfully my husband was away in Apolis for a few weeks, giving me more freedom to pursue my new hobby.

I hadn't meant to stay here so late into the night. But I'd gotten carried away, excited by this new prospect that lay out before me. A few more rocks. I'd heave a few more from their place and then head home before the servants grew too suspicious. Though they'd never suspect this. They'd likely think I was having an affair, not that uncommon. I lifted another rock and down it went, tumbling away and thudding into the soft green grass of the highlands surrounding me. It wasn't like I'd ever actually have an affair. I'd only been married half a year and already hated it, hated my husband, but I wouldn't stray from our marriage. I'd made a commitment, and I would stay true to it.

It was the least I could do to honor my mother, to honor her dream for me. The dream that she'd never see now.

My hands, sore with blisters, wrapped around another heavy stone when a sliver of wood peeked through. I gasped and dug through the rocks, pushing them aside. A box lay there in the rubble. I gripped the smooth wood, pulling it out and examining its chestnut top.

A voice cut through the air. "Hello, little rabbit."

I stilled, clutching the box tighter as that low timbre sent a shiver down my spine. It was a clever nickname given my white fur cloak, but I wasn't in the mood for games.

"Are you a stalker or something?" I asked without turning around. "Not very original, I have to say."

He tsked, and still, I didn't turn.

The sun had sunk below the horizon, a band of purple streaking across the dark sky, the faint outline of stars emerging overhead.

I slowly turned, and a man stood at the bottom of the pile of rocks. He wore a black cloak, hood covering his head and hanging far enough over to keep his face, any identifiable features, hidden. Same as me with my fur cloak.

"What do you want?" I asked, still sitting atop the tall pile of rocks, clutching the box tight. "To turn me in? Do you work for the frost queen or something?"

She'd caught wind of my extracurricular activities, and for whatever reason, had decided to make it her personal mission to catch me. Never mind there were actual murderers out there, threats looming in other courts, pedophiles, but sure, focus on me and my harmless hobby.

"Maybe I'm a fan," the man said, which took me aback.

I'd been doing this for exactly six months, started the day after my mother died. But no one had seen me, noticed me. Which was the way I preferred it.

"A fan of what, exactly?" I asked.

He shrugged, and even though a cloak covered him, I could tell his shoulders were broad. "You're a treasure hunter. You collect hard-to-find objects."

"Have you been watching me?" The thought gave me chills. If he'd seen me, I had to wonder who else might have.

"Maybe just a little," he said, amusement in his voice.

I slid down the pile of rocks with as much grace as I could. "Well, you can stop. I have no interest in whatever it is you want. If you're going to turn me in, then do it now. Get it over with."

I'd fight him, of course, but it wouldn't be hard for him to slip the hood from my head, find out my identity. Ruin my life. Not that it was much of a life to ruin.

"I told you, I'm a fan."

I rolled my eyes. "What do you want? My autograph? I'm not interested in having a fan. I'm interested in being left alone."

He stepped forward. "Are you sure about that?"

This man was getting on my nerves. "Yes, I am."

"I've got a better idea."

Of course he did. Like every other man he thought he knew best. Typical.

"A game," he said. "A competition. Every year, we meet at a different historical site to hunt for an artifact. Whoever gets it wins."

"Wins what?" I asked.

"Well, the object," he said like it was the most obvious thing in the world. "And gloating rights for the entire next year."

This was absurd. I couldn't believe he'd thought of this. "So it's a game you want to play?" I asked. "Why?"

"Oh, come on." He took a step forward, his black cloak fluttering behind him, revealing black trousers that hugged thick thighs. "I've seen you. Your drive. Your passion. Your excitement. I bet you're competitive too. I bet this would inject some thrill into this hobby of yours."

He was right again and that was really beginning to irk me.

He raised his hands in the air. "We'll have rules of course. No personal information is ever exchanged. We won't seek out each other's identities. We won't seek each other out outside of the competition."

I raised a brow, even though he couldn't see it. "Does that mean no more sneaking up on me like this?"

He tipped his head, the shadow of his hood extending further over his chin. "I think you like it a little more than you're admitting."

"I don't," I said, voice dry. "What are the other rules?"

"We keep it clean when we compete. No fighting dirty."

"So I can't knee you in the balls?" I asked.

"That would be correct."

I studied my nails, caked with dirt. "Mm, pity. But I guess it makes sense. Who picks the location? And if we don't ever meet outside of the competition, then how will we communicate?"

"We'll use a neutral place to drop notes that give all the details needed. As for the location . . . I propose we make a list of famous artifacts that haven't been excavated for various reasons: location, risk, danger, you know, all the fun stuff."

Now that was intriguing.

"We drop the artifact names into a jar, hide the jar, and then every year we meet and pick an artifact. We both find out at the same time what we're after. Maybe we give ourselves a month to prepare, then we meet at the site of the artifact on a chosen day. First person to get away with it wins."

Very, very intriguing.

His head tilted down, and I realized he must be studying the box I'd found.

I drew it to me protectively.

"Do you know what that is?" he asked.

"Well, I was on my way to figuring it out before you interrupted me."

He laughed. "You have to use your magic to open it. It's a special lock that only responds to elemental magic."

That was clever and gave me an idea for a way to secure my bunker where I kept all my hidden artifacts—except my most special ones. Those got to go in a box hidden in my house.

He held out his hand and fire streamed from his fingertips. I tensed, worried his magic would set the box on fire, but he directed it right at the little black lock. The box clicked open to reveal a beautiful blue scarf, shimmering with a dust I'd never seen before. It sparkled and glittered, coated the inside of the box.

"Wow," I breathed.

"Congratulations," he said. "I think you just found a scarf made by Spirit Sky for one of his lovers. It's been documented in several ancient texts, but no one has ever been able to find it."

My gaze snapped up at the same time I snapped the box shut. He sounded a little too interested in my find.

He chuckled. "I'm not here to steal from you," he said. "So what do you say about my proposal? You in? Or am I going to have to find another treasure hunter to play my game?"

"Okay," I said before I had too much time to think about it, had too much time to ruminate on all the reasons why this was a terrible idea. "We have a deal."

He stepped forward and stuck out his hand. I hesitantly reached my own hand out and placed it in his. His grip was warm, a tingle spreading through me at the contact.

He gave my hand one firm shake before letting go. "Then let the games begin."

Chapter Eleven

EMORY

As many times as I'd passed the academy, I'd never been permitted to enter. Only students and teachers had that privilege. Now I sat in Maverick's office in awe of this place. I was here. In the actual Academy of Scholars & Historians. Under the watch of the royal guards. My mood soured. I still had no clue why Maverick wanted to bring us here, why he couldn't have just questioned us at the castle, but maybe he wanted to be in a familiar place; maybe he wanted to bring my chest of artifacts to the academy directly. I supposed it didn't matter. He'd given me the gift of time, and I needed to use it.

Maverick stood outside the door, speaking in hushed tones with the guards, while Leoni and Driscoll sat on either side of me, both of them staring at our surroundings.

A large glass desk sat in front of us, everything in its place, neat, organized. Parchment sat in a stack on the corner, next to it, an array of pens for annotating and highlighting. An ink pot sat at the top of the parchment to refill the pens. A magnifying glass lay to the side of the pens, everything else clean, sparkling, immaculate. And there sat my chest. Right in the middle. Glasses perched on the opposite side of the

"

table, and I imagined Maverick wearing them, sitting here long after the sun had sunk, poring over texts and examining artifacts, just like I did in my secret bunker.

I let out a gasp when I saw what was behind the desk: bookshelves spanning from the floor to the ceiling, shoved with books and texts of all kinds.

I stood from my chair and walked toward the shelves, letting my fingers trail over the book spines in wonder. All this knowledge, right at your fingertips. It was unbelievable. Something I could only dream of.

"Are you supposed to be doing that?" Driscoll asked from his chair.

Leoni slumped further into hers. "She murdered her husband, ran from the crime scene, and assaulted a royal guard. Not to mention she's stolen priceless artifacts. I don't think touching a few books is going to make much of a difference at this point."

I swallowed at all the accusations she'd hurled my way.

"Allegedly murdered," Driscoll pointed out. Leoni glared at him, and he snapped his mouth closed.

"I just got the position of captain of the guard, and now I'm going to lose it because of you." She set her gaze on me.

"I didn't murder my husband," I said.

Leoni raised a brow. "And all the other accusations?"

I straightened my shoulders. Well, those I couldn't deny, but I was not going to let her ruin this moment. I spun around and my gaze landed on a book with a blue spine. I'd heard of this one. It contained supposed diary entries from a farmer who'd lived in the Old World, documenting his crops slowly dying as the world around him fell apart. It was one of the few primary sources we had about the actual end of the Old World and demise of its people. And it was just sitting here. For me to read.

My hand hovered in the air. Leoni was right. I was already doomed, so I might as well enjoy my last moments of freedom. I grabbed the book and slid it out.

"You're reading right now?" Driscoll asked as I slowly opened the journal.

Then disappointment welled up in me when I realized it was in a different language. Othala: the language of the Old World. Which I didn't know because only those who attended the academy were taught how to read it.

"What are you doing?" a quiet voice asked.

I spun to see Maverick in the office, door closed behind him. He'd discarded his coat, and it hung on a hook behind him. Now he stood in his grey fitted trousers, his white shirt tucked in, suspenders strapped over his broad shoulders. He rubbed his stubbled jaw, that, along with his muscular chest, made him look rugged. Maverick Von Lucas. I was standing in his office. I was meeting one of the most famous scholars on the continent of Arathia.

He stalked forward, and a breath caught in my throat as he stopped right in front of me, his gaze dipping to my thin nightgown, then trailing slowly to the book clutched in my hand. He reached down, hand brushing mine, then snatched the book from me and shoved it onto the shelf over my head, face now inches from mine.

"Why would someone like you want to read a book like that?" he asked, voice low.

"What, ladies can't read?" I asked.

His gaze never left mine, and he was so close I could see the copper tone to his brown eyes. "That's not what I meant and you know it. That book you were holding, that you were flipping through, why did you pick it up?"

I swallowed, remembering that to him, I was just Lord Growley's wife, and I needed to act more like it if I wanted to get out of here. The last thing I needed was Maverick Von Lucas discovering my secret identity. Then I'd most definitely be doomed.

"Told you it wasn't a good idea," Driscoll mumbled.

Maverick stared at me with assessing eyes, and I cleared my throat and shrugged. "Pretty cover. The blue reminded me of the sky on a stormy day."

Maverick just huffed and gestured to the empty chair between Driscoll and Leoni, and I scuttled backward, sinking into it as he sat in his own padded leather chair behind his desk. He rolled the white sleeves of his button-up tunic, revealing his muscled forearms riddled with scars and burn marks. He leaned forward and steepled his hands together.

I thought he was going to speak, to ask me questions, to maybe reprimand me for the objects I'd stolen. Instead, all he did was stare. Not at Leoni. Not at Driscoll. At me.

I squirmed in my chair under his scrutiny. I didn't understand what in the Seven Spirits he found so interesting about me. Maybe it was my nightgown. That was probably it, and it made me angry.

I crossed my arms over my chest. "I'm not just a pretty object to be ogled."

Driscoll leaned over and whispered, "You could use that to your advantage. Maybe just tug that nightgown a little lower."

I scoffed.

Leoni reached over the back of my chair and smacked Driscoll in the head. "I'm going to start a sleaze jar," she said. "Every time you say something outrageous, you have to add a coin to it."

Driscoll scowled. "I always say outrageous things."

"Perfect." Leoni leaned back in her seat. "I'll be rich, and maybe it will teach you to think more before you speak."

"Sounds boring," Driscoll responded.

Maverick was going to throw us in prison just to get them to stop bickering.

But he ignored them both, reaching across the table and lifting one end of the scarf still wrapped around my neck. His gaze seared into me while the scarf glittered under the rays of the sun. "Where did you get this?"

My heart wrenched at the question because it wasn't about where I got it that made this scarf so special. It was about why I kept it in my chest full of my most treasured artifacts. About the fact that this scarf reminded me of the first time I'd ever met the bone collector. Who I hadn't seen in almost two years, all because I'd ruined our friendship. Pushed away the only friend I had. Possibly the only person in this world who ever understood me. Tears pricked my eyes, and I blinked them away. Except I couldn't say any of that to Maverick Von Lucas. First, because he wouldn't understand, and second, because I wouldn't compromise the bone collector like that.

I opened my mouth, realizing I still hadn't answered Maverick's question about where I got the scarf, then decided I didn't have to. I snapped my mouth closed and raised my chin.

Maverick rubbed his stubbled jaw, frustration coiled in his shoulders. "I don't have time for this. I'm leaving on a trip in a few hours, and I'll likely be gone for months." He leaned forward and pushed the chest out of the way. "So save us both the trouble and tell me where you got the scarf. Where you got all of these objects. Did you steal them from someone?"

A desperation laced his voice that I didn't quite understand.

I ignored his question. "Where are you going?"

"We're going to prison if you don't answer his question." Driscoll threw up his hands. "Who am I kidding? We're going to prison either way."

"It's none of your business where I'm going." Maverick pressed his hands onto the glass table. "Where did you get this? Was it from her? From the white rabbit?"

I reeled back at his use of my secret name. Of course Maverick Von Lucas would have heard of the white rabbit since he worked directly with the queen, but the fact that he knew these objects belonged to her . . . I was in more trouble than I'd realized.

I should've just answered his questions. But after a lifetime of doing what I was told and gaining absolutely nothing from it, I was sick and tired of obeying.

I raised my chin. "Tell me where you're going, and I'll tell you where I got the scarf."

I didn't know why it mattered so much, but for some reason it did. Just being here in the academy filled me with so much anguish. I yearned for this life Maverick lived, wanted it so badly it burned through my ice-filled veins. If he was going on some adventure to find a new historical artifact, I wanted to know about it. To sit in this office and dream of the life I could have had if things had turned out differently for me. For just a few moments before those guards took me away to prison, where I'd likely be for a long, long time.

There he went, staring at me again. Did this man have a problem? Or was he just a pervert? But he wasn't staring at my nipples, which were absolutely visible through my thin nightgown. His eyes never left my face. Just studying me with this perplexed expression like I was a puzzle he couldn't figure out.

"So it's a game you want to play?" he said slowly, carefully. It felt like this was a test of some sort. He gave a subtle nod. "Then let the games begin."

I peered at him, the words he'd just said reverberating in my mind. Not just the words. The tone. The cadence. The playfulness. My entire body went rigid.

Driscoll looked at Leoni. "Do you know what's happening between them right now?"

Suddenly, I was in another time, another place, where we'd said those exact words to each other the first time we'd met.

My gaze locked onto Maverick's frowning face. It couldn't be. This had to be a coincidence. The feeling stirring in my gut told me otherwise. It told me he was exactly who I thought he was. His voice, his words . . . my gaze dipped down to his hands laying flat on the desk, his forearms . . . even those looked familiar. How many times had I seen the bone collector use them when we'd been vying for the same artifact or relic? When we'd been playing our game?

I could barely breathe. Barely think. If I was right, it could only mean one thing.

Maverick Von Lucas was the bone collector.

Part Two

"Curiouser and curiouser."

Chapter Twelve

EMORY

Maverick and I stared at each other, the sound of my heavy breaths filling my ears.

The guards rapped on the door, and I jumped, breaking our staring contest.

Maverick nodded at me, an understanding passing between us. "I keep my office warm," he said. "If it gets too drafty in here, feel free to open a window. If you'll excuse me." He pushed back his chair and exited the room, closing the door behind him with a click while I gaped.

The bone collector, and he knew I was the white rabbit. It was why he'd brought me back here. To confirm my identity. After all these years of us not knowing anything about each other, after how I'd left our last meeting . . . he must hate me. Except he wasn't looking at me like he hated me.

I didn't know how to feel about that. About him.

"Well that went about as well as the time I tried to climb a tree while drunk," Driscoll said.

Both Leoni and I stared at him.

He cleared his throat. "I fell from a branch and broke my ankle."

I jumped from my seat, glancing at Maverick's outline through the stained-glass pane of his door as he spoke with the guards.

"Feel free to open a window."

That was what he'd said. He was helping me.

Without wasting any time, I ran to the window and looked down. Far, far down at the snowy expanse below. I gripped the bottom of the glass, rattling it, using all my muscle to shove it upward.

"Listen, I know you're from the frost court and love the cold, yada, yada, but I'm freezing my balls off here, so if we could keep the window closed, I'd appreciate it," Driscoll said.

I spun to face him, back flattening against the sill. "We're escaping," I said. "We have to go. Now."

He rolled his eyes. "We already tried that. Remember a very similar situation where we escaped out a window and then got caught?"

Leoni crossed her arms, studying me. "What's going on?"

My gaze shifted to Maverick, still speaking with the guards just outside this office. "I know this is going to sound crazy, but I think he's the bone collector."

Driscoll whipped toward the door. "The hot nerd? The hot nerd is the bone collector?"

"Will you stop calling him that? Just because you barely know how to read doesn't mean he's a nerd because he likes books." Leoni stood, staring at the door. "The bone collector. Maverick Von Lucas? The most celebrated scholar in Arathia? Why would he be the bone collector?"

"I don't know." I shrugged helplessly. "I don't have any answers, but I'm almost certain it's him, and he's giving us a chance to escape." I emphasized the last two words.

Driscoll frowned. "You think he's out there talking to the guards on purpose?"

"Yes," I said, exasperated. "So will one of you get over here and help me open this window so we can get out of here and then figure out what in the bloody frost he's doing with Spirit Sky's bolt?"

Driscoll looked at Leoni. "We're probably going to die, aren't we?"

"Probably." She huffed and stomped toward me. "Let's get going."

I sputtered as she and Driscoll shoved past me and worked to push open the window, which was frosted shut. "We're not going to die. Why would you say something like that?"

Driscoll grunted. "Because we've almost died approximately five thousand times in the last few months. You kind of get desensitized to it after that."

He looked at his fingers and yelped.

"What?" My pulse spiked. "What's wrong?"

"Relax." Leoni's face turned red as she pushed and pushed at the window. "He broke a nail."

Driscoll held up his pointer finger and scowled. "I just got a manicure."

I elbowed him aside right as the frost around the edges of the pane cracked, and Leoni and I shoved the window open. A shuddering wind blew in, rattling the parchment on the desk. It whipped up and flew around the room in swirls. Maverick stiffened outside the door, the conversation between him and the guards going quiet.

"We have to hurry!" We would not get another chance. I spread out my fingers, ready to use my frost magic to get us down below. A warning bell rang in the distance, and the clearing below emptied as everyone scurried to their classes. "Perfect timing," I said, looking behind me again.

"Oh no." Driscoll stepped up. "I'm already cold enough. No way I'm depending on your frosty powers."

I rolled my eyes as the door handle turned, the panic in me rising to a peak. "Then what's the alternative?"

He sighed and muttered, "I'm just supposed to be the sidekick, but here I am, once again saving everyone else's asses."

"Well, save our asses faster, please!" Leoni crossed her arms.

Maverick stepped in front of the guards, speaking in low, urgent tones, and I wondered what in the bloody frost he was saying.

Driscoll held out his hand, a vine slithering out the window. It looped around a statue that stood on a ledge outside Maverick's office window. The statue held a book in one hand, the other raised into a fist, the vine curling around it and tying into a thick knot.

The door burst open, and the guards shouted from behind us.

"Hope you both have been working on your upper body strength," Driscoll yelled as he clambered through the window and onto the vine.

"Not really," I shouted back.

Ice shards flew at us as Leoni and I grasped onto the vine, and suddenly we were swinging through the air. I looked back to see Maverick's face in the window, the guards behind him, all of them so shocked they didn't move.

Maverick held out his hand, a ball of fire appearing, his gaze trained on me. Of course he'd have to use his magic. He needed this to be convincing so it didn't look like he had any hand in our escape.

"He's going to burn our vine!" Driscoll yelled as my stomach heaved, the vine swinging us wildly back and forth.

"Where are we going?" Leoni asked from above, her hands white as she gripped the vine tight. "What is the plan?"

"Do I have to do everything?" Driscoll yelled.

We swung toward the rooftop below Maverick's office. His fireball flew past us, barely missing us.

"Really doesn't seem like he wants us to escape," Driscoll shouted.

"We're going to have to jump." I unfurled my fist and summoned my magic. Ice crackled into a ramp from the rooftop, unraveling toward the ground. "And your balls are about to get a whole lot colder."

When the vine hung over the roof, I dropped from it, landing onto the icy ramp I'd created and sliding down. Faces peered from all the windows of the academy, students watching in fascination as professors barked for them to return to their seats. Driscoll screamed as he dropped onto the ramp behind me, and Leoni followed with a thud.

"Spirits below, ice is hard!" Driscoll yelled from behind me. "I think that broke my ass!"

I slid, the ice slick, the cold of it seeping into my skin, which absorbed the chill and gave me renewed energy. I landed with an oomph on the snow-packed ground, Driscoll and Leoni toppling over me. We lay in a heap, all of us breathing heavily when the doors of the academy burst open, the guards and Maverick yelling as they raced toward us.

The guards shot out daggers of ice that flew in our direction.

"I'm really questioning all of my life choices right now," Driscoll muttered.

We struggled to our feet and ran through the courtyard. I ducked as an ice shard flew over my head, crashing into a tree.

Leoni raised her hand, and water unfurled into a tall wall between us and our pursuers, similar to the one she'd made in the street earlier. The shards and fire that flew our way dissipated in the water.

We raced off the campus grounds and into the street, now clear of the thick snow, glistening, damp cobblestone underneath. Leoni's wall fell with a crash behind us, the water washing over the snow.

Driscoll groaned. "They're going to catch up eventually." He bent over, breathing heavily.

Not if I could help it. I stretched out my hand, ice forming in a shimmering sheen along the street, reaching out toward the guards and Maverick. The bone collector shot another fireball our way right as he stepped toward us, his feet slipping from underneath him. The guards crashed into him and they all tumbled in a heap, trying again and again to stand but losing their footing on the slick surface.

"This way," I said as we ducked into an alley and raced through it, the sounds of our pursuers fading into the background. "I know where we can go."

"Lead the way," Driscoll said, voice resigned, all of us breathing heavy and clutching our sides.

It wouldn't be too far. I only hoped we could stay out of sight long enough to get there.

Chapter Thirteen

We arrived at the little field behind the row of houses that lined my street. Snow reached our ankles, and we trudged through it, slow, all of us exhausted after the morning's events.

"Why are we in the middle of a field?" Driscoll asked. "Are you about to kill us and bury our bodies here?" He stopped, bending over to catch his breath. "Actually, I don't even care anymore. Do what you want."

"No, I'm not here to murder you. I can think of far easier ways to kill you both than bring you out here." I sank down and began digging with my hands, shoveling snow in big scoops.

"What is she doing?" Driscoll asked, but I was too focused on the task to answer. "Is this some weird frosty thing they do for fun?"

"You know, I'm really regretting letting you come with me," Leoni said. "Can you just be quiet for five minutes? Five whole minutes of me not having to hear your voice."

"That's rude," Driscoll said.

I kept digging, my nightgown completely soaked, my boots full of water, my fur cloak weighed down with melted snow. Finally, a cluster of branches and brush appeared under the frothy white, and I cleared it all aside.

Leoni gasped as she stepped up beside me. "Is that a door in the ground?"

I brushed the wet dirt and debris from it. Then I placed my palm in the center, and ice shot out and into the seams. The lock clicked open, allowing me to heave the heavy stone door aside. Stairs led down into the dark bunker.

Driscoll gulped, and I suspected he very much wanted to make a sarcastic comment, but his gaze darted to Leoni, and he clamped his mouth shut, shoving between us and stomping down the stairs.

Leoni looked after him as he disappeared into the dark. "I shouldn't have been so harsh on him," she said. "I'm just cold and tired, and I've been with him for about six months now. Every single day. All day. Full of Driscoll. It's a lot."

I could only imagine.

She bit her lip. "Just to make sure, you're not planning on murdering us, right?"

"No, I'm trying to save us." I gestured for Leoni to enter. "Now can we please get to safety before the guards find where we've gone?"

Leoni swallowed, then nodded and entered. I followed behind, closing the stone door over us. To passersby who weren't paying attention, it would just look like a round rock in the ground, which was why it had made the perfect place for me to hide my collection.

I made my way down the dark stairs until I got to the bottom, the ground hard underneath my boots. I knelt down and felt around for the book of matches I kept . . . Ah, right there. I lit a match and held it to a group of candles I'd situated on the table in the middle of the space.

The flickering light illuminated the bunker, made entirely of stone.

Driscoll and Leoni looked around the small space in wonder. Shelves lined three of the walls, wooden and simple, ones that I'd built. Artifacts lined the shelves, and in the center of the room sat a small table, the candles now burning brightly atop it.

"What is this place?" Leoni walked to a back shelf, running her finger along the rough edge.

"My best guess?" I said. "A bunker that belonged to someone in the Old World when . . ."

"When everyone was dying?" Driscoll finished, leaning forward and studying a golden head, one carved to look like Spirit Earth, evident by the flowers and fungi strung in her hair. "I thought it was a sudden death. Boom. Everyone gone. How'd anyone have time to make a bunker?"

I walked toward the table and sunk onto the chair sitting in front of it, exhaustion filling me as I slumped. "That's what we thought for a long time. But recently, new evidence has surfaced that their deaths may have been slower than we previously believed. That the world began falling apart over a long period of time. I spread my arms around. "Evidenced by bunkers like this found all over the continent. Likely bunkers that belonged to the wealthy, the kings and queens and nobles who could afford to have something like this built." I traced a finger over the cracks in the table. "Maverick was actually the lead historian behind this theory. He was the first to find a bunker like this."

Well, the first that anyone knew about. I'd actually found this bunker long before he'd discovered a bunker located in Apolis. But no one knew about my discovery because no one knew about me.

I cleared my throat. "Once he found that one, other historians began to discover even more. Some connected to other bunkers by a network of tunnels. It was a very elaborate system, but we think they eventually ran out of food and water and died anyway."

Driscoll shuddered. "So this just delayed their deaths."

"Are you going to tell us why you think Maverick Von Lucas is the bone collector?" Leoni paced as I twisted in my chair to look at her. "It makes no sense. He's the most prominent historian in Arathia. He already has access to all these artifacts, gets paid to find them. So why in the world would he risk his entire career to become a notorious treasure hunter?"

Well, when she put it like that, it did sound crazy. And the truth was, I didn't know why. The only one who could answer that question was Maverick himself.

"She has a point," Driscoll said. "It's really far-fetched."

"It's him." I pushed a hand through my blonde hair, which dusted my shoulders. "I know it is. His voice, what he said to me. I said those exact words to the bone collector when we first met."

Driscoll pinched the bridge of his nose. "He does have fire magic, just like the bone collector."

Leoni stepped up next to Driscoll, shaking her head. "The similarities are striking. And his voice." Her brows furrowed. "Now that I think about it . . . I wondered why Maverick's voice sounded so familiar."

I couldn't believe I hadn't put it together before this moment. I knew the bone collector's voice, had spent far too many nights dreaming of it. How could I have not recognized he was Maverick the moment I heard Maverick speak so many years ago?

"Spirits below," Driscoll said. "If what you're saying is true, it would ruin his entire career and discredit all his work. Do you think he has his own little bunker of objects he keeps from the academy?"

"I don't know. I don't really know him." I swallowed down the lie. "But I do know that if I'm right that means he has the bolt."

Leoni's eyes widened. "He said he was going on a long journey, that he'd be gone for months. Do you think that's what this has to do with?"

"It must. He's doing something with that bolt. But what . . ." I murmured, realizing just how many secrets the bone collector had kept from me. It shouldn't have stung after the way I'd ended things between us. But it did.

"It's too powerful of an object for him to have." Leoni wrung her hands together. "He could be in league with the shadow king."

"No," I said, and both their gazes snapped to me.

"I thought you said you don't know him." Driscoll massaged his temples. "Can you please get your story straight?"

"I don't know him, exactly, but I—well . . ." Spirits below, I didn't know how to explain this, how to explain our relationship and connection to each other. "We ran into each other quite a few times throughout the years. We chatted . . . and stuff. I never got the sense he'd be involved with someone so depraved like this shadow king."

It didn't fit, not with what I knew about him. Maybe I was being naive. Maybe I just wanted to believe he wouldn't do something sinister with that bolt.

"You chatted?" Driscoll echoed. "So you two would just happen upon each other while trying to steal the same ancient artifact and then stop in the middle of your thieving for a casual little conversation?"

"That about sums it up," I snapped. "Now can we focus on the issue at hand?"

Leoni and Driscoll shot each other looks that I couldn't decipher. Leoni bit her lip. "Why do you want the bolt?" She gestured around the room of artifacts. "Is it to add to your collection?"

A flush crawled up my neck, staining my cheeks. "I hoped maybe it would get me into the academy. That if I found something that impressive, I could bargain with them for admittance."

Leoni's gaze softened. "But what about your husband? Would he really have allowed such a thing?"

I wrapped my arms around my waist. "I hoped that maybe if I did something that grand, he'd finally see me for who I am, that he'd let me attend. It was foolish, and now I need that bolt to bargain for my freedom since I'm wanted for my husband's murder. Hopefully Princess Poppy is a woman of her word and will convince the frost queen to pardon me—for all my crimes."

They both stared at me for a minute before Driscoll said, "I'm still hung up on this bone collector thing. Can you just ask him?" Driscoll flailed his arms around. "You know, something like 'hey bone collector, do you happen to have an all-powerful bolt hidden somewhere in that office of yours, and if so, what, exactly, are your plans for it?'"

I chewed on my bottom lip. What indeed. Why hadn't he given it up to the academy? This journey he was going on had to be connected to it. I was sure. Maybe the academy knew about it? Was sanctioning this trip? I didn't know. Couldn't make sense of it.

"We don't have that kind of relationship," I said. "We're rivals. We compete. We don't help each other."

That wasn't true, but I wasn't going to delve into our entire history right now. It was too complicated.

"And we definitely don't talk about anything to do with our personal lives," I continued. Also not true. Spirits below, I was lying a lot today. "He won't tell me." Especially after what I did almost two year ago. "If he wanted me to know, he would've already found a way to contact me."

Leoni's face twisted into confusion. "How? If you didn't know anything about each other?"

I waved away her words. "We had a system, okay?" I groaned. "We don't have time for this. Just trust me when I say he's the bone collector, and if he has the bolt, as you've claimed he does, then we need to figure out why."

A new game between us. One I had to win.

Leoni's hand went to the hilt of her sword. "Well, since this is the only lead we have, I guess we have to follow it."

"Follow him," I said.

"Which is great, considering we have no idea where he's headed," Driscoll said.

"So what's the plan?" Leoni asked.

"We're going to track him," I responded. "I've followed the bone collector enough times. I know how to be discreet. I know how he works. We'll find him and steal the bolt from him, then get it to Princess Poppy. That's why she sent you, right?"

They looked at each other again, a tension filling the air that I didn't understand.

"Yes," Leoni said, voice curt.

"Nothing can ever be simple," Driscoll added.

"Well, let's get going." Leoni heaved a sigh. "He said he'd be leaving soon, so we don't have a lot of time."

I stood. "I agree. But first"—I gestured to my nightgown—"I need to change."

Chapter Fourteen

MAVERICK

I paced in my office, glancing at that open window. The white rabbit had been here. In my office. The white rabbit was Emory Growley.

Emory. She had a name. I wanted to say it out loud, to see how it might feel on my lips, taste on my tongue. For years, we'd danced around each other. Years that I'd wondered what lay under that hood. Until she'd effectively cut me out of her life. No explanation. No warning. It still hurt. More than I wanted to admit.

Now I couldn't stop picturing her face. I'd sat across from her, memorizing every single feature of her heart-shaped face with her small pointed nose and high cheekbones while she'd glared at me the entire time.

My lips twitched.

Hopefully I'd given her enough time to escape. She'd need to be more careful. I wondered how the guards had found her in the first place. I never took the white rabbit for someone to make mistakes, to be careless enough to get caught. She pulled a lot of dangerous stunts, but she also covered her tracks.

It didn't matter. I wouldn't have time to find her again. To play another one of our games.

I was out of time. I had to leave. Now. I glanced at the corner of my office, a small leather satchel packed with a few essential items I'd need to survive the next few months.

I stiffened.

The white rabbit had been alone in my office with that satchel. I rushed to open it, then slumped against the floor in relief when I saw the bolt inside, sizzling and sparking with power. She'd bested me enough times, taken items right under my nose. But this was the one item I couldn't let her have.

Spirit Sky's bolt. I still couldn't believe it was real. That it was in my possession.

The door to my office banged open, and I quickly pulled the string on the satchel, tying it closed and praying to Spirit Fire I'd been fast enough.

I stood, running a hand over my hair. "Professor Gungar." I nodded.

"Professor Von Lucas," the older man said, raising his chin and sniffing like I'd somehow already offended him.

I'd come to learn that my very existence offended him, especially ever since the frost queen chose me as the historical advisor on her council over Gungar, a personal blow to the old man who'd been the queen's advisor for as long as anyone could remember. Then there was the fact that I never accepted any invitations from the professors. Not for their weekly outings to the tavern, not for their parties, not for their monthly dinners. I couldn't, not when I was so focused on my career. The only reason I went to Lord Growley's party the other night was because he made large donations to the academy.

"What in the bloody frost happened this morning?" Gungar stepped forward, nose wrinkling as he glared at my clothes while straightening his blue robe, one that all historians and scholars wore to signify our connection to the academy. I wore the robe when I taught but otherwise preferred my own clothing, much to the chagrin of all the elders, so used to their traditions, so stuck in their ways. "I'm told you went against the queen's orders and brought a criminal to the academy for questioning? What were you thinking, Von Lucas?"

He raised a brow, and I straightened my shoulders, rolling them back. "I was thinking that you'd want me to bring the woman here so I could question her about this chest she carried with significant artifacts inside."

His eyes widened as he took in the chest sitting on my desk, craggy eyebrows raising and making all the wrinkles on his forehead more pronounced. "What in the world was she doing with that?"

I wouldn't reveal her identity. I had far too much respect for the white rabbit to do so.

I grabbed my long black coat off the hook behind him and shrugged it over my shoulders. "I don't know. But now it belongs to the academy, which should make the queen happy. Quite a few new additions for the museum."

His face turned red, and he snatched my arm. "And you let this woman escape? She's clearly a threat to the academy. To the queen. She kept these items for herself instead of turning them over. She could be hiding pieces of history from us, finding out information the queen might not want anyone to know."

I snorted. He was starting to sound like the frost queen, so afraid of information getting out, like that wasn't our job as historians.

"Well, you could always chase after her yourself instead of making me your errand boy."

Professor Gungar narrowed his gaze. "Watch it, Von Lucas. I've been here for fifty years. You've been here for six."

I tugged on the lapels of my coat. "Yet I believe I'm the one who's the queen's historical advisor. Not you. And maybe if you and the others listened to me, you'd realize that times are changing. That our methods need to change as well."

He scoffed. "Who was this woman? She needs to be brought to justice."

"Lady Emory Growley." Her name. Emory. It tasted as sweet as I'd expected.

"The ambassador's wife?" He raised a hand to his chest. "Spirits below. That does make sense." He stopped abruptly, gaze slowly raising to meet mine. "Do you know why the queen wanted her for questioning?"

"I assume because of all the valuables she was carrying in that damn chest." I pointed to it, still sitting on my desk. If the queen had taken Emory in for questioning, she'd have figured out her identity as the white rabbit sooner or later, and then Emory would be in deep, deep trouble. Thank the spirits she'd escaped.

"No," Gungar said. "That's not why the queen wanted her."

I leaned against my desk. "Since you seem to know, please, don't keep me waiting in such suspense."

"Emory's husband, Lord Growley, was found murdered in his home this morning. Believed to have been killed by his wife."

Husband. I'd been so wrapped up in my discovery of the white rabbit's identity, in knowing her name, I'd somehow forgotten the rest of it. She was married. That was a punch to the gut that I hadn't expected. And—had he just said . . .

"Murder?" I asked, brain still unable to keep up.

"Early this morning." Gungar's chin wobbled. "Servants found him dead in the cellar after a clear struggle. His wife nowhere to be found."

All the breath left my lungs, and suddenly, it made sense: why she was wearing nothing but a nightgown, why she'd been running in the first place. It wasn't because the guards thought she was a thief. It was because they thought she was a murderer. And I'd been stupid enough to let her escape. All because of my connection to her, because I'd actually thought at one point that there was a world where the white rabbit and I could . . . Married. She'd been married the entire time she'd been the white rabbit. Our last meeting suddenly made far more sense. I suddenly felt very, very stupid.

I pounded a fist on the desk.

Gungar raked a hand through his thinning white hair and glanced behind me at my packed satchel. "What's done is done. Emory Growley is now the frost queen's concern. Not ours. Not yours. Are you ready for this mission?"

The mission. I suspected Gungar was sending me with the hope that I didn't return. I might've been the favorite of the queen—and many students—but Gungar still ran this academy, was still the Arch

Historian, and that meant he had the power to send me on assignments.

"We're getting more and more reports of this white wolf stalking the Glacier Mountains. A wolf like no one has ever seen before. Huge with fangs as big as my fingers, standing near as tall as a fully grown man."

I waved away his words. "Yes, yes I've been briefed. Though I'm not sure why you're sending a historian to trek after this creature and not a hunter." I raised a brow.

Gungar shifted on his feet. "Because the queen wants him in her custody."

Just another obsession of the frost queen's I didn't understand. She cared far more about this wolf than she should have.

"We need someone who can analyze the creature," Gungar was saying, "tell us how it evolved, where it might have come from. Not just some brute who will barge in and kill it. We need some answers about this thing. It's terrorizing small villages on the outskirts of the mountains. It's eating livestock. We're worried the villagers are next."

I shuddered at that and swept my arms around the room. "Well, as you can see, I was on my way out before you barged in. Hastings is taking over my class until I return."

"Very good." He nodded stiffly. "Well, good luck to you then."

I snorted. We both knew he couldn't care less if I found this beast or not. Lucky for him, this mission happened to come at the exact right time. Because I had a mission of my own to complete, one that by pure luck would take me through the Glacier Mountains. One that had nothing to do with the white wolf. A trip that would require that bolt hidden in my satchel. If Gungar knew I had it and was withholding it from the academy, if he knew what I planned to do with it, I wouldn't just lose my job, I'd lose everything. Get thrown in the frost prisons right along with the white rabbit.

But the sacrifice, the risks, would be worth it. This wasn't just a mission. It wasn't like anything I'd done before. Because this journey—it was personal.

Gungar swept out of the office.

I could very well die on this secret mission, but if I didn't do this, well, then I didn't deserve to live anyway.

$$\mathcal{Chapter\ Fifteen}$$

One year. It had been almost one year since I'd seen the white rabbit.

We'd met a few weeks after our first encounter in the highlands, then we'd drawn an artifact, and the games had begun.

She'd bested me in our first competition, stealing Spirit Frost's coveted chalice, then bounding away with glee—and leaving me frozen in a giant ice block. It had taken almost all my magic to melt that damn thing and get free.

"See you next year," she'd said.

And I'd spent this last year thinking of her far more than I liked. Especially when what I needed was to focus on my job. Not some mysterious woman. I had no idea why I was doing this. Why I was risking everything to compete with the white rabbit. All I knew was that I liked it.

Now I paced in the Draje Forest, a wintry mix of wind, snow, and rain pelting me. It didn't matter how many layers I wore in this spirits-forsaken court, I still managed to freeze. It didn't help that she was late. Maybe she'd changed her mind in the last year. Decided she no longer wanted to play our little game. The thought shouldn't have disappointed me like it did.

"Miss me?"

A smile came to my face. I had, actually. Which was weird considering I barely knew the woman. Yet I felt a kinship with her, a respect for her.

I turned, snow flurries blurring the space between us. A scarf covered the lower half of her face, the upper half obscured by her hood. I'd started wearing a scarf as well. Not only to protect me from the damn cold, but because we agreed it would be smart to keep our identities as secret as possible.

"Ready to be bested again?" she asked, but her words felt off. None of that typical bite to them.

"Maybe I let you get that chalice last year," I said, stepping closer to her.

"Sure you did." She crossed her arms, her cloak billowing around her while the wind howled, and I could see that she wore a thick sky-blue wool dress that hung down over brown boots with laces. Not cheap clothes, by any means. Which made me wonder if she had money. I shouldn't have been wondering. No personal details. That had been our agreement.

"Whatever helps you sleep at night." She pointed to the tree next to us, carved with a rabbit and a bone. "Let's just get the jar, okay?"

"Something wrong, little rabbit?"

She scoffed. "You think I'd tell you if it was?"

Fair point, but it bothered me, thinking that something, or someone, may have hurt her. Or maybe she was just having a bad day. I shouldn't have wanted to hear about it, but I did.

"Then don't give me details." Tree branches rustled around us, swaying with the wind. I tugged my hood down farther. "Tell me the summarized version."

It was an exercise I gave my students. So many of them got bogged down with details of historical events, unable to see past it all to the bigger picture. So I'd often ask them to take everything they read and summarize it. Into a neat little paragraph. Many times, it was enough to get them out of their heads and better able to understand the historical context. Then we could dive deeper into the issues, the details to round out the picture. The other professors balked at my methods, claimed I coddled the students. I'd just gotten the job, and if I wasn't careful, I was going to lose it already. Which meant going back home to my father. Something I had no desire to do. Not when I'd finally gotten free.

"It doesn't matter," the white rabbit said, her voice reminding me of chiming bells. "Let's just get the jar and pick our next artifact."

She was stubborn, this one. I'd wear her down eventually. To what end, I didn't know. I could never reveal my identity to her. And I assumed there was a reason she could never reveal hers to me. There was no point in trying to wear her down or get her to reveal more about herself. It would never lead to anything. Yet I just couldn't help myself.

"Well, it's a big deal to me. Can't have you distracted. Kind of ruins the competitive element to our little game. So out with it." I gestured toward her. "Tell me what's bothering you."

She hesitated, and I wondered if she'd refuse again. Tell me to go fuck myself. Her shoulders rose under her white fur cloak as she took a deep breath. "It's the two-year anniversary of my mother's death."

Oh, shit. "I'm sorry. Were you close?" I winced because it shouldn't matter. Grief was grief, and even though I hated my own father, I didn't know how I'd feel if he died. If I'd be sad or relieved. Either way, it would be hard.

"My father was basically absent from my life," she said, and I could hear the wobble in her voice. "Focused on his career, coming home to check on my progress and make sure I was being the good little daughter I was supposed to be. He died when I was ten years old. My mother, however, she was present." She hesitated like she was choosing her words carefully. "Too present. She watched my every move, had . . . expectations of me."

"Did you meet those expectations?" I asked. I knew all about parental expectations.

She wrung her hands together, her skin so pale, her skin so smooth and delicate. "I did. She died proud, all her dreams for me fulfilled. So I guess that's what truly mattered."

I scratched my head through the back of my hood. "Do you want to do this another time? We don't have to—"

"No," she interrupted. "This is good. It's the distraction I need."

"Okay." Now that she'd given me those small details about her life, little morsels, I was hungry for more.

But no. This could never be anything more than the game we played. No matter how intriguing she was. So I'd better make the most of it.

I gestured to the tree. "Go ahead."

She brushed past me and I caught her scent in the air, alpine and pale blossoms. It wasn't like the storm that whirled around us, but like the calm that came after. Like waking up after a night of heavy snowfall and stepping outside to take a deep breath. Refreshing and subtle.

She grabbed the little circle of wood we'd cut from the tree, sliding it out and revealing a small nook where our jar sat. "I chose last time." She plucked out the glass jar and shoved it at me. "Your turn."

I plunged my hand into the jar of small folded pieces of parchment, grasping onto one and pulling it out.

"Well?" she asked. "What's the artifact?"

I unraveled the rolled parchment, my excitement building. "The Terramadeau Scrolls."

"In the ice pits," she said, the excitement also evident in her voice, and I fucking loved that she was up for this challenge.

The historians and scholars at the academy wouldn't dare go near the ice pits, not if it meant risking their precious little necks. They wouldn't let me go either. That would make them look bad. The new young professor showing off and embarking on dangerous missions. I shook away the thoughts. This was supposed to be my escape from all of that.

"Now that we've got that settled." I reached into my cloak, pulling out a scroll I'd discovered recently that laid out ten rules for interacting with the spirits. One of the rules mentioned the Seven Spirits' mythical weapons, stating that the weapons were never to be touched by anyone but a spirit. Though it didn't say why. I wondered what the repercussions might be. I wanted to get her opinion, see if she knew anything about these weapons.

I looked up from the parchment to ask the white rabbit what she thought, but when my gaze lifted to find her, she was already gone.

Chapter Sixteen

EMORY

"Iced tits, it's freezing." Driscoll shuddered at the blistering-cold wind that rattled past us.

"Iced tits?" Leoni shot him a sidelong look from under the hood of her black cloak, a single red tendril of hair escaping from it. "You know, your curse words have gotten more inventive the longer I've known you."

"I'm taking that as a compliment. And also a challenge to invent even more."

"How lovely," I said drily while Leoni just smirked.

We'd been following the bone collector for a week now. One week of trekking through the frost court toward the Glacier Mountains. We'd camped at night, all of us huddled together in whatever shelters we could find, waking up early and finding his trail. It wasn't hard with all the snow, his bootprints fresh and thick. He hadn't bothered covering his tracks. Why would he? He probably would never expect someone to be following him, especially not when he was going toward the mountains, known for their freezing temperatures, harsh terrain—and other threats like snow bears, wolves, and mountain lions.

"Why couldn't he be heading somewhere warm?" Driscoll asked, teeth chattering. "Would it kill him to take the bolt to a beach where I can lay in the sand and drink all day?"

We came to a stop at the base of the mountains, harsh gray stone dusted with snow, the range rising so high and stretching so far it seemed like they went on forever. The wind howled around us, snow flurries swirling, thick and cutting. The closer we came to the mountains, the worse the weather had become. It would only get harder to stay on his trail, and I didn't need any distractions.

I turned toward Driscoll and Leoni. "You're both welcome to turn around at any time. Truly. I'm used to following him. By myself."

I tugged at the blue scarf, still wrapped around my throat, covering my bruises. I let the words hang between us, hoping my meaning was clear.

Leoni scowled. "I promised Princess Poppy I would take care of this. That I'd get that bolt. I'm not leaving until I fulfill my promise."

Driscoll raised a finger. "I, on the other hand, made no such promises. So, you know, it might be time to say my goodbyes."

Maybe with one of them gone, I'd get some peace and quiet. Driscoll was the main talker, Leoni only responding out of annoyance or exasperation or sometimes amusement. I could see that they were close, had formed a bond over the events they'd been through. Not that I knew much about those events. By the end of every day we'd all been too hungry, too tired, too cold to do much talking. Well, they'd been too cold. I'd withstood the elements with much more ease than either of them.

Leoni came to an abrupt stop. The wind gusted past us and lifted the hood off her head, snowflakes catching in her hair. "You want to leave?" she asked Driscoll. "After everything we've been through, how far we've come? You just want to give up?"

"Of course I do! I told you back in the sky court: I'm not a hero, and I don't want to be."

Leoni opened her mouth to respond when I caught sight of a familiar black cloak far above and gasped.

Leoni and Driscoll looked at me.

"What?" Driscoll braced his legs, looking around. "Is it a bear? Or a wolf? Because I'm not into furry creatures that want to eat me."

Leoni raised a brow. "I don't think anyone is."

"No." I pointed at Maverick's form as he scaled the side of the mountain.

"The bone collector," Driscoll said. "We actually found him."

Maverick stopped and slowly turned, but surely he couldn't have heard us from so far above.

"Or he found us," Leoni murmured.

"Can we use our magic to get his satchel?" Driscoll whispered.

I lifted a hand over my eyes, arching my neck to look up. "He's too far. But we know we're on the right path at least."

Leoni cocked her head. "What is he doing?"

He pulled himself up onto the edge of a plateau.

Before, in his office, he'd stared at me with curiosity, with a kind of awe and wonder. Now, all of that was gone, his gaze hard and cold as he glared down at us.

I wondered what had changed. Maybe me stalking him. Trying to best him. But that was nothing new. This was what we did. I wanted to say something, but without that hood over his head, it was like I no longer knew him. Like he was a completely different person. The truth was I didn't know what to say.

I snapped my mouth shut as he slowly raised out his hand, and my stomach twisted into a tight knot.

"Is he about to use his magic?" Driscoll asked.

Fire appeared in his hand, and I squinted. "I think so, but we're so far away, what could he hope to achieve? He can't hit us from this far out."

He knelt down and threw the fireball toward the area underneath the plateau. It blazed, melting the snow.

"Is he thirsty or something?" Driscoll asked. "Kind of a weird time to take a drink. But okay, Hot Professor. You do you."

"He's up to something." I tilted my head. "But I don't know what."

All we could do was stand there like idiots and wait to see what in the bloody frost he was doing. He threw another fireball at the snow, and once again, it began to melt, softening.

"Tell me, white rabbit." His voice boomed. "Have you ever heard of the Battle of Sofor?"

I stiffened. So he'd figured out my identity, and by using my nickname, he'd as good as revealed his. Obviously, I'd already suspected all of this, but now that I knew it was 100 percent true, I wasn't sure how to feel. Relieved that I was on the right track. Confused that this great scholar was the bone collector. For the first time since we started our little game so many years ago, we were laid bare before each other. Officially on an even playing field. It was so odd hearing Maverick's voice, knowing that I could put a face to this mysterious nemesis I'd competed against for so many years.

"The fact that you even asked that is an insult to my intelligence," I said. "It was a battle that happened in the Old World between frost elementals and fire elementals, right here in the Glacier Mountains."

Though they'd been called something different thousands of years ago. Maverick probably knew the official name of those who wielded fire and frost magic, but I didn't.

He threw another fireball at the snow below him. "Look at you. Almost like a real historian."

We'd always made jabs at each other, but this one hit different. It felt like an actual insult.

My nails dug into my fists. "The Battle of Sofor," I said, "where the fire elementals were retaliating after the frost elementals froze their drag-ons. They wanted to steal Spirit Frost's axe and hoped to use it to kill him."

There were multiple sources that told this historical tale. A soldier's record-keeping of this battle was one of the first sources we had that detailed it all.

The fire elementals surprise attacked the frost elementals here, in the mountains, since most of the elementals lived in villages around the base. The frost elementals made it snow on the fire elementals as they attacked from above with their fire magic. The frost elementals started turning the tide of the battle, the snowfall so heavy it reached the fire elementals' waists, making it harder for them to summon their fire magic. But the frost elementals' plan backfired because—"

I stopped, my stomach dropping straight to the ground.

"Well, why did it backfire?" Driscoll asked. "I slept through most of the history lessons in school."

My gaze trailed up to Maverick, to the melting snow. The snow that was now beginning to shift and move.

"The fire elementals melted the snow to cause an avalanche."

A smile spread over Maverick's face. "Very good. I believe that's my cue. Don't follow me again. I'm done playing games with you."

He bounded away, coat fluttering behind him as he disappeared. "*Done playing games with you.*" He was angry with me, and I had zero idea why. I also had no time to think about it as the mountain rumbled above us.

We all froze, and my gaze swept upward, where the snow shifted again, beginning to move, to fall.

"It's an avalanche," I screamed above the thunderous sound.

"Yeah, I kind of got that from the impromptu history lesson," Driscoll said.

The snow heaved, barreling toward us with a thunderous roar, rocks falling from the side of the mountain and crashing down around us. "We have to move!" I yelled.

Driscoll looked around, nothing but a flat frozen expanse behind, the nearest village at least an hour away. "Where?" He waved his hands wildly. "There's nowhere for us to hide!"

I'd lived in frost court my entire life. Climbed these mountains as a child, playing with others, hiding in the crooks and crannies of the giant rock. "We have to climb." I lodged my foot into the stone. "And fast."

I heaved myself up, Leoni and Driscoll joining me.

"It really seems counterintuitive to go toward the avalanche," Driscoll yelled over the sound of crashing snow.

"We have to find somewhere to hide," I said, then my gaze locked on a long ledge jutting from above us. I pointed. "Up there!"

We climbed, boots and hands slipping on the icy rock, making our ascent slower while the avalanche came closer. It would be upon us in minutes.

"Can you use your magic to slow the snow down?" Driscoll's eyes darted upward to the mass of white rolling down the mountain.

"I can't stop an avalanche with my magic," I said. "Something like that is too strong, too powerful."

"Well my magic is useless," Leoni said as she reached an arm up and pulled herself ahead of me.

We both looked at Driscoll and he sighed. "Of course it's up to me."

"What about a vine?" I asked. "Something that we can climb faster than on this mountain?"

Driscoll pushed out his hand, and a trellis of thin wisteria began creeping up the mountain, over the snow and ice. We wasted no time, all of us grasping onto the trellis and climbing as fast as we could. It was much easier to grip onto than the rock had been.

The avalanche crashed toward us, the ledge that we could hide under getting closer.

"I don't think we're going to make it," Leoni said from above me, her words punctuating heavy breaths.

"Well, I can only do so much," Driscoll yelled from below. "If one of you would like to step up, that would be great."

I'd almost been choked to death by my husband. I didn't survive just so another man who didn't see my worth could kill me. Something told me that he wasn't trying to kill me. That he knew my strengths, knew what I could handle. That thought alone gave me the confidence to do what I needed. I lifted my hand and tugged at the magic inside of me. A frozen thread that I could pull, that would unfurl in body and spread through me, then manifest into whatever I needed.

A wall of ice crackled over us, extending the ledge that hung over our heads. "Keep climbing," I shouted to Driscoll and Leoni, who had stopped to watch my magic at work. "It might buy us time, but it won't save us if we don't get to safety."

They heeded my warnings, clambering up the trellis. I was now behind both of them, attempting to climb with one hand and maintain that thick wall of ice that hung over our heads with the other. I would find the bone collector yet. If I survived this entire mess.

The thunderous sound grew to a crescendo, crashing, crunching, chaos, all raining down over us. My magic faltered, and that thread inside of me threatened to snap under the pressure of the avalanche hitting the ice. Leoni clambered onto a little crevice in the mountain below the ledge, then pulled Driscoll up behind her.

I was falling behind.

Crack.

I slowly arched my neck as a long fissure split the ice in half under the unrelenting snow. The thread of magic inside me snapped. Ice exploded into a million pieces, raining on top of me, cutting at my face, battering my body. The rush of snow drowned out Driscoll's and Leoni's shouts, and I flattened my body to the mountain as the avalanche fell straight toward me. Something snaked around me, pushing me into the mountainside, fastening me to it. But it didn't matter.

The snow was too heavy, too smothering, too much. It filled my nose, my mouth. I tried to inhale and sucked in more of the wet, slushy substance. It clogged my airways. My lungs contracted, squeezing, burning, screaming for air. My entire body felt weighed down, smothered. I saw nothing but white, which soon turned to black as darkness washed over my vision.

The last thing I thought before falling into unconsciousness was that if the bone collector and I had been playing a game, I'd finally been the one to lose.

Chapter Seventeen

EMORY

"I s she dead?" a voice asked.

My heavy eyes blinked open to see Driscoll's and Leoni's frowning faces staring down at me.

"If I am dead, then this is definitely the Underearth," I said, slowly sitting up and taking in our surroundings.

Driscoll wrinkled his nose. "Well, now I'm starting to regret saving your life."

My entire body felt like it had been hit by a, well, by an avalanche. A fire crackled in front of me, and I realized we were sitting on the ledge where Maverick had taunted us just hours ago, the sky now pitch black, covered with plump gray clouds. The ledge led into a narrow passageway, two tall cliffs rising on either side. On the other side of the passageway, a thick fog hung in the air, leading deeper into the Glacier Mountains.

Driscoll and Leoni both sat as close to the fire as possible, holding out their hands, fingers tinged by blue. Their boots and thick wool socks lay out, drying.

"What happened?" I asked, taking my own soaked boots off, then peeling away my socks and massaging my feet.

Driscoll threw a log onto the fire. "Leoni and I used our combined magic to hold you against the mountain while that avalanche passed through. When it finally ended we were afraid you were dead. We pulled you up on the ledge and made you as comfortable as we could while I created wood and kindling and Leoni made the fire."

Leoni handed me a waterskin. "Drink," she commanded.

"Looks like your theory was right," Driscoll said. "Maverick Von Lucas. Hot professor. Bone collector."

"Gone," I said glumly, staring at the popping embers. "Now we have no way of finding him. He knows we're after him so he'll be more careful about covering his tracks. Not to mention, that avalanche set us back quite a bit."

"You can't give up!" Leoni rubbed her hands together. "He has that bolt, and who knows what he's planning on using it for. Come on, you're the white rabbit. You're not just some housewife with a little side hobby. You've built an entire reputation around this passion of yours."

I met her hard gaze. I could see why Princess Poppy had named her captain of the guard. She had a commanding air about her, a way of rallying the troops, so to speak. But this particular trooper didn't feel like being rallied. All I wanted to do was curl up in a ball and cry. Then consume large amounts of wine. And cry some more.

Leoni glared at Driscoll, who straightened and cleared his throat.

"Yeah." He punched his arm through the air. "You're not going to let some man get the better of you, are you? Did you hear the way he taunted you? He didn't even think you knew what the Battle of Sofor was. So condescending." He raised a finger. "Still very hot, though."

"If you don't get laid soon, I'm going to lose it," Leoni said. "I cannot hear about another hot man. I really can't."

Driscoll frowned. "Why? Hot men are so fun to talk about."

"You don't just talk about them." Leoni threw up her arms. "You obsess. Conversations with you are sixty percent gossip, thirty percent hot men, and maybe ten percent other things?"

"And?" He twirled his hand. "I'm still not seeing a problem."

I mulled over his words, barely hearing their conversation. "You're right," I said slowly.

"You think he's hot too?" Driscoll perked up.

"What?" I glared at him. I hadn't really thought about it, to be honest. I'd been too busy with my entire world being turned upside down. I'd be lying if I said I hadn't wondered what was underneath that hood over the years. I'd be lying even more if I said I'd been disappointed by what I saw. And okay, fine. Maverick Von Lucas was objectively gorgeous. He'd always been, though as a married woman, I never allowed myself to think about him like that. I admired his work, his tenacity in the field, his accomplishments. His looks? Well, I only admired those in a few . . . interesting dreams I'd had about him.

"No," I said quickly. "I'm agreeing about him being condescending. About not letting a man get the best of me. Not letting anyone get the best of me."

I thought of my parents, of my time at the Academy of Ladies, of my husband, and lastly, of Maverick's patronizing glare as he looked down at me from this very ledge.

"You both are right." I scooted away from the fire. "I can't give up. We can't give up."

Leoni leaned forward, the glow illuminating her reddened, chapped cheeks. "So why do you think he's brought the bolt here? To the Glacier Mountains? There's nothing in this area."

Well, that wasn't exactly true. There was plenty in these mountains. But I didn't think now was the time to tell them all about the threats that awaited us when we walked through that passageway.

"I don't know," I admitted. My stomach grumbled.

Leoni opened up her satchel and threw me a stick of dried meat.

I held it up to her and nodded in thanks, then took a bite. The meat was tough and chewy, and I had to swallow several times to get the bite down my throat, but it was food, and I was grateful.

"At least he's not taking it to the shadow court," Driscoll said. "Doesn't seem like he's in league with the shadow king."

No, it didn't. Sorrengard had fallen into ruin nearly sixty years ago after they'd waged war on the other courts. For years before the Shadow War, many shadow elementals had been practicing dark magic, using their powers to rip away people's shadows—an illegal use of their magic. It had all been sanctioned by their king and queen. The other courts of Arathia punished them with embargoes, banishment, arrests, everything they could think of. It only angered the shadow court, who believed they had a right to use their magic how they wished, even if it was for ill purposes. So they started a war over the whole thing. A war they eventually lost. Though it came at a high price: the star court's decimation. Everyone in the star court died, and it was thought to be because the shadow court used some kind of dark magic to kill them all. The star court had fallen into ruin, been boarded off by the other courts, and was now known as the Deadlands, a place no one dared go unless they didn't want to return.

Which, of course, only made me more curious about that place, about the secrets it might hold, the rich history just waiting to be discovered. The Glacier mountains were the only thing standing in between Fyriad and the Deadlands. If we could assemble a team, get to the Deadlands, we could learn what actually happened there during the Shadow War to kill an entire race of people. No one would ever agree to something like that. No one except maybe the bone collector. And he and I weren't exactly on speaking terms now. Not after the way I left things between us.

Driscoll ran a hand over his short coiled curls. "That shadow king is sketchy. Definitely seems like the type to want a powerful bolt to use against us."

I leaned back on my hands, the fire making me feel itchy, too hot. "Clearly that's not what's happening. The Glacier Mountains are definitely the wrong direction to be going if he wanted to get to Sorrengard."

"Which still begs the question: what is he doing with that bolt?" Leoni asked. "And how are we going to get it?"

Driscoll gnawed on his own slab of jerky. "You have to know something about the bone collector. Why is that even his name?" Driscoll asked.

"The name started after he and I both went after a collection of bones that some farmer had found on his land." That hadn't been part of our competition. Just an accident. "The farmer and his family came running out to see him stealing away with these femurs and skulls. I'd watched it all from the barn where I was hiding after realizing he'd made it there first." I shrugged. "The next day, the paper came out, and a description of him was on the front page, with a sketch and all." Though there wasn't much to sketch other than his black cloak and hood. "They'd dubbed him the bone collector."

Driscoll sighed like I'd disappointed him. "You two are the nerdiest criminals I've ever met."

I wanted to ask just how many criminals he'd come across in his lifetime but thought better of it.

Leoni frowned at the fire, and I took another bite of my dried beef. "You know the bone collector better than anyone. So what's his next move? What's his weakness?"

I sat back, mulling it over. "We goad each other a lot, lure each other into dangerous situations to get the better of the other." I finished my jerky, chewing and thinking. "And that wasn't the first time he quizzed me. He's done it before. Thrown out random years or names or objects to see if I knew the significance. Many times, it was related to what we were going after. What he had planned . . ." I sat up straighter. "The Battle of Sofor," I mumbled.

"Please don't tell me he's planning another avalanche." Driscoll's eyes darted upward.

I shook my head. "After their victory, the fire elementals retreated deeper into the mountains. The mountains looked a little different a thousand years ago, but one thing has stayed the same: the elements. They're harsh. Unforgiving this far up."

As if helping to prove my point, an icy gale barreled into us, the flames of our fire flickering, snow and ice pelting us from all directions.

"It gets worse than this?" Driscoll asked. "Perfect. Just what I wanted to hear."

"So how did the fire elementals survive?" Leoni asked.

"Most didn't," I admitted. "They'd planned to hide out and then sneak back home, but many met their end in these mountains. Except for the few who found refuge in the ice caves. It's the only place in the Glacier Mountains that provides shelter and fresh drinking water. That has to be where he's going. He'll know about it."

"Then that's where we go tomorrow," Leoni said decisively.

I wanted to argue, to tell her we should go now. But they weren't as immune to the cold as I was, and my body still felt like it had taken a thorough beating. To get that bolt, I'd need to be at my best.

Tomorrow, then. We'd find the bone collector, and I would be the one to win the game this time.

Chapter Eighteen

I jolted awake in the middle of the night, a snarling sound infiltrating my dreams until it got so loud it woke me. My chest heaved, and I rubbed my eyes, trying to see in the dark expanse. The fire still crackled, and Leoni and Driscoll huddled together, both of them asleep.

A low growl floated through the air, and two red eyes peeked out of the inky black surrounding us. That didn't bode well. I scrambled to my feet, summoning my frost magic into a long, icy sword.

"Leoni, Driscoll?" I said quietly. "You might want to wake up."

"No thanks," Driscoll mumbled before turning over.

"Wake up," I whisper-yelled, sidling over and kicking him in the back.

He shot straight up. "Ow. What is wrong with you . . ." He trailed off as I pointed a shaking finger in the direction of the red eyes.

He swallowed thickly and nudged Leoni, who slowly sat up, her hair tumbling down past her shoulders, out of its usual bun. "I told you to stop waking me in the middle of the night to tell me about your dreams," she said, voice full of sleep. "I don't care who you had sex with. Unless it's real sex, stop telling me about it."

Driscoll pulled her to a stand, both of them now next to me. Leoni stiffened when she noticed the growling.

"What kind of creatures did you say live in these mountains?" Driscoll's throat bobbed. "Did you mention any nice ones that have red eyes and definitely don't eat elementals like us?"

"No." I swallowed. "No, I didn't."

A massive paw appeared from the dark, a beast emerging, its body covered in white fur, its snout as long as my arm. It bared razor-sharp teeth at us that were as long as my pointer finger.

"That is not any kind of wolf I've ever seen before," Driscoll said.

Me neither.

Leoni summoned a swirling ball of water in her hand. "What do your history books say about that?"

I stared as the giant wolf took a thundering step toward us. "They've never mentioned anything like this. That is not a creature of this world."

"Then what world is it from?" Driscoll asked. "Because it sure as spirits seems like it's here in ours."

The beast took another step, its large paw stomping out our fire, the only light now coming from the faint orange embers still glowing.

Driscoll whimpered again, louder this time. "It just snuffed out our fire with a single step." He audibly gulped. "This is fine. This is fine. This is fine—Oh, it's taking another step toward us!"

"Now is not the time to panic," Leoni said.

"Really?" Driscoll whispered. "Because I think this is exactly the type of situation where one should panic."

I was more inclined to agree with Driscoll. I'd never heard of a creature so large, save for a dragon, and I hadn't seen any of those in my lifetime being from the frost court.

I thrust out my hand, a ball of jagged, spiked ice flying toward the wolf. The white of the ice lit the dark, the wolf rearing its head back and chomping it like it was a carrot. That magic would've knocked an elemental unconscious. But it was a snack for the wolf.

Driscoll cracked his neck from side to side, then summoned two vines that sprouted from the ground and shot toward the beast. They wrapped around its legs, but the wolf simply stepped forward and the vines snapped like twigs.

Driscoll raised his hands. "I'm out."

Leoni stepped forward, dragging her hands up through the air, a thick wall of water rising. "This should provide a barrier between us?" she said, but it was more like a question.

We all stood there, none of us moving, breaths frosting the air. The wolf crashed through the wall of water, making all of us jump back as it prowled forward, long, sharp canines bared.

"I think it's time to run," Leoni said, stumbling toward the edge of the ledge.

"You don't think that thing can catch us?" Driscoll asked. "Because I'm betting it runs faster than we do."

"On the count of three," Leoni said as she shoved on her boots, and Driscoll did the same, the wolf bending its legs, getting ready to pounce.

"Three," I cut in.

We sprinted around the edge of the plateau, running toward the narrow passageway that would lead deeper into the Glacier Mountains. I turned and kicked up a flurry of snow into the wolf's eyes, temporarily stunting it. But that wouldn't keep us safe for long. Driscoll was right. That thing would have no problem catching us. I thought of how we'd escaped Maverick's office, the ice I'd spread across the ground.

I stopped abruptly as the wolf regained its senses and pounded toward us, its roar bouncing off the icy walls of the mountain. No time to hesitate. I wiggled my fingers, slick ice rippling across the ground. The wolf instantly slipped, trying to get up and slipping again. I turned and raced after Driscoll and Leoni.

White sheets of solid ice rose up on either side of us, and it was too dark to see far ahead, to know what awaited us when the passageway ended. I shot out my hand as we ran, more patches of ice forming on the ground. Leoni flung her hand out as well, water splattering to the ground and growing hard and shimmery upon contact.

Our boots pounded on the fresh snow. Driscoll slipped, but Leoni and I grabbed his arms and hauled him upward. The ice would only delay the wolf so long before it caught back up. I only hoped we found somewhere to hide by the time it did.

"How long does this thing go on for?" Driscoll yelled between heavy breaths.

I wished I had an answer to that question.

The passageway began to narrow in, slowing us as Leoni and I continued to use our magic to foil the wolf. Soon I had to turn sideways to slip through the rock, its cold, sharp edges cutting into my clothes, catching on the threads of my white fur cloak.

"If this gets any narrower," Leoni said as she sucked in her stomach while inching forward, "we're going to get stuck. That doesn't happen, right?"

I swallowed.

"Why don't you ask that guy?" Driscoll pointed forward, a heap of bones on the ground, crushed between the walls.

"We don't know that that's what happened to him," I said, the lump in my throat growing.

A howl split the air, and we all stiffened, then shuffled forward faster.

"I think we made the wolf angry." Driscoll winced as the rock scraped across his face.

"I'm pretty sure that's just its general countenance." I grunted, squeezing myself through two sharp points on either side of me. A growl sounded from close by. Too close. It was already catching up.

"Emory, was that you?" Driscoll asked.

"Yes, because I regularly like to growl."

Suddenly, the wolf's head jutted between the rock, teeth gnashing at us. Driscoll screamed while Leoni and I shot water and ice toward the creature to no avail. Its sharp canines broke through our magic, catching onto the end of my shirt. The wolf struggled to get its massive body in between the mountain walls, and we inched forward as fast as we could while the hungry beast snapped and growled at us. Leoni disappeared ahead.

"I'm out," she yelled. "I'm out, I'm out!"

Driscoll squeezed through the bend of rock next, and I came falling out behind him. I wasted no time, turning and shooting my magic at the mountain walls. They rumbled and shook, rock beginning to fall as the wolf tried to shove itself through. It glared at us with red eyes, rearing back, ready to lunge when a large boulder of ice came crashing down on its head. More chunks of ice tumbled down the walls, landing right on the stunned wolf.

The creature collapsed, then disappeared underneath the rubble, rock continuing to fall and pile up until no part of the wolf could be seen.

We stood there, all of us staring in shock, unable to move.

"Well, that's not something I'm keen to experience ever again." Driscoll shuddered.

"Really?" I turned to him. "Because I thought that was a blast."

He made a face at me. "Your sarcasm is incredibly unwelcome right now."

Leoni rolled her eyes as the rocks rumbled and vibrated on top of the wolf. "Let's get out of here before that thing escapes," she said. "We're awake, so we might as well find these ice caves where you think Maverick went."

Driscoll massaged his arms. "Do you even know where they are?"

I thought about the fire elementals' famous march to the ice caves, how it had been chronicled in journal entries I'd read. "I have an idea." My heart still hammered from that harrowing experience, yet somehow I was already moving on to our next challenge. Spirits below, when this was all over, I'd sleep for a week straight.

Despite it all, hope bloomed in me.

We might just find the bone collector yet.

Chapter Nineteen

MAVERICK

Moonlight splintered into the ice cave, and I sat up, swearing at the sight of the waning moon set in the purple-hazed sky. It was almost morning, and I'd slept far later than I'd meant to.

That avalanche I'd caused would slow the white rabbit, but it wouldn't stop her. If I'd learned anything about her over the years, it was that she was stubborn. Hardheaded. She was a survivor. And now she was something she'd never been before: a pain in my ass.

All I'd wanted since our last meeting was to see her again, to know how she was doing. Now that exact wish had come true, and I wanted more than ever to go back. I didn't want to know that she'd been married the entire time we'd played our games. I didn't want to know she was a murderer.

Mostly, I didn't want her to find me.

This couldn't be one of our games. I needed that bolt, and where I was going was one place she could not follow. It was far too risky. I might've been angry with her, angry at what I'd found out about her, but that didn't mean I wanted to put her in danger.

She would come to the ice caves. She'd know this was one of the only safe havens in the Glacier Mountains. I had to be gone before she arrived.

I scratched my head. The only problem was that I didn't exactly know how to get where I was going. I had an idea, had an inkling it had to do with this network of caves, but it wasn't a certainty.

I heard the white rabbit's voice in my head. *"Nothing is ever certain. Not when it comes to history."*

She'd said that to me once, and it had stuck with me ever since.

Enough of the white rabbit. Of Emory Growley. I needed to banish her from my thoughts once and for all.

I reached for my satchel and opened it, the lightning bolt sitting inside, and next to the lightning bolt was a folded note. I swallowed, reaching for it and opening it up.

I'm not crazy. I think my reality is just different than yours, and I have to go find it.

Love,

A

That was it. That was all I had from Annalee. She'd left it on her desk in her dorm room, not addressed to Father or Mother, but to me. A single sentence, and I'd known what I had to do, where I had to go to fix all of this. After all, it was my fault she left.

Now I had to find her. It was no secret where she'd run away to, not when she'd obsessed over the place for years. But how to follow her? That was the challenge. I'd need the bolt to protect myself and get us back out. This was unprecedented territory. A place no elemental had gone before.

Well, that wasn't quite true. Many had gone before, but they'd never returned.

I took a deep breath and stood, stretching out my sore limbs. I glanced around the ice cave where I'd settled. These caves were dug by frost elementals under the order of Spirit Frost. He'd been growing paranoid and had ordered his subjects to build these caves and tunnels in the mountain, a way to hide should they need it.

Most thought he'd gone mad in those final years before he and the other spirits disappeared. I wasn't so sure. If he'd been that paranoid that he'd built tunnels into a mountain, there had to be a reason. But without any proof, I'd never be able to propose a theory so bold. Especially not when all the other professors were so set in their ways, so convinced that if they proved a theory it was set in stone. Unchanging. It drove me mad, but I didn't want to risk my job, so for the most part, I kept my mouth shut.

I snatched my satchel, slinging it around my chest as an icy wind whistled through the cave.

I had to leave. Now. I shrugged on my coat, then grabbed my cloak from my satchel and swung it on, raising the hood and walking deeper into the cave, ready to explore and find my way to Annalee.

"Stop!" a voice yelled, one I'd recognize anywhere.

An icy wall crackled up in front of me, blocking my path forward. I shot fire out, melting the ice, but it wasn't fast enough.

"Give it up," Emory said from behind me.

I turned slowly. There she stood with those two familiar companions.

"Give what up?" I said with an innocent shrug.

This felt familiar, like we were falling back into our roles: white rabbit and bone collector. No Emory or Maverick. No wife or professor.

She scowled, her thick white-blond eyebrows drawing together, and I imagined how many times over the years she'd made that same face from underneath her hood. "You know what I'm talking about: you stole Spirit Sky's bolt, and we want it back."

I shot her a smile. "Finders keepers and all that. You know the rules."

She stepped forward, the hood of her white fur cloak falling back, revealing white-blond hair that matched her eyebrows, wavy and short and grazing her shoulders. Her icy-blue eyes bore into me. "The rules don't apply to this particular situation."

"What rules?" the tall man asked, scratching his head, his gaze volleying between us.

"But you know, I do agree, actually." Emory tapped her chin. "I think finders keepers is an excellent idea."

Before I could guess what in the bloody fire that meant, she was jumping forward, snow flurries erupting from her palms and whirling around me in a storm, clouding my vision, scraping against my skin.

The weight lightened in my satchel, and I stuck out my hands as fire flared in my palms. The storm died down, and I wiped the flakes from my eyes and cheeks as she and her friends were already running away—with my bolt.

Fuck no. I wouldn't let the white rabbit get away with this. Not when it was my only way to save Annalee.

"This isn't a game, little rabbit!" I called after her. "I'm not competing against you. Not this time. I need that bolt."

"Well, so do I," she called over her shoulder. "And you damn well know why."

Because she'd told me. Confided in me. And I'd betrayed that trust.

I gritted my teeth and bolted after them, thrusting out my hands and shooting balls of fire through the cave. One caught on the tall, lanky man's green cloak.

But the shorter woman with the bun opened her hand and water appeared over the fire, putting it out.

"You just ruined a very nice cloak," the man shouted over his shoulder.

"Did I?" I yelled back. "Give me the bolt and I'll replace it."

"No deal," Emory said, bolt sizzling in her hand. "And if you come closer, I'll smite you right off the ground."

I snorted. "I'd like to see you try, little rabbit."

She scoffed as they continued running for the opening of the cave. If they escaped into the mountains, they could go in any direction, and I could lose them for good. I didn't have that kind of time. I'd already wasted so much precious time preparing for this damn journey. Too much time.

Emory and her companions skidded to an abrupt stop, and I didn't even have time to think about why. My gaze stayed trained on that bolt. It was within reach. I could grab it, create some kind of distraction, and slip away. They wouldn't be able to follow where I was going. Wouldn't be able to track me once I got there. I'd be well and truly gone.

I reached for it, slipping it from Emory's grasp, but she didn't even seem to notice, her feet frozen to the ground.

A low growl sounded from the entrance to the cave, and I looked up to see a wolf standing there, legs bent in a crouch, teeth bared, saliva dripping in fat splotches to the ground.

The white wolf. It turned out I didn't even have to find the creature for the queen. It had found me.

Emory whipped around, eyes wild. "Use the bolt. Now!"

I clutched it tighter to my chest. "I'm not going to use this weapon without knowing its full power. I need time to study it, to better understand it. What if I use it and it kills us all?"

The plan was to eventually use it, but she didn't need to know that.

A fury blazed in her eyes as she stepped closer. "Fine. It looks like the wolf is hungry. Do you want to volunteer to be its meal?" She paused. "Better yet, you don't even need to volunteer. I'll let the wolf know he can have you."

The tall, lanky man tugged at his coiled black hair. "In case you two didn't notice, there is a wolf ready to devour us all, so maybe you can save this argument for later."

I rolled my eyes and crouched down, pressing my hand to the ground. A line of fire sizzled straight toward the wolf. It yelped as the fire singed its paw, then it snapped its jaws and let out a roar that shook the cave. The beast was huge. Bigger than any wolf I'd ever seen.

Emory put a finger to her chin. "Oh, excellent. Now you've angered it even more."

I tipped my head at her. "I don't see you using your magic."

She didn't break my gaze as she flicked her wrist, and shards of ice flew through the air at lightning speed. They drove straight toward the beast's eyes, then hit it, and simply . . . broke away.

"That can't be possible. It's immune to our magic?" I asked.

"Looks like it, bone collector," she replied. "Any other bright ideas? Or are you going to taunt it more? Just to make it extra ragey."

The beast took a step toward us that made the ground tremble. Its thick pink tongue lolled from its mouth, peeking out from between massive canines.

"We don't have time for this," the short woman said, racing toward Emory and grabbing her arm. "The best we can do is get away and try to delay it like we did last time."

"Oh good." The tall man rubbed his hands together. "More running."

As if it could understand us, the beast crouched further down, bracing its legs like it was ready to pounce. It hadn't attacked us. It could have by now. But I wasn't all that sure it wanted to hurt us. Which made no sense at all.

Emory and her companions pushed past me as I stared in awe at this thing. Gungar was right. We couldn't kill it. We needed to better understand it, to know where it came from. To understand how it could be immune to our magic.

"Looks like you're offering yourself up as a snack after all," Emory called, jolting me from my thoughts. "Thanks, bone collector. That's so kind of you."

I shot out a wall of fire as I began to run, but when I looked behind me, the wolf crashed through the fire like it was nothing. It whined a bit, maybe got a few burns, but something like that would've incinerated a normal animal. What in the fiery spirits was this thing?

Patches of ice formed on the ground, making the beast slip, slowing it only momentarily, and I realized Emory was using her magic.

I turned and raced as my satchel thumped against my chest, cloak fluttering behind me. The wolf was falling farther behind, thanks to Emory's magic. I'd never actually seen her use it. That had been one of our rules during our competition: no magic.

If this thing caught me, it would be over, and then I'd never make things right with Annalee. I clenched my teeth and pumped my arms so that I moved faster, catching up to Emory as she continued to shoot ice behind her.

"My magic is getting weaker," she said. "I've used too much of it on this thing."

The short woman shook her head. "It's too warm in the cave to use my water magic. It won't turn to ice, and I'm pretty sure the wolf would just drink it up."

"Well, we've seen what that thing does to my plants," the tall man yelled. "And it's not good."

"Will all of you shut up and keep running?" I said, urging them forward.

"Just use the bolt," Emory said.

"It's too risky." My hands tightened around it. "I know you like to live on the edge, but surely even you can understand why that's a bad idea."

"You don't know anything about me," she snapped.

"I know you better than you think, little rabbit," I said as I continued to run.

The three of them skidded to a stop abruptly, taking me by surprise. I tried to stop myself but couldn't, careening forward, unable to halt my momentum. Suddenly my feet met air, and I was tumbling into a large hole in the wall. I grasped onto the edge with one hand, keeping the bolt tucked tight under my arm with the other, trying desperately to get my footing.

Emory's face appeared over the edge of the hole. "Give me the bolt," she said, her hair curtaining her face.

"Help me up, and I will."

She knelt. "So you can pull me into that hole with you?" She shook her head, then glanced at the taller man.

"Driscoll, use your magic. Grow a vine or something and snatch the bolt from him."

This Driscoll frowned. "I mean, shouldn't we, like, help him a little bit? We're just going to take the bolt and let him fall? That's cold." He paused for dramatic effect. "Oh, come on. She's a frost elemental. That's cold?" He looked around at everyone's unsmiling faces. "Tough crowd."

The shorter woman turned to him. "Will you stop with the jokes? We're most likely about to die. That wolf is going to catch us, and we need to get that bolt."

My hand slipped on the edge of the hole, my muscles burning with the effort to not let go of either the bolt or the rock.

"What is your problem, Leoni?" Driscoll planted his hands on his hips. "All you've done lately is snap at me and gripe about pretty much everything I do."

Emory stretched out her arm, reaching into the hole for the bolt, but I held it tighter.

"Careful, little rabbit," I said. "I will drop it."

"Don't call me that," she snapped, her fingertips almost grazing the weapon.

"I've called you that for six years, and you just now have a problem with it?"

Her glare sharpened. "Yes, I do."

"I'm just tired of you not taking anything seriously," the woman, Leoni, said. "You started this whole journey so you could be a hero. Now you don't want to be a hero. So you said you'd be a sidekick and help me. But all you've done is complain. And you were ready to cut and run earlier. If it hadn't been for the avalanche, you were going to turn around and go home."

"Of course I was!" Driscoll shouted, throwing out his arms. "This is terrible. Every single thing about it is terrible."

Emory's hand brushed against the bolt, and she grunted. I jerked, my hand slipping farther, legs kicking toward the rock, trying to find a groove. If I fell down this hole, I had a distinct possibility it would be my end.

"That's my point. You don't take anything seriously." Leoni flung out her hand. "Not even people. You don't form any attachments. You just flit from thing to thing. I'm just another one of those things."

The wolf burst out around the bend of the cave, growling and rushing straight toward the trio. Driscoll screamed as the woman jumped in front of him, summoning a sword of water that she slashed at the beast.

Emory stayed where she lay half her body now inside the hole, hand reaching again for the bolt. She swiped a hand at it, and I clutched it tighter.

"You know, now is not the time to be stubborn," she said as Leoni continued to fight the wolf and keep it at bay.

"Hurry up and grab the bolt," Leoni yelled.

"Have you not learned your lesson about that over the years?" Emory asked.

"I think it's the perfect time to be stubborn," I argued, ignoring her reference to the time I'd refused to give up on a game neither of us could win, ending up injured and almost dead—if it hadn't been for the white rabbit.

Behind Emory, whose arm was still outstretched, the wolf was backing the woman and Driscoll toward the hole.

"Let it go," Emory yelled, not paying attention to anything but me.

"No," I said back to her.

I wasn't sure how this could end well for any of us, but I couldn't let that bolt go. It was partly why it took me so long to leave on this mission. Because I knew I'd need a weapon with insurmountable power to survive all of this, to beat the odds no one else had.

The wolf licked its chops, red eyes gleaming as it prowled toward us, knowing it had caught its prey. With a cry, the short woman surged forward, right as Emory grunted, her fingers curling around the bolt. She yanked it from my grip.

"You know, I'm really hurt by what you just said about me," Driscoll said to the woman as she slashed at the beast, letting her water sword splash to the ground as she drew the sword of steel strapped to her side. She and the beast circled each other, its backend now facing us.

"A little busy right now," Leoni grunted out. She jabbed at the beast and pushed it back.

And right into Driscoll.

He, in turn, stumbled into Emory, losing his footing and crashing down over her. The bolt slipped from Emory's grasp, and I watched with horror as it flew up into the air and over our heads right into the hole.

"No," we both said at the same time.

The short woman jabbed the wolf again, and it jumped backward, toppling into Driscoll and Emory, the final force needed to push them both right over into the hole. Right into me.

I lost my grip, all of us tumbling straight into the darkness.

Chapter Twenty

EMORY

I was falling, and the only thing that made me feel better was knowing that the bone collector was falling too. Was it petty of me? Yes. Was it justified? Also yes. I'd never thought myself to be such a competitive person—not until I met him.

My arms and legs flailed, my body banging against the sides of the hole. I tried to grasp for anything to stop my fall, but I was falling too fast, too furious. I braced my body for an impact that never came. I just kept falling down this dark hole as Driscoll's screamed echoed around me.

So my death was going to be drawn out then. Fantastic. More time for me to think about all the ways this could have turned out differently. All the regrets I had. How much this was going to hurt.

And the bolt. I'd dropped it. Maybe it was for the best. We didn't deliver it to Princess Poppy for safekeeping like we'd planned, but that didn't really matter.

No one would find it down here. This mysterious shadow king wouldn't be able to use it for whatever he was planning against the other courts.

That gave me some comfort. I could die knowing I'd made a difference in this world. That my life had meant something after all. Something more than what my mother had wanted it to mean.

Driscoll's garbled screams continued to bounce off the walls of the hole, while I heard nothing from the bone collector. Maybe he'd already reached the bottom and was dead.

The thought didn't fill me with nearly as much satisfaction as I wished it did. In fact, it didn't fill me with any satisfaction at all.

Suddenly, my body slowed its descent. What in the bloody frost? Maybe I'd already died and it had happened so quickly I didn't realize it. I was floating, suspended in the air by something. Then my feet were touching the ground, and I was standing in darkness. Not going splat. Okay, this had officially passed weird and gone to downright crazy.

Flickers of shimmery blue, red, green, and orange lit the space, but not enough that I could see much else.

"Hello?" Driscoll asked from somewhere beside me.

"Seriously?" I said. "I die and now I'm spending an eternity with you?"

"Is it Kick Driscoll When He's Already Down Day?" Driscoll asked. "Because between you and Leoni, it really feels like it." He went silent. "Wait a minute. Leoni?" he asked.

There was no response.

"Do you think she's okay?" His voice had gone from sarcastic to frantic, and I wanted to make him feel better, but I couldn't. I had no idea if Leoni had fallen with us. If she was okay.

"Quit talking," a low voice said.

Maverick.

"Well, that confirms it," I said. "I've definitely died and gone to the Underearth."

I took a step forward, sticking out my hands and feeling my way through the dark. "Did anyone else get a weird sensation when you dropped down here? Like your body was suspended or something? We should be dead, right?"

Neither of them answered.

"Where is the bolt?" Maverick asked, the sound of his hands patting the ground echoing around us.

"Why isn't it cold?" Driscoll asked. "I'm actually feeling a little hot." His cloak whooshed through the air, and I assumed he was taking it off.

"The bolt," Maverick said, voice growing frantic. "Where is the bolt?"

My pulse spiked, an icy dread filling me. "Okay, let's all just calm down."

Something was wrong. Very wrong.

A sizzle hit the silence, and suddenly a yellow light glowed brighter, illuminating the space where we stood. My gaze took in the area: it was like someone had collected all the elemental powers and splashed them around this cave. Vines writhed and wriggled along the walls and ground. Fire sizzled in jagged, red lines across the floor. Water glistened on the walls, the droplets falling in splats on the ground. Jagged spears of ice jutted up from the floor—and the wind. It whirled above us. It must've been what caught us when we'd fallen.

I'd never seen anything like it. "What is controlling this?" I asked, shooting unsure looks at the others, but their gazes were stuck on something else.

The bolt. Clutched tight in the wolf's mouth. It stood in front of a tunnel, the only way out of this cave. For once it didn't attack. Instead, it turned and ran.

"The bolt!" Maverick snatched up his satchel and ran after the wolf.

I shot a questioning look at Driscoll.

He heaved a sigh. "Let's go."

We raced after the bone collector and the beast. The wolf bounded through the tunnel. All the while, the magic was alive and moving across the walls, the floor, the ceiling, in constant motion, slinking everywhere I looked but not attacking us.

I tore my eyes from it to focus on the wolf, which barreled far ahead into the distance, the bolt clutched in its mighty jaws. Maverick reached out his hand, fire snaking along the ground toward the creature, but the wolf was too fast, and his magic couldn't reach it in time.

A silvery light bled into the tunnel, and I realized I was looking at an opening ahead. A way out of this place. Thank the spirits. I pumped my arms, eager to break free of this cave and figure out where we'd fallen and what in the bloody frost was going on. The wolf leapt through the opening, his howl echoing around us, and Maverick stopped at the entrance, bending over, clutching his sides. Both Driscoll and I reached him, stopping on either side, the wolf nowhere in sight.

But somehow, a ginormous white wolf stealing our bolt after falling hundreds of feet wasn't the most shocking thing I'd seen today.

I gaped at the world around us.

"Whoa," Driscoll said, voice full of awe.

It was like our world but not like it. Everything twisted, different, familiar yet not . . .

Trees peppered the ground around us, the size of my hand. Flowers stretched up as tall as trees, their petals all varieties of bright colors. Mushrooms spread across the ground, same height as me, bright orange with red spots, lavender with blue spots, fuchsia pink with black spots. Hills punctured the distance, the grass covered with a black shimmery dust that I could not make sense of. Wind picked up and lifted the dust so it swirled around us.

I rubbed my eyes. "Are you both seeing what I'm seeing?"

"So we are dead," Driscoll said, swallowing thickly. "We're in Galaysia. Or the Underearth." He swallowed again.

"No," Maverick said, voice hard as he stared out at this strange world. "We're not in either of those places."

I threw a glare at him. "Then please enlighten us, O Wise One. Where are we?"

His gaze didn't waver as he brushed past me, stepping outside the tunnel. "We're in the Deadlands. Welcome to the star court."

Part Three

"We're all mad here. You're mad. I'm mad."

<h1 style="text-align:center">Chapter Twenty-One</h1>

EMORY

A roaring sound filled my ears, and my vision went hazy. Maverick had said the Deadlands. We were in the Deadlands. That couldn't be true. No one went to the Deadlands. Not after it had been closed off all those years ago after the horrors of the Shadow War.

My heart hammered in my chest so hard it ached, and I was having a hard time catching my breath. I faintly heard the sound of a body thumping to the ground, of Maverick grumbling to himself, but it was hard to focus on anything but his words echoing in the empty chambers of my mind.

"Welcome to the star court."

"Will you help me, for spirits' sake?" a voice yelled, distant, hard to focus on.

"Welcome to the star court."

If we were in Shiraeth, then we'd never leave. We'd fallen through a hole to get here. A hole we wouldn't be able to climb back up. I whirled around and my vision cleared as I saw the entrance to the tunnel we'd come out of closing, vines and ice and fire and water all mixing to create prison bars that looked impenetrable.

"Welcome to the star court."

"Help me get him up, damnit!"

Everything snapped back into sharp focus. Maverick knelt on the ground next to Driscoll, who was unconscious, his head bleeding. I ran to him, lifting his head, parting his coiled hair to look at the wound on his scalp, a bloody rock next to him that he must've fallen on.

"It's not deep," I said. "Just a superficial cut. He likely fainted from shock, not blood loss."

"I told you not to follow me." Maverick glared at me from the other side of Driscoll with those coppery brown eyes that held so much passion, so much ire. All directed at me.

"I told you this wasn't one of our games," he continued. "Why wouldn't you listen? Now you've made a complete mess of everything."

He shrugged off his coat, revealing his white button-up with those damn fitted trousers and suspenders that hugged his muscled arms and chest.

"Me?" I placed a hand on my chest. "I've made a mess of things? You're the one who had to drag me into your office and question me."

"I saved you." He scoffed. "If I hadn't insisted you come with me, you'd be at the frost castle right now, likely being arrested and thrown into the ice prisons."

That was a valid point, not that I'd ever admit it.

"And you stole the bolt," I said. "You stole it from them." I gestured to Driscoll's unconscious form, shifting so that his head lay in my lap.

"Only so you couldn't steal it first." He shoved the sleeves of his shirt up to his elbows, revealing his muscled forearms. Scars and red markings covered his arms and hands. I knew every one. He'd told me about them. I'd witnessed him get some of them as the bone collector.

I could close my eyes and I'd still see them, know them as well as I knew my own features.

Blood and frost. How had I never put this together?

I swallowed, meeting his gaze and flushing when I realized he'd caught me staring. I ran a hand over Driscoll's head in a soothing motion.

"I told you in confidence I was looking for the bolt," I snapped. How stupid of me to think I could trust him. How stupid of me to open up to him like that. But that was when I'd thought he was someone different. Someone like me. "So you just wanted it to get the best of me? How mature."

"Why I wanted it is none of your business," he snapped back. "You're not the only one after that bolt. It doesn't matter anyway because now you've gone and lost it. Not only lost the bolt but also the white wolf."

It hurt that I'd trusted him with that information. I still remembered how we'd lain together on that hill in the highlands. Side by side, both our hoods up, darkness cloaking us, and I'd told him my stupid aspirations, that I'd hoped to use the bolt to gain entry into the academy. He must've been laughing at me the entire time, knowing he wasn't just part of the academy—he was the face of it.

I shook away the memory, shook away the tears threatening to fall.

Instead, I summoned another glare that I hurled his way. "I think we have bigger problems on our hands. Like how in the bloody frost we're supposed to escape this place."

"You can do whatever you'd like." He stood abruptly, wiping his hands of the peculiar black dust coating them, coating the ground. "I have no intention of leaving."

I stilled and slowly came to a stand. "You wanted to come here?"

His gaze was hard, unwavering, and his expression betrayed nothing.

I gazed around the strange landscape, unable to make sense of any of it. "Why would you want to come to the Deadlands? Everyone knows there is no escaping this place."

Yes, I might have fantasized about exploring the mysterious former star court, but I never would've been crazy enough to do it.

His jaw ticked. I'd struck a nerve, but I didn't know why. "As usual, little rabbit, you have no idea what you're talking about."

"Don't call me that," I said. At one point, the term had felt like an endearment. Now it felt like a mockery.

"What would you prefer I call you?" he asked. "Lady Growley?" He tsked. "Ah, but no. You can't be called that anymore. Not after you murdered your husband."

I flinched like he'd slapped me. "Now who's the one with no idea what they're talking about?"

He crossed his arms. "This is where we say goodbye. It's your fault you're here, so you can deal with the consequences of your actions."

It was as if he were a different person. The teasing, fun bone collector gone. In his place was a serious, very annoyed man. It was as if I'd never known him at all.

He scooped up his satchel and stalked away, feet crushing the little trees scattered across the ground. They squealed as his boot crunched over them.

"Where are you going?" I called, unable to help myself.

"None of your concern," he called back. "And if I were you, I wouldn't follow me again. You can see how well that worked out for you the first time."

"In case you haven't noticed, I'm not very good at taking orders," I said.

He didn't respond, just continued his way through the path of giant flowers. Some of them shuffled as he walked past, others dipping like they might brush against him. He paid no mind to any of it.

I couldn't believe he'd come here on purpose. Was this for his job? Some research expedition? He had to know it was a fool's errand. A one-way trip.

One of the flowers dipped down, its bright purple petals unfurling and hovering over his head. He stilled, looking up and shooting out a hand. Fire erupted from his fingertips, sizzling against the flower, which shrieked and straightened.

"You guys, I had the weirdest dream," Driscoll said, sitting up and rubbing his head where he'd hit it. "Maverick said we were in Shiraeth. Can you imagine? That would basically mean we're dead. Like completely dead. I'm talking no chance at surviving—" He stopped, eyes widening as he took in the landscape around us, gaze slowly working up to the twilight sky above. The dark purple twinkled with stars, ribbons of green undulating through the sky.

My breath caught in my throat. I'd heard about this, how the sun never shone here, the sky always dusky and twinkling. Even sixty years after the star court was destroyed, that still held true.

"Oh, fuck me." Driscoll's eyes widened. I held out a hand and helped him to a stand as he said, "That wasn't a dream, was it?"

I shook my head. "No, I don't think it was."

He scratched his head, frowning. "Why is everything so . . .?"

"Off?" I finished for him, then sighed. "I don't know. I have no clue what's going on or why anything is the way it is. I don't know what we might face here, what the dangers are. I don't know how we'll ever escape."

He planted his hands on his hips. "You're the white rabbit. Figure it out. That's what you do, right? You research and find unfindable things and somehow manage to steal them and hide your identity."

I straightened at his description of me. He was right. I'd never let anything stop me from getting what I wanted. Not my mother. Not the Academy of Ladies. Not my husband. And certainly not the bone collector and his mysterious motives. Now, at a time in my life when I most needed to step up and be the white rabbit, I was shrinking away, acting like some hopeless, lost woman.

I was better than that. Stronger than that. I'd been through too much to give up. Now was not the time to fall. It was the time to rise.

I threw my arms around Driscoll, and he stiffened. "I don't know you that well, but thank you for reminding me of who I want to be."

His shoulders slumped. "Great, does this mean you're going to save us?"

"Yes, yes it does."

I unwrapped my arms from him, and he pointed. "Hey, where's he going?"

I glared at Maverick's form, shrinking into the distance as he stalked farther away. "He's not our concern anymore. He can do whatever he likes. My only motivation is getting us home safe."

Driscoll raised a black brow. "What about the bolt?"

It would pain me to leave something like that behind, but we couldn't go traipsing around the Deadlands looking for it. What I'd said was true. I knew nothing of the dangers here. No one did. And this . . . this strange world where nothing was as it seemed . . . it wasn't a place I wanted to be for any longer than necessary.

"Our goal is to survive," I said.

"Maybe Leoni will get help." Driscoll shrugged. "Then again, we had our worst fight ever before I fell, so maybe not. Maybe she's happy to finally be rid of me."

I didn't know what to say to that. They'd bickered a lot, but there seemed to be a fondness there. "I'm not good at relationships," I said slowly. "The only ones I've ever had involved people who didn't care about me, who only wanted me to exist for their benefit."

My mother had reminded me again and again how a good husband would provide for me. That she'd spent our life savings for me to attend the Academy of Ladies and find a wealthy husband so I wasn't a burden on her. That's all I ever was to anyone.

If only she were still alive for me to prove her wrong.

Then, of course, there was the one relationship that had been the most real in my life. The one where I'd felt safest, where I felt like I could be myself. And it had all been a lie.

"Well, that sucks." Driscoll kicked some of the black dirt, and it flew up in the air, a puff of ebony motes floating before us. "I'm not good at relationships either. Clearly. Probably because I'm too selfish."

So Leoni's words had gotten to him.

"Well, screw them," I said.

His head shot up. "Who, exactly, are we screwing?"

"Everyone who doubts us." I spread out my arms. "We'll prove them all wrong."

"I like your spirit. So where do we start with the screwing?" His face twisted. "Yes, I did just hear how that sounded."

I took a deep breath, looking around this land of wonder. "I had some old maps of the star court stashed in that bunker. I've studied them a time or two, though not as well as I studied maps of the frost court and the sky court." I crouched down, using my finger to sketch a rough outline of the star court as I remembered it.

"Wow, he must think highly of himself." Driscoll nodded to my drawing.

I tilted my head, realizing it definitely looked like a very well-endowed man. "This is Shiraeth," I clarified.

"Oh." He knelt beside me. "Did not get that at all. Thought you were doing something with that screwing analogy. You know, like an erotic picture—"

"I get it," I cut him off, then glanced behind me at the massive mountains that rose to the sky. We'd come from the Glacier Mountains that bordered the former star court. I dragged my finger to the border. "We're here," I murmured, trying to remember the important locations.

The star castle was in the west part of the court. We were in the north. But where was the library? I remembered staring at drawings of it and being mesmerized by the structure. It had been so beautiful with its tall silver walls, ivy hanging down. And the inside. It had stairways that led to levels upon levels, secret passageways where one could get lost but find the most amazing books. It had levels upon levels, and more books than any other library in the seven courts. And it had been destroyed during the war.

"Are you okay?" Driscoll shot me a concerned look. "Is the shock finally hitting you? Are you realizing that we're probably going to die? It's okay. Let it come." He cocked his head. "Hey, what's that?" He pointed at something glinting on the ground.

I reached out and grabbed what looked like a chain, lifting the object up from the swath of dust surrounding it. A pocket watch. Silver and tarnished, the glass cracked, but the hands ticking away. I studied it. Ticking backward.

"Oh good, a broken clock," Driscoll mumbled. "Just what we need."

"Maybe it's not broken." I looked up at him. "Everything else in this world is warped. Maybe the clock is too. Maybe it's supposed to tick backward. Like a timer."

"Except what is it counting down to?" Driscoll gulped.

My stomach twisted. "I don't know." I stuffed it in the pocket of my trousers. Just another mystery to solve. But not the most important one currently.

"So what's the plan?" Driscoll planted his hands on his hips.

I pointed to my drawing. "We're here. The old library is somewhere around here." I pointed south of us. "That's where we should go."

He wrinkled his nose. "I don't think now is the time to go check out books. Besides, everything has been destroyed."

"History is never truly gone," I said. "It gets buried, misplaced, lost. But it can also be found. We're going to that library and we're going to get answers about how to get out of here."

Chapter Twenty-Two

MAVERICK, FOUR YEARS AGO

A wintry blast of wind blew the hood off my head, and I had to quickly tug it back up. Snow and ice pelted me from all directions. I fucking loathed this place, yet here I stood, on the frozen Halfstard Lake, waiting for the white rabbit.

I stuffed my hand into my cloak and pulled out the last note she'd left me, my smile growing as I imagined her voice reading this.

On a scale of 1-10, what is the likelihood that Spirit Sky's infamous Tower of Terror exists? To answer your question about the spirits' weapons, why they didn't want anyone to touch them . . . well I'm not sure we'll get those answers unless we actually find one of those mythical weapons. I'm not saying one of them is located in the tower. But I'm not not saying that either. I do wonder if the spirits were just incredibly possessive. Or maybe someone touching their weapons would spell doom—

for them or for everyone else. I just don't know which.
A little something for you to ponder, BC.

In other news, I'm bored. Maybe that's revealing too much of myself? But I feel like the year between our competition drags on and on so that I'm spending my days counting down the minutes until I get to best you all over again. Luckily, the day is approaching. I look forward to seeing you soon.

Yours,
WR

I wasn't sure how the notes had started. A few weeks after we'd picked our first challenge, I'd come back to our spot and saw a note stuck inside the little hole in the tree where we'd hid the glass jar. I'd opened up the folded piece of parchment, surprised to see that it was addressed to me. From the white rabbit. Some inquiry about a type of wooden paddle she'd come across and what period it might date back to.

So I'd replied. Then I went back a few weeks later, and sure enough, there was a response. I couldn't count how many notes we'd left each other at this point. I sensed she was as eager to hear from me as I was to hear from her. I loved reading her thoughts, hearing about her escapades outside of our challenges, the artifacts she found, the theories she had.

She was brilliant. She would be an amazing addition to the academy. Something I wished I could suggest to her without somehow giving too much of myself away. In our notes, we avoided any personal details, but somehow, that didn't matter. With every piece of her I took, I, in turn, gave her a piece of me. She might not have realized it, but it was too late to turn back. I'd never stop this challenge, never stop writing to her, not when it was the only connection I had to the white rabbit.

A connection I desperately needed in what felt like my increasingly empty life that was solely focused on this damn academy job.

The job my father wanted so badly for me. The job I took because I thought I wanted it for myself. But I didn't feel anywhere near as alive in that academy as I felt out here, doing these challenges with the white rabbit.

I shivered as the wind howled, wondering where in the bloody fire the white rabbit was. I shoved the note back into my pocket and pulled up the scarf that covered the lower half of my face until it rested just under my eyes.

"You're here early." The white rabbit emerged from the snowstorm, hood raised, a white scarf covering her face as well, that white fur cloak billowing around her.

Snow rested on my cloak, the fabric already damp.

"I think you're late," I said, taking a step toward her.

White blanketed the vast expanse around us, nothing but snow and ice as far as I could see. The chill seeped under my clothes, my toes and fingers already numb. If I wasn't careful, I'd get frostbite. Not something I was eager to experience.

"You can summon your fire magic if you want," she said, the wind carrying her voice. "You're at a bit of a disadvantage here."

"I never let that stop me before. Besides I'm not going to use my magic and then spend the next year hearing you talk about how that's the only reason I won."

Even through the thick cloak and tunic, I could see her shrug. "You're already planning on winning? Cocky, bone collector."

She whirled.

"Where are you going?" I called after her.

"Oh, I'm sorry, were you just here to chat?" she yelled over her shoulder as thick flakes swept around her. "Because I'm here to find the lost diadem. May the best historian win." She wiggled her delicate fingers in the air, making me smile.

The diadem was supposedly underneath the frozen lake in the exact center. No one ventured out here, too afraid of the creatures who lurked beneath the surface.

The white rabbit had already disappeared from my sight, a curtain of heavy snow blocking my view. I wasn't even sure which way the middle was. Every way I turned looked the same, making it hard to get my bearings.

But I couldn't let the white rabbit best me again. Not after she'd gotten those damn scrolls at our last challenge. Something she'd spent the last year taunting me about through our notes.

I reached into my satchel and drew out the saw I'd brought with me, one that many ice fishermen used in Fyriad. I'd learned that when I visited a few of them at the docks of the Silver Seas and asked how they went about catching fish. We weren't allowed to use our magic in these little challenges; otherwise, I could've just melted the ice. Though that might have been risky. A saw seemed like the better choice. I wondered what the white rabbit had planned, then I pushed her from my mind. Something that was increasingly hard to do these days.

Another blast of wind made me stumble, but I regained my footing and stalked across the lake in the direction I believed was toward the center. The wind was unrelenting, and I pulled my cloak tighter around me, not that it did a damn thing.

If I got the diadem today, I wondered what I'd actually do with it. I hadn't thought that far ahead when I'd proposed this little game of ours two years ago. It would be odd to keep something like that to myself, but I also couldn't exactly waltz into the academy with a diadem that I hadn't been authorized by the queen to find.

The ice trembled under my feet, and I looked down to see a long sleek body slithering through the water underneath. It should have been a terrifying sight, but instead of fear, a thrill shot through me. A sense that this was what I was meant to do. I wasn't meant to be in a classroom, lecturing students, going on safe expeditions to fields and caves and hills that had been pored over already. There was so much history out there, history the white rabbit was uncovering herself. She was taking things into her own hands and finding amazing artifacts, uncovering important information.

Information that would help us learn about our past and how to approach our future.

But I didn't want to lose this job. I didn't want to have to go back home to my father. To his overbearing presence. To see the way he treated my sister so terribly. Especially if I'd lost a job. He'd focus all his attention on making her suffer for my mistakes.

So what to do with the diadem if I found it? I'd worry about that later. The ice shuddered again, a blue-spotted eel swimming right underneath me. These were the largest species of eel, sometimes as long as a ship and with an appetite to match a dragon. They typically ate fish, but they also weren't picky about their meat or where it came from.

I blew out a breath, keeping my gaze trained on the ice for any signs of this diadem. In the distance, ice shattered, an explosion and a shriek splitting the air. My heart stopped in my chest as the white rabbit let out another blood-curdling scream.

I stuffed the saw in my satchel and took off, all thoughts of the diadem gone as I ran as faster than I ever had toward the sound. The eels normally didn't surface to find prey. Not unless there was a lack of food below. Bloody fucking fire.

I hurried through a wall of flurries and slid to a stop right as the eel's monstrous head erupted from the ice. Huge chunks of the frozen lake floated in the crystal-blue water, the ice jutting up as the white rabbit scrambled backward. She fell onto her back, and in her hand was the diadem.

Of course she'd found it.

The eel wasn't after her. It was here to protect the diadem, which supposedly belonged to Spirit Frost's wife. She'd worn it proudly until his mistresses tried to steal it. Out of spite, she put the diadem right in the center of this lake and instructed Spirit Frost's pet eel to guard it. She might've died almost two thousand years ago along with the rest of the Old World, but these eels lived up to three thousand years.

I ran toward the white rabbit, shielding her with my body as the eel shrieked, thrashing its head in the air.

"Just give it the diadem," I yelled, summoning my fire magic to ward off the eel.

It let out a low hiss, its black eyes flashing with fear, but it didn't retreat.

"No," she snapped. "I came all the way for this. I'm not going to let it go because of some threat. Are you really so easily scared away, bone collector? Because I have to say, I'm a little disappointed."

"Disappointed?" I laughed in disbelief. "That I don't want to lose my head to a centuries-old eel? It's just a game."

"It's not, and you know it."

The eel lowered its head and blew out a frosty breath that extinguished my fire. I rolled out of the way before it could pull me into the icy depths of that lake, and I landed on my back next to the white rabbit.

She held up the diadem as the eel reared back, readying itself to strike. "This is history. It's a living, breathing thing that can teach us something. So I'm not giving it up."

The eel plunged toward us and we both rolled in opposite directions as it barreled into the ice. The frozen layer exploded, cracks webbing out toward where I lay, toward the white rabbit. The eel dove down beneath the surface, its body disappearing into the depths below.

"We're not going to get so lucky next time," I said, breathing heavily. "It's puncturing the ice, trying to get us to fall in with that diadem."

The white rabbit struggled to her feet. "Then I suggest you run." And with that, she took off.

Ice exploded around her in quick, short bursts as the eel's tail shot up. Eels didn't have the best sense of sight, relying on body heat to hunt their prey.

"Fuck." I took off running after her, jumping over the gaping holes in the ice, shooting out fire at the eel as it plunged its tail upward again and again and again, narrowly missing the white rabbit every time.

She was quick on her feet, but this lake was massive, and I wasn't sure we were even going in the right direction. The eel let out a deafening shriek that made the ice trembled as its tail once again broke through, creating another huge hole.

The white rabbit shot a look behind her. "Having fun yet?" she yelled.

"Not even a little bit." It was a lie. This was the most fun I'd had in, well, ever.

The eel erupted from below, blocking the white rabbit's path. Except she wasn't looking forward. She was looking back. At me.

"Watch out!" I roared, but by the time she turned, it was too late.

One minute she was running, the next, she was slipping on the ice, falling into the lake. Her white cloak fluttering in the air. And then she was gone.

No. No, no, no, no, no. I shot out a long rope made of fire at the eel before its large body could slip underneath to kill her. The rope lassoed around its neck, and it bucked against it. I held tight, keeping the eel from diving back under, giving my little rabbit time to find her way back to the surface. If she found her way. But of course she would. She was a fighter. She could do this.

My muscles strained as I held tight onto the fiery rope, the eel struggling against it. I braced my feet against the ice, but the creature pulled me slowly toward it, my feet gliding with ease across the slick surface.

"C,mon, little rabbit," I said under my breath.

She wasn't surfacing. Soon she'd run out of air. Muffled cries sounded from below, barely heard over the eel's roar, and I looked down to see two fists beating against the ice right underneath my feet.

Fucking fuck.

The eel stilled, head tilting. It had heard her, and I couldn't keep restraining it, not when she needed air. Now.

I gritted my teeth, letting go of the rope and whipping the saw from my satchel. I lowered it to the ice, cutting away while the eel let out a screech that shook the entire lake, slowly sinking into the water. I tugged at the thread of magic inside of me, summoning the biggest ball of fire I could muster. One that would deplete nearly all of my magic.

The fists pounded with more urgency.

Then I struck. I hurled my magic at the eel, who opened its mouth in surprise, right as the fire flew into it. The eel yelped, sinking away from view. That ought to keep it away long enough for us to escape.

"I'm coming," I yelled, sawing through the ice as fast as I could. My muscles quivered, and despite the chilly air, sweat gathered on my brow.

Her fists stopped pounding.

"No," I breathed. "Hold on. Just hold on a little longer, damnit!"

I sawed over halfway through the circle, then stomped on the ice, breaking it open. Pieces of it bobbed in the water, along with a white fur coat surfacing. I gripped the back of her coat and yanked her out. She landed on her stomach, and for one heart-wrenching moment didn't move. I was just about to flip her over and pump on her chest, when she came to her hands and knees, sputtering and coughing out the blue lake water.

"Took you long enough," she rasped, back still to me.

The diadem lay at her side, a curious blue dust surrounding it. I didn't have much time to ponder it as the white rabbit, soaking wet and still on her hands and knees, reached for the object.

She was safe. Alive. Joy filled me, and so did a competitiveness. I scooped up the diadem and took off.

"Are you kidding me?" she yelled. "That is not fair!"

"Well, considering I just saved your life and defeated the giant eel," I yelled back, "I'd say it's plenty fair. Until next year, little rabbit."

The diadem wasn't the only thing I'd managed to get away with. I also had the kernel of an idea. That I could do this. I could be this at the academy too. If the white rabbit could be this brave, this bold, then so could I. I was going to change the trajectory of my career.

I was going to be as fearless as my little rabbit.

Chapter Twenty-Three

MAVERICK

I shouldn't have cared so much about this woman. I didn't want to think about her. She'd murdered her husband. I clearly didn't know her as well as I'd thought.

I stalked through the flowers, and every time one of them rustled or moved, I let my fire magic flare to life. I might die here, but I'd be damned if it was because a giant flower ate me.

I couldn't say I was entirely surprised by this strange world. Annalee had prepared me for it, after all. Not that I'd believed her. I'd been too preoccupied with work, with getting a job at the academy, to pay her any time of day. Just another way I'd failed her. Another reason this was all my fault.

I reached into my satchel and pulled out her final note, staring at it before carefully folding it and putting it back. The field of flowers ended, opening up to a forest of blackened trees, all of them with branches in the shapes of . . . arms. Eyes peeked out from the darkness, but as I got closer, I realized it wasn't random creatures lurking in the forest like I'd assumed. It was the trees. They had eyes, all colors of irises, staring, following my every move.

I had to blink a few times just to make sure this was real.

Oh Annalee, I'm so sorry for ever doubting you.

And now I didn't even have the fucking bolt. Because of Emory. Without the bolt and its power, I didn't know how I'd fare here. I did have something, though. I had Annalee's stories. Everything she'd told me about this place when I'd actually bothered to listen.

The seeing trees and the singing flowers and the lake that told you your future and so much more.

And I'd brushed it all off as nothing but fanciful tales. Just like my parents had. Only I was worse. Because, in the end, I left her.

Now I was here, but I had no idea where she was in this spirits-damned land. She hadn't prepared me for that part.

I entered the dark forest, the eyes all swaying in my direction. If I didn't already have a mission to complete, I might stop and take the time to study these marvels.

Trees with eyes. Flowers as tall as mountains. Mushrooms the likes of which I'd never seen. I didn't understand how a world like this was possible, how it had been created, or where it had come from. None of it made sense, and I wanted to get some answers. Maybe Annalee could supply them when I found her. If I found her. No, no, I did not come all the way here just to doubt myself now. I'd done the impossible. Made it to the Deadlands. I owed Annalee more than to doubt. I owed her everything.

"Looking for something?" a voice said.

I stopped, summoning my fire magic and letting it flow through me, alight in my palm. My magic wasn't as strong here, but I was used to that having lived in the frost court for the last seven years. Elemental magic was always strongest in the court where you were born, tied to. At least my magic worked here at all.

"Who goes there?" I turned in slow circles, looking for the person speaking.

"Up here," chirped the high, girlish voice.

My head snapped up to see a woman draped around one of the tree branches. I squinted. Not a woman. Not exactly. Purple fur covered her entire body, and whiskers sprouted from her human nose. Orange stripes slashed across her fur.

She smiled at me. "What's the matter? Not used to seeing so much gorgeousness wrapped into one package?" She gestured to her body and dropped from the tree, landing in a crouch. She wore no clothes, her orange and purple fur providing enough cover over her human body. I had never seen anything like this before, yet I knew what she was. Because Annalee had told me about this catlike woman who had a penchant for mischief. Even with that knowledge, it was hard to believe what I was seeing.

The cat woman stalked up to me, using a long purple claw to lift my chin. "Well, you're not very fun. I barely get any visitors, and now that I do, you can't even talk to me?"

I eyed her and stepped back, the fire hovering over my palm.

"Does she know you're here?"

"Who?" I asked.

"The queen of hearts."

Just the name sent a chill down my spine. "I'm not concerned with the queen of hearts."

The cat woman narrowed her yellow eyes. "You should be. She runs this place, you know. Doesn't have a lot of tolerance for those who misbehave." She stuck out her bottom lip. "She banished me to this forest."

I wondered why but wasn't sure that was a rabbit hole I wanted to dive down.

She wiggled her clawed fingers and slashed at the fire still in my palm. "You're gonna have to put that away, or I'm going to use more than my claws." She flashed a set of sharp teeth at me.

I had a feeling if she wanted to attack me, she already would have.

"Fine," I said and closed my hand into a fist, extinguishing the fire. "I couldn't see very well and needed a light."

And a weapon, but she didn't need to know that part.

She circled me, her tail whipping behind her, then curling around my leg. "What's a handsome man like you doing in my forest?"

"I'm looking for someone, actually. Maybe you've seen her?"

She tapped her chin with a long claw. "Maybe."

This was already getting tiresome. I was used to challenges, but the stakes had never been so high. The stakes had never been

Annalee's life. "She's got black hair, long, thin braids that hang down past her shoulders. I don't know what she's wearing, probably a dress?"

It had been that long since I'd seen her. I didn't even know if she liked dresses anymore.

"She's nineteen." I lined my hand with my chest. "Comes up to here."

Maybe. She might've grown. Bloody fire. I couldn't even give a proper description of her.

The cat woman's tail had wrapped tighter around my legs as she flashed a big smile that revealed all those shiny sharp teeth. "Come to think of it, that does sound familiar."

I raised a brow.

"I believe she went . . . that way."

She pointed east with her tail, west with one finger, and south with the other. Every direction except north, the way from which I had come. There was always a catch.

"You can't even give me a clue?" I asked.

Her yellow eyes narrowed to slits. "A clue." She pursed her lips, whiskers twitching. "Yes, a clue. What a fun idea." She glanced at her hands and tail, still pointing in all different directions. "Two of these ways will lead to her. One will lead to your death."

I flashed her a tight smile. "I'm not sure you know what the word 'clue' means."

She hissed at me, and I held up my hands. Annalee had told me this cat-like woman could be temperamental.

Also not very helpful.

One way would lead to my death, but the other two ways would lead to Annalee. That's what she'd said. That gave me a two-thirds chance of going the right way. In any other situation, I might have liked those odds. But not when my life—and Annalee's—was at stake. I stared at the ground, at my black boots that blended in with the shimmery black forest floor.

I opened my mouth to ask the cat woman another question, but when I looked up, she had disappeared. Maybe this land was doing something to my mind, making me see things like Annalee had. My jaw locked. I'd gone down that path before. I hadn't believed her. I'd failed her. I wouldn't do so again.

I turned in a semi-circle, seeing through the black trees to a road that wound around what looked like ginormous plants with thick green stalks, each as tall as a tower. And at the top of the stalk were huge red heads, wide and flat, no eyes or ears, but they did have gaping mouths lined with thorny teeth. A skeletal bird flapped past them and they all dove their heads toward it, jaws hinging open, all of the plant heads fighting to get the creature. One of them stretched its neck high and chomped the bird from the air.

Not ideal. I peered to my left, where the forest thickened with bramble. Instead of trees, thorn-saddled bushes filled the area, a green substance spitting from their points. Splats of it landed on the ground, sizzling, the ground melting away, gaping holes forming. Also not ideal. When I turned the other way, the trees were bent, their branches reaching toward the ground with sharp, claw-like ends.

It looked like every damn way led to death—except the way I'd come. Maybe the cat woman was just toying with me, playing games. Maybe it didn't matter which way I chose in the end. So I just needed to choose.

I stared ahead at the chomping plants, which had calmed down now that the skeletal bird was gone, their stalks slumped and relaxed, their giant plant mouths closed.

That way it was. One step closer to finding Annalee.

I steeled myself and walked toward the plants. A branch cracked underfoot. Their stalks straightened and their mouths began snapping at the air. I froze, waiting and watching as they slowly settled again, slumping down. So they reacted to noise. If I could be quiet, I could sneak past them. Feeling more confident in my plan, I inched forward, taking slow, measured steps.

I held my hands out to steady myself, working my way out of the forest and onto the black-dusted path that wound through these strange, strange plants. As with everything in this world, I'd never seen anything so wondrous and terrifying, and I had a burning desire to know what created all of this. Dark magic, maybe? I knew of the magical items that lay in the jungles of Sorrengard. The shadow court was infamous for them, objects created when a shadow elemental used their magic to rip someone's shadow from their body. The objects ranged from mirrors that could answer any question to cups that were always lined with poison to necklaces that could make one invisible. Some brave souls ventured to the shadow court to steal those items. They held great power, but the magic always came at a cost. The price could be anything. Could it be something like this? Did someone use dark magic and the Deadlands paid the price, everything becoming deformed and twisted?

Another step.

I'd never heard of the dark magic wielding that much power. The cost was proportional to the magic used. If you used the dark magic to take a life, for example, the cost could be another life. If you used the dark magic to heal a small wound, the cost might be less—like losing your magic for a few months. But a cost that could turn an entire court into this? Something that could twist everything so it became distorted, monstrous? The dark magic used would have to be astronomical.

Another step.

It didn't make sense.

The snapping plants loomed over me, stalks slumped, mouths drooping down, and . . . soft snores filling the air. So I'd been right. They reacted to sound. As long as I stayed quiet, I could stay undetected.

I lifted my feet carefully, step after step after step, following the dusty path while threads of green twisted through the twilight sky above. Snores echoed through the space, and air puffed from the plants' mouths, rancid and foul. The path twisted through the stalks, turning and winding, splitting into three different ways. Of course.

I slowed, studying my choices. The right and left paths led through the plants, no end in sight, whereas the path that went straight led to an end. Well, at least that was an easy decision to make. Tall blades of grass filled the field in the distance, looking far less threatening than these man-eating plants.

So close. I was so spirits-damned close. I glanced behind me at the sleeping giants just as a body collided with mine. I tumbled to the ground at the same time as I heard a voice swear.

Not just any voice. I sat up. The white fucking rabbit. The plants all stiffened, stalks going ramrod straight, their hungry mouths hinging open and ready to devour their newest victims.

She'd found me, and in that moment, I realized that maybe the cat-woman had given me a good clue, and I'd chosen wrong. I'd chosen the one path that would lead to my death after all.

Chapter Twenty-Four

MAVERICK

Emory glared at me, her white-blonde eyebrows arched. Driscoll stood behind her and pinched his fingers together. "We were so close."

They'd appeared out of nowhere and rammed right into me.

Snorts and squeals filled the silence, and Emory's gaze trailed up, mine following it. The plant mouths opened wide, teeth all like sharp spindles poking from their wide mouths.

"Why does it feel like I'm constantly in danger of getting impaled?" Driscoll asked as one of the mouths dove straight toward us.

"Move!" I yelled, and we all dove from the crescendo of plants barreling for us, jaws snapping, spindly teeth puncturing the ground, black dust flying up in swaths. If we could just make it to the end of the path, we'd be safe.

Driscoll stumbled, tripping over a ridge in the ground, but managed to stay on his feet as he ran forward, while on either side of Emory and me, the plant eaters dove down, their long stalks bent, their mouths chomping, creating a barrier between us and Driscoll, their attention no longer on him.

I glared at Emory as she ran next to me, both of us ducking under the green stalks, jumping over them, avoiding the mouths plunging at us. It was like a never-ending maze, and all I could see were the thick green stalks in loops and circles and curves, some of them even getting twisted and tangled together. The plant eaters writhed, mouths greedily snapping at us.

"I told you not to come after me," I growled at Emory as we both climbed over one of the green stalks, then landed on the other side and immediately dropped to our stomachs to wriggle under another stem. "Think you can keep up?" I asked.

Emory shot me a look. "Oh, I know I can."

"Well, I guess we'll find out, little rabbit."

And just like that it felt like we were back in those familiar roles: white rabbit and bone collector. Competing. Playing another one of our games. Despite the fact that we were fighting for our lives, it felt good.

We both pushed to our feet, the long, lean stalks constricting like snakes, the maze of them so thick I couldn't see above me, in front of me, or behind me. Had no idea where the next attack might be coming from. I wasn't even sure we were going in the right direction anymore, the path no longer visible in this twisted green field.

Suddenly the stems parted, revealing a cavernous mouth that had sunk its teeth into the ground and gotten stuck. It pulled and pulled, its spindly teeth lodged firmly in the dirt. We both clambered over its large, misshapen head as more mouths appeared over us. I summoned my fire magic and shot it at the plants. A few of them hissed and shrank away, but the fire seemed to have very little effect. More mouths appeared, their long limbs stretching and bending to chomp at us. I'd never seen such a flexible plant before.

"You know"—Emory flicked her wrist, a sword of ice unraveling in her hand that she slashed at a plant—"I'm really angry at you."

I shot her a look, my fire magic flaring higher in my palm, keeping the plants from biting my head off. "Same. Also, if you're so angry with me, then why do you keep following me? Feels like you're stalking me."

Her mouth dropped open, and her magic faltered, ice sword crumbling right as a plant hinged open its cavernous jaw. Without thinking, I crashed into her, both of us toppling to the ground, my body sprawled on top of hers.

Driscoll stumbled into the field ahead and bent over. "Save it for the bedroom and get your asses up."

He twisted his hands, and the plants that stood between us and that field hovered overhead, mouths open, sticky saliva dripping in long strings, all of them frozen. He was using his earth magic.

"I won't be able to hold them for long," he called. "They're strong, and my magic isn't very effective here."

I gritted my teeth and glared at Emory, still laying underneath me. "You are a pain in my ass. You always have been."

She smirked. "Yes, I can tell how much you hate me." Her gaze dipped to my body as I lay over her. "Last time I checked, I'm not the one who threw myself on top of you."

Fuck. Now that was an image. One I liked far too much. "As far as I'm concerned, you're the one who can't stay away from me."

I stared down at her, her pale hair splayed out behind her, brows arched, pink lips pursed, mischief dancing in her icy eyes.

"This is really a bad time to be having whatever conversation you're having," Driscoll yelled, and a string of green saliva landed next to us, some of it splashing onto Emory's face.

We slowly looked up at the plants, all of them trembling and vibrating, working against Driscoll's magic as they fought to break free.

"We have to go," I said.

"Well, then you're going to have to get off of me."

Bloody fucking fire. I stood and heaved her to her feet, and we set off.

"My magic is breaking!" Driscoll shouted.

The ground trembled under our feet as the plants began to punch through the magic. At the same time, Emory and I both summoned swords, hers of ice and mine of fire. We raised them and slashed at all the plants that dove their mouths toward us.

Almost there. We were almost there.

One of the mouths caught hold of my shirt collar, its spindly tooth puncturing right through the fabric, yanking me backward. I landed on the ground with enough force to knock the wind from my lungs. A plant twisted over me. All I could see was the endless black of its open mouth, all the pointed spindles that would stab me and slice me open. Annalee's face flashed in my mind, tears in her eyes as she watched me walk away from her, begged me not to go.

Then another vision appeared. Emory's face, scowling down. "You are not dying here. Not this way. Not if I can help it."

She grabbed my suspenders and yanked me upward, then pulled me forward right as the plant dove its head straight toward the ground. It smashed into the dust with a shriek.

A thought popped in my head. A memory. Annalee telling me about plants that had mouths, of how much they loved being sung lullabies. Lullabies. It sounded ridiculous, but . . . at this point, what did I have to lose?

I opened my mouth and began to hum.

Emory stared at me like I'd lost it. "What are you doing?" she hissed.

The rustling slowly stopped, the plants stilling, and Emory's eyes shifted back and forth.

"What is happening?" she asked.

So Annalee had been telling the truth about this as well. She'd told me the story of the snapping plants who could be lulled to sleep with a song. A fucking song. I hummed louder, widening my eyes at Emory. She swallowed, then rolled her eyes and hummed along with me.

The plants' mouths slowly closed.

"Spirits below," Emory mumbled, then kept humming until all the plants were asleep, their snores once again permeating the air.

The confusing maze cleared as the plants unentangled, straightening, heads drooping, snores filling the air.

We could stroll right out of this place.

So we did, humming the entire time, Driscoll staring at us with an open mouth as we came to a stand in the field. I wanted to take a moment to process the fact that Emory had just saved my life. I wanted to understand why it had felt so good when my hard body had hovered over her soft one.

But I couldn't do anything of those things because right when we stepped into the grassy field, a low growl echoed around us. The white wolf had found us.

Chapter Twenty-Five

EMORY

The white wolf sat there, a low rumble escaping its mouth as we stood in the grass. Beyond the grassy field, what looked like a maze of mushrooms shot up, all of the spotted fungus reaching taller than our heads, an odd red haze drifting from their button tops.

"So everyone is seeing the wolf, right?" Driscoll asked.

Maverick and I both shot him a look.

"Well, I just had to double check since neither of you seemed to notice the giant head-chomping plants that were about to decapitate you while you were snuggling on the ground, staring into each other's eyes." He took a deep breath. "That felt good, actually. Thank you for letting me get that off my chest."

"We weren't snuggling." For spirits' sake. Why was I arguing with him?

"In case you two forgot," Maverick said as he summoned his fire magic, "we've got bigger problems than the plant-eaters." He nodded toward the white wolf, who prowled through the grass toward us.

"I really, really hate it here," Driscoll said.

I didn't disagree. I summoned my frost magic, ice swirling above my hand in swooping circles, even though our magic seemed to have little effect on the wolf. Not to mention, my magic was weaker here, that thread I wanted to pull at getting harder to grasp.

Driscoll raised his hands. "I used the rest of my magic trying to save your two asses, which was a complete waste." He mumbled that last part. "So you two are on your own."

"Let's back away slowly," Maverick said out the side of his mouth. "Running will only trigger its predator instincts."

The grass brushed against my knees as I slowly walked backward, while the wolf's red eyes watched us.

"Why isn't it attacking?" Driscoll asked. He glanced around. "Also, does this grass seem way too much like regular grass to belong here?" He scratched his head. "Other than the fact that it's purple."

He was right. The wolf wasn't attacking. It had growled at us, but I was starting to think that was just the sound it made.

"Maybe it wanted us to come here?" I suggested.

"It doesn't matter what it wants." Maverick eyed it warily, flames dancing over his palm, flickering out. "It's a wild beast. It will kill us if we give it the chance."

I swiveled my head. "Do you look at everything with such a narrow mind?"

He scoffed. "I use something called observation. Maybe you've heard of it?" He gestured to the wolf, who now looked between us, head cocked, ears pointed straight up. "It's a wolf three times the size of a normal wolf, and it has already tried to kill us once."

My hands curled into fists. "It's also very likely from this place. Where trees have eyes and plants eat people. It might not be what it seems."

"You guys are worse than me and Leoni," Driscoll muttered. "We're never going to get anywhere with you two."

"If all you're doing is judging based on what you know, then what kind of critical thinking is that?" I asked.

Maverick gave me an odd look that I didn't entirely understand. Then he looked down at his boots and shook his head. "I don't have time for this. I didn't die, which means I'm going the right way."

Well, that made no sense. He was just as confounding as this world around us, which I still couldn't make head nor tail of. If we could get to that library, maybe we'd have a shot at getting answers, at making an actual escape plan. I glanced back at the giant plants, their mouths now closed, all of them sleeping soundly. If we lived long enough to make it there. I couldn't imagine what still awaited us.

Maverick began walking past me. His gaze darted to the wolf as he attempted to inch by it.

The wolf let out another growl, nudging its head.

"Did it just shake its head?" Driscoll asked.

Of course it did. Because why wouldn't a wolf understand us?

Driscoll stroked his chin and glanced at Maverick. "I don't think it wants you to go that way."

The wolf took a step forward, all of us taking a step back.

"I don't think it wants any of us to go that way," I said.

"So then what does it want?" Maverick asked, a bone-weary exhaustion filling his voice.

The wolf took another step forward, nudging its head again.

"You know when I said this grass was pretty normal?" Driscoll asked, then pointed behind us.

Maverick and I both turned.

"Well, I think I was wrong."

A door stood in the middle of the field. Plain brown with a round silver handle.

Something poked me in my butt, and I jumped, shrieking as I turned to realize it was the white wolf's cold, wet nose.

Maverick smirked.

"Jealous?" I asked.

His smirk turned to a glower, and Driscoll whistled low.

I hadn't meant to say that. It sounded so flirtatious. Something I had no interest in doing when it came to the bone collector. Actually, I'd flirted with the bone collector many times and enjoyed it a little too much. It was Maverick Von Lucas I had no interest in flirting with.

Driscoll strode toward the door. The white wolf lifted his head and howled, and Driscoll stopped in front of the door, then took three steps around it and peeked his head back out. "And it gets weirder," he said.

"Something I didn't know was possible after seeing trees with actual eyes."

I tugged at the ends of my hair. "What does the wolf want us to do?"

Maverick stalked ahead of me. "I'm guessing he wants us to open it."

"Go ahead." I flung out an arm. "Be my guest."

Driscoll came back around and crossed his arms. "Let me guess: he's going to open the door and then it'll fall on him. Or he'll try to open it, but it will actually trigger an explosive that will blow us all to pieces. Or maybe—"

"Can you turn him off?" Maverick said over his shoulder, stopping in front of the door and leaning down to inspect the handle.

"He doesn't have an off button. Otherwise, trust me, I already would have tried it."

Driscoll looked between us, frowning. "You know I can hear you both." He glanced at the white wolf and shrugged. "At least you're coming around."

The white wolf flashed his fangs.

"Never mind," Driscoll mumbled.

Both of us came to a stand behind Maverick, peering over his shoulder.

"Are you sure about this?" I asked right as he was about to turn the handle.

"No, I'm not sure about this, but I don't think the wolf is giving us many options."

Driscoll swallowed, his throat bobbing.

Maverick grasped the handle, and he slowly twisted it, the door swinging open.

I blinked several times. That wasn't possible. The door opened to a completely different place. All stone and rubble, the wind whistling with an eerie tune.

Driscoll raised a finger. "I vote we stay in the field."

Before any of us could respond, the white wolf crashed into me, propelling all of us straight through the opening. We stumbled into the new world, and I whipped around to see the door slamming shut and disappearing.

My pulse spiked, all the hairs on my arms raising.

I stood with Maverick, Driscoll, and the white wolf on some kind of stone . . . building? Temple? I couldn't tell. Piles of stone had toppled over. Statue heads and other concrete limbs were scattered across the area. Pillars lay on their sides. Hills surrounded the stone structure, all different colors of the rainbow.

"Why did he want us to come here?" Maverick asked, glancing at the wolf, who just stared with its red eyes.

"Why don't you ask him?" I said, gesturing to the creature. "And while you're at it, maybe offer yourself up for a snack."

"I get why everyone was annoyed with me and Leoni now." Driscoll massaged his temples. "You two are like an old married couple."

We both glared at him, and he raised his hands. "You're right, I'm staying out of it."

The stone trembled under our feet, debris rattling around us. We all moved in closer, our shoulders pressing in together.

"What is going on?" Driscoll asked.

The white wolf just sat there on its haunches, like it was waiting for something.

"I think we should run, figure out where we are, and make a plan," I said quietly. "Something is very, very wrong."

But before we had a chance to move, a fissure split the stone under us, and then, we were falling.

Chapter Twenty-Six

EMORY

I was falling. Again. And once again, I blamed the bone collector. Was this technically his fault? No. But I was angry and needed someone to direct that anger toward. So Maverick it was. In truth, I still hadn't figured out exactly why I was angry at him. It was a buried wound, one I didn't want to unearth right now.

Thankfully, this fall wasn't as long as the previous one.

My body hit the hard, rough ground with a force that rattled my teeth.

"Watch out!" Maverick yelled from somewhere beside me, and just as I blinked, my vision clearing, the stone from above came crashing down over us.

I quickly rolled, the stone pummeling into the ground, blasting apart into thousands of little pieces that rained over us. Dust filled the space, thick and suffocating.

I pulled my tunic up, but the dust still managed to infiltrate my nose, ears, mouth, stinging my eyes and burning my throat.

I tried to make out the forms of the others through the thick dust. "Driscoll?" I asked. "Maverick?"

"I'm here," Maverick said.

"Present," Driscoll added glumly. "Oh, and the wolf who maybe, probably, wants to kill us is here too."

The dust settled over the black shimmery ground, the wolf's slumped form laying there in the middle of the space. Stones had fallen over it, knocking it unconscious. I scrambled to the creature and lifted the stones off its legs and side.

"What are you doing?" Driscoll asked. "Maybe we don't help the wolf that tried to eat us."

"Maybe it's changed," I said over my shoulder, petting its matted hair.

"Or maybe you're delusional," Driscoll shot back.

"Oh, she's definitely delusional," Maverick said.

I finished lifting the rocks off the wolf, then slumped back against the wall, peering up to see the hole we'd fallen through, too high to reach. My magic would be no use, so depleted after how much of it I'd used over the last day.

Driscoll and Maverick sat with their backs against the opposite wall.

"I don't suppose you can grow a vine to get us out of here?" I asked.

"No." Driscoll gave me a pointed look. "I'm afraid I used up the last of my magic trying to save your two sorry asses."

"Right." I tugged at the ends of my hair. "So we wait until our magic strengthens again, and then we can escape."

"Or maybe it won't return." Maverick spread out his arms. "We have no idea what this place might do to our powers. Look what it did to everything else here."

I tugged at the scarf around my neck, not wanting to think about being stuck here without my magic. I raised my chin, refusing to give in to these negative thoughts. "We don't know anything for sure, and without evidence to corroborate that glum theory, we will just have to wait and see."

Maverick's head thumped against the wall, but for once, he didn't argue.

"What do you guys think happened here?" Driscoll gestured to the world above us. "I mean, we were never taught about this in school."

I snorted, thinking about my self-made education. "We weren't taught a lot of things in school."

"That's because the early schooling for the masses isn't intended to be specific," Maverick said, an edge to his voice. "You learn basic history, how to use your magic, and then you go your specialized route when you're done."

"I know how it works," I snapped, a bitterness coating my words.

I remembered all too well when I'd finished my basic schooling after ten years. Everyone started school at eight years old and finished when they turned eighteen. In that time, you lived with your parents, went to the local school that was free for all to attend. After that, it was off to either apprenticeships or an academy.

There were many scattered throughout Arathia: Academy of Healers, Academy of Scientists & Thinkers, Academy of Engineers & Architecture. Academies were expensive to attend, and most could only afford to go if they were part of the upperclass, children of royals, council members, ambassadors, advisors, high-ranking military officials. My father had been the general of the Fyriad Army and had enough saved to send me to an academy. He'd promised I could go to the Academy of Scholars & Historians. Then he'd died on assignment and my mother panicked.

I'd turned eighteen and hoped she would entertain the idea of me applying to the Academy of Scholars & Historians. All those hopes had been dashed when it became clear she intended no such thing. I was sent to an academy, just not the one I wanted. She forced me into the Academy of Ladies. Where I stayed for four soul-sucking years, learning how to sew, how to run a household, how to plan a dinner party, and my personal favorite, how to please your husband. The academy even made us matches. It was a guarantee that came with the schooling. They were the ones that had arranged the marriage between me and Gregory.

"I hated school," Driscoll said, and I realized he and Maverick had been talking this entire time. "Failed out after a year at the Academy of Scientists & Thinkers, much to my parents' dismay. Disappointed them. Disappointed myself. Disappointed everyone, really." He shrugged a shoulder. "And now it's all led to this. My death in some strange land."

"We're not going to die," Maverick and I both said at the same time.

Our gazes met, and I quickly looked away. His white shirt had lost a few buttons, now opened farther, revealing more of his muscled chest, while his suspenders hung at his sides, gray pants tight and hugging his thighs.

I cleared my throat and caught Driscoll's eye as he cocked an eyebrow and smirked. I returned that little smirk with a glare, but it didn't seem to deter him from waggling his brows.

I glanced around the space, hoping he'd knock it off before Maverick noticed. I stood, wincing at the aches and pains shooting through my legs. I'd run more in the last day than I had in my entire life, and my body was paying for it.

The space was dark and dank, the smell of moss and death permeating the air. Dust covered the rough stone, and this place seemed to stretch on and on, darkness swelling over everything so I couldn't see much beyond where we sat.

My instinct was to explore, but if this place was like the rest of the Deadlands, I wasn't sure that would be smart. I had no idea what I'd encounter underground.

My gaze caught on a heavy circular stone that lay on the floor, fractured into pieces. It lay in front of an entrance to a circular nook. The stone had clearly been covering the nook, and I walked over to it, crouching down and realizing it was embedded with iron. The metal twisted through the rock like thick veins. Iron was typically used in prisons to dull elemental powers so prisoners couldn't use their magic to escape. I squinted at the stone, running my hand over its ridges and bumps.

"This is likely a crypt," Maverick said from behind me, and I turned, crossing my arms.

"Well, all the bones and skeletons did kind of give that away." I pointed to one of the skeletal figures that Driscoll had rested his head on.

His eyes slowly traveled to the skeleton, and he jumped. "Oh, bloody earth. Why did no one tell me I was cuddling with actual bones?"

Maverick shrugged. "Some people are into that."

"Well, not me. I haven't gotten that desperate. Yet." He looked over at the skeleton, its mouth gaping wide open. "Although I haven't had much luck finding anyone else to love me. Maybe this is the best I can do."

"At least the bones won't talk back." I shot a withering look Maverick's way. "So other than the dead people everywhere, what tipped you off that this might be a crypt?"

He tsked, taking a step toward me. "There could be skeletons for any number of reasons." He ticked off his fingers. "A cave-in, a plague, some kind of mass murder. You can't just make assumptions."

"Except my assumption is right," I said, my annoyance turning sharp and spindly in my chest. "It is a crypt."

Maverick gritted his teeth together. "Yes, but not for the reasons you assumed."

"Then what are those reasons?" I gritted back. Spirits below. Had he always been so argumentative?

He pointed at the nooks dug into the walls, all of them closed, covered by big, thick stones. "Those of the Old World believed that it was important to be as close to Galaysia as possible after one died in order for the soul to travel there. So they buried their loved ones far under the earth. As far as they could go." He spread out his arms. "They'd often make these crypts underneath important temples and religious monuments dedicated to the Seven Spirits."

I hadn't known that. Had never come across it anywhere in my readings. I hated the way it made me feel inferior to him, even though I'd come to the same conclusion about what this place must be. But he was right: I'd missed facts, the evidence. Jumped to a conclusion too quickly.

"So what do you make of this?" I gestured to the stone on the ground. "Why go to such elaborate measures to bury someone in here with iron?" I traced one of the iron veins.

"Maybe they were buried alive," Driscoll said. "Closed in and trapped."

I chewed at the inside of my cheek, then stepped toward the nook. Before I could enter, Maverick grabbed my arm. "What do you think you're doing?"

His hand was warm and firm. Just days ago, if someone would have told me I'd be in a crypt from the Old World with Maverick Von Lucas,

I probably would've fainted. Then woken up and fainted again. I'd spent so long dreaming of the day I'd get to talk to him, to pepper him with questions, to be treated as his equal. Then I'd actually met him, and everything changed between us. My dreams shattered. That seemed to be a recurring theme in my life.

I wrenched my arm from his. "Oh, you know, I just thought I'd close myself in there. Maybe then I'll finally get some peace and quiet."

Driscoll snorted. "Ooooh . . . burn." He'd moved away from the bones and now sat by the wolf. Still unconscious. Or possibly dead. I hadn't checked its pulse. He reached out a tentative hand and stroked its head, then glanced up at us. "I already made the frost joke. Now I make a burn joke and still nothing from you two?" He shook his head, mumbling what sounded like insults, but I couldn't be sure.

Maverick pointed to the crypt. "You can't just waltz in there and disturb a historical site."

"Well I would fly, but I'm missing essential body parts for that to work."

"Can you be serious for one moment?" His stubbled jaw worked back and forth.

I leaned forward. "I think you're serious enough for the both of us."

I moved to step forward and he shot out an arm to block me. "You might disturb important evidence that could help us better understand who was trapped in here. Step on a bone or cause the entire structure to collapse. We need light, we need proper tools—"

"Oh, please." I threw up my arms. "In case you haven't noticed, we're in the Deadlands. This is a once-in-a-lifetime opportunity. If we escape this place, we're not coming back. So you can get over your haughty attitude and either help me or leave me alone."

His mouth dropped open. "It's not haughty. There are procedures in place for a reason."

I ducked under his arm and into the nook. "And have you always followed those procedures? Mr. Bone Collector?"

His jaw locked. "That was different."

"Right. Just you playing pretend." I whirled, not realizing how close he was, our noses now inches apart. "It sounds like you're okay with exceptions, but only when they come to you."

A fire danced in his eyes. "You are so . . ."

"I can't tell if you guys are turned on or angry, but this is actually getting pretty entertaining," Driscoll said from behind us.

I quickly stepped back. "You're welcome to join me in here, unless you're afraid of breaking too many rules."

"I'm not letting you in there by yourself," he said. "I don't trust you."

Like he hadn't spent years trusting me. When I was the white rabbit. Now that he knew my true identity, he wanted nothing to do with me. That was the crux of it. That was what was bothering me.

I made a face at him and turned to examine the area, but it was too dark to see anything. "Do you have enough magic to light this space?" I asked.

I expected him to argue since that was all he seemed to know how to do, but instead a small fire lit his palm, and the dim glow casting over the nook.

I sucked in a sharp breath. It hadn't just been the door threaded with iron. It was the walls, the ceiling, the floor under our feet. Iron spikes jutted from every inch. Iron spikes that I'd been just about to step onto. Maverick's magic faltered, and I pushed him out of the nook.

He scowled.

"You have to stay out there so your magic doesn't weaken. I'll look around and report back." He was already opening his mouth to argue, but I cut him off. "Do you want answers about what this is or not?"

His brows furrowed, but he stepped far back, holding out his firelight so I could see.

"What do you notice?" he asked. "Even down to the smallest detail."

"Well, other than the giant spikes . . ." I glanced around. "And dust."

I swiped a finger over the ground, that same black dust that covered the land here too. I cocked my head. And it looked like another color of dust was mixed in, but it was so dim, even with Maverick's magic, that it was hard to tell. This dust. Something about it was bothering me, but I couldn't figure out what.

"So someone was put in here alive. Most likely. Or they were dead and didn't deserve a proper burial? But then, why even go through the trouble of the iron and the stone door?" Maverick murmured, his question clearly rhetorical. "That would mean this was a dangerous elemental, then. Very dangerous from the lengths gone to entrap this person."

I stood and looked at the edges of the nook. My gaze went to the round stone. "I bet if we lifted this stone, it would be a perfect fit, and look at the serrated edges. It's like a dagger or knife was used to cut it open."

Maverick shook his head. "What kind of dagger could cut through iron and stone? What kind of weapon could be that powerful? More importantly, what escaped from here?" He looked at the other closed nooks, their stones still in place. "And what lay in the rest of these nooks?"

I had no idea. The more I studied this crypt, the less I understood anything about it.

"Uh, guys?"

We both whirled to see Driscoll standing there, his mouth gone slack, his face ashen. He swallowed. "I might know who was trapped here. And I think maybe it's time I tell you."

<h1 style="text-align:center">Chapter Twenty-Seven</h1>

MAVERICK

Emory stepped out of the nook, and Driscoll gestured to the ground. "You two might want to sit or risk fainting when I tell you the truth."

"What truth?" Emory asked as she sank to the ground, stretching out her legs and tucking a stray wisp of white-blond hair behind her ear.

Dust and soot covered her pale skin, her blue eyes as searing as ever as she set them upon Driscoll. After years spent wondering what she might look like, I wasn't sure I could've conjured up a face like Emory's if I'd tried. Those delicate features, her high cheekbones and straight nose, her full pink lips. I looked away as I sat against the opposite wall. Also a murderer. A liar.

I hid my identity from her because it could jeopardize my entire profession. She'd hid hers from me because . . . because she'd been married. I couldn't get it out of my head. I couldn't make the sharp thorns of that betrayal dull. Married. Another man touching her, kissing her, loving her. It wasn't fair to her to be angry about her marriage. I knew it wasn't. She'd just been following our rules. And she'd never crossed any lines with me. I'd been the one crossing lines.

But murder? I could be angry about murder. It was just so unlike her. That was the part that hurt. It made me feel like I really hadn't known her at all.

Driscoll sat next to Emory. "It's a really long, sordid tale that I'm going to skip so I can get straight to the plot twist. A revelation. Something Leoni and I discovered on our journey together with Princess Poppy."

I sat down, drawing up a knee and roping my arm around it. "What revelation?" I asked.

Driscoll took a deep, steadying breath. "The shadow king is actually Spirit Shadow."

My heart stopped, and the floor tilted under me.

Driscoll waved his hand. "The gist of it is that we found Queen Priscilla, queen of the shadow court, and she confirmed Spirit Shadow is alive and well."

But Queen Priscilla died along with her husband and baby during the Shadow War. At least that's what we'd all believed.

"Queen Priscilla found Spirit Shadow's dagger. She also found Spirit Shadow's crypt, right here in Shiraeth. She'd wanted to release him and beg for his help in the Shadow War, which they were losing, hoping he'd help change the tide, help Sorrengard win. So she used the dagger to release him from the tomb where he'd been trapped. But things didn't go as planned. After she released him, he tore through Shiraeth and destroyed everyone and everything before returning to the shadow court, where he's bound until the other six spirits are freed as well."

I blinked, staring at the ground, then looking back at that opened tomb, then back to the ground. This couldn't be true. This wasn't possible. The spirits hadn't been trapped. All evidence pointed to the fact that thousands of years ago they'd made the decision to leave, to go to Galaysia, where they waited to greet souls to the spirit world, to welcome them in death. They'd been meddling too much in human lives, and the elementals of the Old World were becoming too violent, too greedy with the powers the spirits gifted them. So the spirits destroyed them and disappeared. Then our direct ancestors found Arathia a thousand years later and settled here. The spirits decided to give us humans a second chance, to gift us their powers. But this time, they stayed away. No meddling. No getting involved.

What Driscoll was saying . . .

I looked at him; he was still petting the wolf. "How did Spirit Shadow get trapped?"

"I don't know how he got trapped or who trapped him." Driscoll shrugged. "Queen Priscilla died after revealing all of this information to us. But she said the other spirits are trapped too. The spirits' weapons are the keys to freeing them all."

Emory stood, pacing now. "So what does he want?"

Driscoll swallowed. "Queen Priscilla claimed he wants to free the other spirits. But he needs the weapons to free the other spirits. He has some of them already." He ticked off his fingers. "His dagger, Spirit Water's trident, and Spirit Earth's bow and arrow. He's trying to gather the weapons so he can set all the spirits free and they can get revenge for being trapped so long ago."

Emory stopped, hand floating to her mouth.

This couldn't be happening. And everyone at the academy had missed all the signs somehow. Or they didn't want to see the signs.

"We have to get that bolt back," Emory said, likely thinking the same thing as I was.

"What about getting out of here?" Driscoll threw his hands up. "You guys just can't help yourselves."

"You two don't need to do anything else." I cut my hand across my body. "Leave and I will take care of finding the bolt."

Emory stared at me, planting her hands on her hips. "So you can get all the glory? Find the bolt and be the hero? No, I don't think so. That bolt could be the only thing that saves me at this point." She raised her chin. "I can use it to bargain for my freedom."

"That's what you care about right now?" I snorted. "Not that our entire world is in danger of going extinct, exactly like what happened to the Old World?"

"Is that why you want the bolt, then?" she asked, accusation in her eyes.

I looked away. "That's none of your business. And the frost queen won't bargain with you. She's not the bargaining type. Not the forgiving type. She's been humiliated by you for years. Time and time again you've gotten your hands on valuable objects that you've taken right from under her nose. She won't let you go free."

"We'll see about that," she said. "Maybe if I give her the name of the bone collector, it will change her mind."

I stiffened at that threat. Stubborn, stubborn woman.

"Wait." She faced Driscoll. "Is that why the king of Apolis called that conclave? Is that what he wanted to tell all the rulers?"

Driscoll nodded. "And it doesn't sound like it went well. The frost queen stormed out."

"Because she's in denial. But why?" Emory said. "To defeat this threat, we're going to need all the courts to band together."

I agreed, but I'd have never been so brazen to say something like that out loud. Not when she employed me, held the key to my future—and was known to imprison those who spoke against her. All the rulers of Arathia were bad about sweeping things under the rug, ignoring threats, but the frost queen might have been the worst of them all.

"We've found where Spirit Shadow was trapped," Driscoll said. "This is huge. And also really bad. Especially because the only people with this information are currently in a crypt somewhere in the Deadlands with a giant wolf who's probably going to wake soon and be very grumpy—and hungry."

Emory swiped the dust from her pants. "Well let's just hope our magic returns before that happens."

"Let me know if it does. I'm exhausted and tired of you two and your bickering. I'm going to take a nap," Driscoll lay down and rolled over. "Let me know if wolfy wakes up."

"You can sleep too," Emory said to me. "I'll keep watch."

"I'm not tired." I should have been, but my mind was racing with theories, reeling from all the information Driscoll had just shared.

"Me neither," Emory said.

The sound of Driscoll's snores filled the crypt, his chest already rising and falling in a slow rhythm.

Perfect. So it was just me and the white rabbit, then.

Chapter Twenty-Eight

Perfect. Just me and the bone collector, who was quickly becoming the pain-in-my-ass bone collector. I could've probably come up with a cleverer insult if my brain hadn't felt like mush after Driscoll's revelation.

He slept soundly, cuddling with the wolf, which was a weird turn of events, while Maverick and I sat in complete silence, both of us lost in our own thoughts.

Maverick stared at the ground, brows furrowed, so I could only see the top of his short black hair. Rays of green lit up the crypt as ribbons undulated through the purple sky so far above. My magic was growing stronger, but at this point, it might be safer to stay here. The thought of going back up into that unknown, strange world terrified me.

I drew my knees to my chest.

Maverick Von Lucas. Over the last week, we'd been constantly moving, trying to get that bolt, running from the white wolf, then falling straight into the Deadlands.

But here in this cave, without anything threatening me, I could breathe and . . . feel the tension of the situation creeping over me.

In the past, I'd sit with the bone collector in silence and feel so at ease. I could spend hours talking to him. Had done both those things multiple times. But doing either of those things with Maverick Von Lucas? I didn't know how.

I squirmed, trying to get comfortable.

"It's hard to rest when you're just sitting there staring at me," Maverick said from across the space, shifting and stretching his long legs out in front of him with a groan. He lifted his hand, to scratch his jaw, blood coating it.

"Damnit," he said, examining his fist, skin ripped and seeping.

It must've gotten cut open when we'd fallen. With all the adrenaline pumping from our discovery, I could understand how he hadn't noticed yet. I stood and crossed the space, kneeling in front of him, grabbing his hand—bits of raw flesh hanging from it—cradling it in my own. It had been on instinct, natural. Yet I realized a moment too late what I'd done.

He stiffened.

"We need to clean this and wrap it in something," I said quickly.

I grabbed the waterskin peeking out of his satchel, pouring it over his knuckles. "It's the best we can do right now." I unwrapped the scarf from my neck and wound it around his hand. At this point, it didn't really matter that the scarf was priceless, an amazing piece of history. It had been muddied, snowed on, torn. It was a wonder I could even still see the blue color of the fabric.

I tsked, staring at Maverick's hand. "You really did a number on this one. Let's hope it doesn't get infected since we have no access to medicine, not to mention no healers, no herbs, not even a poultice . . ."

I trailed off when I looked up to see his brown eyes trained on me. He was probably about to scold me for how I'd mistreated this scarf, further desecrated his precious life's work by not taking better care of it. But I realized he wasn't looking at my face. His gaze was stuck on my neck. The blood drained from my face as I remembered the reason I wore the scarf: to cover all the mottled bruises inflicted by my husband. They'd faded over the last week, but from the way Maverick was staring, I knew however faint, they must still be there.

He pushed away my hand before I could finish tending to his wound, the scarf hanging down, blood still trickling from his knuckles, but he paid no mind to any of it. He reached out, fingers brushing my skin so delicately, a breath escaped me. I couldn't move. In all the years I'd known him, he'd never touched me, not like this.

"Who did this to you?" he asked, voice low like a growl.

"My husband." I stepped back, putting distance between us. "Ex husband," I clarified.

His brows furrowed, muscles bunching under his white shirt. "Your husband," he said with deadly calm. "Is that why you murdered him?"

"I didn't murder him, you ass." I shot Maverick a scathing look. "He was about to murder me, if you must know, and then he had a heart attack, which is the only reason I'm standing here today. I know you have a low opinion of me, but I didn't realize your opinion was so low that you think I'd murder my own husband. I thought you knew me better." I stopped abruptly as tears burned at the back of my eyes, and I stood, retreating until my back pressed against the opposite wall.

It hadn't hurt when Leoni or Driscoll accused me of the same thing. They didn't know me. But the bone collector? After our games, our notes, our conversations . . . I'd expected so much more from him. A fact that I hated.

The tears threatened to spill down my cheeks, and I dashed them away before he could see.

But he didn't even appear to notice. "That fucking bastard," Maverick said under his breath. When he glanced up at me, his eyes were full of fire. "Arch Historian Gungar said something about it, and I . . ." His hands clenched at his sides. "I was so shocked by your real identity. I'd met Lord Growley before. Met you. We'd been in the same room so many times, and I never knew."

"That was kind of the whole point." I crossed my arms. "You know, what we agreed to. Also, learning your identity wasn't exactly easy on me, and I didn't go straight to thinking 'murderer.'"

"Fucking bastard." Maverick still stared at my neck, making me itch to cover it again.

I took a steadying breath. "Sorry to shatter your illusion of him."

"I'm not," he said quickly. "Sorry, that is. I'm not sorry about that. I'm definitely not sorry that he's dead. Not when he did that to you."

The words took me aback. I didn't know what to say. Everything about this interaction stung, reminded me how little I actually knew of the bone collector. How stupid I'd been to think I'd ever known him at all.

"Is that why you became the white rabbit?" Maverick asked after a beat. "Because you needed an escape from him? Was he always like that?" He gestured to my neck.

I shook my head. "Not in the physical way. He just . . . wasn't a very nice man."

The fire in his eyes blazed once again at those words.

I rubbed my arms. "I became the white rabbit after my mother died."

His gaze softened. "Ah, I remember you telling me about that."

"I wanted something for myself in a world where it felt like I had nothing. Where not a single thing, not my body, my heart, my mind, belonged to me."

Sorrow shone in his eyes. We'd always had a fun, playful relationship where we were on equal footing. I wanted it back. Especially in this moment.

He leaned against the wall, crossing one ankle over the other.

I didn't want to talk about this anymore. I didn't want to think about Gregory. "Now you know why I became the white rabbit, so what about you? How did Maverick Von Lucas become the bone collector?" I tried to keep the accusation out of my voice, but I failed. "I mean, I don't really get it. You're already famous. You already have all the resources and access you could want. So why would you create an entire secret identity to go steal objects that you get to play with for your job? Why would you ever risk that?"

He crossed his muscled arms over his chest. "Maybe that's what I was missing from my job. Risk. Excitement. Adventure."

"What does that mean? I've heard your stories as Maverick. You've been chased by pirates, battled with dragons, swam with seafolk. What more could you ask for?"

He sighed and rubbed his temples.

"Oh, I'm sorry. Am I annoying you? Do you have better things to do in this dark crypt than talk to me?"

He raised a brow. "I could be sleeping."

"You said you weren't tired. Getting your stories mixed up now, bone collector?"

"Fine." His eyes locked on my legs, then traveled up my waist, to my collarbone, resting for just a moment on those bruises, before meeting my gaze. "It was you. You're what made me want to be the bone collector."

I stilled at that. "What?" I could barely get the words out. "What does that mean?"

"Do you remember that night you were digging in the field behind the academy?" To my surprise, Maverick laughed. "When you found that soldier's golden helmet?" He grabbed the end of the scarf and finished wrapping his hand with it.

"I remember." My voice came out scratchy, huskier than I wanted it to. "But how do you know about that?" It had been my very first find.

"Right behind the academy," he said fondly. "Risky, little rabbit."

I raised my chin. "It was in the middle of the night. No one was supposed to see me."

"Well, I'd been working late." He tilted his head. "In my office, and I was just leaving when I looked out the window and saw a hooded figure in the distance, digging for something. I was curious. So I decided to investigate. Imagine my surprise when I came across someone in a white fur cloak holding that golden helmet. I suspected it was a helmet worn by a general in the Old World army."

"Then he must've died," I continued, "and his family buried the helmet along with him to honor him."

"Exactly." Maverick's eyes glittered, then he sighed. "My job is a privilege. I love it. But when it started, it came with a lot of restrictions. A lot of rules. I wasn't even allowed out in the field until later in my career. Just in the last two years, actually. I craved excitement. Adventure. And when I saw you digging in that field in the blistering cold, late in the night—a thrill shot through me. I found you again. And again. I watched you work. Watched you find treasures and artifacts. Then I decided it was time to formally introduce myself."

That day in the highlands when I'd found the scarf now wrapped around his hand. Whatever I'd been expecting him to say, it wasn't that.

"After that run-in with the eel at Halfstard Lake," he continued, "I realized something in my life needed to change. I went straight to the frost queen the very next day, right over the head of Arch Historian Gungar. I told her there were amazing artifacts out there just waiting to be discovered, but we had to be brave enough, bold enough, to go after them. She agreed, only if I reported directly to her. She must've liked something about me because she asked if I wanted the role of her historical advisor. She removed Gungar from the position and appointed me, and well, you know the rest."

I did. He started going on dangerous missions to find rare artifacts, started gaining a reputation and following as Maverick Von Lucas, explorer extraordinaire. And it had been because of me.

"So why did you keep doing it?" I asked. "Once you started becoming the famous Maverick Von Lucas. Why keep being the bone collector?"

His shifted. "There's something I need to tell you about why I'm here."

That wasn't an answer to my question, but I was intrigued, so I stayed silent.

"You wanted to know why I took that bolt. Why I went after it. It wasn't to best you, little rabbit. I needed it because I knew I'd be coming here, and I also knew that in order to survive and escape, I'd need something powerful."

"What could possibly be that important that you'd risk coming here?" I asked.

"My sister," he said quietly, still staring at the ground. "She's here, in the Deadlands, and I have to find her."

Chapter Twenty-Nine

EMORY

Yet again, the bone collector had surprised me.

"Your sister?" I repeated.

I wanted to be angry that this man swooped in after I'd confessed my plans to him and stole that bolt right out from under me. But I couldn't. Not when he'd done it for such a noble reason. His sister. His sister was in the Deadlands. I had so many questions. Maverick Von Lucas had a sister. It shouldn't have been shocking. He was just a person after all, but I'd never seen him as just a person. I'd always seen him as this larger-than-life figure.

"I'm sure you'll find her." I blew out a breath. "It's just a matter of time. We'll get out of here, and you can go your way, and I can go mine."

"What if that's not what I want?" he asked, then rose to a stand and prowled toward me, a predatory look dancing in his eyes.

There was nowhere for me to go, my back already pressed to the wall, as he stopped right in front of me, his face inches from mine, his eyes searching.

"I'd say you don't have much choice in the matter." I attempted to use a haughty tone, but my voice came out breathy.

His gaze traveled over me, starting at the top of my head and rolling down my body like a slow-moving wave. "You're angry with me." His breath was warm on my cheeks.

My jaw locked. "As if you haven't been angry with me."

"I'm sorry."

The apology sounded so genuine.

"I thought you'd murdered your husband, Emory. It felt like a slap in the face, I guess. Like a betrayal. And it was so stupid of me to think such a thing about you. I should've known better. I was just so caught up in everything else happening around us. So caught off-guard."

I still didn't answer him, our gazes fused together, his swirling with so many different emotions.

"So?" he asked.

"So what?"

"Why are you angry with me?"

"You were supposed to be like me." The words came out as a whisper.

Confusion flashed in his eyes, but he didn't move, still pinning me to the wall.

I wasn't sure I realized why I was angry until the words had spilled out. But the truth of it hit me, and the words kept coming. "Do you know what it's like to feel so alone in the world?" My voice wobbled. "To have no control over your own life?"

"No," he said quietly. "I don't."

"Exactly." Tears pricked my eyes. "And the entire time we played our games, I thought you did. I imagined that you were trapped like I was. I thought that maybe, for once in my life, I wasn't completely alone in this world. That there was someone else out there like me." Tears trailed down my cheeks. "Someone who understood me."

Maverick's jaw ticked.

"And the entire time, you were the most celebrated historian on Arathia. You were just playing pretend."

"No," he said fiercely, thumbing away a tear. His touch left a searing burn on my cheek. "That's what I was trying to explain earlier. Before you came along, I was just going through the motions. You showed me how much joy and excitement and passion there is in this job. I wasn't playing pretend. Never with you. It was my real life where I was pretending." He took a deep breath. "You asked me why I kept being the bone collector once my career took off. Why do you think?"

His gaze bore into me.

I didn't know what to say, could barely speak with him staring at me like . . . like he wanted to kiss me.

"I want to propose a new game." He reached out and tucked a strand of hair behind my ear, and I had to repress my shudder when his thumb grazed the skin behind my ear.

"What did you have in mind?" I asked, wanting to feel his touch again, against all better judgment.

"Instead of working against each other, let's work together to find my sister and the bolt. Help me get my sister, and you can have that bolt."

My eyes widened. "You want to work with me?"

He let out a laugh. "With the Lady Emory Growley? Oh yes, I'd very much like that."

"I'm not a Growley anymore." I hesitated. "Not now that my husband is dead. I don't know who I am."

That fire in his eyes intensified. "You still have time to figure it out, little rabbit."

He cupped my cheek, and I leaned into the touch, sparks jolting through me. Spirits below, that touch, the way it ignited me . . . This was dangerous.

"Emory," he said, voice low, head leaning toward mine. "There's something else we should really talk about."

A conversation I wasn't ready to have because I was almost certain it involved us . . . and whatever had been simmering between us for years.

"Could you two stop yammering for five minutes so I can actually sleep?" Driscoll groaned and sat up, and we both jumped apart.

Bloody frost, I'd forgotten there was another person in this crypt.

Next to him, the wolf stirred, its body twitching. Just when I'd finally been able to breathe, of course the wolf was waking up.

I tilted my head. Except something strange was happening.

Maverick must've noticed it, too, because he stepped forward, gaze trained on the creature.

It began to yowl, paws lifting and thumping, tail thwacking the ground, the twitching turning to full-on convulsions.

That woke Driscoll up as he scrambled back and toward Maverick with wide eyes. "What in the blood and earth is going on now?"

The beast's torso twisted, its legs bending in awkward angles, back hunching over. I watched in horror, afraid to so much as move. The whole time its eyes stayed closed, but it cried out in pain.

Driscoll and Maverick watched, mouths agape with the same horror I felt. The wolf's back paw transformed to a long pale foot. Then the same thing happened to the other paw. The two front paws split open, revealing two hands. Fur fell in clumps to the ground, each bald patch revealing pinkish-white skin.

Driscoll whimpered. "I really, really hate it here."

"So you've said," Maverick murmured, transfixed on whatever was happening with the wolf.

Soon all the fur had fallen away to reveal a pale back with a spine. The tail shrank into the creature's tailbone. The wolf's snout shrank into a straight nose, the fur on its head changing to a shade of blond hair, the long teeth fell away, smaller ones sprouting from the gums. When the transformation was complete, I realized it wasn't a creature I was now staring at. It wasn't a feral beast.

It was a man.

Chapter Thirty

"What in the actual flying fuck did I just witness?" Driscoll asked. He put his hands in front of one side of his body. "There was a wolf." He shifted his hands to the other side of his body. "Now there's a man. My brain is not processing this."

The man groaned and stood, his, well . . . everything . . . on full display. He blinked a few times, stretching out his muscular arms.

Driscoll cocked his head, staring at the man's very large appendage approvingly. "Okay, well my brain is processing that."

Maverick cleared his throat, and Driscoll quickly looked away.

The man looked around, his gaze landing on each of us. "Oh, hello," he said.

"Hello?" I echoed back. "Hello? That's all you're going to say after spending days terrorizing us, almost eating us? Forcing us into the Deadlands?"

He frowned. "Oh no. Did I hurt any of you in my wolf form?" He scratched his head through his straight blond hair, which fell in a careless sort of way over his forehead. "I don't have the best memory when it comes to my time as a wolf."

He said it like it was the most normal thing in the world. Like "his time as a wolf" was just a mask he slipped on and off.

"Tried to hurt us is an understatement." My hands balled into fists.

Maverick stepped forward. "I think what she's attempting to say is that we're a little confused."

I glared at him. "I think what I'm trying to say is perfectly clear and doesn't need to be explained."

He had the decency to wince at my words.

"I do apologize if I offended you," the man said.

"Didn't offend me," Driscoll piped up, gaze darting down once again to the man's long length that hung between his legs.

"Can you put on some clothes?" I asked, waving a hand toward him.

"Or don't," Driscoll suggested, then shrugged. "Whatever you prefer."

Maverick pinched the bridge of his nose.

"What?" Driscoll threw out his arms. "I'm just trying to make sure he feels comfortable."

I rolled my eyes. "I'm less concerned with him feeling comfortable and more concerned with who he is and why he just shifted from a wolf!"

"I agree with Emory." Maverick rubbed the back of his neck.

The man's brows furrowed. "I have to admit, I don't understand this situation." His pale blue eyes shifted from Driscoll to Maverick to me. "You three shouldn't be here."

"We shouldn't be in a crypt full of bones and dead people?" Driscoll asked. "Yes, I would tend to agree."

"Let's give the man a chance to explain," Maverick said.

"How did you get into the Wilds?" the man asked, brows knitted in confusion.

I threw up my arms, growing increasingly frustrated with the way this conversation was making less and less sense. "What are the Wilds?"

The man scratched his head. "It appears you three are not from here."

"Of course we're not from here," I said. "Are you from here? You fell in the same hole that we did."

The man's frown deepened. "A hole?"

Maverick stepped forward, holding out his hands. "Okay, let's just start from the beginning. We're not from here." He gestured between himself and me. "My name is Maverick Von Lucas, and I'm from the fire court. This is Lady Emory from the frost court. And that is Driscoll Bayliss from the earth court. We were in the Glacier Mountains when you chased us, making us fall into a hole in the mountains that led us to this place, which we call the Deadlands since the Shadow War that happened sixty years ago. You do know of the Shadow War?"

Understanding lit the man's eyes. "Ah. I'm sorry." He gave a slight shake of his head. "It appears there has been a grave misunderstanding."

At that, my anger ebbed away. He was clearly as confused as we were and doing his best to figure this situation out. "I'm sorry for yelling," I said. "I'm confused and overwhelmed and a little frightened, if I'm being honest."

Maverick stepped to my side, his hand coming to my shoulder and giving a gentle squeeze. Our gazes locked. He gave me a nod, none of the anger or hatred that I had been so used to seeing these last few days etched across his face.

"My name is Aron." We jolted, both our gazes snapping to the man as Maverick stepped away from me. "I do not know this Deadlands of which you speak, but we call this place the Wilds."

"Who is 'we'?" I stepped forward.

A ribbon of green swam across the crypt, highlighting Aron's face and hair with an emerald shade.

"Those of us who live here, who survived the Shadow War."

"There were survivors?" I breathed.

Maverick and I both shot each other glances. My stomach turned. The courts had closed off the Deadlands after the war, believing everyone dead. The frost queen had been the one to lead the endeavor, insisting it must be done. Under her guidance, they'd put up walls, actual borders. She'd sent teams of frost elementals to explore the Deadlands, to see if anyone was left. None of them returned, so she'd called a conclave, gone to extreme lengths over the years to tell everyone that entry to the Deadlands was forbidden, that if you chose to come here, you wouldn't live to make the journey back.

Of course there were those who didn't listen, who were curious or greedy or just plain stupid, and decided to come here anyway, and just as promised, no one ever returned. But this whole time, there had been people trapped here.

I squinted at Aron. He couldn't have been much older than me. He looked to be mid-thirties at the most. Which didn't make sense. "The Shadow War happened sixty years ago. How are you so young?"

It felt like something in my brain was permanently broken.

"I don't have my shadow," Aron said, then his blond brows furrowed together as he stroked his clean-shaven jaw. "Well, that's just one part of it. I'm also cursed. Like everyone here who survived the Shadow War."

The room started spinning, and I stumbled into a wall, having a hard time breathing. None of what he was saying made sense, and I couldn't catch my breath enough to ask the other two if it was just me or if this was getting really weird. By the look of shock on Maverick's face and the way Driscoll's mouth had dropped open, I was guessing they were feeling about the same as I was.

Before I could ask any more questions, clothes fluttered down through the opening of the crypt, the green ribbons casting their light through the thin fabric. I peered up and realized a woman's face scowled down at us. Cascades of black hair fell over her shoulders, almost raven in the light.

Aron looked down at the clothes, then up at the woman. "Ah, El is here at our meeting place. She might be better at answering your questions than me. I, admittedly, need some work in the communication department."

Driscoll pointed at the brown tunic and trousers. "Are those for you? Because if you're not comfortable putting them on—"

"Driscoll." I massaged my temples. "Just let the man get dressed."

Maverick smirked, the first smile I'd seen on his face since we'd met.

The woman continued to scowl down, not saying anything as Aron tugged on his brown trousers and stretched a tunic overhead. Then two black boots dropped down and thudded on the ground. He pulled one on each foot and looked up expectantly. Next a thin rope dropped, swaying until Aron caught hold of it.

He grabbed on with his powerful hands and shimmied up as we watched, too stunned to move. Aron got to the top, and the woman, El, pulled him out.

He poked his head back in. "Well, are you all coming?"

Chapter Thirty-One

Blood and frost, it was scorching. Sand, dunes, and rocks surrounded me as I stood in the boiling land of Gilraeth, the sun so hot it shimmered in the air, making the horizon waver in my vision. I swiped an arm across my brow and adjusted the scarf I'd draped over my hair and the one covering the lower half of my face. I'd traded my fur cloak for the traditional clothes of the fire court: baggy harem pants with a light, long-sleeved linen shirt to keep the sun from burning my skin.

When the bone collector and I had met to draw the artifact for our annual challenge, we'd picked a dagger located in the highlands of the sky court.

I'd immediately stuffed the paper back into the jar and proclaimed I had a better idea, one I was very much coming to regret as perspiration dripped over my brow, stinging my eyes. I'd known my husband had an upcoming trip to Gilraeth to speak with the council members, who were ruling in the absence of their cursed queen. Or trying. A sorceress had risen up, rumors swirling she was from the shadow court. She'd taken control of the castle, was using her shadow magic to wreak havoc, and no one had been able to best her.

Gregory was here to represent the sky court, to show them they had Valoris's support, but to also remind them they needed to get their shit together—and fast. With no official ruler named in Princess Seraphina's absence, a decision needed to be made before the realm sunk into chaos. We'd see if my husband was successful in his dealings with the fire court council.

A vulture soared overhead, then dove toward what looked like a snake carcass, landing and picking at it.

With my husband's upcoming trip in mind, I'd suggested an alternative to the bone collector. When we'd first started this whole thing, I'd made it clear we needed to stay within the parameters of the frost or sky court. I wouldn't be able to venture farther than that. But with my husband's trip, I figured why not?

Sweat trickled down my back, in between my breasts, down the sides of my face. I wished I could go back in time and kick myself.

"Look at you," a voice said, and I turned to see the bone collector standing before me. "A little out of your element?"

"Well, it's only fair." I spread my arms wide. "You've been out of yours a few times now in Fyriad. Time to even the playing field."

He wore all beige, his signature black cloak gone, his clothing similar to mine. Those copper eyes that reminded me so much of the burnt oranges of the desert sparked with delight. "How do you know I'm out of my element in Fyriad? I'm always in my element, little rabbit."

I snorted.

"Is this your first time here?" he asked, strolling toward me.

"That sounds like a personal question, bone collector."

He raised an eyebrow, then ticked fingers. "I know that you think eyeballs are disgusting, but you're perfectly fine with mummified bodies. I know that you have a weakness for sour berries. I know that your most prized possession is a golden helmet because it was the first item you ever found." He cocked his head. "I know that you are impatient, stubborn, that you're always running late. Yet asking if you've ever been to Gilraeth is too personal?"

I held back a snort. He'd learned more about me than I'd realized these last few years. The frequency of our notes had increased. I was traveling to that little spot with our hidden jar more often than I'd like to admit. It happened to not be too far from my house in Fyriad, and it was so tempting to make the short walk and check if the bone collector had left me a new note. We talked about so much and hardly anything at all. We never revealed personal details, yet it felt like he knew me better than anyone.

I shot him a smile, even though the lower half of my face was covered. I could always tell when he smiled, could see it in the crinkle of his eyes. So maybe he could tell too. "Let's just get going."

I had a dinner to attend later with my husband. I'd told him I wanted to get out of the manor where we stayed, explore the beauty of the court. He had barely heard me, so excited to go to the meeting with the council members and speak on behalf of the sky crown that he couldn't care less what I did, so long as I showed up at the right times to look good on his arm and, in turn, make him look good.

"Well, I only asked because I wanted to warn you of the dangers that lurk in the fire court," the bone collector said. "But if you're so reluctant to give me any personal details, I guess you'll just have to find out for yourself the risks of going after The Book of Yaraho."

With that, he spun and strode toward a cluster of caves that nestled into a tall, rock structure. It stretched along the flat piece of land, dunes surrounding it. The Book of Yaraho was rumored to be here, in this area, buried somewhere in that cave.

I ran to catch up. "I'm aware of the risks. So how did it go with the sunken ship?"

"Ah, I forgot to update you," he said from beside me. "Too busy packing for our trip."

Our trip. Like it was a holiday we were taking together, like my husband wasn't in the picture at all. Guilt niggled at me. Going behind my husband's back to create a secret identity, stealing priceless artifacts and hiding them in our home, lying to him for years—none of that made me feel bad. But something was growing between me and this bone collector, and that felt very wrong.

I swallowed. Nothing was happening. We didn't even know each other's names, for spirits' sake. I didn't even know what he looked like.

We were friends, and my husband couldn't fault me for making a new friend who happened to have the same interests as me.

"And that's when the shark found me," the bone collector was saying.

Oops. He'd been talking this entire time. Answering a question I asked.

We came to a stand in front of the dark cave.

"Did you know that shark teeth have poison on their tips? One bite is enough for the poison to make its way to your heart and stop it. Unless you find the antidote first."

"So where did you find the antidote?" I asked as we ventured inside, the sun blocked out by the cave walls and ceiling.

"Why do you assume I got bit?" He stopped, turning to me.

I crossed my arms. "I thought that was the point of your story."

He leaned closer, the movement exhilarating, his face so close to mine that I could see the small freckle beneath his left eye. "The point of my story was that I got the treasure chest from the Losotros shipwreck."

A famous shipwreck. The Losotros were a clan from the Old World who exclusively lived on their massive ships, but a calamity at sea caused their entire fleet to be wrecked, all of them wiped out from a single natural disaster. All the Losotros's ships had been destroyed except that last one, which was nearly impossible to get to because of the location: right by a vortex in the sea where the water constantly moved, anyone who came too close at risk of being sucked in and drowning.

The bastard did it.

I envied him in moments like these. The fact that he could travel to the edges of the continent, to access places like that while I was limited to Fyriad and Valoris, made me burn with jealousy.

"Well done, bone collector." I whirled and moved farther into the cave, which split into three different paths.

He pointed to the left. "I'm going this way."

I nodded to the right. "You'll be seeing me again as I'm running away with The Book of Yaraho."

His back was to me as he stalked in the opposite direction, yelling over his shoulder, "You always have been too arrogant for your own good."

I rolled my eyes, continuing on my chosen pathway through the cave. I reached into the pocket of my pants and pulled out a match, which I struck and lit, illuminating the narrow space. Hopefully I'd chosen the right way. I didn't like being in these enclosed spaces where it would be so easy to get stuck, buried alive, caved in. Many things could go awry. Again, I wondered what in the bloody frost I'd been thinking when I suggested this.

The fire burned brightly on the match, giving me just enough light that I could see in front of me, watching the ground to make sure there were no sudden drops or ridges. Skitters and patters echoed around me, and I wondered what creatures dwelled in this place. I knew of some: snakes, fire lizards, desert rats. But other texts I'd read in my research alluded to more ancient creatures that lurked in these caves across Gilraeth.

Hopefully they'd died along with everyone else in the Old World.

Still, that familiar thrill threaded through my veins at the challenge, the excitement of it all, propelling me forward as the path wound down, getting so steep I had to sit on my bottom and scoot until I could go no farther, the rock dropping off in a sharp decline. Hopefully this path didn't go too far underground. I didn't even want to think about the climb back up. I dropped my match and watched as the fire fell through the air, so far the light disappeared.

I really couldn't be late for dinner. In the past, I'd planned these little escapades when my husband would be out of town, when I had plenty of time. This was different. Stupid of me. I'd been so eager for something new I hadn't thought about all the risks. Yet the thought of finding that book kept me going. Except I'd just dropped my match and had no light to see in front of me. My legs hung over the rock, and I bit my cheek, wondering if I should just start climbing down and see what happened.

As if the universe heard my thoughts, fire erupted in the air. Flames dotted the air, floating lights decorating the space before me. I sat on the edge of a jutting ledge, and my eyes widened as I realized what I was seeing: a huge cavern. Round and bottomless. Cave openings dotted the upper parts, circling all around, and jagged ledges protruded from the caves.

Even with all the light illuminating the vast space, I couldn't see the ground below. But I didn't need to. A tall rock rose up in the center, and there on the rock lay the book.

It was said to have been written by Spirit Fire himself. A tome full of his mandates. It could tell us so much about the Seven Spirits. I blinked a few times, the flames that hung in the air seeming to move.

"Of course you're already here." The bone collector appeared in the opening of one of the caves on the opposite side of the cavern.

"Well, I won't be here for long." I pointed to the column of stone where the book sat, noticing a series of smaller columns leading to it. I could easily hop from each one. This was already going in my favor. "Just going to grab the book and be on my way."

"I don't think it's going to be that easy, little rabbit."

He pointed to the flames, a few of them floating closer. Enough that I could see they had eyes . . . and sharp teeth. Not flames at all. Fire sprites. They filled the space, and they didn't look happy.

I'd heard about the sprites that lived in the mountains and caves of Gilraeth. The winged creatures were the size of my hand but could ignite on a moment's notice, incinerating their victims. I'd also heard they had the ability to steal someone's magic, to absorb it into themselves, though I didn't know if that particular rumor was true. Either way, I had no desire to find out.

I racked my brain as a few sprites bared their black pointy teeth. This didn't bode well. Sprites were created by Spirit Fire, answered to him alone, and once he disappeared, they retreated, supposedly waiting for his return before reemerging into society. In the meantime, they guarded his treasures, any artifacts connected to him, fiercely protective. Which was why no one had gone after that book.

I held out my hands. "Please, I'm just here for the book."

One of them hissed, and every single sprite turned their wide eyes, which took up nearly half their faces, on me. Behind them, the bone collector began climbing down from his cave opening.

"You miss your master, right?" I asked, the sprites slowly congregating around me. "Well, I'm a scholar. A historian. I'm trying to uncover truths about him, about his history. I want to understand what happened to Spirit Fire and all the spirits. I want to better understand the way they lived, the way they ruled."

The sprites' flames licked and leapt around their bodies. If I used my magic, I'd forfeit. The bone collector won our last game, running away with that diadem that I'd found on the lake. I did all the hard work, almost died, and he got the glory. The competitive side of me refused to let that happen again.

The bone collector fished a rope out of his satchel, making a loop at one end and lassoing it. He missed the first few times, but eventually, the rope landed around the tall column. Meanwhile, the sprites' attention was all on me.

"You'd do well to turn around and go back where you came from," one of the sprites said, her voice low and raspy, like smoke drifting through the air. Her bright fuchsia eyes flashed, promising danger if I didn't listen.

By now, all of them had me surrounded, and I could barely see over the flames flickering from their little bodies. Together they looked like one massive ring of fire. Just over the blurring heat of the flames, I could see the bone collector swinging through the air and latching onto the rock.

Damnit. Time to play dirty. Just like he had at Halfstard Lake.

"I would, but I kind of want to see how this plays out."

The fuchsia-eyed sprite stiffened. "How what plays out?"

The bone collector scaled the column, so close to reaching that book laying at the top.

"If he gets the book or not." I gave an innocent shrug.

All the sprites whipped around at once as their gazes locked onto the bone collector.

"Don't let him get the book!" a sprite yelled, and they all rushed forward.

"Thank you for that," the bone collector called as he froze on the column, right near the top.

I smiled from underneath my scarf, and then backed up and took a running leap through the air, landing on a shorter column that jutted up from the darkness. I landed on my feet, the force shoving up into my bones, and making me bite down on my tongue. Ow.

The sprites swarmed the bone collector right as he pulled himself to the top of the column and grabbed the book.

"Don't come any closer," he warned. "Or I'll destroy it."

He wouldn't dare. He'd die before letting any harm come to such an important text. But they didn't know that. The sprites froze, all of them at a standstill. The bone collector slipped a dagger from his boot and pointed it right at the center of the book.

I leapt to the next column, wavering on my feet before regaining my balance. One more to go. I reared back my arms and jumped again, crashing into the column and wrapping my arms around it. My muscles ached, already fatigued, but I was so close now.

The sprites closed in around the bone collector, but none of them moved to strike against him, his threat working nicely in his favor. Still, he had no escape plan, while one was forming in my mind.

I worked my way to the top of the column, boots and hands finding every crack and crevice they could lodge into. My arms and legs shook, and sweat drenched me, the scarf around my head and face sticking to my skin. I'd have a lot of explaining to do to my husband about my current state.

I wouldn't think about that right now.

Focus on the mission. I was not Emory Growley. I was the white rabbit, and I would get that book.

"Set me on fire, and the book gets set on fire," the bone collector was saying. "Push me and the book falls with me. Stab me, and I stab the book. Quite a conundrum."

"You can't stand here forever," one of them hissed. "You'll tire eventually, and you will hand over that book."

Finally I reached the top, peeking over the column. The bone collector teetered there, his eyes flicking down to me. I gestured for him to throw me the book. He gave a slight shake of his head, and I widened my eyes meaningfully.

Yes, this was a game we both wanted to win, but we also wanted history to prevail. We both cared far too much about these objects and preserving them, learning from them, to let our egos get in the way.

"Drop the book," I mouthed, *"and I'll help you escape."*

My muscles quivered with exhaustion, and I wasn't sure how much longer I could hang onto this thing.

His jaw locked. He closed his eyes, paused for what felt like the world's longest minute, and let the book go with a heavy sigh. I snatched it from the air, then quickly flattened myself to the column as the sprites shrieked and dove headfirst into the darkness, both of us forgotten as they flew deeper and deeper, their shrill, panicked yells filling the air until they were finally far enough away for me to let out a breath.

"You're welcome," I said as he grabbed one of my hands and heaved me up. We both slumped down, sitting back-to-back, legs hanging over the side. "Also, I win."

"I'll let you have this one, only because you saved my life," he said, voice weary.

"I'd say we're even now."

The sprites' flames disappeared as they dove deeper down, so far below I truly wondered if there was a bottom to this place. When they finally did hit the bottom, they'd realize the book wasn't actually missing.

"How long do you think it'll take them to search for that thing?" the bone collector asked, leaning his back against mine.

"Long enough for us to rest before climbing back down." I stretched my arms overhead, cracking my neck.

I could feel the hard muscles of his back, the broadness as it stretched against mine. I looked down to see dust shimmering on the pedestal where we perched. Red and glittery. I swiped a finger over it, wondering if it had come from the sprites. I hadn't seen dust like this before, and I was about to ask the bone collector about it, when he spoke.

"Twice now we've almost gotten killed. Why do I feel so exhilarated by that?"

I reached behind and nudged him in the ribs with my elbow. "Maybe it's in us to be thrill seekers. Sometimes I think I love the pursuit, the chase, as much as I love actually getting the artifacts."

He smelled like sweat and embers, and I took a deep inhale of it.

"What's your favorite part of it all?" He shifted, his back rubbing against mine.

I stayed silent.

"What? Is that too personal, little rabbit?"

"I'm thinking, you ass."

He chuckled, and the sound rumbled down me, vibrating into my skin.

I looked down at the thick leather-bound book in my lap. "Don't get me wrong, I love exploring, traveling to dangerous places, not knowing what I'm going to face. But this." I held up the book, even though he couldn't see me. "This is my favorite part. The potential. What I'm going to learn from this. Not just from reading it but from studying the writing, the ink used, the type of parchment, the binding. There's so much story here. A story I get to unfold."

"Wow."

"What?" I said, wondering if I got too carried away.

"That's it. The potential. That's my favorite part too." He paused. "So what do you do with all these items you collect? Do you just hoard them away, plan to sell them off on the black market."

"You insult me." I scoffed, then swiped the back of my hand over my soaked brow. "If you really want to know, I would love to open a museum one day. A place where I can offer this knowledge for free. Funded by the frost court so any citizen who wants to learn can do so." I waited for the sarcastic response, for him to tell me it was never going to happen, but he didn't.

"You're just full of surprises, little rabbit."

I wasn't the only one. The more we talked, got to know each other through these challenges and our notes, the more I was beginning to realize the bone collector might be more like me than I ever realized. In a world where I'd always felt so alone, he made me feel like I had someone. And that was terrifying.

Chapter Thirty-Two

MAVERICK

My mind should have been reeling over the events that had just occurred. It should have been reeling over the fact that a wolf changed into a man right in front of us, and then said wolf told us he was cursed like it meant nothing at all. My mind should have been focused on the fact that Aron and this El couldn't be trusted, that we shouldn't have been following them away from the ruins and toward a "safer" area like Aron claimed. My thoughts should've been centered on every single one of those things, and more, but instead all I could think about was Emory. When I'd cupped her cheek with my hand in that crypt, she'd reacted, curled into my touch. Like maybe she wanted me as much as I wanted her.

I couldn't deny it. Not anymore. I'd tried to keep my distance, I'd tried to tell myself that whatever I felt for her was impossible. Then I'd seen those bruises on her neck, and I knew that I would burn this world if it meant keeping her safe. I'd burn this world for her. And I'd enjoy doing it.

She wasn't a murderer after all, and guilt speared me that I'd ever thought she was. She was right. I might not have known her name or her face, but through the years, through her notes and our encounters, I'd known her.

That was the problem, in the end. I was the problem. I'd done the same thing to my sister. I hadn't had faith in her, and it had ultimately been my fault she ended up here. Just like it had been my fault Emory ended up here. Yes, she chose to come after me, but that was because she needed that bolt to bargain for her freedom. If I'd stood up for the white rabbit, gone to the frost queen directly and pleaded her case, the whole thing could've been taken care of, and Emory wouldn't be here in danger.

But I'd put my career first. Helped her escape in secret instead of going directly to the queen and risking losing my position. I scrubbed a hand down my face.

Aron, Driscoll, and El walked ahead of me. Aron had told us it would be better to get to safety before we talked any further.

El had stayed silent the entire time as we trekked from the stone ruins and onto a black-dusted path that led through sweeping hills. Driscoll had wandered too close to one of the hillsides, and Aron had grabbed him and told him in a very matter-of-fact voice that the hills tended to eat anyone who stepped foot on them.

After that, we kept to the middle of the path.

Now we stood in a forest that looked more like what I was used to: brown trunks, green leaves, branches that didn't have claws or talons. They'd led us to a spot that was flat, protected by the trees and the towering canopies and had enough space for all of us to pick a spot to sleep. It was the best we could hope for right now. Better than any other areas we'd come across so far.

Aron took Driscoll hunting for some dinner while El got to work making a fire. She collected branches, leaves, and twigs, then sat down, the skirts of her simple red dress floating around her. She concentrated on creating a spark with two rocks she gripped in her hands, while her long black hair curtained her face, falling in thick waves around her golden skin.

"I can help." I gestured to the sticks, then flipped my palm over and summoned my magic. Flames appeared, dancing over my palm. The woman just glared and continued using the rocks to catch a spark.

So much for helping.

Emory stood at the edge of the clearing, arms folded over her chest, back to me. I should've been peppering El with questions, figuring more out about this land, about how to find my sister. But when it came to Emory, "should've" had never mattered much. I threw "should've" out the window the first time I'd seen her. And I'd never looked back.

She held something in her hand that she was studying.

"What is that?"

I reached her side, and she shot me a sideways glance. "I'm really not in the mood for arguing. Aron will be back soon with Driscoll, and I am thinking through all the questions I have for him and El."

"That didn't answer my question." I nodded at the watch in her hand, glass broken, silver chipped and scratched. It was attached to a long silver chain that she'd looped around her neck. "Do you typically use broken clocks?" I lifted the pocket watch from her palm, studying the little hands, all ticking backward. But the tick was slow. Much slower than normal. It wasn't counting seconds anymore.

"I found it when we first got here. I think it's counting down to something," she said. "Let's just hope it's not as ominous as everything else here."

Emory let go of the pocket watch, and it thumped against her chest.

She turned, gaze shifting to El and back to me. "Maybe we can ask El and Aron about this. See if they know anything. You heard Aron, right?" Her voice dropped to a whisper. "He said he was cursed. What in the bloody frost does that mean?"

Spirits if I knew. Fuck, it was hard to concentrate with her standing so close to me, that freshly fallen snow scent clinging to her, making me want to lean in just a little farther . . .

"Who would have cursed this place?" Emory asked. "And how?"

I ran a hand over my hair. Right. She was thinking about the logical things, not about us. Not about the revelations we'd made to each other. Not about the fact that our lips had been closer than they ever had in the seven years we'd known each other. My gaze trailed down to those lips, and I wondered exactly what it might be like to feel them on mine.

I needed to get a fucking grip on myself. Annalee needed me to.

"I don't know," I finally said. "I can't imagine how this world came to be. I've never read nor heard of anything like these Wilds or Aron or the cat woman I saw in the eyeball forest earlier."

"Now that's a sentence I never thought I'd hear. Cat woman?" She raised an eyebrow. "Do I even want to know?"

I leaned against a tree, crossing my arms. "Oh, it was just a woman that looked like a cat and talked and also purred. And she had a tail. You know, normal stuff compared to men who shift into wolves."

That got a smile out of her. The first smile I'd ever seen from Emory. It lit up this entire damn forest. It lit me up. Forget the fire. Forget food. I just needed her to keep smiling like that, and it would be enough to sustain me for all my days.

"Hello?" Emory snapped her fingers, and I jolted.

Right. I was falling apart ever since her identity had been revealed. Maybe it was this world, or maybe it was the fact that my sister was missing. Everything was upside down right now, including my brain. Once I found Annalee and got the spirits out of here, all would be right again. Everything could go back to the way it was.

Except this. Except the one thing I didn't want to go back to normal. Her. Me. Us. "Sorry." I rubbed my stubbled jaw. "Still processing all of this."

"Do you think we can trust them?" Emory whispered, chewing at her bottom lip.

A breeze brushed through the forest, leaves and branches rustling. El almost had the fire going as she struck the two sharp rocks together, sparks flying.

"No," I said, then hesitated. "And I'd appreciate if you could keep what I told you about my sister being here between us. I don't want to put her in any more danger than she's already in. Until I can trust them, I don't want them knowing anything."

Emory leaned closer, her fresh snowfall scent wafting toward me. "You don't think they could help?"

"Maybe." I thought of the cat woman who'd purposely misled me. "But I don't want to take that chance. I'd rather get information from them without revealing my sister's whereabouts."

She looked unsure but nodded. "Okay. I won't say a thing. And our deal. Is it still on?"

I laughed. "We just made it an hour ago."

"Well I'm just making sure you're not going back on it." She scowled in a way I imagined she had so many times over the years when I'd frustrated her.

"Have you ever known me to go back on a deal?"

She pointed a finger into my chest, and it did things to me that I never knew such an innocent touch could do. Suddenly I wanted that finger trailing down my entire body.

"Hello?" She'd withdrawn her hand and now stared at me like I'd lost it.

I very well might have when it came to her. Fuck. "Sorry, didn't hear you."

She rolled her eyes. "The time on Halfstard Lake when you used your fire magic, even though it was against our rules?"

"I used that magic to save your life," I said. "To defeat a giant eel that was going to make you its lunch."

"And then you took the diadem I found."

"You got your payback with that book in the fire court."

Her lips twitched. "I suppose."

Whatever happened in that crypt, I was grateful for it, because it felt like we were finally getting back to our normal selves. To the person I wanted to be when I was around her. My best self.

Shadows passed over her face, and she crossed her arms and stepped back, already retreating away. Like she'd done so many times before.

"What's going on?" I asked, voice low. "You can tell me."

"If we don't find that bolt, I'm as good as dead. I have no one in this world. All alone." She murmured the last part like I wasn't supposed to hear it.

It broke my fucking heart that she actually thought that.

I hooked a finger under her chin and forced her to look at me. "I don't know what the future holds, but I do know one thing for certain."

"And what's that?" she asked, those blue eyes so bright, so pale they almost looked like snow.

"You're not alone. You've never been alone. Not since the day I met you."

Her eyes flashed in surprise. She opened her mouth to speak when a bush started shaking across the clearing, and we both braced ourselves, magic flaring in our hands. The bush shook harder, and finally Driscoll and Aron emerged, Aron holding what looked like three rabbits, all of them with claws that stretched as long as my fingers as Driscoll chattered away.

"You really knew a woman who did that to a statue?" Aron asked. "Doesn't sound very comfortable."

Driscoll nodded. "I know. Crazy, right?"

They both stopped, gazes turning to us like they were just realizing they had an audience.

"Anyone hungry?" Driscoll asked.

Chapter Thirty-Three

EMORY

"*You're not alone. You've never been alone. Not since the day I met you.*"

That's what Maverick had said to me, his words so sincere that I wondered if it might actually be true. But I didn't have much time to think on it. Not when there was so much else to dissect.

We sat around the fire, bellies full, that same twilight sky as always stretching over us with rays of emerald green slicing through the canopies. When the star court was at its full power, it must've been beautiful, a true sight to behold.

Questions burned through me. So many spirits-damned questions, but neither Aron nor El seemed to notice. Aron had tended to Maverick's wound, properly dressing it, the tattered scarf I'd used now shoved in Maverick's satchel. Then we'd eaten and he'd asked us what we'd encountered so far in the Wilds. We told him everything, none of it appearing to shock or surprise him. El said nothing, her brown eyes, so dark they were almost black, watching us as she chewed on the rabbit meat, spitting out bones and flicking them behind her into the forest. She looked like she might very well belong in the Wilds, like she'd been born from it, her hair curly and disheveled, black dust coating her cheeks, her eyes with a feral glint to them.

I shifted, crossing my legs underneath me. "We need to talk," I said.

El lifted her hands and formed a series of shapes with her fingers. I tilted my head, studying her as she lifted her pointer finger, then bent it and slashed her hand in a vertical line down her stomach.

"El agrees," Aron said.

So she couldn't speak, but she could hear us? Just another question to add to the growing mountain of them. This was not the most pressing one, though, not by a long shot.

"What is this place? How is it possible?" I looked at Aron. "How are you possible?" I winced. "No offense."

Aron didn't look remotely offended. More like he was pondering the question along with me. He might have been the most even-keeled person I'd ever met.

Maverick leaned closer, and the fire illuminated the sharp edges of his stubbled jaw, the straight line of his nose, his copper-brown eyes that swirled with questions. I quickly looked away when I realized I was staring.

There would be none of that. I hated the way my gaze kept darting to him, that I was constantly looking to see how he reacted to something new, constantly wanting to ask his opinion, constantly wanting to banter back and forth like we always had. I'd revealed far more of myself than I'd intended to in that crypt.

"What do you know of the spirits?" Aron asked in response to my rapid-fire questions.

Driscoll, Maverick, and I shot each other loaded stares. I heaved a sigh. To get answers, we were going to have to give a few ourselves. "We believe the Seven Spirits were trapped long ago. That they didn't leave the Old World of their own volition like we've always been told. We know that Spirit Shadow was freed from his tomb sixty years ago and resides in the shadow court, where he's trapped. We know he wants to free all the spirits, that that's the only way he can be free himself." I took another deep inhale. "We also know that he's using his shadows to search for all the weapons needed to free the other six spirits."

I waited for any flicker of surprise on their faces, for shock, bewilderment, fear. None of that came. Instead, El gave a grim nod and flipped her long, black hair over her shoulder.

"This place is cursed," Aron said. "Everything here was born of that curse."

We all stayed silent, listening intently, but my mind worked through what he was saying.

El signed. Aron's eyes flicked between her hands and us while he translated. "When Spirit Shadow was freed, he tore through the star court, destroying everything in his path. He tore shadows from bodies, taking the shadows with him to the shadow court." Aron tilted his head. "Many, many elementals died because of Spirit Shadow, the way he so viciously ripped through Shiraeth. Most of the star court, in fact, and anyone else who was here fighting in the war. But a few of us didn't, by pure luck. Right place. Right time. Survival involved many factors."

"Okay." Maverick scratched his head. "So after the Shadow War, a few survivors remained, including you two. What in the fucking spirits below made everything into this?" He gestured around his head.

Aron spread his hands out. "A curse. That's what we call it. It warped everything. We don't know who cast it or how, but it had to be powerful magic."

El began signing again, and Aron glanced at her, then translated, "Within days after Spirit Shadow's rampage, the transformations began. Trees that started to shrink. Flowers that grew as tall as mountains. Bark that formed eyes. And the elementals who remained, turning into monstrous creatures." El paused and placed a hand on Aron's arm, giving it a soft squeeze.

Aron looked at us. "She's worried she has offended me, but I am what I am. I accept I am a monster of sorts. I also accept that part of my past self remains, a semblance of humanity."

"Do you remember your human life?" I asked. "Do you remember anything of yourself before you became this wolf? Can you still use your frost magic?"

Aron tipped his head to the side. "Yes, yes, and yes. It took time. Years. And not everyone is so lucky. Some creatures here don't remember anything of their former lives, can't access their elemental magic. Some can. I still can't control when I shift."

This was so hard for me to wrap my head around.

"At first, I was more beast than man." He tipped his head. "But I met El and she took me in, took a lot of us in. Slowly my humanity returned, as did my frost magic, though it doesn't work well here. Elemental magic tends to be repelled by this world. You can use it, but it probably won't save you if your life is being threatened."

We'd definitely experienced that.

Aron leaned forward, steepling his fingers together. "El gave us a safe haven, a place to just be monstrous. Slowly, my memories began to return. I lived in Fyriad, came to Shiraeth to fight in the Shadow War. But I am not that same person. Not anymore."

I studied El. "What about you?" I asked her. "You don't seem . . . monstrous."

She returned my gaze, her own brown eyes hard and cold as she signed, Aron translating, "That's because I was born shortly after the curse was cast."

Maverick studied her, and I followed his gaze, realizing her shadow stretched over the ground. That was why she had her shadow. She'd been born after all the tragedy that had struck Shiraeth. Likely born from one of these creatures. I wasn't even sure I could process the logistics of that. Who her father was. Who her mother was. I didn't know if it would be rude, painful, even, for her to talk about her parents, so I asked a different question instead.

"What magic do you have?" I asked. "What court are you from?"

"You're looking at it," Aron said.

Driscoll's mouth dropped open, and he worked to close it. "The star court? You're from here? You have star magic?"

El's jaw locked, and she glared at Aron. It seemed like she hadn't wanted us to know this information, but it was important.

"Everyone assumes that all the star elementals are dead. But there's one of you left. Are there others?" I asked.

"None that are still elementals," Aron said, and I understood his meaning.

They'd transformed into one of these cursed creatures, no longer their former selves.

El looked to be a bit younger than me, maybe in her mid-twenties at the most.

"If you were born shortly after the curse," Driscoll said slowly like he was thinking along the same lines as me, "then why have you not aged? I mean, shouldn't you be like at least fifty?"

"We assume that's part of living here." Aron spread his arms wide. "She's aged, just very slowly. The rest of us haven't aged at all, not without our shadows."

El's gaze went watery, and suddenly, I felt a tenderness in my heart. It couldn't be easy reliving all of this for complete strangers.

I reached across our circle and lay my hand over hers. "I'm sorry. You won't be forgotten about any longer. Not if we escape this place."

She stared at me for a long moment before she slipped her hand from mine and nodded.

"Who is the queen of hearts?" Maverick asked abruptly. "Is she welcoming of strangers like us?"

I hadn't heard of this queen of hearts, and I wondered where that question came from. Driscoll frowned like he was wondering the same thing.

"The queen of hearts," Aron repeated.

Driscoll sighed. "Why is there a woman called the queen of hearts? Let me guess, she rips people's hearts from their chests and eats them?"

El signed, eyes dancing. "Oh yes," Aron translated. "She doesn't just eat them. Makes the hearts into pulp. Drains her enemies of their blood and uses it in pies, tarts, bastes, soups. Can't get enough of it."

We all stared, horrified, until El's lips twitched, the closest thing I'd seen to a smile on her face.

"Apologies," Aron said. "She can be mischievous."

"So you're joking?" Driscoll asked El. "Please tell me you're joking."

"She's called the queen of hearts because she has been known to rip out a few hearts," Aron admitted. "But it was to protect those she's taken in. She also has a big heart of her own. She's selfless, fearless, and you're sitting in her presence."

I stared at El, dumbfounded.

"You're the queen of hearts?" Maverick asked. "So you're in charge here?"

"As in charge as anyone can be of a place like the Wilds," Aron said.

El glowered at us.

"Um." I bowed my head, not knowing the proper way to greet her. "Your Majesty."

She rolled her eyes and crossed her arms.

"She prefers El," Aron said.

"Okay, El," I said, looking at her, then Aron. "Can you two help us get out of here?"

All the amusement disappeared from her face. Aron cleared his throat. "That's going to be difficult since we've been trying to escape for the better part of fifty years."

Maverick leaned forward, gaze pinned on Aron. "But you did escape."

"I've only escaped once, and it was in my wolf form." Aron scratched his jaw. "Like I said, I don't remember how I got out. According to El, I left one month ago. She looked everywhere for me, couldn't find me. I have very few memories of my time in Fyriad."

"So you don't remember the bolt?" I asked.

Aron's brows drew together. "The bolt?" he echoed.

My heart sank, and Maverick met my gaze with a sympathetic smile. I didn't want to reveal too much to these strangers. Didn't want them to know Spirit Sky's bolt was somewhere in the Wilds. They'd saved us, but that didn't mean they could be trusted with such important information.

"Never mind," I said quickly.

"So we're stuck here." Driscoll used a small bone to pick his teeth. "Perfect."

"No." I leaned back on my hands. "We will find a way out. We'll go to the library like we planned, and we will read every book we find if that's what it takes."

El signed something, a questioning look in her eyes.

"She wants to know what library you're referring to," Aron said.

"The Library of Astrias," I said. "The most famous library in Arathia. I know it's likely been razed to the ground, but there must be something left that can help us."

El's face darkened as she made a series of quick hand gestures.

"It's too dangerous." Aron watched El, translating. "If you want to lose your life, go for it. But I will have no part of it. I haven't stayed alive this long just to die on some foolish mission."

"So you'd rather just stay here and do nothing?" I shot back, temper flaring as El and I glared at each other. "What is the point of being alive if you're not even living? You're just surviving." I gestured around us. "This isn't a life."

Her jaw locked, and she stood abruptly, flipping her wild black hair over her shoulder and stomping away.

I slumped back. "I'm sorry," I said to Aron. "I shouldn't have lost my temper like that."

"She has many wounds she hasn't yet healed from. She's lost her whole family, her whole life ripped from her in a single moment. It's not an easy thing to move on from."

"What about you?" Driscoll asked.

Aron shrugged one shoulder. "There's not much more to add than what I've already told you." He stood. "I'll find El and talk to her. It might be best to travel with us back to our home. You can get the supplies you need before you leave for your journey to the library. Or wherever you need to go. But for now, you should rest. You all look tired."

That was an understatement. I could sleep for three days straight and still not be well-rested.

"We'll be safe here?" Maverick asked, an eyebrow raised.

"Ah." Aron's eyes lit with understanding. "This forest is dangerous but only during the day. The trees sleep at night, so as long as we leave before morning, we'll be okay." He pointed upward. "The stars tell us what time of day it is by their movement. We're well-accustomed to using them as our guide." He nodded and disappeared into the dark, leaving the rest of us once again lost in thought, not sure what to make of our new companions or their revelations.

Chapter Thirty-Four

EMORY

I sank down into the silver-hued water that was surrounded by small boulders. Steam curled into the air, and I moaned. I actually moaned out loud. It had been over a week since I'd had a proper bath, let alone a hot one.

Aron had eventually returned with El, who seemed in better spirits. Such good spirits that she'd told me about some hot springs in the forest that were a safe and private place to bathe.

She'd probably been able to smell me from across the fire. I'd planned to wait until everyone was asleep to slip away, but Aron and Driscoll had stayed up later than I anticipated, both of them huddled together, Driscoll entertaining Aron with gossip that Aron seemed genuinely interested in. He asked actual follow-up questions. He also got Driscoll to open up about himself. I'd learned that Driscoll had four siblings. Four. I thought he was an only child. Aron had this calm presence that balanced Driscoll's chaotic one.

They'd still been chatting when I snuck away and followed El's directions, half worried the queen of hearts was leading me astray.

Now those worries melted away as I lay back in the water, hair floating around me, another moan escaping my mouth as the heat of it soothed my aches and pains, my creaky joints.

As tired as I was, I wasn't sure I'd be able to sleep anyway. Not after learning so much about the Wilds, about all these creatures here. So they'd once been survivors who somehow transformed into something else. It was almost like they'd been given another chance at life, but in these monstrous forms, I wasn't sure what kind of life that might be.

I also wondered if the other courts had any idea about what truly lay in these Wilds. The frost queen had proclaimed there was nothing left here but death and destruction. How had she missed all of this? Missed the survivors like El and Aron?

Aron might have been a wolf, but he was kind and helpful, and he didn't deserve to waste away in a place like this. At least, I thought he might be wasting away. I actually didn't know if he aged in this form. It didn't seem like it, but I hadn't actually asked.

Another question, another mystery.

They'd answered a lot of our questions, though, even if the answers hadn't been what I wanted to hear. I'd hoped they would know more about a way to escape, but we would still have to figure that out on our own. I wasn't sure where we went from here. El made it seem like going to the library was a fool's errand. But if we went with them to the safe haven they'd created for their people, we'd be wasting time.

Maverick was determined to find his sister, and we'd made a deal. I'd promised I would help, and in exchange he'd let me have the bolt. The bolt we no longer had in our possession. I sighed in frustration.

I could go back on my promise to Maverick, but the thought of his sister being out here alone, possibly already dead, was enough to motivate me. I couldn't leave her. Whatever had happened between me and Maverick, I knew his sister meant everything to him, and for some annoying reason, that meant she meant something to me too.

The plan formed easily in my mind. We'd find Maverick's sister, we'd scour the lands and find the bolt, and we'd use it to escape this spirits-forsaken place. Once we found it, maybe we could even offer to help El and her people escape. Though that would present a whole new problem. I had no idea what place these creatures could have in our world. It wasn't a very accepting one. We didn't like conflict. We didn't like things that made us uncomfortable. We didn't like change. Especially not the frost queen. These monstrous creatures were all of those things, and I didn't know what would happen to them if they escaped the Wilds. It was such a mess, and right now, all I wanted to do was sink under this warm water and let it wash away every thought from my mind.

Nothing had disturbed me so far, so maybe that meant I was actually safe here, that I could relax.

A splash sounded, and I stiffened, standing up in the water, which barely covered my breasts.

I was naked, no weapons on me, but I had my magic. I summoned a dagger of ice and gripped it tight. A cluster of rocks that sat in the spring blocked my view from the sound. Water splashed again as I rounded the pile of stone and ran right into Maverick Von Lucas.

He stared down at me, surprise flashing in his eyes.

"Stalking me again, little rabbit?" he asked, voice low.

Our bodies were plastered together, so close I could see the water droplets clinging to his eyelashes, rivulets dripping down his nose, landing on his full lips.

I shoved myself from him, then quickly lowered into the water when I realized my breasts were on full display.

"Emory," he said, gaze dipping with my movement. "I think we need to talk."

"We agreed to work together," I said quickly. "I'll help you get your sister. You help me get that bolt. We don't need to talk beyond that unless it has to do with planning, which"—I gestured to my naked body, now covered by the silvery water—"now's not really the right time for."

His eyes flashed with heat as they followed my hands, and I realized I was pointing directly at my breasts, the swell of them still visible. I cleared my throat and sank lower until the water reached my chin, hair now floating around me.

He was so damn close, his chest broad and hard, his abs carved by muscle. Scars laced his arms, and I wanted to trace every single one, which only made me back away farther.

"Why are you running from me?" His voice was low as he stepped closer, towering over me. "We were . . . friends. All those years spent passing notes back and forth, adventuring together."

"You never knew me," I said. "And I never knew you. Not really."

"You know that's a lie," he murmured. "You can taste the bitterness of it on your tongue, on your lips." He reached out and brushed a thumb across my lower lip.

A shudder rippled through me, heat pulsing at his words.

"How else would I know that as much as you're afraid of this place, you're also enticed by the adventure? You can't help but want to know more about the Wilds." He stood in front of me now and lowered himself in the water until his face was inches from mine. "You want to explore as much as I do. You want to figure out what happened to the star court as badly as I do. Because you and I, we're the same."

I stared at him, the way the purple sky shone over his umber skin, the way the water lapped at the hard muscles of his chest. I wanted to take the leap, to close the distance between us, but I stayed frozen to my spot.

"What are you afraid of?" he asked, his gaze so intense I thought I might combust under it.

"I don't know," I burst out. "I'm not used to this. Okay? I'm not used to letting others in. The only person I ever let in was—" I stopped.

"Me," he guessed.

"The bone collector," I said, and he winced.

"It's humiliating, you know. How much I shared with you about my stupid dreams of working at the academy one day. I'd never shared that with anyone. You must've thought me such a fool."

"No." He grabbed my shoulders and gave me a small shake. "I thought you were the bravest person I'd ever met. The fiercest. The smartest. The prettiest."

I raised a brow. "Now I know you're lying. You didn't even know what I looked like."

"I knew you were gorgeous." His lips twitched. "And I was right." His face sobered. "Did you not listen to a word I said in the crypt or the forest? You're the entire reason I was brave enough to become the Maverick Von Lucas. You're my inspiration. My muse. I was in awe. But I was never ever laughing. Not at you, Emory."

My heart squeezed, my body flooded with heat. Those were the words I needed to hear ever since I found out his true identity. To know I wasn't just some joke to him, that maybe Maverick Von Lucas and the bone collector had more in common than I realized.

I'd never thought the day would come that my real name would be on his lips. Then it wasn't just my name on his lips. He leaned forward and brushed his mouth against my jaw. I couldn't move, so intoxicated by whatever was simmering between us, had been simmering between us for years.

"If you don't want to talk, then maybe we can do something else," he murmured.

Then I was turning my head, letting his mouth press against mine. His lips were soft, warm, so impossibly perfect.

"This is much better than talking," I agreed and moaned against him as he deepened the kiss.

He probed my mouth open as his hands wound around my back, pressing into my slick skin, sliding down and cupping my ass.

Before I knew what was happening, I was wrapping my legs around him, his hard length pressed right against my entrance. Blood and frost, things had escalated so quickly. Then again, considering how we'd been dancing around each other for six years, maybe not.

The area between my thighs ached as our mouths moved together. I'd never felt anything like this. With my husband, it had been the same every time. I'd lay in bed, he'd roll on top of me, shove up my dress and push inside. A few pumps later, he'd be done.

If my husband had siphoned the light from me, Maverick was shining it back in. He was the light himself.

With every thrust of his tongue, every touch of his hand against my bare skin, I felt more alive than I had in years. His fingers slipped down below the water, and he dragged them up my slit, making me cry out against him.

"Is this okay?" he asked.

"Yes," I breathed.

Yes, yes, yes.

He rubbed up and down my center in slow, languid motions.

"Have you ever had an orgasm before?" Maverick murmured against my lips.

"Mm-hmm," I gasped out as his finger swirled in a circle around my clit. "When I touched myself." I could barely get the words out.

His lips went to my ear, and he nibbled at the lobe as he added more fingers, circling my sensitive bundle of nerves.

"What did you think about, little rabbit? When you touched yourself?"

I swallowed, knowing my answer immediately. I'd thought about a man in a cloak. I'd never pictured his face. Never needed to. Just his hands. Pictured them on me. Pictured the way they'd roam over my breasts, tweak my nipples, the way they'd slip under my own cloak, under my tunic. The way they'd slide down my legs and in between my thighs. Only I never could've imagined just how good they'd feel kneading the pleasure from me like he was doing right now.

His finger plunged inside of me, and I gasped. "What did you think about?" he asked again.

"You," I said without hesitation. "I thought of you, of shoving that hood off your head, your cloak off your body. I thought of unlacing your trousers, letting you take me in the middle of whatever current challenge we faced. I thought of how it would feel if you were buried inside of me."

"Fuck," he said.

It was all true, even though every time I touched myself and came thinking about the bone collector, guilt had riddled me afterward.

"Good, little rabbit. So good." He added another finger, pumping them in and out while his mouth went to my neck. "Because I thought of you too. Every single time I stroked my cock. Every time I came, it was you I pictured."

My entire body clenched tight, sparks dancing in my belly, his words wringing the orgasm from me as it made my insides quake.

I cried out, unraveling around his fingers, my release rushing through me with his words. He captured my mouth again, holding me tight to his hard body while I became a puddle in his arms. I clutched tight to him, breathing heavy as my release ebbed, and all I could do was cling to him, mouth still pressed to his.

He lifted his head so I could see his face, his smile. "I never thought I'd get to hold you in my arms like this, to see your perfect face as you came apart. To be the one to make you come apart."

I cupped his cheeks with my hands. "I didn't either. I never thought this could be my reality. Not when . . ."

I trailed off, not wanting to mention my husband, not wanting to even think of him in this moment, but it felt like his was a presence I couldn't ignore.

Maverick tucked a strand of wet hair behind my ear. "I'm sorry you had to endure so many years with him. I'm sorry you were stuck in a marriage with that monster. All that time I was a professor at the academy. Do you know how many times we were in the same room and I never knew it was you . . . I don't know what I would have done if I had known. What I could have done. Not when you were a married woman and I had a job at the academy."

"It doesn't matter anymore," I said. "That's in the past. Now we can make our own future." I realized how much I wanted that. It was like this light-bulb moment. Of course I did, and I could have it. I didn't have to run from him anymore. "If I'm not in prison, that is."

"I won't let that happen," he said fiercely, pulling me tighter and letting me feel every honed edge of his body.

Heat gathered between my legs again. Blood and frost, I already wanted more of him.

"Does this mean our games are officially over?" I trailed a finger down his chest.

He leaned down and pressed a kiss to that sensitive spot behind my ear. "I think it means we're just going to be playing a different kind of game."

I reached under the water and ran my hand down his shaft as he shuddered. "Now that I can get on board with."

Chapter Thirty-Five

MAVERICK

Emory and I lay on a smooth flat rock in the middle of the hot spring. We'd haphazardly thrown clothes over our bodies in case anyone came across us, but it would be too easy to reach over and lift the tunic draping her midsection, to roll my body on top of hers and bury my cock inside of her.

I couldn't count the number of times I'd dreamt of this over the years. The amount of times I'd imagined lifting that cloak of hers, bending her over and thrusting into her again and again and again. Now she'd been the one touching me, making me come apart in that hot spring as she stroked my cock. This time, when I came it was with her name on my lips, her mouth pressed to mine.

She stroked my chest in slow, even motions. "What are you thinking about?" she asked.

I snorted, then rolled over and pressed my semi-hard length against her thigh. "Does that answer your question?"

She playfully shoved me off of her. "Did you ever think this would happen between us? When you were the bone collector and I was the white rabbit?"

I stayed silent. I wanted to tell her yes. I wanted to admit that I'd dreamt of this for six fucking years. That she'd captivated me from the first moment I saw her in that snowy field behind the academy. But something held me back. I remembered her words in that cave. About her husband, about feeling trapped with him, about never wanting to be trapped like that again.

In all the years I'd known her, Emory had always been skittish. She'd always been the one to retreat, to hold back. I didn't want to scare her or give her any reason to run from me again. So I'd take it slow. I would let her come to me, let her realize that I wasn't going anywhere. And when she was ready, I'd give her my all. Every piece of me that she wanted. I only hoped I was worthy in the end.

"We had our rules," I said finally, avoiding the question. "I figured there was a reason you were hiding yourself from me, and I knew why I was hiding from you. I didn't want to ruin what we had."

"What we had was good," she agreed, then let out a laugh. "We had a lot of fun over the years."

"We did." She rolled to her side, snuggling into my bare chest, and I pressed a kiss to the top of her head. "We can still have a lot of fun. As partners."

As more. When she was ready.

"Partners instead of adversaries. Are you sure that'll be enough of a challenge for you?"

I laughed. "I think you are my challenge. Seeing you in action, seeing your passion, your knowledge. That's what I crave."

She propped herself up on an elbow, the tunic draped across her shifting so that I could see the swell of her breasts, pale skin gleaming in the twilight sky. My cock twitched.

She pointed a finger into my chest. "I can't believe you got to attend the Academy of Scholars & Historians while I spent four horrid years at the Academy of Ladies."

I snorted. "What, exactly, does that entail?"

She grimaced. "Learning how to be a lady, of course. We lived in the dormitories and spent our days learning how to sew, how to plan a meal for a family, how to throw a ball, how to plan an intimate dinner party, a feast if any of us were lucky enough to marry someone who had enough money to host something so grand. We had an entire semester dedicated to learning important topics of conversation so our husbands didn't grow bored of us." She trailed a finger from my chest down my stomach, making my cock pulse with heat. "And don't forget the art of pleasing a man."

I turned onto my side to face her. "Now that I'm quite interested in hearing about."

"Well you got a little taste of it in the hot spring." She smiled mischievously.

"Thank the spirits for the Academy of Ladies," I said, and she swatted at me.

"I had so many dreams," she said wistfully. "And that academy squashed every one."

My smile faded as I thought about that day we'd been trapped together in the fire court. Of the dreams she'd shared. "Did you mean it? When you told me that you dreamt of opening a museum one day with all your artifacts? Of offering classes free to the public? Using all that knowledge you gained for others?"

"Yes, I did." She leaned over and gave me a far too chaste kiss. "There's so many out there like me who aren't reaching their full potential because they don't have the means or the power to do what they want. I met so many women at that academy with dreams they'd never realize, even though there was so much talent. Women would be ruling this continent if so many of them weren't stuck. It's not just women, though. There are men, too, who don't have the money to attend an academy, so they follow in their father's footsteps, take over the family farm or the blacksmith business. If that's what they want, then wonderful. But everyone should at least get that chance, you know?"

I stared up at the dusky sky, watching the ribbons of green twist and thread together. "I do know."

This woman was brilliant. She was going to change lives. Of that I was sure. We just needed to get out of this place so she'd have a chance.

"My sister could've used an advocate like you," I said. "So could I, if I'm being honest."

Emory moved her finger from my chest to my arm, trailing up and down in soothing motions, waiting for me to continue.

"It's my fault she's here. My sister."

Emory's brows furrowed. "What do you mean?"

I swallowed. "When Annalee was younger, maybe around ten, she started talking about a place where the sun didn't shine. Where lakes could show you your future. Where trees were watching you. Where you could whisper commands to the wind. Where plants would eat you unless you knew the right song to sing to lull them to sleep."

Emory stiffened, her finger pausing on my bicep. "That sounds familiar."

I nodded. "She told stories of this place. Talked about it constantly. I didn't realize it was the Deadlands she was talking about at first. We entertained her stories for a while, when we thought they were just stories."

"We?" Emory asked.

"My father, mother, and I. My father didn't like Annalee's fanciful tales, actually forbid Annalee from talking about them. He wanted to send her to the Academy of Ladies, make an honest woman out of her, in his own words. My mother and I protested. We told him that kind of place would stifle her, that marrying her off to a man would kill her spirit. He wouldn't listen. He was steadfast in his plan. Meanwhile, Annalee's stories got wilder, more specific. She talked of people who had scales, fur, fangs. Of elementals who had turned into creatures."

"Maverick," Emory said, concern in her voice.

I scrubbed a hand over my face. "I know. Now that I'm here, I know. She saw it all. Somehow." My jaw locked. "But I realized it too late."

"What happened?" Emory squeezed my arm reassuringly.

"She was growing increasingly agitated as the years went on. Openly defiant when my father told her to stop talking about this place. The Wilds, she called it."

Emory's mouth dropped open.

"She admitted to me privately that it was the Deadlands, that this place was full of trapped creatures, of the most wondrous sights, and I—"

I stopped, the memory filling me with guilt.

"I told her it wasn't real. That maybe it was time to grow up and think about what she wanted to do with her life." My throat grew thick with the admission. "I thought I was helping her at the time. That if she'd just stop my father wouldn't send her to the Academy of Ladies. But she didn't see it like that. She looked at me like I'd gutted her. After that, she retreated completely. Stayed in her room, refused to come out. I'd been offered a job at the Academy of Scholars & Historians by that point. And I left her. I left her, knowing what kind of man my father was. Knowing he wouldn't hesitate to send her away."

"So he sent her to the Academy of Ladies?" Emory asked.

"According to my mother, she didn't even react on the day she left. It was like she was already broken." My voice shook, betraying my emotion. "I visited her a few times, and she was never like her normal self. Didn't talk about the Wilds at all. I begged my father to let her leave. Told him she could stay with me. But he refused. Said this was what she needed."

"Maverick, you can't blame yourself." Emory's pale eyes pierced me. "You didn't know. You couldn't have possibly known what she was saying was real. You were trying to protect her."

"Yet I did the opposite. I didn't believe in her."

Just like I hadn't believed in Emory. I wondered in what ways I'd damaged her mind, her heart, by telling her she was a murderer, by treating her like one. I'd known her for six years, and all it had taken was Gungar, whom I didn't even like, to tell me some rumor, and I'd believed him. I'd thought the worst of Emory, just like I'd thought the worst of my sister.

"How do you know she's here?" Emory asked, breaking me free of my thoughts.

"She left me a note. And I knew immediately what it meant. But before I could go after her, I had to prepare. I needed something strong, powerful, to ensure my survival and hers, to ensure we got out of the Deadlands alive. That's why I took that bolt. And I'm sorry. When you said you were looking for it, I wanted to tell you everything. But—"

"But I ran away," Emory said.

"Yes," I confirmed. "So I went after it and hoped you'd forgive me."

Emory bit her lip. "I do. And we're going to find her," she said.

"I don't doubt it with you by my side. You want something and you just go after it. You rise to every challenge."

She squirmed under my gaze. "Your sister is a lucky girl."

"A woman now," I murmured. "She's nearly twenty."

"Did she ever say how she knew about the Wilds?" Emory asked. "It's remarkable that she had so much information about this place."

It was a question I'd asked myself time and time again. How? How had she dreamt of this? How had she been so accurate in her descriptions? "I have no idea. But if—when—we find her, we'll be sure to ask. She might be the key to understanding why the Wilds is the way it is."

"Maverick," Emory started, worrying at her bottom lip. "I've been thinking . . . what if someone brought Annalee here? What if they sent her those dreams?"

"But that's not possible," I said. "Only star elementals have the power to enter dreams."

And they were all gone . . . Except El. Emory stared at me with a meaningful look.

"You think El could've done this?" I asked.

"Who else?" she said. "You heard her and Aron. There's no other star elementals left."

"That's true, but . . ." I stretched an arm behind my head. "No star elemental has that kind of power. They can enter others' dreams, but only if they're nearby, close enough to see the person whose dreams they want to infiltrate." They could also use their magic to put others to sleep, but once again, they had to be close enough to see the person.

Emory sighed. "True. El wouldn't have the power to enter your sister's dreams when she was all the way in Gilraeth. Not from here, anyway. Just more questions that we don't have answers to."

She paused, a wicked glint in her eyes as she sat up and peeled the tunic from her chest, then rolled her body on top of mine. "So maybe we stop thinking about all those questions. Maybe we do something else instead."

"Maybe you're right," I murmured.

"Mm." Emory pressed a kiss to my lips, her tongue slipping into my mouth as her hand slipped to my inner thigh, barely grazing my cock.

"That means I have the rest of the night to show you what else I learned in that academy."

My cock stiffened as Emory lowered herself down my body, trailing kisses down my stomach, licking, teasing until her mouth pressed against my already moistened tip.

I sucked in a sharp breath, my hand fisting in her hair. Her tongue licked around the tip and then she took my entire length into her mouth.

"Fire and fucking blood," I groaned as she sucked, then released me, shooting a wicked smile my way.

"I might not have paid attention in all my classes, but in that one, I was a particularly good student."

And she spent the rest of the night showing me exactly how good of a student she'd been.

Chapter Thirty-Six

EMORY

"Okay, spill," Driscoll said from next to me.

We walked through a field of wheat stalks that reached our heads, and every time we brushed past one, it giggled.

El and Aron promised they were harmless. They walked ahead with Maverick, El signing to him as he watched intently. Apparently he knew sign language, something that didn't surprise me. Not when it came to Maverick Von Lucas, a man of many talents.

"Spill?" I echoed, cutting a look at Driscoll.

One of the wheat stalks bent down and dipped to Driscoll's ribs, brushing against him as he let out a shrill laugh. "Stop it, no seriously, stop it!"

He swatted it away, and it straightened, letting out its own laugh. He turned his attention on me. "It's annoying, but I'll take it over giant plants trying to chomp me into little pieces. And yes, spill." He pointed to Maverick, then turned his finger on me. "What's going on with you and Hot Professor?"

I rolled my eyes. "You love your gossip, don't you?" I'd heard plenty of it while we followed the bone collector through Fyriad.

"Who doesn't love gossip?" Driscoll asked. His hand brushed one of the stalks, and it shrieked in delight. "Bloody earth, this is so weird," he mumbled.

"Nothing happened." I tucked a piece of hair behind my ear.

"Oh, come on." Driscoll's voice took on a whine. "I gave you so much good gossip." He ticked off his fingers. "The guy who spread that crotch fungus throughout the earth court. The servant who was stealing everyone's underwear. The inn owner who installed peep holes in his guests' rooms." He shuddered. "That wasn't actually gossip. It was illegal, and he was arrested. Pervert. I even told you about the woman caught having sex with statues. Can you imagine getting on top of one of those and riding that hard stone—"

"Okay, Driscoll, I get it."

"So you owe me one piece of gossip." He pressed his hands together. "Please, I'm begging you. We could die here, and the last thing rolling through my mind will be Leoni's words about how selfish I am." Driscoll narrowed his eyes. "You're a bit of a loner, aren't you?"

I tilted my head. "How did you know that?"

"When Leoni and I dropped in on your party in Fyriad, you were the only one standing alone. Everyone around you was talking, drinking, laughing. But you just stood in the middle of the room. Until your husband grabbed you."

I bit my lip. "I suppose loner is a good word for it." My shoulders slumped. "It's hard to make friends when you feel like you have to hide a piece of yourself from everyone around you." I waved my hands in the air. "I always loved history. Since I was little, I loved examining things and learning about them. Finding little clues that could give me insight into their past."

"How'd you get into that? When I was little I was chasing boys and making kissy faces at them."

"My mother," I said softly.

Driscoll's head snapped in my direction. "But I thought your mother was the one who wouldn't let you attend the Academy of Scholars & Historians."

"It's complicated."

Driscoll gestured to the field of giggling wheat around us, no end in sight. "We do have the time, you know."

I sighed, thinking about my mother's own curiosity, her obsession with libraries and museums, and how in the end, that love got crushed by the demands of society. "My mother was much like me growing up. She had a hunger for knowledge, a passion for history. But something held her back from pursuing it. Her parents were willing to pay for her to go to the Academy of Scholars & Historians, and she refused them. She'd met my father by that point, and he offered her a good life. A stable one, I suppose. She chose that stability over the unknown. Over attending an academy that couldn't promise her a job or a future. When I was little I stumbled across her old journals, full of history and theories, stuffed away in a crate in the back of her wardrobe. I pored over them, and they ignited my own love for the subject."

"So what happened?" Driscoll asked. "Did you ever talk to your mother about any of this?"

My biggest regret in life. I crossed my arms, hugging myself tight. "No. I was afraid she'd be angry that I was snooping. Tell me how unladylike I was. Reading those journals was like seeing a side of my mother I hadn't even known existed. It gave me insight, but it also made me sad. She wasn't happy in her marriage to my father. She was safe. And she wanted that same security for me, was so convinced it was the right path. No matter how much I argued." My eyes welled with tears. "So I attended the Academy of Ladies, and three years later, they matched me with my husband. The day after I got married, I found out my mother had died. An accident in a snowstorm. She'd been in a carriage, on her way to visit me."

"I'm really sorry," Driscoll said.

A tear rolled down my cheek at the memory, at getting that letter in the post and being so utterly devastated. "It was heartbreaking. But it was also eye opening. My mother died never getting to live out her dream. She played it safe, and she still lost her life. I decided I wouldn't do that. I wouldn't just take the path of security and stay miserable. I would do something for myself." I sighed. "Except I suppose I was a coward, too, because the academy matched me with my husband, and I married him."

"A coward?" Driscoll turned wide eyes on me. "Excuse you, Miss White Rabbit, you are not a coward. You've made an actual name for yourself. You are living out your dream."

I snorted. "In secret. I didn't go after it. Not really."

"Well, who says you still can't?"

I tapped my chin. "Oh, I don't know, probably the frost queen, who thinks I murdered my husband and who also abhors the white rabbit."

"Well, you didn't murder him. And we'll get that all sorted out." He nudged me. "Especially now that you're taking steaming baths with Hot Professor. Keep doing whatever you did to make him moan your name like that last night, and he'll confess to murdering Lord Growley himself before letting you take the blame."

I laughed and nudged Driscoll back. "Leoni was wrong, you know. You're not selfish. I see the way you talk to Aron, help him fill in the gaps at times when he's not sure if someone is being sarcastic or angry or silly. The way you just reminded me I still have time. The way you made me laugh to make me forget what I was sad about in the first place. You're a good man, Driscoll."

"Yeah, well, Leoni knows me a lot better than you do." He looked at his feet.

"Leoni was hurt, so she hurt you. I don't think she really believed what she was saying. I think she just felt blindsided that you were so ready to leave her, to give up on your mission."

Up ahead, the path curved, finally opening up to what looked like an old village, the silver-brick houses in disrepair with broken windows, caved-in thatch roofs, busted-open doors. This must've been a village in Shiraeth that had been destroyed by Spirit Shadow. My body was already tingling at the prospect of getting to walk through it.

He sighed. "That's because Leoni's a hero like the rest of you. I'm not. I mean I can be." He shot me a side-eyed look. "You have no idea how many times I've saved everyone's asses. But the point is, I don't want to be a hero. Honestly, I don't know what I want to be. I thought maybe I could be a sidekick, but this journey is showing me I don't really want to be that either. I already failed out of school. I hate being the earth court ambassador, mainly because the only reason I got it is Queen Liliath and the fact that I'm one of her best friends. Also, I'm terrible at diplomacy." He threw out his arms. "Maybe I am selfish. I run from place to place, from person to person, never putting down roots, never sticking to anything. Disappointing everyone."

"You don't disappoint me," a voice said, and both Driscoll and I jumped.

Aron stood there while Maverick and El walked ahead, El still signing as Maverick watched her and spoke in a low voice.

"I barely know you." Driscoll eyes shifted back and forth like he wasn't sure who Aron was speaking to.

Aron didn't look offended or put off. "True, but in the short time I have known you, I appreciate your bluntness. You always tell the truth. No matter how harsh that may be. I like that about you. Most don't have the courage to be so honest."

Driscoll's eyes widened, and I had to hide a smile at how Aron had caught him off-guard.

"Oh," he said. "I mean, normally that's what people dislike about me, but wow. Well, um." He shuffled his feet, and my smile grew wider.

I hadn't known Driscoll very long, but I got the sense he was rarely rendered speechless by anyone, and definitely not reduced to this bumbling person in front of me.

"Um," he said again, his brain not connecting with his mouth. "What I mean is . . ."

"Are you trying to say thank you?" I prodded, looking between him and Aron.

"Yes. Those are the words I was looking for." He touched his head. "Just couldn't think of them."

"You're welcome," Aron said, again not seeming phased by any of this. "I just wanted to let you two know that Maverick requested to stop in this village and take a look around before we continue on." He tilted his head toward El, who had her arms crossed, tapping her foot on the ground. "El's not so happy about it, though."

They were such an odd pair, this El and Aron. "How did you two become friends?" I asked.

Aron's lips quirked. "Ah, well, shortly after the Shadow War, I met El in my human form and invited her to the sad excuse of a cave that I called home. I told her I'd make her dinner, that we could talk and maybe find a new friend in this lonely place. When she arrived, she was expecting a man. Instead, she found a wolf. I almost ate her, but she somehow kept me calm in my wolf form until I shifted back. That's how we became friends."

"Right," Driscoll said. "You almost ate her, and then she thought, hey, why not befriend this guy? Totally normal."

"It is if you know El." A faint smile lined Arons' lips. "Anyway, we're going to stop here so you can dig around a little bit. See if you find anything interesting."

"Oh, thank the bloody spirits." I surged forward, excited to explore.

"Nerd," Driscoll muttered.

I spun around. "I don't think I'm the only one who needs to spill."

I looked meaningfully toward Aron, who was marching away.

Driscoll sputtered. "What? Him? Wolf Man?"

"You were enjoying Wolf Man plenty when he was naked." I waggled my eyebrows, and Driscoll scowled.

"Yes because I have eyes. As do you. Who wouldn't have enjoyed that view?"

"I'm just saying"—I held up my hands—"you seemed a little flustered right there."

"Because he's so . . ." Driscoll threw out an arm. "Blunt and literally not phased by anything that comes out of my mouth."

"Like someone else I know?"

He shoved past me. "You know, you should stick to history because matchmaking is not your forte."

He marched ahead, mumbling to himself, but I couldn't help but notice the way his gaze kept sneaking to Aron.

Chapter Thirty-Seven

MAVERICK

Emory crouched next to a pile of rubble, gingerly lifting pieces of silver brick native to Shiraeth, setting each block aside on the black-dusted ground. I loved watching her work, watching the way a little crease appeared in between her brows, her mouth parted, tongue resting on her bottom lip as she puzzled through what all this meant.

My cock stirred, already hungry for more of her. Her hands, her mouth . . . I'd give her my everything. She already had my everything. She just didn't realize it yet.

I hoped I could show her without scaring her away.

Aron and Driscoll wandered past a few houses, their roofs partially caved in, and stepped inside as Driscoll chattered away to Aron.

"You know, Wolf Man, you're not so bad."

"I think that's a compliment," Aron was saying before they disappeared through the doorway.

I crouched down next to Emory. "Find anything?" I asked.

She trailed a finger over the bricks she'd laid aside. "No, nothing of much significance. Though I'm sick of this black dust." She held up her finger, the black specks glittering on it. "What in the bloody spirits is it?"

I wished I knew, but this dust was as much a mystery to me as everything else in this land.

I felt a tap on my shoulder and jumped, then turned to see El behind us, signing something.

I knew the language. It had originally been used in the Old World as a secret form of communication between the Seven Spirits that eventually got documented by scholars. When our direct ancestors founded Arathia, they came across the texts with the documented language. We'd adapted it, using it for those who could benefit from it rather than as a secret form of communication. I'd taught myself over the years, using it to communicate with my sister. A way for us to talk in the presence of our father without him knowing what we were saying. Mainly it was so when my father was berating her or lecturing her, I could sign to her, make her laugh, distract her. It infuriated my father. It was my own way to be rebellious without directly rebelling.

El signed again. *"We stop for little while. Then we go."*

I nodded. "We just wanted to look at a few things here. It's not everyday we get to see a destroyed village in Shiraeth. We don't get to see a lot of things here."

El just scowled, which seemed like a permanent expression she wore. *"Be careful what you look at. I once looked too closely at something and it foretold a future I wasn't ready to see."*

Emory gave me a questioning look, and I translated what El said.

"What did you look at that told you your future?" Emory asked, eyes alight with curiosity.

El signed her answer dismissively. *"A crystal blue lake."*

"A lake," I told Emory.

"What was the future?" she asked El, but El was already crouching, tracing her finger through the dust and ignoring the question.

Emory glanced back down, then squinted at something through the pile of rock. "Wait a minute. I think I see something."

I saw it, too, a glint of silver through the rubble.

We both grabbed brick after brick while El sat on the ground beside the rubble, watching us intently. I winced as the sharp edge of a brick caught on my hand, scraping against my wound. Emory stood, bending over and wiping away the black dust that covered the object. I still couldn't tell exactly what it was. Emory leaned closer, grabbing it and lifting it out slowly. She kept her hands on the outside of the object, her touch light, careful not to damage it.

"It's a painting," she said, holding out the rectangular-framed canvas.

She was right. Scratches dragged down the front so it was hard to make out the image. Emory lay it on the ground and we both studied it. The background matched the twilight sky above us, purple and black twined together with glittering specks of silver dotting the canvas. A faint ribbon of green stretched over the top of the painting. A group of people stood on grass, but deep gashes made it hard to see who the people were or what they were doing.

I glanced up and El signed, *"It's the royal family. King and queen of Shiraeth with their children."*

I repeated what El said to Emory, and her eyes flicked back to the painting. "Yes, that makes sense. I can see the faint background of the castle in the distance. And the swans." She pointed to what looked like feathered birds sitting in a pond next to the family, though so much of the paint had peeled away, it was hard to tell. "The king of the star court was known for his beautiful swans." She brushed some wisps of that white-blonde hair from her forehead, misted with sweat.

I'd never heard that. "Swans?" I repeated.

"Oh yes," Emory said with a faint smile. "The king loved them. His favorite animal. Every party he threw, he'd make sure to have a little pond where the swans could be on display for everyone to see. They were his most prized possession."

El listened intently, eyes misting over, then she blinked, gaze hardening.

"I read about it in the history books," Emory said. "Apparently the obsession started when the king was taking a stroll through his court one day. He happened upon a pond full of the lovely creatures. He was enamored with them, with their graceful, long necks and soft downy feathers. The swans belonged to a man who owned that land, The king bought all the swans from the man and hired him as the caretaker for them. That caretaker worked for the king for twenty years, became his good friend . . . up until the Shadow War."

"The history books lie," El signed, fire in her eyes. *"You two know nothing of the star court or the royal family."* She looked away, jaw locked. *"We need to go."*

Emory and I glanced at each other as El stalked off to find Driscoll and Aron.

"Well, she's pleasant." Emory glanced down at the pocket watch hanging around her neck as it counted backward, ever closer to the twelve.

I ran a finger around its edge. "Neither El nor Aron knew what this pocket watch represents nor what it's counting down to. El said it's likely just a broken watch and nothing more."

Emory looked at it, biting her lip. "I can't help but feel like it's significant somehow." She let go of it. "How much longer are we traveling with them before we break off to find your sister?"

I looked to the distant horizon. Hills surrounded us, all different colors, and I wondered what might await over each of them. What dangers lay out there.

"I don't know," I admitted. "My instinct is to trust them. But at the same time . . ."

"I understand. We'll do whatever you want." She gazed longingly at the painting. "I hate leaving this here, but it can't come with us. It would be nice to restore it. To have something from the star court when we return home."

I held out my hand and helped her to a stand as El, Aron, and Driscoll emerged from the little house where they'd been. "Maybe one day we can come back. Explore this land and all its hidden treasures. A true expedition."

"Together?" she asked.

I pressed my forehead to hers. "Together."

Chapter Thirty-Eight

EMORY

Nothing about this land made sense, yet my mind couldn't help but constantly try to explain the impossible. To make it possible.

El and Aron knew the exact spots to avoid walking, places where mud would suck you in or vines would reach out and suffocate you, where skeletal birds would dive from the flowers where they perched and pluck out your eyes. They knew the shadows to stick to and the best areas to drink water that wouldn't show you some future you didn't want to see.

We'd stopped to camp for the night, Aron and Driscoll off hunting for dinner once again, while El and Maverick were speaking, Maverick likely telling El we were parting ways with them come tomorrow. A crystalline lake sat in the distance, surrounded by the hilly Wilds.

I didn't know how to feel about separating from them. So far they'd kept us safe, but that didn't mean we could trust them.

In the distance, six knotted trees spread out in a circle, trunks thick and twisted, long branches threaded like braids, vivid red leaves sprouting out. They were so vivid, gorgeous. With nothing else to do, I walked toward the massive trees, the foliage so thick you couldn't see into the clearing they surrounded.

The trees looked harmless enough, though I approached cautiously and lay my hand on one of the trunks. The red leaves rustled, but otherwise the tree didn't move. I rounded the large trunk and walked inside of the sheltered clearing.

Two arms wrapped around me, and I stiffened.

Lips brushed against my ear. "This is an excellent idea, little rabbit."

I smiled as Maverick nuzzled my neck, heat stirring between my legs. "What idea is that?"

"To come somewhere private and dark and away from prying eyes."

I turned in his arms as he walked me back into a tree. "And why would we need to be away from prying eyes?"

"So I can do this." He pressed a kiss to my collarbone, and I shuddered. His hands slipped inside the waistband of my trousers. He stroked a finger down my center that made me gasp. "And this."

"Mm," I said in agreement.

"I've missed you," he growled, trailing kisses over my neck while his hands worked slow, steady motions over my clit.

"We've been together all day," I panted out.

"Not like this."

His lips found mine, and we kissed with a kind of insatiable hunger I'd never felt before. I fumbled with the laces of his trousers, undoing them and wrapping a hand around his hard length. He groaned as I pumped my hand up and down, loving this effect I had on him.

He braced one hand against the tree behind my head while his fingers continued to work my clit. An aching throb pulsed in my core, and bloody frost, I wanted more.

I arched my back, lifting a leg to wrap around his waist, and he circled my clit with his finger while I dipped my hand lower, giving his balls a light squeeze. A low rumble escaped his mouth.

He swiped his tongue over mine, deepening our kiss.

I never knew pleasure like this existed. At the Academy of Ladies, all we learned was how to please our husbands. The right ways to touch *them*, to make *them* fall apart, to make *them* happy and satiated and wanting more. Always wanting more. I'd done it all with efficiency for my husband. But I'd never wanted to. It was always out of duty.

This, with Maverick. I wanted this. I wanted to hear all the sounds he made when I touched him. I wanted to explore his body and memorize every single part of it. I wanted him. All of him. In a way I hadn't wanted anyone before.

Something slipped down my back, under my tunic, trailing down my skin. I moaned out again at all the sensations sparking through my body, igniting my blood. Maverick's fingers plunged inside of my wet heat while I rubbed my hand over his shaft, a thick bead of moisture coating my fingers, making them slick and easy to slide up and down him.

"Fuck, I love how wet you are for me," he murmured against my lips.

"I need more of you," I said. "I need all of you. Inside of me. Now." I positioned his cock right at where my entrance would be if I weren't wearing pants.

Heat lit his eyes. "Emory," he said, face taking on a pained expression. "That is so, so tempting."

I let go of his cock and wound my arms around his neck, lifting my other leg and wrapping it around his back. "Then what are you waiting for? I'm right here."

"Because, little rabbit"—he pressed his hard length against my thigh—"when I fuck you for the first time, it isn't going to be against a tree. As much as I absolutely love the idea of burying myself inside of you, fucking you until you're so sore you can't walk—this isn't where that's going to happen."

That area between my legs ached with his words. "Well, then you're going to have to do something with those fingers right now because I need you."

Our mouths crashed together again, and he let one of my legs go, pushing me further up against the tree. One hand trailed back down to my aching clit. The other cupped my jaw. Tingles shot across my back again as something stroked it.

I stilled. If one of Maverick's hands was currently stroking me, and the other was cupping my jaw, then what was touching my back?

"A threesome with a tree. Huh," Driscoll said. "That's a new one. And good piece of gossip. Don't worry, I'll keep you both anonymous."

"Get away from the tree!" Aron yelled.

Cold doused me as Maverick jumped back. He fumbled with his trousers, lacing them while shooting murderous glances toward Aron, Driscoll, and now El, who'd emerged into the clearing, her usual glower on her face. Oh, wonderful. So we had a whole audience for this.

I tried to move but couldn't, and it didn't take long to realize I was stuck to the tree, a branch dipping down the back of my tunic.

Maverick's eyes went wide when he had the same realization. "Emory!"

"Is the tree eating her?" Driscoll asked, tilting his head. "I don't see a mouth anywhere."

"Not eating, exactly," Aron responded. "Absorbing. These trees are coated with a sticky sap that traps their victims, and they slowly squeeze them into their bark." He gestured upward. "They don't need water to survive. They need blood. It's what gives their leaves that color."

"Can we take a break from the history lesson and figure out how to save me before the tree absorbs me?" Fucking spirits below.

"How do we get her loose?" Maverick rushed forward, yanking me to no avail. He ran his hands over my body like there might be some key hidden that would unlock me from this situation.

My heart thumped furiously, but it seemed like the more I struggled, the tighter I became fused to the tree, my back already aching from the pressure.

"Oh, I see how it works." Driscoll stroked his jaw. "She's slowly sinking into it." He pointed. "Look how her body is disappearing as the tree presses her tighter."

"Why are you so blasé about this?" I yelled.

"Would you rather I be freaking out?" Driscoll studied his nails. "Honestly, I cannot win with you people."

El signed, and Aron and Maverick both watched.

"Be still," Maverick said. "The more you struggle, the faster the tree absorbs you." He swallowed, his Adam's apple bobbing. "We will get you free. I promise."

My chest tightened, making it hard to breathe.

"So how do we save her?" Maverick asked again through gritted teeth.

Aron pointed. "We need to tire out the tree enough that it'll lose its strength so she can get free. As I've said before, elemental magic isn't very effective here."

"Let me guess." Driscoll raised a finger. "That involves fighting the tree the old-fashioned way."

Wolf Man didn't answer. He simply slipped a dagger from his boot and lunged at the tree. One of its long branches swept down toward him as he swiped at it. El brandished her own dagger and threw it straight into another branch. The tree flailed above me, shaking this way and that.

Driscoll rolled his eyes, then gathered an armful of rocks, pelting the tree with them. A few stuck to the trunk over my head.

"The branches," Aron said through heavy breaths, driving his dagger into one of the tree's branches. "You need to go for the branches, and whatever you do, don't touch the trunk."

"Yeah, I gathered that from the fact that Emory is currently stuck to it." Driscoll aimed higher, launching rocks up at the branches.

One of the branches swung down, attempting to knock Driscoll off his feet, and Maverick jumped onto it, climbing up it and tearing leaves from it. Blood sprayed down over us as the leaves floated to the ground.

The tree shrieked, branches flailing harder, but Maverick kept his footing, staying away from the trunk and continuing to yank leaf after leaf away, letting the blood flow down. I thrust my body forward but still couldn't move.

Around me, my companions continued to fight. Branches slashed and shook furiously. One hit El and she flew across the clearing and landed on her back with a thwack. My heart stopped, but she popped back up, a determined scowl on her face as she rushed forward with her dagger clutched tight and drove it straight into the branch that had just hit her. Leaves continued to pepper the ground, blood dripping from the trees' branches in fat splats.

I wiggled my shoulders. "I think it's working," I called out.

"Thank the spirits." Driscoll launched another rock at the tree. "My arms are killing me."

Aron sliced at a thinner branch, the blow so forceful the branch cracked in two and came tumbling down.

I shoved forward with all my might, straining as the tree's grip on me loosened. My shirt stretched from my back, and I dug my legs into the ground, screaming as I lurched forward and fell to my knees. I didn't have long to rest before Maverick was grabbing my arms and launching me up, all of us running from the little clearing and back toward the flattened area around the lake.

We all collapsed, breathing heavy, chests rising and falling. None of us spoke, but Maverick reached over and grabbed my hand, squeezing it tight. Tears pricked my eyes as my heart slowly returned to its normal rhythm. I'd almost died. Again. It would be a miracle if we made it out of this place alive.

Maverick sat up, his white shirt completely unbuttoned, revealing his hard chest, gleaming with sweat. He rubbed his stubbled jaw, now splattered with blood. Everyone else sat up, too, all of us covered in dirt and grime, clothes torn, scratches adorning our bodies.

"We're looking for my sister," Maverick said abruptly.

I stiffened, and Driscoll shot me a questioning look.

Maverick took a deep breath. "If we're going to find her, we'll need your help."

Aron crossed his arms over his chest, while El stared at the ground, then made a series of signs.

Maverick nodded in understanding. "She came here two months ago. It took a while before I could get here to find her. That's all I want. To rescue her and escape. I didn't trust you, which is why I never told you. But it's become clear we won't survive this place without help. We won't find Annalee without help."

"We're looking for a girl also," Aron said slowly.

"Why are you looking for a girl?" Maverick's voice had turned from pleading to deadly.

El signed, motions fast and furious.

Maverick's scowl dissipated the longer El signed. "So this entire time, that's why you've been out here, away from your safe haven? You've been looking for her as well?"

El nodded.

"We've heard reports throughout the Wilds about a girl who suddenly appeared a few months ago. A girl with fire magic. We wanted to find her and keep her safe, though she seems to be doing okay on her own from everything we've heard."

Maverick stiffened. "Have you heard what she looks like?"

Aron swiped the blood from his cheek. "Black hair in braids, comes up to my chest. Very social. Gets along well with many of the creatures here apparently."

I laughed in disbelief. "Well that would make sense given how much she seemed to know about this place."

Hope shone in Maverick's eyes. "Do you know where she is?" he asked.

"We have an idea. El was tracking her before you arrived. Planning to find her and bring her to safety."

"So you'll help us?" The relief in Maverick's voice was palpable, and it wrenched my heart. He wanted to find his sister so badly, and this was the first piece of good news we'd received since arriving here.

El signed, and Aron nodded. "We'll help you. We believe she might be located in the old star court arena, where the gladiator fights would take place."

"How far is that from here?" Maverick asked.

"A few hours' trek."

Maverick blew out a breath and looked up at the sky. "Thank you," he said. "I don't know how I'll be able to repay you for helping us find her."

"We do not need payment," Aron responded. "We'll help you find her because it is the right thing to do."

Maybe once we found Annalee, we could ask them about the bolt. For the first time since arriving here, I wondered if everything actually might work out in the end.

Chapter Thirty-Nine

EMORY

Later that evening, I trekked to the lake with a bucket to collect water. Aron and El had warned us not to look into the lake, but we could collect the water to bathe and drink. They hadn't explained any further, both on the verge of sleep when I'd decided to get clean. El had mentioned many times a lake that could tell you your future, and I wondered if this was that same one.

I was willing to take the risk. I wanted the blood, the grime, the reminder of my near-death experience, gone. Then tomorrow, we'd find Maverick's sister. We'd work with El and Aron to find a way out of this place.

And, maybe, just maybe Maverick and I could start planning a future together. I had no idea what that might look like. A life with Maverick. I imagined it would be filled with a lot of this: adventure, danger, passion. The thought of spending my days with him, of having an actual partner, terrified me, but it also exhilarated me.

I walked along the lake's edge, keeping my gaze ahead to the flat clearing that surrounded us to the hills in the distance. I knelt by the lake's edge, dipping the bucket in the water, careful to keep my eyes averted. I just needed a few bucketfuls to wash all the mess from my skin and clean my cuts.

Something flashed on the edge of my vision. I shook my head, ignoring it and continuing to fill the bucket. A streak of silver shot through the water. White-blond hair floating on the peripherals of my gaze. My brain screamed at me to not look.

Do not turn your head. Do not turn your head.

It was like an otherworldly force was controlling my body, and no matter how hard I tried to keep my eyes on the ground, they slowly shifted over until I could see through the crystal-clear water.

I gasped when my gaze landed on what I'd been trying so hard to avoid.

It was me. Or someone who looked like me. She floated under the surface, staring at me with light-blue eyes.

I didn't even register what I was doing. My legs straightened and began moving toward the lake, bucket forgotten. One slow step at a time. I told myself to stop. To turn around. To not look. But my body had other ideas. I took off my boots and dipped a toe in the cool water. All the while my gaze stayed trained on the woman. She swam backward under the surface. Her white-blond hair fanned out behind her, eyes sparkling with mischief. She beckoned for me to follow. Every instinct screamed at me to stop, to turn around, but the water felt so good.

I needed to go deeper, to immerse myself in it. To discover its secrets. Water Emory twisted her body like a sleek mermaid, her pale skin bright and glimmering, a thin white dress draping around her body. I lowered myself into the lake, my hair splaying out and floating on the surface, the water now up to my shoulders.

Water Emory wiggled her fingers at me from below, then curled one, once again beckoning me. She hadn't just wanted me to come into the water. She wanted me to follow her. Yes, that's what I would do. I would follow and discover everything this lake had to offer.

I took a deep breath, then plunged under the surface. Water Emory took off, legs kicking and arms wheeling as she glided along. I followed, the water so clear I could see her easily, even with how far ahead she swam.

Stones covered the bottom of the lake, all brightly colored, like a rainbow had fallen from the sky and splashed down among them. Other than Water Emory, the lake was empty, no fish, no plants, no life at all.

Water Emory stopped abruptly, then turned, her smile growing wider as she waited for me. I pumped my arms and legs, swimming to her, burning to know what this lake wanted with me. What knowledge it would give.

The water swirled, a cyclone rising up and spinning faster and faster and faster, blurring my view. The cyclone pushed me this way and that, turning me so many directions, I was no longer sure which way to go. Then it all stopped, once again clearing. Water Emory had disappeared, and I found myself staring at the bottom of the lake. Stones covered the lakebed. Slowly, the colors of the rainbow stones began seeping out, bleeding into each other, mixing, creating new colors. Creating a picture. No, not a picture, exactly.

A vision.

One of me. I was standing inside the Academy of Scholars & Historians at the back of one of the classrooms. Students filled rows and rows of desks, all arranged in a stadium style.

My heart hammered, blood pumping in my veins.

I'd dreamt of standing in one of these rooms so many times over the years. Maybe I was a professor in this vision. Maybe I'd finally accomplished everything I wanted in life. The students' backs were to me, parchments, pens, and ink pots sitting on their wooden desks. At the front of the room stood a podium and a large smooth stone wall where professors used chalk to write as they lectured. The room was magnificent, domed ceiling with beautiful stained-glass windows that depicted famous historical events.

My lungs squeezed, but I ignored the burning pain, the way spots dotted my vision as I tried to concentrate. I stood at the top of the stairs, wearing a long wool blue dress, much like what I wore in my everyday life before falling into the Wilds. This had to be a vision of me as a professor. I'd made it. I was seeing it all play out before me. Everything was going to work out exactly like I wanted.

In the vision, I walked down the steps, students turning toward me and nodding. Future Me nodded back, smiling at them. I couldn't help but notice the sadness reflecting in her gaze. An emptiness. My stomach clenched. If I was living out my dream, then what was the matter?

The spots around the edges of my vision grew bigger, but I blinked them away, determined to see this through. When Future Me got to the bottom of the stairs, a voice boomed out.

"Ah, there she is. The lady of the hour. My wife."

The word shot sparks through me. My blood heated at hearing it because I knew exactly who had spoken it.

"My wife."

Maverick Von Lucas appeared in the doorway and strode down the stairs behind me, smiling at students. He looked so handsome in his fitted grey trousers, black shirt tucked in, a few buttons popped open at the top, grey suspenders stretched over his broad shoulders. When he turned his gaze onto me, his smile widened, those copper eyes filling with warmth.

Maybe we were teaching a class together. How amazing would that be? The spots returned, and that burning in my lungs worsened, spreading across my chest and up to my throat, but I ignored it, needing to know what happened. To unlock whatever message was being sent to me.

Maverick met Future Me at the bottom of the stairs, kissing her on the cheek and turning to his class. "My wife. I don't know what I'd do without her," he said. "Can't teach without my lucky watch."

She reached into the pocket of her dress and pulled out a watch, a silver chain connected to it. The same watch I'd found here, in the Wilds. Future Me handed it to Maverick, and he attached the chain to his belt.

"Thank you, my love," he said. "I'll be home a little late for dinner tonight." He turned his attention to the students. "Alright, everyone turn to page thirty in your books."

Future Me gave him a strained smile, one that didn't quite reach her eyes. She turned without a word, marching up the stairs, back ramrod straight.

This couldn't be right. The black spots grew, the vision growing hazy, but not before I caught the tear rolling down Future Me's cheek as she dashed from Maverick's classroom.

No. That wasn't supposed to be my future. My lungs screamed at me now, darkness cascading over me as all the colors separated, seeping back into the stones, no longer blending. I needed to swim, to get air, but I was too weak, too tired. My body was already failing me, and I hadn't even realized it, so sucked in by the vision.

My head grew heavy, my eyelids like weights. I lifted an arm, but it felt like trying to move through heavy mud. My consciousness began to fade right when a hand grabbed my arm, yanking me from the water and onto solid ground.

A distant voice called my name while a hand thumped my back. I coughed, water burning its way up my throat and out of my mouth. My stomach heaved, and I retched up more water, that darkness slowly ebbing and clearing.

"Emory," Maverick said, voice urgent.

He rolled me onto my back after I'd gotten all the water from my stomach and lungs.

"What in the bloody fire happened?" His concerned face stared down at me.

My entire vision came back to me. Maverick. The Academy. *His wife.*

His. Wife.

That was my future. El had told me about this lake, about how she saw her own future in it, that she wouldn't wish it on anyone. I'd just seen my future, and it was my worst nightmare. I slowly sat up as Maverick cupped my face, staring at me with such intensity.

"Emory, what happened? What—"

"The lake," I said, voice raspy, throat still on fire. "It—don't look at it."

"I'm not looking at anything but you," he said so gently it made me want to cry. "I'm not taking my eyes off of you ever again." He leaned forward and pressed his lips to my cheek.

Exactly the same way he had in that vision. His wife. I was Maverick Von Lucas's wife. But he hadn't set me free like I'd hoped. No. In my future with Maverick, I was just as trapped as I had been in my past.

Chapter Forty

EMORY, TWO YEARS AGO

I lifted the mask of Spirit Sky, studying it and smiling with glee as the bone collector lay next to me on the rocky hills of the Valoris highlands. The grass was soft and spongy, and we'd collapsed onto it after escaping the lighthouse where we'd just come from.

"You cheated," he said from next to me as a chilly blast of wind howled past us.

I raised my nose. "You're just jealous, Bone Collector. I outwitted you. Two years in a row now."

I wished I could see his face in this moment, that I could know if his reaction was to roll his eyes or furrow his brows or frown deeply—or smile, more amused by my comments than annoyed.

I lifted a hand and tugged my hood further over my head, lower half of my face covered by the scarf.

"It wasn't two years in a row," he said, hands resting on his stomach. "I got that book last year."

"That's funny because I'm pretty sure I was the one who walked away with it."

"After I dropped it to you to save my life and keep the fire sprites from incinerating me to death."

"All I'm hearing are excuses," I said, lowering the delicate white mask, covered with blue dust that I blew off. It poofed into the air, shimmery and dancing in the waning sun rays.

I was starting to think there was something to it. That maybe the dust came from the spirits themselves? Or maybe it came from their magic? I couldn't be sure, would have to gather more evidence to come up with a concrete theory. But this dust had to come from somewhere. It didn't seem to have any magical properties itself, but it emanated this otherworldly glow that nothing I knew of could create.

The mask was beautiful. Delicate with a firm mouth and strong nose. I wondered under what circumstances Spirit Sky might've worn it. Or if he gave it to his high priests or priestesses to wear. There had only been one in the little lighthouse perched on the edge of the isle, which led me to believe if it did get worn by someone, it would've been Spirit Sky. Maybe during a masquerade ball. He was known to love throwing those.

I couldn't wait to get this back to my little bunker and study it in more detail. Add it to my collection.

The sun sank below the horizon ahead of us, the sky a melting pot of pinks, oranges, and purples.

We fell into a comfortable silence. No pressure to speak when both of us needed to retreat into our own thoughts. It was nice, and I'd come to appreciate these moments.

Far below the ocean crashed against the tall cliffs of the sky court, the sound thunderous and roaring.

I turned to face the bone collector, once again this odd sensation pulling at me, making me wish I could reach out and tug that hood off his head. I didn't know what was coming over me. We'd been leaving more notes for each other than ever before in our secret meeting place. I had hundreds from him at this point.

Notes that talked about his theories about certain artifacts, silly stories, mundane stories, and sometimes, even stories about his childhood, his favorite things to do. Those notes kept me going. Every week, I'd return to our secret spot with something to look forward to.

Just a month ago, my husband had commented that I'd better start smiling again or he was going to shove me off our cliffside home. It might've been a joke, but underneath the teasing, there was a warning to his words. He wanted a wife who would meet his every need, who would be sunny and happy and not burden him in any way. Instead of asking me what was wrong, his instinct was to threaten me if he saw any signs of anger or sadness. Little did he know, I'd been sad because I hadn't heard from the bone collector.

"So what's next for the white rabbit?" he asked.

I bit my lip under my scarf, not sure if I should even tell him about my crazy plan, but if there was anyone I could talk to about this, it would be the bone collector. "I think the Seven Spirits mythical weapons might be real, and I want to find one of them."

I felt him go completely still.

"I've found evidence pointing to the existence of Spirit Sky's bolt. I just don't know exactly where it's located, but I'm getting closer to finding it." I took a deep breath. "And once I do, I'm going to use it to gain entry to the Academy of Scholars & Historians."

I waited for him to tell me I was crazy, for him to laugh, anything. But he just sighed. "If anyone can find it, little rabbit, it's you."

The compliment filled me with joy. I didn't even realize I was seeking his approval until this moment, but it meant everything.

"Until next year, then?" I sat up, realizing it was already getting dark.

The bone collector sat up as well, and I waited for his usual sarcasm, some response about how next year I wouldn't get so lucky—even though luck had nothing to do with me getting this mask today.

"Do you think it's odd that we've known each other for four years, and I've never seen your face? Don't know your name?"

I stilled, pulse spiking. "That's our agreement. We have those rules in place for a reason."

"What if I wanted to know?" He leaned forward, his black cloak rustling as his voice dropped low. "What if I was willing to tell you my name? To show you my face? To trust you?"

I scooted back, putting space between us. "Then I'd say you're a fool. What we're doing is against the law. We've been stealing artifacts that belong to the academy."

He snorted. "The academy doesn't do nearly as much for history as we've done."

My annoyance flared. "The academy is amazing. Its entire purpose is to preserve history and to teach young scholars how to thrive as historians. What we do is . . ." I trailed off, not knowing what I wanted to say.

Not pretend. It was real enough. But we weren't helping the world. What we did was shrouded in secrecy and anonymity. I hoped to use it for good one day.

"What we're doing is brave," the bone collector finished for me. "Far braver than any of those historians sitting in their pretty little academy, sending out treasure hunters to collect artifacts for them to study. They miss so many details by not getting the objects themselves, and half of the artifacts come back broken, pieces gone."

"Not Maverick Von Lucas," I challenged. He was a rising historian and scholar at the academy. I'd seen him speak a few times, and each time, his passion and excitement for the profession bled into me.

"You know, I bet Maverick was inspired by us," the bone collector said, crossing his arms.

"What are you talking about?" I let out a laugh of disbelief.

He shrugged. "It wasn't until our own reputations spread to the frost queen that he started going on his adventures. He's the face of the academy because none of the other historians and scholars are willing to do what he does. They don't really care about history, you know. They care about telling the frost queen's story, the one she wants to perpetuate."

"Stop," I said. The academy had been my dream for as long as I could remember, and I wouldn't let the bone collector ruin it. "We all have different values, different places in the world. Maybe one day we can be the historians, the collectors, we want to be. We can share this knowledge."

"I think you're trying to avoid my question," he said like I hadn't spoken at all.

Another gust of wind blew past us, and a flock of birds soared overhead through the dusky sky. Even though my husband was away on business, I needed to return home before the servants got suspicious.

"What are you talking about?" I stood, dusting the shimmers from my cloak, descending down the hill and toward the stone-paved road that wound through the highlands. "Did you hit your head a little too hard in that lighthouse?"

"No, I'm thinking very clearly. Maybe clearer than ever before." He followed behind me. "And I want to know what you think."

"About what?" I asked, acting exasperated, but I knew exactly what he was referring to. The question burned a little too hot in my blood. Seeing his face would be amazing. Knowing his name would be like a gift. But it would also be dangerous. So very dangerous.

"Have you ever wondered?" He gestured to his body. "What's under this cloak. Because, little rabbit, I've wondered so very many times what's under yours."

Heat flushed my neck and cheeks, and I thanked the bloody spirits my face was hooded and covered.

I kept my voice light, teasing, even though it felt like a butterfly had taken up residence in my stomach. "That eager to uncover my secrets, Bone Collector?"

He didn't miss a beat. "Every single one." He stepped closer, so close I could reach up and tug down his hood. "I want to know the secret to this." He lightly touched my hood. "I want to know the secret to this." He ran a featherlight touch over the scarf covering my face. "Mostly, I want to know the secret to this." He lay a palm flat in the middle of my chest, right over my beating heart.

He must've felt the way it thundered like a stampede. The pound of it reverberated in my ears. I wanted that too. All of it. It would be so easy to reach up and take off my hood, to tug down that scarf covering my face. To unveil him. And then what would come next?

Spirits below, what was I thinking?

I stepped back. "Well, I can't go giving away all my secrets. Where would be the fun in that?"

He didn't move, didn't say a word. I spun on my heel before he could persuade me because I had a feeling the day he actually touched me, I'd lose all restraint.

"I'll see you next year, Bone Collector." I waved over my shoulder, not looking back as tears spilled down my cheeks.

As soon as I'd rounded a curve in the road, I flattened myself against one of the grassy hillsides and let the tears come. I'd taken this too far.

It was supposed to be fun. Meaningless. There was nothing meaningless about this, and I knew it. I didn't know how it happened. I didn't know when. Maybe it wasn't an exact moment I'd fallen for him, but in all the moments. In the challenges, the competition, the way he pushed me to new levels. In the way he understood me. In the way he encouraged me, never held me back. The way he said "little rabbit" like it was a gentle caress.

I liked the bone collector. A laugh bubbled from me while the tears still ran down my cheeks. It was ridiculous. I didn't know his name, for spirits' sake.

The laughter died when the next thought came. I was a married woman. This was so far out of bounds. It didn't matter that my husband didn't love me. That I didn't love him. That we'd been matched by the Academy of Ladies, our marriage a simple transaction. That he had countless mistresses.

None of that mattered. Because he had the power in our relationship, and if he found out about this—not me being the white rabbit—but me having feelings for another man, he'd ruin me. His ego wouldn't survive something like that. My world was supposed to revolve around him. It did revolve around him.

Until the bone collector.

This had to stop. Nothing good would come of this, whatever *this* was. My heart felt like it was being wrenched from my chest. I didn't know the bone collector. Not really. Even if I was entertaining the idea of leaving my husband for him, who was to say I wouldn't just be controlled by another man in another relationship? Same problem, different man.

I pawed away the tears. Because one thing was certain: if I ever escaped this marriage, I'd never allow myself to become trapped again.

Chapter Forty-One

MAVERICK

Something was wrong. Other than the fact that Emory had fallen into a lake and almost died. When I'd arrived, she'd just been floating at the bottom of the shallow water, staring at the glassy rocks, eyes wide open, bubbles escaping her mouth. Like she was in a trance.

We sat by the lake, our backs turned to it, and she shivered, her tunic and trousers still soaked, staring at the ground. I couldn't get her to tell me what she'd seen. Her eyes were puffy and red, her cheeks blotchy. And she was still the most beautiful woman I'd ever seen.

The wind blew again, dust swirling up and sticking to her cheeks, smudging them with black.

"I wish I had sky elemental powers right about now," she said. "I'd command this wind to stop."

A memory surfaced, one of Annalee. We'd been sitting in the court-yard of our home, Annalee telling me her latest dream about the Wilds.

"I almost fell off a cliff chasing that pesky rabbit," she'd told me. *"But in the Wilds, everything is always listening. Including the wind."*

She'd said that all she had to do was whisper, and the wind listened, keeping her from falling over that cliff.

"My sister taught me a trick." I eyed Emory. "Might as well try it." I cupped my hands around my mouth, then whispered, "Calm."

The wind instantly settled around us, no longer blowing, the dust falling to the ground.

Emory's eyes widened. "That's quite a trick."

"Annalee has no idea how many times her stories have helped us in this strange, strange world."

Emory swallowed, the brief light in her eyes dimming again.

When I'd first come upon her, lifeless in the water, I'd feared the worst. I'd thought she was dead, and I knew in that moment, I couldn't lose her. I couldn't live without this woman. Not since the day she came into my life. I couldn't live without her sarcasm, her taunting, her courage, her ferocity. She made me better, more.

She was everything, and I needed to tell her. I couldn't wait any longer. If the Wilds had taught me anything, it was that the next day was not guaranteed.

So I would lay my heart bare before this woman and hope that she felt the same way. Except . . . I knew she felt the same way I did. It was obvious from the way she looked at me, eyes shining and full of happiness. The way she opened up to me about her past. It was in the way she touched me and kissed me, like she needed me as much I did her.

I wasn't afraid she didn't return my feelings. I was afraid she'd run from them.

I wrapped an arm around her shoulder and pulled her tight to me. She buried her head in the crook of my arm.

"You don't have to talk about it," I said gently, "but if you need to . . ."

She shook her head, nose rubbing against my chest.

I pressed a light kiss to her wet hair. "Hey, can I talk to you about something that's been on my mind?"

She sniffled and nodded, scooting out of my hold.

"This probably isn't the best time to do this," I started.

"Do what?" She wrinkled her nose.

I licked my lips. "It's just that we're always in danger. Every single fucking day here could be our last. We've almost died about a hundred times since we got here. You almost just died."

She swallowed.

"When I saw you in that water, and I thought you were dead, I felt like my heart had been ripped from my chest."

"Maverick," she started, but I held up a hand.

"Just let me get this out, and then you can say whatever you need to." I took a deep breath. "The thing is, we belong together, Emory."

She sucked in a sharp breath.

"We always have. You're my person. You get me in a way no one does. With you it's okay that I obsess over my work, that all I want to talk about is nerdy history things, as Driscoll would say."

Her lips ticked up at the corner.

"No one has ever made me feel the way that you do. I loved you before you had a name. Before you had a face."

At that, her expression went slack, so I forged on.

"I know you've been hurt in the past, but I want to be your future. A bright future full of happiness and love and really good sex."

She still said nothing, which only made me ramble on more.

"I know this isn't the traditional way marriages are proposed. I don't have any family heirlooms to present to you. I don't have a wedding bracelet. I have nothing but my promise to love you until my dying day."

I wished Annalee were here. She'd absolutely love this moment, the spontaneity and whimsy of it all. Mostly she'd just love Emory.

"You asked what I saw in that lake," Emory said slowly, gaze trailing up to meet mine. "I think I need to tell you."

"That's not quite the answer I expected," I said, voice teasing, but she didn't return my smile. My stomach sank.

She took a deep breath. "I saw my future." She waved a hand in explanation. "El mentioned a lake that foretells your future. She said to not look into it, and I tried not to. I tried to resist, but it drew me in anyway." Her voice trembled, and I reached for her, but she scooted backward, drawing her knees up to her chest.

Her hair was still plastered to her head, rivulets of water trailing down her cheeks.

"What did you see?" I asked, not sure I wanted to know.

"I saw you."

My heart swelled but immediately deflated at the sound of her voice, at the sadness in her gaze. Whatever she saw didn't sound good.

"I saw you and me. Married."

I let out a laugh. "That sounds perfect given I'm proposing a marriage to you right now. That's what you saw? Our future together? Emory, you don't know how long I've dreamed of that. With you—"

"Stop!"

The force of her words took me aback.

Tears filled her eyes again. "I saw a marriage in which I was trapped. You were teaching at the academy, professor to adoring students, and I was just your wife. Once again, I was just somebody's wife."

"No." I shook my head. That couldn't be. I wouldn't do that to her. "I don't want to trap you. I want you to be free, Emory. You know that. Your passion and dedication to being a historian is what I love most about you."

"You say that now, but you have no idea how things will change once we're married. You're going to need someone to run your household. You're going to need someone to support you in your career."

"I've gotten this far in life by myself." I spread out my arms. "I don't need anything."

Except you. I didn't say those words out loud. Not when she was already retreating.

"You know the worst part about that vision?" Emory asked, ignoring what I'd said.

I swallowed the growing lump in my throat. "What?"

"I could see how I'd become a shell of myself again, just like I was in my marriage to Gregory. You remember that day in the highlands? After I got Spirit Sky's mask?"

I nodded, feeling numb, afraid if I opened my mouth, every single emotion and feeling would pour out, and then I'd lose Emory for good. This scared her, but I didn't really believe it was because she thought I'd trap her. She had to know I never would. Something else was holding her back. I just didn't know what.

She played with the frazzled end of her tunic. "We were laying side by side, and you wanted to see my face."

I remembered. It was the day I realized I didn't just want to spend one day a year with her. I wanted to spend every spirits-damned day with her.

"It scared me at the time." She reached over and grabbed my hand, the brush of her fingers shooting sparks through me like it did every time we touched. "Because I realized I had feelings for you. And I was a married woman."

My jaw locked. "You never betrayed your husband. You did nothing wrong."

"No." Her eyes were so bright, so full of anguish. "That's not what I'm saying. I don't feel guilty for falling in . . . for falling for you." She slipped her hand from mine and straightened. "You made me feel seen in a way no one ever had, and I will always be grateful for you. But that day I realized how trapped I truly was. I couldn't reveal my face or name to you because doing so would jeopardize my horrible, pathetic life."

I hated that she ever had to go through that. Part of me grateful Annalee escaped the Academy of Ladies, even if it meant coming here. That fate would've suffocated her. Whereas Emory found a way to carve out a piece of this world for her, I wasn't so sure Annalee would've been able to do the same.

"I ran away from you in the highlands," Emory continued, "and I vowed that if I ever got free of my husband, I would never, ever put myself in a situation like that again."

My heart twisted. "And you truly think that's what I would do? Trap you?"

"I saw it," she said, voice barely a whisper. "Please don't make me say it, Maverick."

"Say what?" I rubbed my jaw just as a ribbon of green twisted throughout the purple sky.

"Don't make me say no to you."

I gave a stiff nod, and she stood, water still dripping from the ends of her hair. "I'm going back to camp. It's been a long day, and I need some sleep."

I met her gaze but said nothing, too numb to speak, to feel. She padded past me without looking back.

I didn't dare look at the lake, but whatever she'd seen, it wasn't real. It couldn't be.

Then again . . . Doubt filled me, a voice whispering that I'd done it time and time again. I'd put work before those who mattered most. I'd done it to Annalee. I'd left her in a horrible situation for a job. I'd neglected relationships, kept others at bay, all for the sake of my career. So who was to say I wouldn't do it again in the future? Maybe Emory was right to say no. Maybe I wasn't what she needed after all. Maybe I truly had to let her go.

And that was the most painful realization of all.

<h1 style="text-align:center">Chapter Forty-Two</h1>

EMORY

I watched as Maverick walked ahead with Aron and El, El signing something to him, her red dress muddy at the hem, swishing around her boots. The long sleeves had been cut, hanging in shreds around her arms. Maverick watched her intently, and I wondered what they were talking about.

We'd barely spoken over the last two days while we continued our travels through the Wilds. We'd come across a few different places where El thought Annalee might have been, only to come up empty, no Annalee in sight. I saw the disappointment in the downturn of Maverick's lips, the way he stared hard at the ground like if he just looked closely enough, he could find his way to her. I wanted to reach out to him, touch him, kiss away his worries. But I couldn't. Not after I'd so thoroughly rejected him.

It hurt me as much as it did him, but I doubted that would be any kind of comfort. So I stayed away, gave him space, and I hoped that one day maybe we could be friends.

Something told me I could never be just friends with the bone collector. Not after everything we'd been through together.

I tugged at the pocket watch hanging around my neck, the hand nearing the eleven. We still didn't know what it was counting down toward, but I was growing increasingly concerned about what might happen when it ticked all the way back to the twelve.

"Was it the sex?" Driscoll asked from next to me.

"Excuse me?" I dropped the pocket watch, and it thudded against my chest as my head snapped in his direction. We walked under thickets of vines that had twisted and fused together to create a tunnel that arched above our heads. I hadn't asked what danger they posed as we'd entered, but when I looked up at their wriggling forms, I wasn't sure I wanted to know.

"You and Maverick have barely spoken for two days." Driscoll tilted his head, studying Maverick. "So was it the sex? Not what you expected? Did he call you the wrong name? Was it bent? Or maybe he just got on top of you and a few pumps later it was over. That's definitely happened to me. Major turnoff. One time—"

"No, Driscoll." I lowered my voice, darting glances to our companions in front of us. "We haven't had sex."

He gasped. "You and Hot Professor haven't even had sex yet?"

"No." And now I'd never know what it felt like.

"That actually makes more sense," Driscoll said. "I can't imagine Hot Professor not being good at sex. He kind of seems like the type of guy who's good at everything, you know?"

"I really don't want to talk about this." I crossed my arms.

Up ahead, Aron glanced over his shoulder, those blue eyes trained on Driscoll, before he turned back around.

I shot a curious glance at Driscoll. "You know what I think?"

"Um, no, actually." He tugged at his curly hair. "I'm not a mind reader."

I made a face at him. "I think you busy yourself with everyone else's lives so that you don't have to think about your own."

"That's rude." Driscoll pointed to me. "And also a little true."

"Is there something going on between you two?" I gestured between him and Aron.

His eyes widened. "Between me and him? The big, objectively gorgeous blond man who also happens to be a wolf?" He scoffed. "No."

"Why not?" I nudged Driscoll. "I think he's into you."

"He's too nice for me." Driscoll waggled his eyebrows. "I like the bad boys."

"And where has that gotten you so far in life?"

"Fair point." He tipped his head. "Aron is nice, and we all know how he looks naked, but no. I don't think I'm the relationship type, you know?"

I stared him down as he avoided my gaze. "This is still about what Leoni said, isn't it?"

"She's supposed to be my friend." He threw out his arms. "If my own friend thinks that about me, then it must be true."

The vines slithered over each other, weaving in and out, knotting and twisting so it was hard to see where any began or ended.

"You think we should be concerned about those?" Driscoll pointed upward.

"I think we should be concerned about everything in the Wilds."

The tips of a few of the vines poked out.

"Blood and earth, this place is so weird," Driscoll mumbled.

"So why can't you have sex with the hot wolf?" Aron turned around again, glancing at Driscoll.

He nudged me. "Because he's nice, and I ruin nice things, okay? I talk too much and I'm too direct and I don't have any kind of filter and—"

"And because you're selfish," I finished for him.

He rolled his eyes. "Fine. Maybe I still can't get Leoni's words out of my head."

"Well, I'm not going to be able to convince you. All I can say is that if you find a spark of passion in this world, you should grab hold of it. If you have any interest in Hot Wolf Man, and he has interest in you, then go for it. Life is too short not to."

"Hot Wolf Man?" Driscoll's lips twitched. "Are you stealing my nickname system?"

"There's not much of a system involved. You basically insert hot before some descriptive words."

He stuck out his tongue at me, then straightened. "Well done." He did a slow clap. "You completely distracted me from talking about you."

I skipped a few paces ahead, then turned. "I don't want to talk about me."

The vines above us rustled, dipping a little lower. The tunnel curved around, no end in sight. El had insisted this was the best path forward. Apparently the other route was through a field of flowers that emitted scents that drugged their victims so they could then trap and suffocate them.

"Oh, come on." Driscoll pointed at me. "You both went to that lake, and we all assumed you were having sex, finishing what you started up against that tree. But then you came back all weird and distant."

I sighed, slowing so Driscoll could catch up. "He asked me to marry him," I admitted.

"What?" Driscoll shrieked. "Spirits below, are you having a wedding? Am I invited? Oh, please let me be invited. I love weddings. The alcohol. The sad mopey single people just begging to get laid. Did I mention the alcohol?"

"Shhh." I clapped a hand over his mouth. "There's not going to be a wedding. I said no."

"What?" His shriek was even louder this time, making Aron, El, and Maverick turn to stare.

We both gave them strained smiles as they slowly faced forward once more.

"Why would you ever say no? You two are like a nerdy match made in paradise. You're both obsessed with the most borings things. The other day, you debated if an old chipped cup was likely from the Hotoath or the Yaramo period." He shuddered. "It was about as interesting as watching two turtles race."

I pinned him with a look. "Are you done?"

"No, I actually have a lot to say on the topic. Is that foreplay for you both? Like do you get naked and talk history before going down on each other?"

I continued staring at him, and he zipped his lips. I blinked a few times.

"I have more to say, but I'll be quiet now so you can talk."

I didn't want to get into the vision I'd seen in the lake. It was too painful to recount again. So I'd tell as much of the truth as I could.

"I spent seven years trapped in a life I didn't want. My entire identity revolved around someone else. I can't let that happen again."

Driscoll wrinkled his nose. "Who says that's going to happen again? You know not all men are sadistic, self-centered assholes, right? I mean, most are, to be fair." He pointed at Maverick. "But that guy? He's not one of them. He worships you."

My stomach twisted at his words.

"Hot Professor has got it bad for you."

The vision didn't lie. That future I saw, it was so real. Everyone could say what they wanted, could deny that that's how my life would turn out with Maverick, but I couldn't shake the haunted look in Future Me's eyes as she'd walked up those stairs while he was living out her dream. My dream.

"You can't tell the future, Driscoll." But the lake could. "You don't know what's going to happen to us. Maverick has always been wrapped up in his career. It's the most important thing to him."

"Well, until you came along," Driscoll said.

"You don't get to where he is by not being that passionate, that dedicated. I don't blame him. I really don't. I understand. I just can't risk losing my identity again. Especially not when we have so much going on already."

"I get it." Driscoll laid a hand on my arm. "I can't imagine what it would be like to be forced into doing anything. Especially marrying someone."

I nudged him again. "That's why it's important that you live this life you have, Driscoll. Stop living through everyone else's stories. It's time to live your own."

I glanced ahead at Aron, and Driscoll chewed on his bottom lip.

"We'll see. I'm still not sure Hot Wolf Man can handle me." His throat bobbed as one of the vines dipped down and wrapped around his arm. "Uh, what's happening here?" he called ahead.

El turned and signed, her movements fast and jerky, like the vines taking notice of us was an imposition to her. She was definitely feisty, had hardened edges and tall walls I wasn't sure anyone could break down. I supposed a place like this would do that to a person.

"The vines react to your fear," Aron said. "Do not fear them, and they won't harm you."

"Oh, is that it?" Driscoll whimpered as the vine wrapped tighter around his arm, more vines taking notice and slinking down. One caressed his cheek.

Aron took a few steps toward us as more vines slithered around Driscoll's body, tightening across his waist, his chest.

"If you're afraid, there is another way to get the vines to release you." Aron studied the slithering plants.

"What?" Driscoll asked, voice reaching a frantic pitch. "Magic? Fire? Frost? I can't summon my earth magic without my hands." He wiggled his fingers under the constriction of the vines.

"Not magic. If we attack, all the vines come down upon us. Just give them a secret. Each secret you give will make one vine return to its place."

One of the vines wrapped around the back of Driscoll's neck and rubbed behind his ear. His eyes widened. "Secrets? I don't have any secrets."

"Okay, don't panic," I said.

Maverick summoned a ball of fire, ready to launch it, but Aron held out a hand to stop him. "Everyone has secrets."

"Not me." He glanced around wildly. "I'm an open book. I tell everyone everything. That's literally my entire personality."

El signed impatiently as the vines wrapped tighter around Driscoll. A few more dropped down, one tickling my head, another poking Maverick in the shoulder.

"I have a secret," Aron said. "I retain a lot of my wolf traits in my human form."

One of the vines around Driscoll's neck loosened. "What does that mean?" he choked out.

"It means I hear sounds impossible for human ears to comprehend. Including the conversation between you and Emory just moments ago."

Driscoll's eyes bugged out of his head, but the vine released his throat and retreated upward.

Aron stroked his jaw. "Another secret? I enjoy your openness.

Another? You're not going to ruin me. I've already been ruined. You don't bring out the beast in me—you bring out more humanity than I feel like I've had in years. You don't hide what you're feeling. You don't say something but mean something else. I like talking to you and knowing that what you are presenting is what you're getting. I like you as you are, Driscoll."

Driscoll's mouth fell open along with mine as the vines around his waist unraveled, slinking back. A few of the vines still wrapped around his hands and chest.

That was so damn romantic. Tears pricked my eyes at all of Aron's revelations. I knew something was going on between them. My gaze flicked to Maverick. I was happy for them. They deserved this.

El signed something, and Maverick glanced at her, then translated, speaking almost to himself. "I haven't just been looking for your sister because I heard of her and wanted to keep her safe." He stilled as he said the words, processing them while El kept signing. "I want to find her because if she found a way in, then maybe that means she can lead us out."

Maverick's jaw locked as he finished speaking, but El held his stare, almost as if challenging him to say something to her.

Another vine slithered from Driscoll's chest and up into the tangle of plants overhead. It was working, but I didn't know how to feel about El's admission. It made me wonder what other secrets she might be keeping, and by the look Maverick had given me, he must've been thinking the same thing.

Maverick cleared his throat. "I'm afraid I'm not capable of loving anything more than my work."

There it was. The dagger to my heart. Exactly what I'd feared all along. I looked away, folding my arms across my chest. I supposed I needed to supply a secret as well. I opened my mouth to say something, but then Driscoll spoke.

"I'm free." He patted down his body. "I'm free. I'm free. Now can we please get the bloody spirits out of here?"

Chapter Forty-Three

EMORY

We finally trudged through the tunnel of vines, no more almost-suffocations happening, the vines satiated with all the secrets that had been spilled.

The five of us stood in a circle on the pathway, everyone breathing heavy and wild-eyed after yet another near-death experience. Black dust lifted and swirled, and I blinked a few times as some of it got in my eye. The pathway wound around a hill, and I could've sworn I saw more of those cat-like creatures lurking about, tails flicking out from the tall grass, eyes peering curiously. But every time I blinked, they were gone.

"Why didn't you tell me about wanting to find my sister?" Maverick asked El, hands on his hips. "What else are you keeping from us?"

El signed, pointer and middle fingers sticking up, then she raised her pinky and swiped her hand in an arc over her chest.

"That's not good enough," Maverick said, fists balled. "I don't care if you thought it might anger me, if you didn't want to risk us running away to find her ourselves. You should've told me from the beginning. What are you planning on doing? Marching her through the Wilds so she can show you where she got in? What if she doesn't want to? What if I say no?"

El glared at Maverick, making a quick succession of signs.

"Yes," he responded. "Of course we want to escape, but not at the expense of my sister. It's not her job to be your personal guide. And why do you want to escape anyway? As twisted as this place is, it's your home. So why do you want to leave?"

El broke eye contact, pale skin flushed with anger. Another secret.

"Ah," Maverick said. "So you're willing to share a few secrets, but not all of them."

"We should calm down." Aron held out his hands. "I think we might be close to finding your sister."

Maverick pointed a finger at El. "She's not getting anywhere near my sister. Not until she tells me every secret she's keeping."

El threw her hands up in the air, stalking down the path, her back to us.

A buzzing noise filled the air.

Driscoll rubbed his temples. "What is that?"

"We need to stay quiet," Aron said, voice low. "They're blind, but they do react to sound."

"Oh good, so another plant-eater situation," Driscoll said.

Aron frowned. "These are flying bugs that latch onto your neck and suck out your blood, so quite different from plants."

Driscoll sighed heavily.

"Okay," I said as Maverick still stood rigid, El with her back to us, arms crossed. "What do we do?"

The buzzing morphed, turning to chimes and humming. I tilted my head. It sounded like a song.

"Are the bugs in a band?" Driscoll scratched the back of his neck. "Do they tour the Wilds and put on shows?"

"No, that's odd." Aron frowned. "The buzzing indicates they're about to attack, but it seems to be . . ."

The buzzing faded even more, the other sounds growing louder, a melody that floated through the air. Fun and fast. It made me want to dance, to join in on whatever party was happening beyond this pathway.

El straightened, then started toward the sound.

"El, wait!" Aron said, but she didn't listen.

"I think I'm going to need my heart checked if we ever get out of this place." Driscoll laid a palm to his chest. "It's just one thing after another here."

Curiosity got the better of me, and I followed El. A hand grabbed my arm, and I whipped around, face inches from Maverick's.

"You don't know what's around this hill," he said. "Maybe it's better to let her go first."

I shook my arm from his. "Afraid of a little challenge, Bone Collector?"

"Oh, I live for challenges. I also prefer to keep my head." His eyes flashed, and for just a moment, it felt like we were back.

A violin struck up a chord, and we jumped apart.

"Might as well go check it out." Driscoll huffed and shoved between us.

Aron and Maverick looked at each other, and Maverick sighed, relenting. We followed the path around the hill. The music grew louder as we approached, and laughter pealed through the air.

I gasped as we rounded a curve, a thicket of thorns and tangled brush creating a large canopy that arched over a girl. A woman. Young, in her early twenties if I had to guess. She clapped and laughed again. Bugs hung in the air around her, as large as my hand, their translucent wings fluttering nonstop.

She pointed at one. "You're not keeping up the harmony, Atticus."

As if it actually understood her, the bug lifted higher and made a sound like a drum that beat in rhythm to its flapping wings.

I blinked a few times, unsure of what, exactly, I was seeing.

Maverick pushed past me, stumbling forward. "Annalee?"

My head snapped to him, then back to the girl.

The bugs continued their harmony while Maverick entered the canopy, ducking to get inside. Annalee patted the spot next to her and gave him a toothy grin like she'd been expecting him this entire time. Aron, El, Driscoll, and I stayed outside, all of us watching with rapt fascination.

"Maverick!" Annalee clapped her hands. "I was hoping you'd find me. Do you want to join my tea party?"

"Your what?" Maverick snapped.

I took in the entire scene. Annalee sat on a checkered blanket, chipped and dusty cups surrounding her. A top hat sat next to her bouncing up and down.

"Would you like some tea?" Annalee held the cup to the hat. It flipped upside down and she poured the tea inside.

"This is the weirdest shit I have ever seen." Driscoll stared at the scene, wide-eyed.

"Annalee, what are you doing?" Maverick asked, standing over her.

She glanced up at him, her brows folding into a scowl. "Well, at least sit down. You're being rude."

Aron's gaze swept the area, then he stepped forward and sat down next to Annalee. So matter of fact, as always. El's face had softened as she stared at Maverick's little sister, and I wondered what was going through her mind.

Annalee gave Aron an approving look and offered him a cup, then grabbed the teapot and tipped the tea into it. "Welcome," she said brightly.

Maverick crossed his arms, boot tapping on the ground.

Driscoll shrugged. "Whatever. When in Arathia. Or, in this case, the Wilds." He sat next to Aron, and Annalee reached over and handed him a cup.

El huffed, then sank down, her red dress floating around her. I followed suit, sitting next to her while Maverick stayed standing.

"Annalee, this place is dangerous." He crouched next to her. "What are you doing in the middle of the Wilds? Have you been hurt?"

She raised her pert nose, offering tea to both me and El. We accepted while Maverick ran a hand over his head. My lips twitched. I imagined his sister tested his patience quite often, and it was entertaining to watch.

"This tea is actually really good," Driscoll murmured, taking another sip while the bugs continued their melody.

"How did you get the blood beetles to play this music?" Aron asked Annalee.

She tugged on one of her braids, all of them spilling over her shoulder as she leaned forward. "Oh, that's easy. They like parties."

Driscoll's cup froze inches from his mouth. "Parties?" he echoed. "The bugs like to party?"

She nodded eagerly. "Any chance for them to play some music instead of making that awful buzzing noise. They only make it when threatened."

She gave us a pointed stare.

The hat flipped back over, bouncing next to her. "Hatter, where are your manners?" She tsked at it.

Aron stilled. "Hatter? As in the Mad Hatter?"

"Who is the Mad Hatter?" Driscoll asked, voice resigned.

"Don't let the hat anywhere near your head," Aron said quietly. "It's known to make people who wear it go mad."

The hat jumped higher, and Annalee shot Aron a glare. "Don't be rude. Mad Hatter is behaving and drinking his tea."

El sighed heavily.

"Enough," Maverick said, grabbing Annalee's arm and pulling her to her feet. The tea she held splashed out of her cup.

"Mav," Annalee protested as her brother hauled her upright. "You're ruining a perfectly nice tea party."

"Annalee, this is serious," Maverick said. "Do you understand how much danger we're in? How many times we've almost died trying to get to you?"

Her eyes widened, the exact same shade of copper brown as Maverick's. "Did you not listen to all my stories over the years? I thought when you came, you'd be prepared."

"Bloody fire," Maverick muttered.

"I didn't mean to lead you into danger." Tears filled her eyes. "I figured you'd follow me here, and I could finally prove this place was real. That I haven't been making it up."

Maverick stared at her for a long minute before yanking her into a tight hug. She buried her face into his chest, and I looked away, wanting to give them this moment of privacy.

"I knew you'd come for me," she whispered.

Driscoll wiped away a tear. "It's a little dusty in here is all," he said as we looked at him. More tears spilled down his cheeks. "Okay, fine, I'm crying. This is a very sweet reunion, and you all are emotionless voids of humans."

El rolled her eyes and signed, Aron clearing his throat and translating, "Now that we've found the girl, are you all going to accompany us back to our home? Or are you going your own way?"

Maverick still hugged his sister tight, but she turned. "Oh, I'd love to go with you. Can we, Mav? I can show you around a little more. Introduce you to some friends."

"Friends?" Driscoll squeaked.

Maverick sighed, massaging his temple. "Does your home have a bath, by any chance? And food? And a decent place to sleep?"

For the first time since I'd met her, El smiled and held up two fingers, both of them pressed together. I'd learned enough to know that meant yes.

Maverick slung an arm around Annalee's shoulders. "Then let's get going, and once we're there, we have a lot to discuss." He met El's gaze, and she stared at him for a long moment before giving a sharp nod.

"Does that mean the tea party is over?" Driscoll asked.

The bugs quieted, slowly floating to the ground while the hat slumped. Annalee ducked under Maverick's arm and patted the hat. "Don't worry. We'll have another tea party again soon."

Maverick opened his mouth like he wanted to argue, but then he snapped it shut.

El signed, and Maverick nodded. "Okay, let's get going, then." He reached for Annalee's arm. "Want to take a walk with your big brother?"

Annalee gave him the brightest smile. "Absolutely."

He roped an arm around her shoulders. El turned and began walking, all of us following. I only hoped this place was safe like El claimed. I wasn't sure my heart could take any more. I chanced a glance back at Maverick. Not when it was already so thoroughly broken.

Chapter Forty-Four

MAVERICK

I held Annalee's hand tight, not wanting to let it go for even a second. I looked over at her as she smiled, her light brown skin dewy with a glow to it that I didn't recognize, her eyes so bright and full of life.

This was a side of Annalee I hadn't seen in a long, long time. She seemed so at home here, which should've been . . . impossible. This place wasn't a home. It was a wasteland, where death and danger awaited around every corner, yet Annalee had no problem navigating any of it.

"Hey," I said as we walked through a field of trees that had been razed to the ground, nothing left but their stumps and dead leaves and branches. "I owe you an apology, you know."

She arched her neck to look up at me. "It's okay. I know I was asking a lot of you, of Mama and Father. I knew it all seemed impossible." She gripped my arm. "But that's why I wanted you to see it."

I let out a laugh of disbelief. "How did you even know I'd follow you? That was a huge gamble to take."

She bit the inside of her cheek. "I had to come here, no matter what.

Every time I slept, I dreamt of this place, Mav. And it felt like the longer I stayed away, the more it was eating me alive. I almost believed I was crazy, just like Father said. But everyday when I woke up, back to reality after a night spent dreaming of the Wilds, I lost a piece of myself."

She jumped up onto a tree stump, then stepped down, her blue-checkered dress swaying with the movement.

"Do you know why you had dreams of this place?" I asked, still not able to put any of it together. "How could you have known what was here? The madness? The wonder. I—" I rubbed my jaw.

"I don't know," she admitted. "I don't know why I started dreaming of the Wilds or these creatures. I don't even know what happened here after the Shadow War, how Shiraeth became this." She gestured to the field of stumps. "But I think, in a way, I was meant to come here. To understand the Wilds and its inhabitants. To help them. You know they wouldn't ever be accepted in Arathia. If word got out what existed here, they'd send armies to slaughter everyone and burn everything."

For a moment, I wondered if that might be such a bad thing.

Like she could read my thoughts, Annalee swatted my arm. "There's some beauty here, you know," she said. "I've found it, and everyone else can too. There's been no one to govern these creatures, no one to lead them or show them how to behave. They need help, not to be wiped from existence."

"How did you get so smart?" I pressed a kiss to Annalee's temple. "And when did you grow up?" I'd missed so much after I left for the academy, and Annalee had gone through a lot without me by her side.

From an early age, she'd been having these dreams about a place no one else believed was real, she'd had to deal with my mother's wild emotions, my father's stern hand. She'd been called crazy and been made to feel like she was lying, making all of this up for attention. And all the while, she'd been steadfast in her beliefs.

I swallowed my rising guilt, then glanced behind me at Emory, who walked alone, Driscoll and Aron behind her, while El marched ahead of us all.

I caught Emory's eye and gave her a nod, then turned.

"Who's the pretty blonde?" Annalee asked.

"A friend." I kept my voice curt, my answer short.

"Really? Because while we were having our tea party, you kept looking at her like a sad puppy who got its toy taken away."

I shoved Annalee as she laughed.

"Just worry about yourself."

"I can't. You might be my older brother, but I'm always going to worry about you."

"Hey." I stepped over a tree stump as the field sloped upward, peaking at a hill that El already stood on, tapping her foot impatiently. "That's not your job, okay? I'm here to watch out for you."

"I don't need you to watch out for me. I just need you to"—she flailed her hands about—"be there for me. To support me. I just want to know that you'll have my back."

"I do," I said quickly. "Always."

She tipped her head back toward Emory. "Have you kissed her?"

I groaned. "Can we drop this?"

"Should I ask her?" Her smile grew mischievous. "Maybe she'll be more willing to talk."

I stopped, tapping her nose. "You wouldn't dare."

"Well, I made friends with blood beetles and the Mad Hatter. I don't think speaking to Emory is going to be so scary compared to that." She widened her eyes innocently.

I sighed heavily as we began the trek uphill, El staring down at us, her gaze practically burning holes into my head. She might have been eager to get home, but I was tired and I was going to take my damn time getting up this hill while I talked to my sister.

"Emory and I have a complicated history." Annalee didn't know I was the bone collector. It wasn't like I was worried she'd reveal my identity to anyone, but it wasn't my place to tell her that Emory was the white rabbit. I didn't even know if she'd heard of us, our secret identities. We were mostly known to the frost queen, those connected to her. "She's a historian like me. Except she's far braver."

If only Emory could see that.

"She loves a good challenge. She'll jump over snake pits, dive into piranha-infested rivers, cross frozen lakes—anything to get hold of rare artifacts."

Annalee's breathing growing heavy as we continued to ascend the hill. She lifted her skirts when we came upon a muddy spot that she stepped over. "Sounds familiar."

"Yeah." I laughed. "We like to compete, challenge each other. Over the years we became friends, and then recently, it became something more."

"So what's the problem? She sounds perfect for you."

"I'm the problem," I said. "I care too much about work, my profession. I don't know how to have a life outside of it, how to let others in. I put it above everything." I swallowed the thick knot in my throat. "I put it above you. Went off to the academy to my job, even though your dreams were beginning to become more frequent, and Father was getting more and more frustrated with you."

Annalee stopped and turned. "Is that what you think? You think you abandoned me?"

"I did abandon you."

"Mav." She shook her head, scowling. "You saved me. You wrote to me every single week. You listened to all my dreams, my ramblings. You asked questions. You didn't treat me like I was crazy. Not ever. Not like everyone else. You came home and visited, even though it meant long trips and missing work. You even tried to get Father to let me come with you up north." She put a hand on my arm. "It's okay to be passionate about something you love." Then she moved her hand, laying it right over my chest. "Your heart can grow, you know." She bobbed her head. "Not literally. But you can make room for more. You're not selfish, and if she believes that, then she doesn't know you. She doesn't deserve you."

We continued up the hill, and Annalee clutched her side.

"Do you need to rest?" I asked.

"No." She nodded toward El, who was pacing back and forth, hands balled at her sides. "I think she might actually push us back down the hill if we take any longer to get up there."

I looked behind me. Driscoll, Aron, and Emory had stopped to look at a plant sticking out of the ground that was puffing smoke into the air.

"They better be careful," Annalee said. "That stuff will give you hallucinations."

"She's not the problem," I said quietly, gazing at Emory as she laughed in delight at something Driscoll said. "She was married before. To a terrible man. He hurt her." I thought of those bruises on her neck and had to swallow back my anger. "She's scared. She's afraid to be in another marriage like that." Annalee opened her mouth, but I continued on, "She's worried she'll be trapped again. Her husband kept a tight rein. So she had to hide that part of herself from him. She doesn't want to risk losing herself all over again."

"Hm," Annalee said. "You know, when no one believed me about the Wilds, I'd almost given up. Father sent me to that terrible Academy of Ladies, and I was so resigned."

My heart broke at the words. I'd known this, but hearing her say it hit differently.

"I was going to just go and finally be the good girl. Shut up and forget about these dreams and forget about the Wilds."

"So what changed?"

"You did." She laughed.

"Me?" I said, arching a brow.

"Yes, *you*. You started taking more risks, going after what you wanted, trying to make an actual change at the academy instead of going along with those old, stuffy professors. You became this amazing adventurer, and it made you happy in a way I had never seen before."

"Because I met Emory. Because she changed me."

"So show her that," Annalee said. "Don't stop proving yourself until she realizes you're going to love her the way she deserves to be loved. Go after her like you've gone after all those rare artifacts sitting in that fancy academy museum."

My lips twitched because when she put it like that . . .

"If you love her, then it's worth the fight."

Of course I loved her. She'd become so entwined in my life, in my thoughts, in my very being, there was no me without her.

Annalee was right. I'd never scared easily. I'd never let anything stop me from getting what I wanted. And there was nothing I wanted more than Emory.

We finally arrived at the top of the hill, and Annalee gasped.

"That's your camp?" she asked, mouth agape.

I took in the view below. A sparkling blue lake spread out in front of a towering castle. Silver walls that shimmered and glittered rose into pointed peaks. Large balconies jutted out with billowing white curtains draped over the windows. A drawbridge stretched over a river that fed into the lake and wound around the castle.

"Your camp is the castle?" I asked with a raised brow.

El just shrugged as the rest of our group caught up, and Driscoll hunched over, hands on his knees. "I get to stay in the star court castle? Are you kidding me?" He turned to El. "Do you have hot water?"

She nodded.

He sank to his knees. "Oh, thank the bloody spirits. I don't think I've ever been so happy in my entire life."

"Is it safe?" I drew Annalee back toward me.

"It is," Aron said. "The castle is where many of us have resided for the better part of sixty years. We keep it fortified." He nodded toward the castle walls, and I could just make out the forms of guards keeping watch from the towers, all of them with something slightly off about them. I swore one of them had wings instead of arms and another's body was covered with black fur. "You'll be safe. I promise."

That was good enough for me. Maybe without constant threats to my life, I could finally have some time and space to figure out exactly how I was going to win back Emory and make her mine.

Chapter Forty-Five

I stood at our tree, holding out the little glass jar as thick snowflakes fell from the sky. The snow came up to my calves, and I shivered, the wind a constant barrage. She was late. As usual.

For a moment, I worried something was wrong, but then my eye caught on the little piece of paper sitting atop the other folded pieces in the jar. It was a different color, shaped into a triangle instead of in half like the others.

A note. My heart kicked up its pace. Maybe she'd written to tell me she couldn't make it today. Maybe she'd had some other commitment and needed to reschedule our choosing. Something in my gut told me that wasn't it. Not after she'd practically run away from me ten months ago in the highlands. Right after I'd admitted I wanted to reveal myself to her.

The thing was I didn't regret it. If I regretted anything, it was not chasing after her. I'd spent the last ten months thinking about that moment.

Over and over.

Wondering what it would've been like if I had slipped that hood

"

from her head, tugged that cloak from her body. I never would've done it without her permission, but maybe if I'd chased after her, I could've shown her that I wouldn't give up so easily.

At this point, I'd thought so many times about what she might look like, but the truth was it didn't matter.

I knew her heart. Her soul. Both sang to me in a way nothing else ever had.

I took a steadying breath and plucked the little triangular paper from the jar, then unfolded it to see her familiar handwriting. I loved the way she signed it: WR. How she curved the Ws at the corners and looped the R to connect it. I could hear Annalee's voice in my head, teasing me about this infatuation, how I was so head over heels for this woman that I'd even fallen for her handwriting.

I studied the piece of paper, and my heart sank when I read the rest of the note. It didn't take long. It was only a single sentence.

I can't do this anymore.
WR

That was it. After five years of playing our game, this was all I got. I ran a hand over my head, shivering and wishing I'd brought my damn cloak.

But I'd wanted to give her a show of good faith. To reveal myself to her and expect nothing in return. I could've just worn my cloak and not pulled the hood up, not worn the scarf covering my face, but no. I decided to be dramatic about it all and show up in just my damn shirt and trousers.

Now I was freezing—and alone. The white rabbit wouldn't step through these woods and see my face for the first time ever. She wouldn't hear my speech about how I didn't want to be anonymous anymore. About how I wanted to be more than friends.

Branches cracked nearby, and I whipped around, heart pounding, hoping this meant she'd changed her mind. Any moment she'd step through the trees and run straight into my arms.

But it wasn't the white rabbit who appeared in between the thick tree trunks, boots sloshing in the snow.

It was the frost queen.

Her white hair sat atop her head in an elaborate updo of braids that looped around to make a heart shape. Her maroon cloak draped her frail shoulders. Wrinkles and folds lined her ancient face. I didn't know her exact age, but she'd been queen since the Shadow War, when the reigning king and his entire family had been killed. She'd been a distant cousin, someone who never had hope of ruling, but the war had changed everything for her.

She only came up to my chest, but she stood tall, raising her age-spotted nose in the air. She used a cane that she leaned on as she stepped forward.

"Maverick Von Lucas," she said. "Now this is a surprise."

I thanked the bloody spirits I hadn't worn my cloak, the cloak that would give away my identity as the bone collector. The queen would never understand. I'd lose my position as her advisor, lose my job at the academy. My reputation would be ruined beyond hope of ever redeeming it.

I bowed. "Your Majesty."

"I came here expecting to see the white rabbit." Her eyes narrowed in on me. "You are not the white rabbit."

No. The queen couldn't catch the white rabbit. She'd throw her in one of the infamous ice prisons. Blocks of thick ice that surrounded iron bars, trapping prisoners inside, many of them freezing to death before they even got any kind of audience with the queen to discuss their crime. The white rabbit had frost magic, so she likely wouldn't freeze to death, but the thought of her in one of those cells—I wouldn't stand for it.

"The white rabbit?" I asked, stepping forward, mind working quickly. If she found out I was the bone collector, I'd never be able to protect the white rabbit. I cleared my throat. "Yes, I came here for the same reason. I've been tracking her."

The frost queen raised her chin, eyeing me with approval. "Of course you have. This is exactly why I made you historical advisor to the crown. You take charge. You don't wait to be told what to do. You're a pioneer in this field, you know." She spread out her skinny arms, hands threaded with veins under paper-thin skin. "So what have you found about this white rabbit?"

I had to tread this dangerous ground very, very carefully. "Not much. She's clever. Cunning."

"What does she know?" The queen's voice came out sharper than I'd expected.

She always exuded such calm, an impenetrable wall of ice that couldn't be chipped or cracked by anyone. The white rabbit had her rattled, but I didn't know why. Yes, she was a criminal, stealing artifacts that were supposed to be handed over to the academy. But there were many criminals. An entire black market that thrived under the noses of the crown. The fact that the frost queen had come here herself meant that the white rabbit was a direct threat to her. What I didn't know was why.

"I'm not sure," I said slowly.

Her gaze hardened. "We cannot allow her to continue this little charade. Who knows how many valuable items she's taken? What kind of stories she might be spinning about them."

She was clearly afraid of the white rabbit finding out something.

"History doesn't lie, Your Majesty," I said. "It would be hard for this white rabbit to completely fabricate something based on an object she finds. And who is she going to tell? Revealing a new find or a new theory would out her to the crown."

The frost queen started pacing, her red cloak whipping behind her, her boots sinking in the thick carpet of snow. "Maybe she doesn't care about being outed. Maybe she has some vendetta against me, against the crown. Maybe she just wants to find a way to make me look bad, to discredit me."

I'd never seen the queen so beside herself before. Something else was going on here. I just wished I knew what.

She whirled on me, blue eyes blazing. "You will find her. You will bring her to me. And you will reap all the rewards. I will make you the head of the Academy of Scholars & Historians."

I stilled. I was being offered everything I'd ever wanted. Everything I'd ever thought I wanted. Until I met her.

This might just be the best way, the only way, to protect the white rabbit. So I'd do what I needed to do, and I'd find a way to make sure the queen never found her. Maybe it was best our game ended for now, as much as that thought was a dagger to the heart. I could pretend I was tracking her. Feed the queen false information. It would be risky. It could cost me everything. But if the white rabbit got caught, then none of that would matter anyway.

Mind made up, I took a step forward. "Anything for Your Majesty. If you want the white rabbit found, then I'll find her. We'll make sure she doesn't discover any secrets you don't want discovered."

I tested out the words, hoping I hadn't prodded too much, gone too far, but the queen just tipped her head with a knowing smile. "Good. Very good, Maverick. I know you won't disappoint me."

With that, she turned and disappeared behind the curtain of flurries. I stood there, staring after her, mind running through our conversation. One thing was clear: the frost queen had a secret, one she didn't want found out, and that made me want to know it all the more.

Chapter Forty-Six

EMORY

"Watch out for staircases that don't lead anywhere. Doors that open to odd locations," Aron said as we crossed the glass drawbridge that stretched over a sparkling blue river, all of us staring up at the tall silver walls of the castle that shimmered and glittered under the twilight sky.

Maverick's arm was still wrapped around Annalee, drawing her into him as if he was afraid to let her go.

Aron reached the sleek silver double doors and opened one, allowing us all through in a single-file line. We entered into the foyer, black dust covering the floor that looked like the surface of a pristine lake—or at least it would have without all the dust. A chandelier hung from the ceiling, filled with stubby candles, dried wax dripping down the sides. A hallway sat to our left, doors stood in front of us, and a bridge stretched out to our right, leading to another part of the castle.

I gasped when I saw a room beyond the foyer, the entire floor painted to resemble a huge chess board. Life-sized pieces stood on the floor, moving of their own accord.

"I do not recommend playing with them," Aron said from beside me. "They tend to crush anyone who loses." He shot a glance at El. "The queen of hearts plays regularly, but that's only because she's never lost."

El studied her nails, flicking a piece of dust from her dress.

Long scratches dragged down the walls, fissures and cracks spread everywhere. The castle might've looked impeccable from the outside, but on the inside, it was a mess.

"I'm afraid the castle has fallen into disrepair," Aron said, turning to look at our group. "We haven't had the proper supplies to restore it."

El made a series of signs with both hands.

"Or the interest," Aron added, and it was clear that was El's words. Aron cleared his throat. "Let me show you to your rooms. They're not much, but we do have hot water, beds, and food."

"You had me at hot water," Driscoll said.

El disappeared through the doors in front of us, and I thought I saw a flash of water, a glimpse of white feathers, but the doors closed so quickly I couldn't be sure. Maybe it was more of the odd creatures that populated the Wilds or the swans the star king obsessed over. Could they still be alive? Or were they warped like everything else?

I shuddered at the thought of swans with long, sharp teeth who wanted to eat me.

Aron led us to the right, over the bridge. The railings were cracked, tree roots jutting up in random spots. We picked our way across and into the other part of the castle. Stairs greeted us, spiraling upward in a narrow tower. This place must've been a marvel to behold before the Shadow War.

We silently made our way up as I looked at the glimmering silver stone walls. I could just imagine how much this stone would go for if Shiraeth still existed. The wealthy would pay premium gold to have it in their homes. Kings and queens would travel from the human lands to procure it for their castles. I traced a finger down the rough brick, and it came away with the black dust that I was growing so sick of. If I ever got out of here, I feared I'd find dust in various places on my body 'til the end of time.

Finally we arrived at a hallway filled with doors on the right and left sides. Worn gray rugs lay on the glassy floor.

Aron spread his arms out. "There's only a few functioning rooms on this floor, but you can take them. Our residents reside in the floor above this one."

Boards creaked overhead, and I thought I heard a growl. I wondered exactly what kind of residents they'd invited to live here. If Aron could shift into a wolf, what other types of creatures had been borne of this curse?

I tilted my head. "How did you choose who to invite to the castle?"

Aron frowned. "Anyone is welcome. But many do not want to come here, feeling more comfortable staying out in the Wilds, living amongst nature, in environments that better suited them. Not everyone wants to be confined to the walls of the castle. Not everyone remembers their old lives or wants to. And we do have rules. Some have been kicked out for not abiding by them."

"Rules?" Driscoll echoed.

"No killing." Aron ticked off his fingers. "No stealing. No lying. No conspiring. If any of those rules are broken, they face the red queen."

Annalee gasped. "I've always wanted to meet the queen of hearts. I've heard so much about her."

"You already met her," Maverick said drily.

"El," Annalee guessed. "That makes perfect sense." She studied Aron. "Though I have a feeling you're the one who keeps things running around here."

Aron gave a sharp shake of his head. "I simply follow orders."

Annalee made a face like she disagreed but didn't say anything.

Driscoll was already striding toward a door, opening it, and slipping inside. "No offense," he said, "but I'd rather take a bath than stand here talking with you all." He paused. "Actually, I really don't care if I offended you." With that, his door slammed shut, and he was gone.

Annalee followed suit, picking the room next to Driscoll's and almost disappearing inside before Maverick surged forward and grabbed her arm.

She gave him a look full of exasperation. "I'm just taking a bath, Mav. Promise I won't go anywhere, okay? I just need a break from your hovering."

"I'm not hovering," he said calmly.

She raised a brow.

He rolled his eyes

Aron scratched his head. "I assume you two will take the final room left?" He nodded to the one across the hall. "All the others are in disrepair."

Of course they were.

Maverick shifted from foot to foot, and I tried my best to look anywhere but at him.

"Emory can stay with me," Annalee chirped.

Before I had a chance to respond, she reached for my arm and pulled me toward her door.

Maverick glared at her, and she just smiled wide, a mischievous gleam in her eyes. "We're just going to have some girl time." She shooed him away. "Go take a bath and maybe a nap because you've been a little grumpy ever since you interrupted my tea party."

Aron looked between all of us. "Does this mean you've chosen your rooms? I have other matters to attend to, but I will check on all of you in a little bit."

"Yep," Annalee said quickly, then yanked me inside the room and shut the door in Maverick's face before he could say another word.

I turned and gave her my best smile. I could use some girl time. Relaxing, bathing, napping, but Annalee clearly had other ideas.

"We need to talk," she said.

Chapter Forty-Seven

EMORY

"You can have the bath first." Annalee gestured to the open bath chamber off to the side of the room. My gaze swept around the small room, a bed pushed against one wall that was big enough for two people. A wardrobe sat against the opposite wall, the wood knotted and twisted, woven with such craftsmanship it looked exactly like a few of the trees we'd encountered in the Wilds. The walls gleamed silver, the floor that pristine glassy material that gave the illusion of standing on a frozen lake. The ceiling, which had three big glass skylights that gave a view of the twilight sky.

"Thank you," I said to Annalee, giving her an unsure smile. "I haven't had a proper bath in days."

I walked across the floor into the bath chamber and gasped. A tub sat, water already filling it, a stream of water pouring from a chute that jutted from the wall.

I approached the water, holding out my hand, feeling the warmth of it slide against my skin. I'd read about these famous baths in various texts and books. The chutes were made from a type of wood that was always warm, heating the water automatically and depositing it into the tub. The chute connected to a network of pipes that were inside the walls of the castle. Only the very rich in the star court could afford something like this.

A drain sat at the bottom of the tub. Water swirled into it, flowing through pipes and back out to the lake outside the castle. Bacteria-eating fish cleaned the water before it was filtered back to the chutes. It was a magnificent system, and I'd always wanted to see it in person.

I shed my clothes and lowered myself into the tub, groaning as the water soothed my aches and pains.

"How is it?" Annalee called from the other room.

"Glorious," I said. "I promise I won't take too long."

I reached up and grabbed a bottle of purple liquid off a shelf, popping open the cork. The scent of lavender filled the air, and I took a deep inhale of it before pouring the liquid in my hand and massaging it into my hair.

"So you're the white rabbit, huh?" Annalee said.

I jolted in the tub, and water sloshed over the sides, spilling onto the gleaming tile floor. "Maverick told you that?"

"Of course not," Annalee said. "He hasn't even told me he's the bone collector."

My mouth dropped open, and it took me several seconds to regain my composure. "Then how did you find out?"

I moved directly under the cascading water and tipped my head back, letting it wash away the soap. Maybe we hadn't been as careful as we thought with our secret identities.

"He was kind of obvious about it." Her giggle floated through the air.

I lathered the soap in my palms and spread it over my body. "What do you mean?"

She paused. "Before all this bone collector business, Maverick was always so focused on the Academy of Scholars & Historians. Probably because of my father. It was drilled into Maverick that he had to get into an academy, get an honorable profession, not disappoint my father. Especially when it became clear what a disappointment I was. It was all my father cared about. But Mav had a seriousness about him. A severity, like he was doing a duty more than living out a passion."

A heavy silence filled the air, and I chewed the inside of my cheek, waiting for her to continue.

Her voice wobbled with her next words. "Sometimes, I think Maverick saw how my father treated me, and so he worked even harder to become better, to do better, in an attempt to make my father happy. He never said this out loud, but I know he thought that he could shield me from my father's wrath if he did enough. If he was enough." She snorted. "My father is an asshole. No amount of achievements is going to change that."

I slumped back in the tub until the water came up to my chin. Maverick had told me enough about his father that I already hated the man, but I'd never stopped to actually think about why Maverick put his work above all else. He did it to try and protect his sister, and maybe along the way, he lost sight of how to do anything else.

"One day, at the Academy of Ladies, I'd overheard a few girls talking about the bone collector, who'd they'd heard about from their parents —friends of the frost queen. It was curious, but I didn't think too much of it. Then my brother visited, and he was so full of life. He had this energy about him like nothing I'd ever seen before. He'd always loved history, but never like this. Now it was like he was actually enjoying his profession, not just going through the motions."

I swallowed, watching the water fall from the chute and pool into the tub.

"I didn't tell him my suspicions," she continued. "He was so happy, and I was afraid I'd ruin it. That he'd get it into his head that if I knew, our father could find out, others could find out as well. Of course, I didn't know who the white rabbit was, not until I saw you and Maverick together today. It was fairly easy to piece it together from there."

"You're very clever," I said. "I'm impressed."

"He loves you, you know," she said softly.

I stiffened at that. The word sat like a stone in my gut. Love. "I'm not trying to hurt him," I said. "You must hate me."

"I don't," she said quickly. "I know you're not trying to hurt him. You're trying to protect yourself from being hurt. Mav told me a little about your past. I don't exactly know why you're so sure he's going to trap you like you were trapped before, but I can tell you with certainty he won't."

"And how do you know that?" I asked.

"Because he's already shown you that he'd put everything on the line for you—including his job. He became the bone collector. Do you know what a risk that is to his reputation, to his career? And why would he even be the bone collector? His adventures as Maverick Von Lucas are proof enough that he never needed to be the bone collector to do what he loved, to feel alive. So what was the one thing that kept him in that role?"

Me.

The answer was obvious. Maverick had admitted as much. Of course that was why he'd continued our little game, continued doing dangerous stunts under the guise of the bone collector. Because as Maverick Von Lucas, he couldn't have had anything to do with the white rabbit.

Tears pricked my eyes.

"I don't know as much about the white rabbit, I'll admit. But I'm guessing you served as somewhat of an inspiration for my brother," Annalee continued. "I'm guessing you two had quite a few run-ins, got to know each other over the years."

"Yes," I whispered, tears spilling down my cheeks as I thought about all our adventures.

She was right. Clever, clever girl. Yet it didn't change what I saw in the lake. What I knew to be our path should Maverick and I ever choose a life together.

I stepped out of the tub and wrapped a fluffy white towel around my waist. My skin felt wrinkly and clean. Now all I needed was a long, long nap and maybe I'd feel just a fraction better. When I emerged from the bath chamber, a freshly laundered dress lay on the bed. Red, yellow, and pink roses were embroidered across the bottom of the skirt. The fabric was a nude color with a black lace overlay, and the sleeves were thin straps that I assumed would hang around my biceps. It was beautiful.

Annalee shrugged. "Found it in the wardrobe if you want something clean." Her eyes gleamed.

She was still scheming, but I didn't know exactly what she had planned. If she hoped I'd put on the dress, and Maverick would see me, then we'd fall into each other's arms, she was going to be sorely disappointed. It would take more than a pretty dress to fix the issues that lay between us.

"Go talk to him." She gazed up at me with wide copper eyes, so full of hope.

"Annalee," I started, but she stood from the bed, rushing forward and taking my hands.

"Fine, don't go talk to him, but I heard his door click open while you were bathing, and if I know my brother, he went exploring, probably hoping to root out some secrets from this place. Discover new artifacts, unveil hidden histories. You wouldn't want him to have all the fun, would you?"

She'd poked at my competitive spirit, and damnit, it had worked. Maverick and I hadn't gotten to play our game in almost two years, and I missed it. I snatched the dress from the bed as Annalee squealed and clapped her hands.

I shoved it over my head, then pointed at her. "Don't get too excited. I'm just going to explore a little. I might not even run into him."

She widened her eyes innocently. "Of course."

My gaze caught on the pocket watch laying on the bed, still counting backward, a little past the eleven now, close and closer to the twelve. Annalee trailed a finger down it. "Not long until the opening closes again. Maybe two, three days, at most."

I stilled. "You know what this watch is counting down to?"

Her gaze bounced back and forth. "Don't you?"

"No," I cried, rushing forward and picking it up by the chain. It dangled between us. "We've been trying to figure it out this whole time."

"Oh." Annalee frowned. "I learned about it from one of my friends. A caterpillar, actually."

I didn't even want to know.

She studied it. "There is a way out of the Wilds. The same place where I got in. A hole in the border. But it only opens every few months. The clock counts down to when it'll open again."

Holy fucking spirits below. I looped it around my neck. "We have to tell the others." And come up with a plan to leave. I gazed at the bath chamber longingly. Which meant no more hot baths and nice, comfy beds. We'd be back out in the Wilds before I knew it.

Annalee nodded, lips pursed. "Maybe at dinner tonight?" She bit her lip. "My brother is going to want me to leave with you guys. I don't know if I want to."

I knew what it felt like to be pushed into something that you didn't want for yourself. "Annalee?" I grabbed her hands.

She watched me, a wariness passing over her face.

"I can't pretend I know what you've been through with your father, but I do understand what it's like to feel like no one cares about what you want for yourself, like no one has faith in you or your dreams." I paused. "Figurative and literal. You're beyond brave for forging your own path, for coming here, doing something most wouldn't dare. You're kind, and I can tell you have a special bond with the creatures here. A way with them that I suspect no one else has. No matter what happens moving forward, don't let anyone take that from you. I can't tell you what to do, but I can tell you to follow your heart. It's gotten you this far."

Her eyes welled with tears. "I think we have more in common than I realized."

I winked. "I think you're right."

She slipped her hand from mine. "Now get out of here. Before Aron comes by and has a chance to stop you. I'm going to enjoy a nice, warm bath."

I nodded and shoved my feet in bright red slippers that sat by the door. Time to go explore . . . and try to avoid the bone collector in the process.

Chapter Forty-Eight

MAVERICK

I slipped down the hall, looking behind me to make sure no one had seen me. Aron had warned us not to wander, and El would likely be furious if she knew what I was up to, but there were secrets surrounding this castle, surrounding El, and I intended to find them.

Especially when they had to do with my sister. El had wanted to find Annalee, and my gut told me it wasn't just about Annalee leading her out of the Wilds, that there was more to this story. I just didn't know what. Yet.

The hallway split, one way leading to another hallway with more closed doors, the other leading to stairs that spiraled downward. I hesitated but took the stairs. Voices echoed above me, likely some of the residents, far enough away that I shouldn't have to worry about them.

I'd studied the layout of the original star court castle over the years. We had them on display in our museum. I'd seen them enough times that I could picture it in my head. Not every hallway or room, but the more important ones: the prison cells underneath the castle, the throne room, the king's and queen's chambers.

History usually got buried, so I'd go to the bottom of the castle, see if I could do some unearthing. Honestly, I had no idea what I expected to find, but my instincts told me something was lurking down there. Maybe a secret. Maybe an artifact. Maybe a skeleton. Perhaps a key. Something that would give me answers about El and her motives.

I crept down the stairs, passing a level that led to the throne room. I kept going, the stairs growing steeper, the path growing darker. I tugged at the thread of magic inside of me. Fire burst to life in my palm. I held out my hand and the fireball floated before me, a guiding light as I descended into the belly of the castle.

I shook my head, questions rattling my mind. We'd gotten many of them answered, but so much still didn't make sense. Why had Annalee dreamt of this place? Where had the lightning bolt gone? Who was El? She'd given very few details about herself over our time together.

I didn't think I'd get all the answers today. But I had a feeling I could at least get some.

The fireball floated down and illuminated a dirt ground. An area spread out before me that I assumed was once the dungeons. Aron hadn't mentioned keeping prisoners here, so it should be empty, but I'd be cautious all the same.

A body slammed into mine as soon as I stepped onto the flat ground, and we both went tumbling down. I hit the dirt with a resounding crash, pain splitting through my elbows and knees.

I groaned, still not sure what in the fuck had just happened, until I slowly rolled over to see Emory staring down at me with her wide blue eyes.

She gave a guilty shrug. "Well, I couldn't let you have all the fun, could I?"

I sighed as she scrambled off of me. "I thought we weren't playing any more of our games."

She crossed her arms, and I came to a stand, wincing at the shocks of pain in my bones. Then I took in the sight before me: Emory in a dress. It cinched at the waist, highlighting her curves, the bodice was cut low, the skirt swishing just around her ankles. Fucking fuck. She was always gorgeous, but now, she was . . . something that I couldn't even describe. Words wouldn't do her justice.

"Your sister insisted I wear it," she said, her cheeks flushing.

Ah. Of course she did. Annalee had plans of her own for Emory and me, no matter what either of us wanted. My sister didn't understand my little rabbit, how timid and scared she could be when it came to relationships. If Annalee pushed Emory too hard, she might run for good.

"What are you looking for?" she asked.

I jolted, my gaze shooting up from her waist to her eyes. "I don't know," I admitted. "I just have a feeling that El isn't telling us everything. That she has information we don't. And I want to know what it is."

Emory bit her lip, eyes shifting back and forth as she took in the space. Iron cells lined the walls next to us while tunnels burrowed deeper into the ground, cloaked by darkness. Emory marched to the wall, where a torch was mounted, covered in dust and cobwebs. She grabbed it, then held it right over my fire magic.

"Do you mind?" she asked as she was already lighting it.

I spread out a hand. "Go ahead."

She held the torch to the flame, and it lit up, bright and crackling, providing extra light that Emory shone in all directions. "Well this place isn't creepy at all," she said as the light illuminated a pile of skulls stacked in one corner.

"Maybe that's from Spirit Shadow?" I suggested. "Or the Shadow War."

"Or something else," Emory murmured as she brushed past me. She knelt to the ground, running a finger through the dirt, then lifting it.

Purple dust covered her finger, similar to the black dust coating everything in this land.

"What do you think this is?" She looked up at me from where she crouched. "Do you think it's connected to some kind of ancient magic that no longer exists?"

"It must be something from the Old World," I said. "Every time we've encountered this dust, it's been through objects, artifacts, historical sites."

She pinched the purple dust between her finger and thumb, studying it, brows furrowed, mouth pursed. So fucking adorable. I loved watching her think. I loved seeing the way her mind worked.

She dusted her hands, standing. "But why would it be in the dungeons? Maybe you're right. Maybe there is something here that's important."

She swung her torchlight, then sniffed the air. "Do you smell that?"

I wrinkled my nose. All I could smell was the scent of fresh snowfall and pale blossoms. It smelled like Emory. It smelled like home. My heart clenched.

"Hello?" she asked, brows raised.

Right. I rubbed the back of my neck. "I don't think so."

"It smells like something burning."

"Down here?" I asked, doubtful. "There's nothing to burn." I stalked to a wall and placed my hand against the damp stone. "It's too wet, Emory."

"I've smelled this before," she said slowly. "It's not like a burning fire. Or burning flesh." She shuddered, tapping her chin. "It's more like the smell of a lightning strike . . ."

As soon as the words were out of her mouth, we both stiffened, our gazes locking.

"A lightning strike," I echoed.

She swung the torch again, and I shoved out my hand, forcing my fire magic forward as we followed the scent. Now that Emory described it, I recognized the smell of a sizzle permeating the air.

"You don't think . . ." I couldn't even finish the sentence.

"Why would the lightning bolt be down here?" Emory asked, following my train of thought as we walked in the dark space toward the tunnel, the smell becoming stronger.

"Well, what's a reason to hide something?" I pushed out my hand, making my fire magic fly further along to illuminate our path while Emory's torch lit the immediate area.

"What do you think these tunnels were used for?" Emory asked, raising her torch to light the stone ceiling.

I shrugged. "Well, tunnels like these are common in all the castles. They were built in the Old World as an escape should any attacks happen. They usually lead out of the castle to some undisclosed location. I'm guessing this one does the same."

"I don't want to be spit out somewhere in the Wilds." She swallowed thickly. "Not when it finally feels like we're safe. Even if it's just temporary."

And I had no desire to be separated from my sister once again. "That's not going to happen," I assured her. "We'll see if our suspicions are right, if the bolt is this way, and if it is, then we're going to have a lot to say to El."

Emory shot me a look. "And Aron. He's the one who took the damn thing."

I rubbed my jaw. "You know, I'm starting to think Aron's not capable of lying. He said he didn't know anything about the bolt, and I believe him. He disappeared for hours with that bolt. He probably doesn't remember any of it."

The smell of burning grew stronger, and now it wasn't just fire that lit our path. A bright yellow glow sparked ahead of us, a familiar glow.

Emory walked ahead of me, faster, and I grabbed her arm. Just that simple touch sent a jolt through me. Now that I'd gotten a taste of her, I craved more. Craved what she wasn't ready to give. What she might not ever be ready to give.

She whirled, eyes flashing. "Worried I'll get there first?"

"I'm worried about you."

She faltered, then raised her chin. "I'll be fine, Bone Collector."

I winced at the use of my nickname. It felt like a step backward. Too anonymous. I sighed and let her go, and she turned, continuing down the dark path, the yellow glow growing brighter and bigger the closer we got.

Emory passed my fireball, still holding out her torch, but the light was limited.

"Stay close," I barked.

"You really can't stand me winning," she said over her shoulder, the stubbornness in her voice loud and clear.

"What I can't stand is seeing you hurt," I said back. Spirits forbid something worse happened.

Silence followed, and I wondered if I'd said too much.

"Well, I guess I'll just have to gloat when I win," she said, ignoring my words.

"You really never stop." I took a cautious step forward.

"Not when I'm having so much fun." She raised her torch in the air.

I twisted my hand, making my fire magic twist downward, to light the ground better. "Glad you still have fun with me."

"The bolt!" Emory gasped. It lay in an iron cage that hung from the ceiling of the tunnel.

My gaze followed the trail of the firelight.

"The lightning bolt is in an iron cage." Emory pointed to it. "It'll deflect our magic. El must've done this, right?"

"There's only one way to find out."

We needed to talk to El.

Chapter Forty-Nine

EMORY

I walked out of my room, wearing a new dress—this one floor-length, maroon, and long-sleeved. The bodice molded to my curves, and the sleeves hung across my biceps, leaving my collarbone and shoulders on display. While we'd been foraging in the dungeons, Annalee had been foraging every wardrobe in this castle. She'd found a whole array of dresses and insisted I wear this one. Apparently she was becoming my personal stylist.

We'd been summoned for dinner, but all I wanted to do was trek back down to those dungeons and get the lightning bolt. I'd given up hope that I'd ever find it in this wasteland, and here it was, the key to my freedom. Right underneath this castle.

I took a few deep breaths as I walked to Driscoll's room and knocked on the door. A muffled sound escaped, and my heart picked up its pace. Driscoll sounded like he might be in trouble. Like he was being attacked. My hand hovered over the doorknob, and I was unsure what to do when a scream split the air.

I couldn't take any chances. I turned the handle and burst in.

"Are you okay?" I yelled, then abruptly stopped when I saw Aron kneeling behind Driscoll, who was on all fours. On the bed. Naked. Very naked.

"Oh spirits below." I covered my eyes and wheeled around. "I'm so sorry. I heard sounds, and I thought you were in trouble."

"Oh, I'm in a lot of trouble," Driscoll said. "And Aron is making sure I'm adequately punished for my bad behavior."

The sound of shuffling, trousers being pulled on echoed behind me while I stood there, absolutely mortified.

"I should go," I said. "Again, so sorry for interrupting—"

A heavy hand landed on my shoulder, and I peeked open an eye to see a fully clothed Aron standing there.

Driscoll sat on the edge of the bed behind him, also now clothed, smirking at me while Aron just had the same matter-of-fact look on his face that he always had. Absolutely no shame.

"I should go. Dinner will be served shortly, and El doesn't tolerate tardiness."

"We have a pretty good excuse for being late," Driscoll said in a singsong voice.

Aron patted me on the back and left the room, closing the door behind him.

I pressed a hand to my forehead. "I just completely ruined that, didn't I?"

Driscoll pointed a finger at me. "If that wasn't our third round, I'd be really really mad right now." He cocked his head. "I mean, I'm still a little mad, but you thought I was getting attacked so I can forgive you."

"I did." I took a tentative step forward.

Driscoll waggled his eyebrows. "Technically, I was getting attacked. By Aron's penis."

"Okay." I held up my hands and sat next to him on the edge of his bed. "I get it. You were having great sex." I nudged him. "What changed? I thought you were anti-relationships."

Driscoll tugged at the hem of his forest-green tunic. "Well, someone very wise told me that it was time to start living my life. So I decided to stop worrying about why you and Maverick can't just figure it out or why El has seven swans waddling around her castle. Or why Annalee keeps looking at El like there's something she wants to say . . ." He shook his head. "Anyway. Decided to stop thinking about all of that and just focus on myself."

I laughed in disbelief. "Good for you. Aron is good for you, I think."

Driscoll pinned me with a look. "Calm down. It's just sex."

"Mm-hmm. Sure it is."

"Are you having sex with Hot Professor yet?" he challenged. "Annalee said you two disappeared somewhere together earlier."

I crossed my arms. That girl was downright mischievous. "No, we were doing some investigating."

"Of course you were." Driscoll stood, walking over to his wardrobe and opening it. He grabbed a black jacket that was far too big for him and shrugged it on. "So I listen to your wise words, but you won't listen to mine?"

"I did listen. It doesn't mean I have to take your advice." I strolled across the room to look out the window, but my feet got tangled in something, and I tripped, falling to the ground with a crash.

"Emory!" Driscoll ran to me, crouching down.

"What in the blood and frost . . ." I trailed off, seeing that the strap of a satchel was wrapped around my slippers. Maverick's satchel.

"What is that doing in your room?" I asked Driscoll.

"Oh." He crawled to it, unentangling it from my feet and lifting it. "Aron brought it to Maverick's room, but you all were off on your little adventure, so I told him I'd keep it in here until Maverick got back." His face turned thoughtful. "So really I have Maverick to thank for our sexcapades. I wouldn't have invited Aron in and had the best sex of my life if it weren't for Maverick forgetting his satchel—"

In his attempt to free it from my slipper, it had opened up, all its contents dumping out onto the ground.

"Oh, spirits below." Driscoll knelt down to pick everything up. He lifted a folded piece of parchment. "Why does he have so much parchment? Was he planning on writing a ton of letters while he was here? Sending them off in the post?" He scoffed.

I stared at all the parchment on the ground. Hundreds of little notes, folded. Not just any notes.

Mine.

I scrambled forward, picking them up and opening them in a frenzy. Reading them. My handwriting. My words. And he'd kept every single one. He—brought them with him.

"You know, that's kind of an invasion of privacy." Driscoll stuffed a few back in Maverick's satchel. "I'm all for snooping, but I think I'm actually going to have to put my foot down here."

"I wrote these." I held one up, showing Driscoll the WH.

His eyes widened. "You wrote these?" He glanced back down at the papers scattered everywhere. "And he kept them? And brought them on his journey? Hot Professor is a romantic."

I sat back, surrounded by all the notes I'd written over the years, stunned.

"This has to change your mind, right?" Driscoll asked, shaking one of the pieces of parchment. "If you don't kiss that man, I might."

I gave him a look.

"Okay, I probably won't because of all the sex I'm having now, but Hot Professor deserves to be kissed by someone! Preferably the woman he loves. He risks his life for you, risks his career for you, and now this?"

I stopped abruptly, Driscoll's words hitting me.

"Hello?" Driscoll waved a hand over my eyes. "Is anyone in there?"

"You're right," I said slowly. "He's risked his life for me over and over. He risked his career helping me escape from the frost guards. He risked his career just by being the bone collector."

"Uh, yeah?" Driscoll scratched his head. "I know."

"No." I stood and began pacing. "You don't understand. It's not just that he put me before his job, he puts my life before his. Constantly."

"Uh-huh," Driscoll said. "Everyone knows this. I told you he's kind of obsessed with you."

I thought about that vision in the lake. It supposedly told my future, and I'd believed it. I'd believed it over not just Maverick's words, but his actions. He'd shown me time and time again that he was willing to put me before everything.

"You're having a huge realization, aren't you?" Driscoll asked, then waggled his finger at me. "I can tell by the way your eyes have gone as wide as saucers. About time, by the way."

"I love him," I said, grabbing a handful of the notes. "And he loves me. And I don't care what a stupid lake showed me. That won't happen to us."

"You've lost me on the lake thing," Driscoll said. "But it sounds like you're ready to finally sex up Hot Professor, so yay?"

"I have to apologize. I have to tell him how I feel."

"After dinner, right?" Driscoll asked. "I'm really hungry, and I don't want all the drama to cause a delay."

"Driscoll!" I grabbed his arm and pulled him toward the door.

"What? You heard Aron. El does not tolerate tardiness. And I get grumpy when I'm hungry, so can you just wait until after dinner to make your big declaration of love?"

Dinner. It was in just a few minutes. Everyone would be there. Well, not everyone. Just those of us who'd arrived today, plus El and Aron. I hadn't actually seen any of the other residents who lived here. Just heard them.

Maverick wanted to question El about the bolt. Maybe Driscoll was right. My declaration of love could wait until we found out exactly why El was harboring Spirit Sky's lightning bolt.

Chapter Fifty

MAVERICK

When they said "feast," I'd expected a little more. A long snake lay in the middle of the table, cooked, split open, its green scales glinting under the light of the twilight sky, visible through the glass ceiling above.

We sat around a long table, easily big enough to seat thirty of us, but with our small numbers, our group gathered at the very end, El heading the table.

The sleek black thrones that sat behind her were cracked in half, toppled to their sides, the stairs leading up to the dais broken and splintered. Overhead a chandelier hung sideways, threatening to tumble down at any moment.

A green, murky pond sat next to the thrones, laid in the ground, swans flapping their wings, splashing the water. Emory had been right. The king's swans were still here, and they seemed so . . . normal. No sharp teeth or enlarged eyes or warped bodies. They looked and acted like swans, and it made me wonder about their lifespan. I hadn't realized swans could live so long.

The chandelier swayed, creaking, and Emory gulped, gaze flicking upward.

Aron leaned over and whispered to her, "It hasn't fallen in sixty years, so you should be safe."

She gave him a small smile but glanced up at it again. I sat on her other side while Annalee and Driscoll sat across from us. Emory's snowy alpine scent wrapped around me, and I balled my fists under the table. It took all my self-control not to reach over and place my hand on her leg. Our adventure earlier had been fun, but it had also reminded me far too much of our time as bone collector and white rabbit. Back when we had no chance.

"Snake." Driscoll grimaced at our dinner. "How delightful."

"Our resources are limited here," Aron said.

El raised her hand, folded it in half, then shoved it up in the air. *"You're welcome to shove it up your ass."*

El might not have been able to speak, but she had no problem getting her meaning across.

Driscoll looked from Aron to me. "She just cussed me out, didn't she?"

Aron cleared his throat. "El said that no one is forcing you to eat."

I smirked, and Emory sent me a knowing look.

Aron reached forward and stabbed the middle part of the snake, using his bent fork to pry the meat from its body. Driscoll gulped, a look of horror on his face.

I shrugged and lifted my fork, stabbing into the snake as well. Roasted snake was common in Gilraeth. Not so much in the other courts. Those from Elwen preferred deer and bear, so Driscoll was definitely out of his element.

I plopped a huge chunk of the snake meat onto my plate while Driscoll just continued to stare.

"We have other options I can find for you," Aron offered. "But you probably need your strength after our rigorous activities this afternoon."

I choked on my bite of snake while El just rolled her eyes. Well, this was a new development. Driscoll and Aron. Together. Annalee shot me a sympathetic look that I hated. I didn't need my baby sister feeling sorry for me. I could be happy for others finding love, even if my own love life was in shambles.

"I think I've lost my appetite." Driscoll pushed his plate away, then caught Aron's eye. "Not for sex, just to be clear. We can have all the sex you want, Wolf Man."

A faint smile lifted the corner of Aron's lips. "Noted."

"This is the weirdest dinner conversation ever," I mumbled, and Annalee hid a smile behind her hand. "And it's about to get weirder." My gaze landed on El. I didn't care if it was impolite to talk about this while eating. I couldn't wait any longer. "We know you have the lightning bolt."

All the air got sucked from the room, everyone going completely still. El's expression revealed nothing.

Aron's brows scrunched, an utterly perplexed look pasted across his face. "Lightning bolt?" He frowned at El, who looked away, her long black hair curtaining her face. So Aron hadn't known, and I'd wager a guess that El felt guilty for not telling him.

Annalee's lips pursed, and she looked as confused as Aron.

I nodded to Emory. "Emory and I went on a little stroll and stumbled across the bolt in your dungeons."

"Holy fuck." Driscoll straightened. "It's here? Spirit Sky's lightning bolt is here?"

"Spirit Sky?" Aron echoed. "I am not following."

"Neither am I," Annalee said, propping her chin in her hands.

The swans flapped their wings, feathers ruffling, and I followed Emory's gaze as she stared at them with a parted mouth, then looked back at El, and then back at the swans. I knew that look. Her mind was working through something. Solving something. A puzzle of some sort.

"You're the princess of the star court," she said slowly, turning her wide eyes onto El.

I stiffened, while Aron's brows furrowed, and Driscoll's mouth dropped open.

El huffed and rolled her eyes, signing in quick succession. Aron translated for everyone, but his voice fell into the background as I watched El, reading her movements.

"*Close,*" she said to Emory. "*But no. I'm not Shiraeth's princess. She died with her brothers, her parents. Like I told you.*"

My shoulders sank. It had been a good theory on Emory's part, and it had made sense.

Emory leaned forward. "Okay, maybe I'm wrong about your exact identity, but I'm right about something. You're connected to these swans . . ." She snapped her fingers. "The caretaker."

El's jaw locked, her impassive face still revealing nothing. She was hard to read. Had years of practice hiding her thoughts, I'd wager. But the question was why did she ever need to? What was she afraid of us finding out?

El glanced back at the swans, tears filling her eyes. "*My father,*" she finally signed, her movements slow and careful. Measured. She sniffed, and it was the most emotion I'd ever seen from her. "*Caretaker of the castle swans.*"

Emory had been right. My clever little rabbit.

El continued signing: "*You're wrong. About history. King didn't buy swans. King stole swans. My father begged the king for them back. When the king refused, he begged for a job instead. As caretaker. King agreed. He loved the swans. He fed them, bred them, healed them. My older brothers grew up in castle. Helped father.*"

El stood and walked to the creatures, kneeling at the edge of the pond and laying a hand on one. It bent its long neck into her touch. She looked back, fingers picking up speed in their movement. "*When Spirit Shadow escaped his tomb, he ripped through everything. Everyone. Then the curse happened.*" She gestured to the castle walls, to something far beyond the palace. "*Everyone started transforming. Except Father and brothers. Father said they lucky. Hidden away. Protected. I was lucky too. Protected in my mother's womb.*"

That would have to be some kind of luck. Not only did El's brothers and father live through Spirit Shadow's attack, but on top of that, when this mysterious curse came and affected everyone else here, it somehow didn't hurt them? I understood why El was protected, still in her mother's womb. But the rest wasn't adding up, and based on everyone else's confused expressions as Aron translated, I wasn't sure it made sense to them either.

"Mother was not so lucky," El signed. *"She turned to a creature. Forgot herself. Father kept her imprisoned until she gave birth to me. After she had me, she escaped. Now she tricks travelers who come to her forest. Clever cat."*

Emory met my gaze. Her mother was the cat woman I'd run into. I couldn't imagine the pain of knowing your own mother was alive but no longer herself, no longer with her own mind or faculties. Maybe not even recognizing her own daughter.

"My father, brothers, me lived in the castle for ten years," El signed. *"A safe place. Until* she *came."*

I didn't know who *she* was, but the haunted look in El's eyes as she signed the word sent shivers down my spine.

"I never liked her, never trusted her, but my father fell in love. Like my mother never existed, like she wasn't out there. It made no sense. My brothers were wary, confused, but they trusted my father."

I watched El as she signed, trying to understand where this story was going.

"The woman was cruel to us. Mean. Kept our father away. Dangerous accidents happened to brothers, to me. One of us would take a tumble down the stairs. Were fed a poison berry. Involved in a wild animal attack."

Emory and I exchanged concerned glances while Driscoll and Annalee did the same. Aron just sat back, translating in his calm voice for everyone else. Emerald ribbons lit up the room, casting their hue over everyone's faces.

El still crouched by the pond, more swans gliding over to be near her. *"Father was becoming a shell of himself. Like a ghost. Someone I no longer recognized. He was angry, temperamental, withdrawn."*

El paused, taking a shuddering breath that rippled through her body. No tears fell, but her eyes shone with them.

"Me and my brothers planned to leave, go into Wilds. Get my father away, start over. She caught us, right by the lake outside castle. My brothers forced me to hide, lied to her, saying I escaped. I watched her use a magic item." Her hands flailed for a moment before she spelled it out letter by letter. *"N-E-T. Threw it over my brothers."*

My brows furrowed and Emory looked at me and mouthed, *"Net?"*

It must've come from Sorrengard. That was the only place a net with magical powers would exist.

"When she lifted the net, my brothers had turned into swans. It wasn't a coincidence that those were my father's favorite animal. The curse was a punishment, a mockery. But I didn't know why. She disappeared with him. I haven't seen them since. But I've never stopped asking myself why. Why did she hate Father so much she did this to his sons?"

El swallowed, still not a single sound coming from her.

"My brothers have been trapped as swans for fifty years."

Annalee's eyes shone with tears. "I'm so sorry."

El's jaw locked. *"For months I didn't know what to do. I was alone. Sad."* She strode back to the table and lay a hand on Aron's arm. *"I met Aron. It was his idea to welcome other creatures, to lead them. He gave me community. He gave me purpose. But now I want revenge."*

"Against your stepmother?" I guessed.

El shook her head, eyes flashing with mirth and malice. She swiped her hand across her body. *"Against Spirit Shadow."*

"Spirit Shadow?" I asked. "You're planning revenge against him? Why?"

She gestured around as if to answer the question.

I sat back in my chair. "He's a spirit, El. You don't even know how to kill him. I understand he was responsible for what happened to your mother, for what happened to the entire star court, but this is not something you can take on by yourself."

The set of her pointed chin and raised nose said otherwise.

"That's what you intend to do," Emory guessed. "And you want Annalee to show you the way out so you can do it."

She nodded, then bit her lip, eyes sweeping around our little group as she signed, *"The lake outside the castle—where my brothers turned to swans. We avoided it, always knowing something wasn't right, not since the curse. Last year, my brothers escaped the castle, fled to the lake. I chased them, almost drowning—but the lake showed me future. Not all. Flashes."* She pinched her fingers together. *"Pieces. I learned I can fix my brothers. The lake showed me how. Must not speak. Must knit sweaters made of . . . N-E-T-T-L-E W-E-E-D. Must put the sweaters on my brothers. Then, they will come back."*

My brows pinched together. "The vision showed you all that?"

El nodded.

"Nettles?" Driscoll asked as Aron finished translating, shooting us unsure glances. "Sweaters made of nettles? That sounds awful. They'll pierce your skin. They're full of poison. Your hands will become swollen and bruised."

El's lips thinned.

"She's aware," Aron said gravely. "To undo magic like what her stepmother used takes great sacrifice. She will have to be that sacrifice."

"Do you think your stepmother is the one who cursed everyone here?" I asked, thinking through everything El revealed.

She shrugged.

"We don't know," Aron said. "In all the years I've known El, I've never been able to piece together who her stepmother was or why she came into El's life to wreak such havoc. Nor why she would disappear with El's father. It's clear she must have had a vendetta against El's father, but we can't figure out why."

"So why haven't you started knitting the sweaters?" Driscoll asked. "Or have you? Are the sweaters laying around somewhere?" He glanced around the room like they might be strung up.

El sighed, looking back at the swans.

Aron pushed his plate away, the snake barely eaten. "There's only one court where the nettle weed grows. In her vision, El saw it. The poisonous plant, the shadowy castle, the island and its crocodile-infested waters where they lay."

I drummed my fingers on the table. Only one place like that existed. "Sorrengard," I said.

El's shoulders tightened.

"So you don't just want to go there to get revenge on Spirit Shadow." Emory leaned forward, elbows resting on the table. "You also have to go there to save your brothers."

She signed, *"Solves all my problems. I get my brothers back and kill spirit who took everything away. Then I can focus on my stepmother."*

"Two birds with one stone." I shook my head. "I get it. I still don't think it's smart. If you want to survive, if you want your brothers to survive, you can't make an enemy of an actual spirit. You have no idea the power he wields. You don't even know how to kill him. No one knows how to kill a spirit."

But my words had no effect. I could see in the set of El's shoulders, in the fire behind her eyes, that she wouldn't back down. She'd been planning this for a long time. Now that Annalee was here, she had a way out. If I would allow it.

I peered at her. "So how does this connect to the bolt?"

El shot me a sharp look, then signed, *"No connection. Aron brought bolt. I hid bolt somewhere safe."*

I snorted, not sure I believed her. "You're telling us you want nothing to do with that bolt? That you don't think you could somehow use it to aid you in killing Spirit Shadow?"

Emory stiffened beside me. It wasn't a confirmed theory. In fact, it wasn't a theory at all. Just something Emory and I had pondered over the years through some of our findings.

El gave a vicious shake of her head.

"Okay," I said warily. "Then we'll be on our way with the bolt. Tomorrow. You can come if you're looking for a way out. Annalee will leave with us, so this will be your only chance to escape."

"And we'll have to hurry." Emory lifted the pocket watch from where it lay on her chest. "Annalee knows what this watch does. It's counting down to the next time the border will open. We have days." She glanced at the ticking hand, now halfway between the eleven and twelve. "I think."

I thought I heard Driscoll mutter "great" under his breath.

Annalee glared at me from across the table.

"We have to go home," I said as gently as I could. "We'll find a way to save everyone here. I know you've formed a bond with these creatures, and now you can bring that expertise with you to the outside world."

El looked no happier than my sister. Her jaw worked back and forth, but she gave a stiff nod, then stood, signing *"Excuse me"* before sweeping out of the room and leaving all of us in silence.

<h1 style="text-align:center">Chapter Fifty-One</h1>

EMORY

Maverick stood on the balcony, which was missing half of its thick banister railing. Trees sprouted up through the stone, huge fissures and cracks splintering what once must've been a magnificent piece of architecture.

His back was to me, his clothes now clean, suspenders snapped in place over his crisp white button-up, tucked into his gray trousers. I had to admit, it was a nice view.

His head turned, and I jumped, realizing I'd been caught gawking. "Hi," I said quickly.

He turned fully now and leaned against the part of the railing still standing. "Hi."

I dragged the toe of my slipper over a crack in the balcony suddenly feeling shy. "I kept your notes, too, you know."

"I'm sorry?" he asked.

I gave him a soft smile. "Driscoll accidentally spilled the contents of your satchel, and . . ."

His eyes widened. "And all the notes you wrote me over the years were inside."

I nodded. "I kept yours too. In a little box in the bunker along with all my artifacts. I'd read them over and over, especially on my worst days."

The days when my husband was particularly cruel or life was particularly hard. Those notes were my escape.

He tilted his head. "Why are you telling me this?"

"I'm sorry," I burst out. "I'm sorry about everything. I know you would never trap me in a marriage. I know you would never put your work before me. When I saw that vision, I was scared. It took me right back to my marriage with Gregory, to the worst years of my life. Before I met you. The Maverick you. Well, the bone collector you too. But, well, you know what I mean." I flailed my hands in the air, suddenly not knowing what to do with them.

"Ah." He tipped his head toward the shimmering blue lake in the distance. "So you realized the lake you fell into wasn't the one El was talking about. The one that would show you your future."

I blinked several times. Then looked at the lake he was pointing to. Then back at him. Spirits below. He was right. El had said the lake right outside the castle was where she'd seen her future. She'd been talking about this lake. Not the one we'd encountered on our travels. So what did that lake show?

Maverick took a few steps forward until he was standing right in front of me, then he used his finger to gently close my mouth. "You look surprised by this revelation."

I was. "Somehow, I missed that completely. I was so caught up with the rest of her fantastical story that that detail slipped by me." I searched his face, desperate to know if we still had a chance. Hopeful that I hadn't messed up our relationship so badly that there would be no repairing it. "The truth is, when I started rereading those notes, I realized you would never do any of those things to me that Gregory had. That I didn't care what some stupid lake showed me. We are the ones in control of our fate, and I won't let my past dictate my future."

His lips quirked up, and my heart melted. "Oh yeah?" He stepped closer, his arms wrapping around me.

"Well, your sister and Driscoll might've talked a little bit of sense into me as well."

"My sister can be very, very persistent." He leaned down, trailing his lips over my jaw, and I shuddered.

"Now I know where she gets it from."

"Mm," he said.

"Marry me," I burst out. The second time tonight my brain didn't seem to have any control over my mouth.

Maverick's arm's stiffened, his lips frozen in place over my jawline.

I looked up to meet his gaze, swallowing as my stomach bubbled. "It's okay if the answer is no. I hurt you. I didn't believe in you. I didn't believe in us. If you don't want to marry me anymore—"

He lifted me up and twirled me, his arms tight around my waist. "I asked you first," he said, lips still twitching.

"Is that a yes?" I asked.

He stopped suddenly, arms hugging right under my butt, my hands now propped on his shoulders. I looked down at him with a question.

"Of course it's a yes, Emory Von Lucas."

My breath hitched. I'd been Emory Janey. Emory Growley. Neither names ever felt like me. But Emory Von Lucas. That didn't scare me. It didn't feel like I was losing a part of myself. It felt like I was claiming a part of myself.

I slid down his body until our foreheads met. "I can't believe I get to be your wife. Do you think the frost queen will rescind your position once she knows you've married the white rabbit?"

He stilled, and I hoped he wasn't already regretting this.

"That was beautiful," a wobbly voice burst out.

Maverick and I jumped apart just in time for Driscoll, Annalee, and Aron to appear from behind the thick columns that stood in front of the balcony doors.

"Were you listening to that?" I asked.

"You're getting married." Annalee clapped and jumped up and down.

"Of course we were listening," Driscoll said. "I'm the wedding whisperer. If there's even a hint of a wedding happening, I'm summoned. I can help plan the entire thing. You have no idea how wrong you can go when it comes to dresses, colors, food . . ." He looked us up and down. "Especially you two. Knowing you, you'll want to get married in some ancient, dusty tomb or in the middle of a volcano."

Annalee rushed forward and barreled into Maverick. "I'm so happy for you."

"Congratulations." Aron nodded in our direction. "By the way, the lake we camped at? You are right. It does not show your future."

I quirked a brow. This I wanted to hear.

"It's a reflection of the worst parts of yourself," Aron continued. "It shows you that which you fear the most. That lake actually wasn't made by the curse. It was made long long ago in the Old World. By Spirit Frost. He and Spirit Star were feuding. Spirit Frost was angry and wanted to hurt Spirit Star. He knew the best way to do that would be to hurt her people, so he created a special mirror, one that reflected your worst fears about yourself, then flew high over the star lands and shattered the mirror. It fell into that lake, sinking to the bottom and coating all the rocks. Anyone who looks into the lake sees this ugly reflection of themselves."

My mouth dropped open. So that truly hadn't been a vision of the future.

"What a fascinating tale," Maverick murmured.

It was. But all I could focus on was what a fool I'd been. How I'd hurt Maverick because of my own insecurities.

El clicked open the door, slipping outside and giving us a questioning look.

"They're getting married," Driscoll said. "At some point. If we survive all this and actually get out with our lives intact."

El's eyes widened, then she paused, and slowly signed, catching Maverick's gaze.

He kissed Annalee on the head, keeping an arm roped around her while watching El. "Here? You can't be serious."

"What?" My gaze bounced between El and him. "What did she say?"

He looked over at me. "She said we should get married here. Tomorrow. Before we leave. Make a celebration of it."

Annalee gasped. "Yes, it's perfect!"

"It is," Driscoll echoed. "It totally is. You two should get married."

I frowned. "Tomorrow? But . . . the watch. Time is running out."

Annalee shook her head, black braids falling over her forehead with the movement. "You can take a day. The opening isn't too far from here."

Every protest I might've had never made it out of my mouth as I met Maverick's gaze, his eyes shining brightly. I wanted to be his wife. And I didn't want to wait.

"Tomorrow," I said approvingly.

"We can plan everything," Annalee said, gesturing between herself and Driscoll.

"We can provide the food and music," Aron offered.

"Then it's settled!" Driscoll squealed, and Annalee rushed over to him, grabbing his hands as they whispered furiously.

Maverick held his hand out to me. "So what do you say? Will you do me the honor of becoming my wife tomorrow?"

He reeled me to him, and I choked back a sob. "Of course I will."

He hugged me tight, and I snuggled into his embrace. Tomorrow I would finally get to marry the man of my dreams.

Chapter Fifty-Two

MAVERICK

The next twelve hours went by in a blur. The moment it was decided we were getting married, Annalee whisked Emory away and said they'd need every second available to find her a suitable wedding gown. We'd agreed we would delay leaving by one day so we could get married and celebrate. One day where we could forget everything that was at stake and just find the joy in us.

I hadn't slept a wink. No one seemed to care what I was going to wear, so after all the chaos I'd gone back to my room and lay in bed all night, thinking about my little rabbit. My wife. Driscoll had woken me up early, insisting on helping me dress, stuffing me with food, and prattling on about the importance of impressing my wife on our first night together. I mostly ignored him.

Now that the time to get married had arrived, I had no idea what to expect.

I stood on the same balcony as last night, except it had been transformed. Everyone had come together to lay garlands of flowers across the still-standing parts of the railing. Driscoll had used his earth magic to grow wisteria around the columns, and vines with vibrant pink flowers now draped the space between the columns.

Rose petals scattered across the rough, broken stone of the balcony. This was so surreal. Twenty-four hours ago, I wasn't even sure Emory could ever look at me again. Now she was going to be my wife. Mine. The thought sent a thrill through me.

A slow, romantic harmony filled the air, and I looked over to see Annalee instructing a group of blood beetles as their music vibrated the balcony around us. She winked at me, running a hand over her checkered dress as she swayed back and forth.

Driscoll stood in front of me, and Aron and El stood in the audience.

"We don't have a priest or priestess," I said. They were usually the ones who presided over marriages, made sure wedding rituals set in place by the Seven Spirits were followed so that the marriage was valid.

Driscoll hefted up a heavy book that I just now realized he'd been holding. "Yeah, we scoured this thing last night. Knew you and Emory would probably be sticklers about doing it the right way and blah, blah, blah." He patted it with his hand. "I got you covered. Your marriage will be wholly and fully sanctioned by the Seven Spirits."

The irony behind that statement wasn't lost on me. The Seven Spirits who we'd spent centuries worshiping that might actually have been trapped this entire time and if they just so happened to escape would reign terror on us all. I shook my head. Not thinking about that today.

"We're ready," Driscoll called to the back of the balcony. The heavy curtain of vines obstructing my view of the doors rustled.

Then Emory stepped out from behind them, and I couldn't summon a single thought if I'd tried.

Her white-blonde hair hung in loose curls, just brushing her shoulders. Her pale-blue eyes danced as she met my gaze.

"Your mouth is hanging open," Driscoll whispered.

I snapped it closed. Fucking blood and fire. I was the luckiest man in this spirits-damned world. It was tradition to wear the color of our court during wedding nuptials. I wore a fire-red tunic that Annalee had found, while

Emory wore a long-sleeved glittering, sequined white dress that hugged every inch of her body. I could see the curves of her breasts, hips, ass. The dress looked like it was made from snowflakes. The same ones that flurried around us so many times over the years when we'd met to play our games.

She reached me and folded her hands into mine. Her gaze devoured me as much as I was sure mine was devouring her.

"You're going to have to stop looking at me like that," I murmured. "Or we won't make it through the ceremony."

"Patience, Bone Collector." Her lips twitched. Little vixen. She was enjoying her effect on me far too much. "We have a whole ceremony and celebration to get through."

A growl rumbled from my throat. Driscoll opened the book in front of us, a swath of dust rising in the air.

He waved it away. "Sorry about that!" he said cheerfully, then looked down at the book. "Okay, so we have to say the words, yada, yada, do the hand thing, then thank the spirits for allowing this blessed union, and then comes twining of the magic. Got it." He snapped the book closed and dropped it with a thunk.

Emory and I both winced.

"What?" Driscoll asked, looking between us and the book that now lay on the balcony. "Aren't you ready to get married?"

"It's just . . ." Emory started.

"The book," I finished for her.

"What about it?" Driscoll asked, eyes shifting back and forth.

"Can you pick it up and put it somewhere safe?" Emory gestured inside the castle. "You know, where the elements can't destroy it. I kind of want to look at it later."

"Can you also not drop a centuries-old text like that?" I added.

Driscoll rolled his eyes while Annalee hid a smile behind her hand. "It never stops with you two, does it?"

Aron stepped forward to pick up the book and tucked it gently under his arm. Emory nodded in satisfaction and set her attention back on me, her smile luminous.

The ceremony went by in a blur. I'd been to enough of them that I knew the rituals.

Still, I wouldn't remember the words Driscoll spoke. I wouldn't remember the thanks we gave to the spirits. I wouldn't remember the words we repeated to complete the ritual. I would remember the magic we used. How fire and ice came together, like instead of opposites, they were actually perfect complements of each other. I would remember the smile on Emory's face and the way it promised happiness for all our days to come. I would remember the fire in her eyes and how it flared for me and me alone. I would remember the way her grip tightened over mine, reminding me how she'd never let me go.

I wouldn't remember most of the day, but I would remember how my heart swelled, how it felt like on this day, all my dreams had finally come true.

Chapter Fifty-Three

EMORY

The entire day had been a blur. A long, joyful, tiring blur. We'd finally managed to convince Driscoll that we celebrated, and drank, enough, and that it was time to retire to our room.

Now Maverick clicked the door closed behind him, gaze hooded and sending flutters through me.

"I have been waiting for this moment all damn day." He strode toward me and pulled me to him in one strong, swift move.

"Me too. I can't wait to get some sleep," I said teasingly.

His eyes flashed, then he spun me around and slammed my back to his chest. A gasp escaped my mouth.

"Still tired?" he whispered into my ear as he slowly began undoing the laces on the back of my glittery white dress. "What, exactly, can I do to wake you up?"

Heat flooded between my legs. I was already wet, blood pumping through my veins, but like all the games we played, I was enjoying this one far too much to end it now.

He undid the last lace and pulled my dress open, exposing my back.

His finger trailed down my spine, making me shudder, igniting sparks in the wake of his touch.

He pressed a kiss to my back. "I love you," he said. "I loved you before you had a name. I loved you before you had a face. I loved you when you were just a fur cloak and a lot of sass." His kisses trailed lower, every one making me melt further under his touch.

I'd never liked the heat, always shied away from fire, but this . . . this fire could light me for the rest of my life. I couldn't get enough of it. Of him.

He stopped when he reached the lower part of my dress. "You have far too much clothing."

"Well, I'm still feeling very tired," I said teasingly. "Maybe taking off this dress would help?"

"Oh, I'm sure it would." He whipped me around to face him, then slowly ran his hands up my arms, gripping the fabric that hugged my shoulders and tugging it down just enough to expose my breasts, my peaked nipples. He peeled the dress down until it hung around my hips, my upper half exposed.

He palmed a breast, his lips brushing mine, featherlight, teasing. The heat between my legs flared, the heavy ache growing to a throb.

"Awake yet?" he murmured against my lips.

"I'm getting there." I gasped as he rolled a nipple between his thumb and forefinger.

"Let me try a little harder, then." He dipped his head down and sucked hard on my nipple, his tongue swirling over it in delicious strokes.

I threw my head back, the sensation feeling so damn good. Gregory would never have done something like this. He hadn't cared about my pleasure or making me feel good. Sex had been an obligation, not something enjoyable. Instead of staring up at the ceiling, counting down the minutes until this was over, I never wanted it to end. I wanted to stay holed up in this bedroom with Maverick Von Lucas forever. How I'd ever thought he would trap me was beyond me.

He didn't trap me. He set me free.

"Kiss me," I said, needing his lips on mine.

"Someone's finally waking up." He grinned, and then his mouth crashed into mine.

He teased my lips open, his tongue slipping inside. Both of us grappled at each other while our mouths met again and again, a force of clashing teeth, frantic tongues, and kisses that made that ache between my legs spread to every corner of my body. If I was a fire, then he was the match, lighting me with every touch.

I ripped open his red button-up, the buttons popping off.

"Driscoll's going to be so mad," he said, his eyes twinkling.

"I don't care." I pressed my hands to his chest, feeling his hard muscles, admiring the way the green ribbons of light flooded in through the glass ceiling, dancing over his skin. I shoved down his suspenders, then pushed the shirt off his broad shoulders until he shrugged it off.

He gripped my hips, fingers digging into my flesh and walked me back toward the bed, shoving me onto it and falling on top of me, his hard length pressing into my thigh. A promise of all the things to come.

I trailed my fingers up and down his back as he pressed kisses to my lips, these ones light and feathery, sweet, but just as heated as the others.

"You know, I always thought our first time would be in the bottom of a cave or out in the highlands or in the middle of some dangerous mission," he said.

I laughed, propping myself up on my elbows while he sat up in between my legs. "You thought about our first time?"

It was his turn to laugh. "Are you kidding me?" His gaze unraveled every bit of me, his eyes black orbs as they traveled down my body.

I reached out and tugged at the laces on his trousers, the bulge in his pants stiff, a bead of moisture soaking through the fabric. "When was the first time you thought about it? Fucking me?"

His eyes flashed, and he pounced, his body pushing mine into the soft mattress, arms caging me. He kicked off his trousers, then reached his hand to grab a fistful of my dress, yanking it down and off me. Now the only thing between his hard length and me were my panties, already soaking wet.

"The first time I thought about fucking you?" he echoed, voice low and rumbling. "Was the first night I saw you." He slipped his fingers underneath my panties and stroked a finger down my slit.

I squirmed under the heat of his touch. "That was the first time? But you didn't even know me!"

He chuckled darkly. "I felt like I did. I came up behind you in the highlands, digging through those rocks. So much fire and passion in your voice. I smelled you, that snowy, alpine scent of yours. I knew I had to see you again. Why do you think I created that whole competition?"

My mouth dropped open. "Because you are competitive?"

He pressed a kiss to my nose. "Because I knew I couldn't let you go."

"I can't believe that . . ."

"That night I went home and I stroked myself." His voice dropped low. "I came thinking about the ways I could lift that cloak of yours up and slip inside of you from behind."

"I want that," I said. "Let's do that."

"Oh, we will," he said. "Just not yet. Right now, I want to see your face when I make you come. I want to know what expressions you make when I'm buried inside of you so that the next time I do the same thing from behind you, I don't have to use my imagination. I'll have a perfect picture already there in my mind. And I want you to have that same opportunity, to see what you do to me, Emory Von Lucas."

"Mm," I hummed, reaching down and grabbing his cock. I rubbed my palm over that moistened tip, then gave his shaft a few strong pumps that made him shudder.

I released him, and he pushed his hard length against my slit, rolling the tip around my clit. He was so close to being inside me, and I wanted it so badly . . . but when I'd done this before, it had always hurt, felt so uncomfortable.

I tensed for a moment, and he paused, peering at me. "If this isn't the right time, you can let me know. We have a lot going on. Tomorrow we'll be descending back out into the Wilds."

"No." I cupped his face. "It's not that." I hesitated. "Sex has never felt good for me. I've only been with one man." I groaned. "I don't want to talk about him right now."

His jaw locked. "Neither do I, but I think we need to. Gregory was a sad excuse of a husband, of a man. I'm going to make a guess that most of the time when you had sex with him, you didn't want to. That you weren't wet for him like you are for me."

"No," I said. "Not ever."

He nodded and kissed my forehead. "I think this will be different because you want me." His pushed his cock and it slipped up and down between my folds so effortlessly. "Because you love me."

"I do love you." My smile grew at the words. "So much."

"And I love you," he said. "So if I had to guess, this is going to feel really good for both of us. But if it doesn't—if anything feels off or wrong or painful, you let me know and we'll stop and we'll figure it out. Together."

It was the words I needed to hear, my body already relaxing, melting under his. Gregory never cared how I felt. If I cried out in pain or if I couldn't breathe under his heavy body, he'd just keep ramming into me until he got his release. Of course Maverick wouldn't do that.

I arched into him, just enough so his tip pushed against my entrance, and we both gasped at the contact.

"Do you want to go farther?" he asked.

I nodded. I wanted it so desperately.

Holding my gaze, he thrust in, his hard length sliding into me so easily, my body ready for him, begging for him. He stopped halfway and grimaced, and I knew it was taking all his self-control to stop.

"Does this feel good?" he asked, eyes searching my face.

"Yes." I pulled his face to mine so I could kiss him, and he pushed all the way in. I gasped against his mouth as he filled me, then rolled my hips, and both of us moaned at the movement.

"I want to take this slow," he said. "But I've been dreaming of this moment for six years."

"No." I shook my head, rolling my hips again so that his hard length slipped out and back in.

He groaned. "Oh, fuck."

"Slow has never been our pace," I said through heated breaths. "And I don't want to change that now."

"Thank the fucking spirits," he said, then slammed back inside of me.

He plowed into me in short quick bursts that had my body thrumming. I rocked my body to match his rhythm, his pelvis slapping against mine. He ground into me so that with each movement, his pelvis rubbed into my clit, creating that friction I so desperately needed.

I wrapped my legs around his waist, my arms twining around his neck. He slowed his pace, staying buried in me while shifting his hips to rock in deep, rhythmic movements.

The pulse between my legs grew and spread like a web so that I felt him in every part of my body. It was like I was fire and ice at the same time: melting and hardening and melting again. Over and over until my body was on the verge of shattering in the absolute best way.

Maverick pressed his forehead to mine. "I want to come inside of you. I want you to feel my cock while I'm coming."

Spirits below, that sounded so good. I didn't even know why or what, exactly, those words awoke inside of me, I just knew that I was living for them. That those words were tipping me closer over the edge.

"Maverick," I moaned, and his cock pulsed, showing me exactly what I did to him.

"Say my name again, Mrs. Von Lucas."

I came apart completely, yelling out his name while reveling in hearing mine. He cradled me as I cried out, my release exploding, shattering, breaking me until I was nothing but a limp trembling puddle.

We finally melted into each other, laying there, bodies sticky with sweat and so completely satiated.

After a moment, Maverick slipped out of me and rolled off my body, and I wriggled my back against his chest. One of his arms lay underneath me, the other draped over my bare waist. My heart still hammered, pulse pounding, body buzzing. He nuzzled my neck, and I cuddled deeper into him.

"I don't think I was ready to be apart from you," I said with a smile.

"We're not apart," he said back, laughter in his voice.

"I mean I wasn't ready to not have your cock inside of me."

He choked out a laugh. "Don't worry, little rabbit. We'll fix that soon enough."

And we did. Many, many times over.

Chapter Fifty-Four

MAVERICK

Emory's mouth around my cock might have been my new favorite thing in this world. Besides my cock inside of her. Besides my mouth between her legs. Besides me behind her. Or the sound of her coming. Or the way she said my name when she was at the peak of her release. So maybe I had a lot of favorite things when it came to Emory Von Lucas.

I threw my head back into the pillow as I came with her succulent lips wrapped around my hard length, moaning as she took me, swallowed my release. Fuck, this felt so good. Even better because now she was my wife.

She crawled up my body with a smile on her face. "You ready for another adventure?" She folded her hands on my chest, then propped her chin on them.

"I've come inside of you six different ways. I think that's been adventure enough. Unless you're telling me you have a seventh way? Because I am up for that." I cocked an eyebrow, and she swatted me.

"No, it's something else. Our honeymoon."

I laughed at her teasing, then the laughter died down as she stared at me, dead serious. "You're not joking? How are we going to take a honeymoon? We have to leave the castle in a few hours."

"Our honeymoon was never going to be traditional." She waved her hand. "It's going to be a honeymoon that fits us. We're going to get that bolt."

"And why are we doing that?" I stretched my hands to rest under my head. "El said she'd give it to us before we left."

Emory sat up, bringing the white sheet with her, hard nipples pebbling through the thin fabric. "First of all, I don't trust El, not when it comes to that bolt. Second of all, is that really our style? Being handed something? We don't get anything easily. We fight for it. We risk our lives. That's the fun of it."

She had a point.

I leaned forward and kissed her, then tucked a sweat-soaked strand of hair behind her ear. "So what's your plan, then? That bolt is locked in an iron cage that deflects our magic."

She smiled, then slipped from the bed giving me a view of her smooth, pale skin, lit by the twilight sky. I sat up, admiring my wife, still in disbelief that she was all mine.

She opened the wardrobe and pulled out a hammer and a rope. "I did a little exploring while Annalee was trying to find me a wedding dress. Found this in a closet."

I snorted. My wife was nothing if not resourceful. She set the tools down.

"We're going to use a rope to pull the cage to us, then we'll use this hammer to break it open." She tugged on her trousers, now washed and cleaned by Aron, then grabbed her tunic from where it lay on the floor and pulled it over her head.

"Well?" She grabbed the pocket watch and slipped it over her neck, then tapped it. "What are you waiting for? We're late." She winked. "For a very important date."

We arrived at the dungeon a little while later, and I held a ball of fire in my hand to illuminate our path through the dusty stone prison while the rope was slung over my shoulder and Emory carried the hammer. We passed the pile of skeletons, her hand clasped with mine.

Instead of competing, we were in this together, and it was a new kind of thrill. One I wanted to experience every day for the rest of my life.

"So you think this will actually work?" I asked as we entered the tunnel.

Emory shot me one of those brilliant smiles that lit me up from the inside out. "There's only one way to find out," she said. "That lightning bolt will be ours, and I'll get the frost queen to pardon me."

I thought about the frost queen, the mission she'd sent me on a year ago, how I'd been directly working against her, giving her false leads, pretending I was on the cusp of capturing Emory, only for her to slip through my grasp. I needed to tell Emory at some point. The frost queen was hiding something. I just didn't know what, and right now, it didn't seem to matter all that much, not when there were much bigger things at stake—like our lives. That bolt might very well earn Emory her freedom, but if we didn't have it, I'd find another way.

"Emory, you don't need a bolt to keep from going to the frost prisons."

She sent me a disbelieving look, brow arched. "I don't?"

"No." I drew her to me and pressed a rough kiss against her head. "You have me. And I won't let anyone trap you. Never again."

Her eyes shone. "But your job, your life—"

"You are my life, and I won't let anyone take you from me."

She gave a small laugh. "My fierce bone collector. I was so wrong about you."

"And I was so right about you," I said.

She shot me a curious look. "What is that supposed to mean?"

"I knew you'd come around."

She rolled her eyes and pulled me along the tunnel. "Uh-huh." Her laughter died, smile disappearing as she stopped abruptly.

From out of nowhere, a man stumbled into our pathway. We both took a few steps back, but he lurched forward, eyes wild, his thick salt-n-pepper hair going in all directions.

"She's gone," he said with a shaky voice. "My Bellamy is gone."

Emory and I shot each other concerned glances, Emory letting go of my hand as she tucked a strand of hair behind her ear. "I'm sorry, we don't know a Bellamy."

The man grabbed hold of Emory's shoulders. "You don't understand. She's gone. She's gone and she's never coming back."

"Get your hand off my wife," I said with a deadly calm.

I grabbed the man's arm, ready to wrench him the fuck away from Emory, but she gave a slight shake of her head. My jaw clenched and my grip loosened. The man didn't even seem to notice me. I didn't like it, but I also trusted my wife, and I knew she was capable of taking care of herself.

"I'm sorry Bellamy is gone," Emory said gently. "That must be so hard for you."

He sank his head into his hands. "I failed her. I failed my daughter."

Emory swallowed. "I'm sure whatever happened between you, she'll understand."

"She won't. She's never forgiven me, and I don't blame her. I kept so much from her. To protect her, at first. Then because I was trapped in my own mind, in my own nightmares. Now she'll never know the truth."

The man had been driven mad, that much was clear. He must've been one of the residents here, gotten lost and wandered into the dungeon. Tears filled his eyes and slipped down his pale cheeks, his green eyes so bright and glassy.

"I can't take this anymore." He grabbed his hair and pulled. "Get out of my head. Please. Get out."

He turned and ran in the opposite direction.

"Wait!" Emory reached out a hand and shot me a questioning look.

I sighed and shoved a hand over my hair. "Let's go get him before he hurts himself."

Emory made to move, but I grabbed her hand. "Nothing stupid. No risking yourself for this man. I just married you, and by the spirits, I plan on loving you for a long, long time."

She pressed a brief kiss to my lips, then set off after the man. I shot my fire magic forward and raised my hand to lift it higher so that it cast its light wider, gave Emory a path forward.

"Wait," she called out to the man, who'd disappeared. "We can help you get back to your room, to safety. Please stop!"

We ran deeper into the tunnel, the man becoming visible again as he limped his way forward.

Emory lunged forward and grabbed the man's arm.

He erupted into sobs. "It's my fault. This is all my fault." His gaze landed on Emory, on me. "You're going to die. Both of you. Everyone in this world. She will make sure of it."

"Who?" Emory asked.

He gripped his head again. "Get. Out," he bellowed.

I touched her arm. "Emory, let's just get him back and try again for the bolt a little later." We were running out of time, but this man was unraveling, and I was afraid he'd do something dangerous, turn on us if we didn't get him to safety.

My gaze flicked upward.

That's when I realized a key detail we'd been missing. Emory must've noticed at the same time.

"There won't be a later," she said, raising a shaky finger to point to the space in front of us.

There wouldn't be. Because the lightning bolt was gone.

Part Four

"It's no use going back to yesterday, because I was a different person then."

Chapter Fifty-Five

Aron paced in front of us, his shirt off while Driscoll sat on the bed, now fully clothed, though they'd been naked when we burst in on them, and Driscoll had made it clear he was starting to think I was doing this on purpose. We'd brought the raving man with us, and he sat in the corner, shivering, still crying. Snot dripped from his nose, and he'd folded himself into a huddle, rocking back and forth, muttering to himself.

"You broke my sex toy." Driscoll gestured to Aron, who was still pacing, shooting horrified looks at the man. "Are you happy? I finally find someone kind and amazing who actually likes my brutal honesty and gives it back tenfold—also is hung like a horse—and now he can barely function!"

Maverick's arms were crossed, and he rubbed his jaw as his gaze stayed on Aron.

"Aron?" I asked, stepping forward.

He whirled on me, blue eyes wide. "It shouldn't be possible. He disappeared over fifty years ago."

"Who?" I threw out my arms. "This isn't making sense. Please explain what's going on."

Aron pointed to the man. "That is El's father."

We all stilled, our gazes turning on him.

"He must've survived the Wilds all this time," Maverick said, striding toward Aron and putting a hand on his arm to stop his pacing. "Weirder things have happened."

Aron nodded, his eyes crinkling like he still couldn't believe it. "I've never met him, but I've seen paintings of him in this castle. The king held him in high regard. I'm sure that's him."

I wrinkled my nose. "Wait, so El is Bellamy?"

At the sound of her name, the man began wailing louder.

"Yes," Aron said. "And if the lightning bolt is gone, then so is she." He hesitated. "I should have said something sooner. Now I regret not speaking up."

I stilled. "Said something about what?"

Aron frowned. "I didn't remember anything about it until you mentioned the bolt on our first night together. It bothered me because it seemed so familiar. Then I started having flashbacks to dreams. Dreams I had in my wolf form of that bolt before I left the Wilds. I think that's why I left. To find the bolt."

"And you think El is the one who made you have those dreams?"

He nodded slowly. "I think maybe she kept part of that vision in the lake to herself. I think she may have seen that bolt. Maybe have known it was the weapon she needed to help save her brothers."

"She wants that bolt to kill Spirit Shadow," I guessed. "She lied to us because she knew she'd have to fight us for it. She knew we wanted it for our own purposes." I gasped. "That's why she suggested we get married. To delay us."

"To distract us," Maverick said, a grave expression on his face.

We'd definitely been distracted.

"So El—Bellamy—orchestrated this entire thing?" Now I started pacing, hands clasped behind my back. "She entered Aron's dreams in his wolf form. She had access to him. So it makes sense that she could. She put that bolt in his mind so he'd want to go after it. That's why he ambushed us in the frost court. Took the bolt and brought it directly to her."

Aron's frown deepened.

"Does she even know her father is alive?" Driscoll asked, shooting disturbed glances at the man. "Has he been lurking all this time beneath the castle?"

"She doesn't know," Aron said. "She'd never have left him here."

So I'd been right to not trust El—Bellamy—whatever she called herself.

"As for your second question," Aron continued. "I'm not sure where he's been this whole time."

Driscoll still sat on the bed in a stunned silence. He opened his mouth, then closed it, then opened it again.

I pinched the bridge of my nose as the man continued to rock back and forth in the corner. I gestured to him. "What happened to him?"

"I don't know," Aron said. "This was not how El described him to me."

"Oh, you mean fifty-five years ago?" Driscoll asked.

"We have to find Bellamy," I said to Maverick. "She has the bolt."

"I agree," he said.

"I guess that means the party is over." Driscoll stood. "Safety and food and sex—all gone." He swiped his hand across his body. "Guess it was just too boring to become the norm."

"Driscoll," I said gently. "You can stay here if you want. With Aron." I nodded toward him.

A look of panic crossed Driscoll's face.

Aron didn't seem to notice as he stepped toward me. "I'm coming with you. I have to find El and tell her about her father. She cannot win against this Spirit Shadow. In truth, I never thought she'd find a way out of the Wilds. I never thought she'd find a weapon powerful enough to kill a spirit. It didn't seem probable. I see now I underestimated her. But she won't survive this journey. It's my duty to help her."

"Why?" I asked.

Aron looked at me with that steadfast gaze. "Because she is my friend. She took me in when no one else would. She was never afraid of me, of my wolf form. She saw the beauty in the beast. I will owe her for the rest of my days."

"She manipulated you, Aron," Maverick said. "She kept things from you."

"I'm not saying she's perfect." Aron shrugged. "Or innocent. She's neither. But she is my friend, and she has done a lot of good for many of us here in the Wilds. So I'm coming with you, and I am helping you find her. I will do my best to get that bolt back for you. I don't know why you want it, but I trust that you both will not use it for dark purposes."

Aron was truly one of the kindest souls I'd ever met.

He turned to Driscoll, walking toward him and taking his hands. "You can stay here if you want. Wait for me. I'd like that very much actually."

"Uh." Driscoll let out a nervous laugh. "I'd love to, really. But I have . . . things . . . going on back home." He slipped his hand from Aron's and scratched his head. "Laundry and stuff . . ."

Maverick smirked, and I held back a laugh despite the situation. Driscoll was flustered. And nervous. And I was loving every minute of it. If Leoni were here, I'd bet she'd love it too.

"I understand," Aron said.

"Okay." Driscoll clapped his hands together. "Let's get this journey where we're probably all going to die over with."

"Let me just wake Annalee," Maverick said, stalking toward the door. He reached it, hand hovering over the handle, frozen mid-step.

I met his gaze as he turned his head, and my stomach dropped like a rock. Maverick threw open the door and sprung from the room, but I already knew the horrible truth, which was confirmed when Maverick yelled Annalee's name with gut-wrenching pain.

Bellamy hadn't just taken the lightning bolt. She'd taken Annalee as well.

<h1 style="text-align:center">Chapter Fifty-Six</h1>

MAVERICK

I was going to kill her. When I found Bellamy—and I would find her—I would not be responsible for my actions. I'd told her my sister was off-limits. Annalee had been through enough already. She'd been fed visions and dreams of this place for years by some unknown source that I was starting to think was connected to Bellamy—maybe it was Bellamy herself, though that still didn't make sense since she couldn't have that much power. Maybe it was the mysterious stepmother who'd cursed Bellamy's brothers. I didn't know. But either way, my sister had been led here under false pretenses, and just when I'd found her, when I'd finally gotten her back, she'd been taken from me again.

I forgave Bellamy once, but I would not be so forgiving this time.

"Do we even know where they went?" Driscoll asked. "I mean Bellamy and Annalee have quite the head start. While we've been . . . occupied . . . all night, they've been traveling." He held up a finger. "And let's not forget that Annalee and Bellamy are like the Wilds whisperers. Annalee does the freaky shit where she can get any of these monsters"— he looked at Aron—"no offense—to become like cuddly little puppies, and Bellamy knows this place better than anyone since she's the only one with her full memories intact."

Well, Driscoll had laid it out about as plainly as possible. He was right. None of it worked out in our favor. But I hadn't given up when I'd first realized Annalee had come here to the Wilds. I hadn't given up in finding Spirit Sky's bolt and stealing it. I wouldn't give up now either.

"We're going to find her," Emory said from beside me, giving my hand a squeeze. "We're the ones who find the hard-to-find things, right?"

I gave her a strained smile. "Right."

Aron ignored all of us, crouching on the ground outside the castle, staring at the black-dusted road.

"I'm so sick of all this dust." Driscoll kicked it up in the air, and it whooshed around him, pushing him this way and that. "It's tickly and shimmery and pretends it's all pretty and nice, but really it's like an annoying swarm of gnats you can't get rid of. You're not special!" he shouted at it.

The dust blew around him with the breeze, then fell back to the ground.

"Driscoll, are you okay?" Emory asked, giving him a curious look.

"Fine," he said, tone back to chipper. "Why do you ask?"

"No reason," she mumbled.

"The dust is the least of our problems right now," I said. "And with the wind blowing it all around, we can't even use it to track them."

"Maybe we should just start walking?" Emory suggested, biting the inside of her cheek.

"I can scent them out," Aron said. "Not as strongly as in my wolf form. It's faint, but they were here."

"Of course they were here," I snapped. "We're right outside the castle." I sighed. "I'm sorry. I'm just . . ."

"It's okay." Emory squeezed my arm. "I'm here for you."

I pressed a kiss to her forehead, grateful for my wife. My wife. Even in the turmoil of the current events, those words would never get old.

"So what do we do?" she asked. "Let Aron track them for us?"

"Too bad he's not in his wolf form," Driscoll said.

"Unfortunately, I still cannot control that," Aron said. "And even if

I could, I don't know that I would retain much of myself, be of much help."

"You brought that lightning bolt to El," Driscoll said. "Also, you took us to that crypt. I think you knew we needed El, needed guidance, so you brought us to a place she'd find us all together."

"Perhaps." Aron shrugged. "But I would rather not test that out when we don't have the luxury of time."

Driscoll rolled his eyes. "I'm just saying, I think you have more control in your wolf form than you realize."

The dust blew up in my face again, swirling around me, and I swatted at it. "I'm sick of it too," I said. "Does it ever stop moving?"

"Not really," Aron said. "It's harmless, but it can be annoying."

"Too bad Annalee isn't here," Driscoll said. "She'd probably sing to the wind or something and it would just magically calm the dust down."

I stilled, staring at the dust as it swirled round and round.

"Are you okay?" Emory asked, putting a hand on my arm. "Apart from the obvious reasons why you're not okay."

"Tell the wind which way to blow," I said.

Emory's eyes lit up with understanding. "Yes," she breathed.

"Great." Driscoll threw up his hands. "So let's tell the wind to blow us out of here."

"That's exactly what we're going to do," I said, the realization hitting me as the dust blew with the wind, black motes dancing in the air.

"Well, he's lost it," Driscoll said.

"No." Emory crouched down and swiped at the black dust. "He hasn't. We can tell the wind to blow in the direction that Annalee and Bellamy went. And then the dust . . ."

"The dust will be like a guide, a visual path for us to follow," Aron finished.

"Exactly," I said, feeling just a little less devastated than I had a moment ago. "We might just catch them yet." I glanced at Emory. "How much time do we have?"

She pulled the pocket watch from her trousers, clicking it open. "Not much. We might barely make it."

I nodded. "Then let's not waste any more time."

Chapter Fifty-Seven

Sure enough, that damn nuisance of a dust finally proved useful. We followed its trail, swift and without taking any breaks. It took us hours to get to the border, and Aron was able to keep us from getting eaten by sinking sand, sticky trees, caterpillars as big as logs, and the bright hillsides.

Every time I stumbled, Maverick was right there to hold me up, to keep me going. We'd been through a lot over the years, and at least we'd gotten a few solid days to rest. Well, we were supposed to be resting. I couldn't exactly call all the things Maverick and I had done last night rest. But it had been good. Beyond good. It had restored parts of me I thought lost forever. He'd lit a fire in me that melted all those icy walls I'd put up so long ago. Maybe it was better than rest. It was exactly what I'd needed.

"Up ahead," Aron called from in front of us. He stood at the top of a winding path, the black shimmers of dust blowing past him.

Driscoll reached him, and Maverick grabbed my hand as we ran up the hill as fast as our legs could carry us.

At the bottom, Annalee and Bellamy faced a towering wall of fire, ice, earth, wind, shadow, and star. Vines made up the bulk of it, but they spit out fire, their exterior shimmering hard with ice, which would make it impossible to climb. Shadowy tendrils reached out, lashing at Annalee and Bellamy. Bellamy drew closer, and a blast of wind blew her backward. The seven swans surrounded her, flapping their wings and backing away. Her brothers. So she was taking them with her on this journey.

I admired her grit, but she'd never make it out of the shadow court alive with these seven swans. She'd never knit those sweaters of nettle. I wanted her to succeed. I wanted her to be reunited with her brothers. But not like this. Not when this was clearly a suicide mission.

I gasped as my gaze dropped to the bottom center of the border. There it was: a hole big enough for someone to crawl through. Annalee had been right. Of course she'd been. She was right about everything when it came to this place. That was our chance at escaping. I pulled the pocket watch out. The big hand was one tick away from the twelve. We had an hour, if we were lucky.

"Bellamy, stop!" Maverick's voice rang out, and Bellamy whipped around, her long black hair whipping around her angular face.

"It's okay, Mav," Annalee said. "I wanted to help her."

We all stumbled down the steep hill to the little grassy plain, the black dust that had led us here settling down on the tips of the grass. The wind calmed, Bellamy glaring at us while clutching the lightning bolt tight.

"Give us the bolt," I said as we approached. "It's not yours."

She signed, and I understood enough of it. *"Not yours either."*

I crossed my arms. "Except we're the ones who found it. We need it. I need it. You don't even know if that will kill Spirit Shadow. You have no idea the power it wields. What it might do. The consequences of using it. It needs to be studied, tested, kept in a safe place."

From the hard set of her jaw, I could tell my words hadn't moved her. The clock ticked steadily toward twelve, getting closer. "We don't have time." I showed her the clock.

Her gaze softened, and I thought maybe I'd gotten to her.

"What does the bolt have to do with you, Mav?" Annalee asked, staring at him curiously.

"It's a long story." His gaze never strayed from Bellamy's face.

"El." Aron stepped forward. "I've stood by you all these years. I've never wavered in my loyalty. But this is a fool's errand. Your father, he's—"

Before Aron could finish, Bellamy raised her hand to the sky. The stars brightened, their glow stretching down, shining on each of us, our own individual spotlights that left us transfixed. Suddenly my eyes were growing heavy. So, so heavy.

It dawned on me too late what was happening. "She's using her star magic." I stumbled into Maverick, whose own eyes were fighting to stay open.

And she was using it to put us all to sleep.

I stood in the frost court. My boots sunk into cushy snow. The cold wind soothed me, and I raised my face to a grey sky, thick flakes falling from it. Home. I was home. Then I remembered all the events that had just occurred.

This wasn't real. I was dreaming. Asleep. I pinched myself.

"Wake up," I said. "C'mon, wake up."

I pinched myself again. Harder this time. All I managed to accomplish was giving myself a thick red mark on my hand.

"It won't work," a voice said.

My head snapped up as Bellamy emerged through the flurries. Her voice was low, raspy but smooth. It reminded me of a singer. Her blood-red dress was stark against the snow, and in this dreamworld it wasn't torn or raggedy, but smooth and full and clean. Her raven hair fell in smooth waves past her shoulders.

Her hand moved to her throat. "The only place I can talk. In dreams."

"Your father is alive," I burst out.

Her face went slack for a moment, but then her usual hard mask returned. "You're lying," she said. "Trying to catch me off-guard."

"I'm not," I said gently. "Something's wrong. His brain. He's troubled."

"Then he's already gone." She sucked in a shuddering breath. "I have to focus on saving my brothers. I owe them this. I owe them everything."

Snowflakes swirled between us.

"But not like this. Not when the stakes are so high." My voice took on a pleading tone.

"You just want the bolt," she said. "And you're not going to get it."

I threw out my hands. "Despite what you believe, I don't just care about myself. I do care about you, El."

She flinched.

"I care about you and your brothers."

"Then you know why I have to do this," she shot back.

"So that's it? You're going to leave us while we're all asleep, defenseless? You're going to escape through that hole and keep us trapped here the same way you were trapped so long ago?" Tears welled in my eyes at the injustice of it all.

Bellamy looked away, the wind blowing her black hair so that it covered her face. "I don't have to explain myself to you."

"Yet you want to." I stepped toward her. "That's why you're here, in my dreams." I said my suspicions out loud, even if they seemed impossible. "You're the one who lured Annalee here, aren't you? But why? How?"

I half-expected her to laugh or tell me to stop being crazy. Instead, her eyes widened. "How could you know that?"

"You just put all of us to sleep at once. Five people. There is no star elemental in recorded history with that kind of power. To have the power to enter a girl's dream who lived all the way in the fire court—it would be someone with the kind of power to sink five people into unconsciousness at the same time."

It didn't make sense. Star elementals could enter someone's mind when they slept, to create nightmares or the best dreams. They could put a person to sleep, but typically just putting one person to sleep could drain their magic, except for the strongest of star elementals. To reach out to someone in another court halfway across the continent, Bellamy must've had powers far greater than I understood.

She swallowed, gaze still guarded. "My brothers and I always had powers that far exceeded other elementals of the star court. My father didn't know why. He and my mother were baffled by all of us. Well, my mother never knew me. She had already transformed by the time she gave birth to me. But my father told me that before the Shadow War, when they were just a normal family, they'd agreed that my brothers shouldn't tell anyone about their powers."

I'd never heard of anyone wielding magic like what Bellamy had used.

Bellamy waved a hand in the air. "They instructed my brothers to act like everyone else. They didn't want any attention, afraid of what that attention might bring."

"Haven't you ever wondered?" I asked. "Where that kind of power came from?"

"Of course I have," she snapped. "But my parents didn't want to risk our family being ripped apart, thrown in the star prisons, or worse, executed. You know how the courts could be about anything different, anything suspicious, anything dangerous."

I did. The seven courts were infamous for being terrified of conflict of any kind, terrified the Seven Spirits would swoop down and take our powers away if we acted out in any way. What fools we'd all been.

Bellamy reached out a finger, and a snowflake fell onto it. She stared at it in wonder. I didn't know if she'd ever been out of the star court in her life. She might've never even seen snow before, other than far in the distance on the peaks of the Glacier Mountains.

"That day I fell in the lake and saw my future, I saw the bolt, saw Aron in his wolf form. And I saw the girl who would ultimately help me escape the Wilds."

"Annalee," I said.

Bellamy stared off into the distance, like she was reliving these memories. "I knew what she looked like. I could feel her soul, her magic. I entered dream after dream after dream, spent night and day searching through minds. It took a while, but I found her, and I started filling her dreams with visions of the Wilds, giving her this purpose, this obsession.

I knew eventually she would come and show me the way out. It took five years. But now she's here and fulfilling that vision I saw of my future."

"Futures can be changed."

Bellamy shook her head, her brown eyes swirling with so much anger. "Not this one."

"So you saw yourself killing Spirit Shadow with the bolt? You saw success?"

She looked away, which gave me all the answers I needed.

"This is a fool's mission, Bellamy," I said again. "You're doing all of this, and you don't even know if it will work."

She didn't answer, her jaw set, arms crossed.

"So what happens now?" I asked.

"You'll wake up, and I'll be gone." She pursed her pink lips together.

"You're just going to leave us here?"

She rolled her eyes. "It's only a few months until the border opens again."

"A few months in a dangerous land," I argued. "Where we can't get to the outside world and give them all this information. They need to know about this, Bellamy. This place. Everyone here."

"So they can kill them?" She whipped around. "I don't think so."

We wouldn't let that happen. Change was coming. The frost queen might've been the last leader following the old ways, staunchly against change. New rulers were emerging in every court, and from what I'd heard, they all were on the same page when it came to no longer sweeping the atrocities of our past under the rug. I had to believe they'd choose to protect these innocent souls.

"I'm going to stop you," I called after her.

Bellamy looked over her shoulder as she walked away, her red dress fluttering behind her. "You can't. I'm already gone."

Chapter Fifty-Eight

EMORY

I woke with a gasp, no longer feeling that delicious cold prickling over my skin. Dust swirled in my face, black and shimmery as always.

I blinked a few times, remembering my dream, my talk with Bellamy. Embers spat from the wall in front of me, floating in the air. No hole to sneak through. My heart sank as I looked at the watch, already ticking past the twelve. The opening was closed.

It was over. Bellamy had escaped with the lightning bolt, and we'd be stuck here for at least a few months. There was no telling the damage that would result from this, what Bellamy might do by trying to use that bolt to kill Spirit Shadow, what her actions might do to incur his wrath in return. He might be trapped in Sorrengard, but we had no idea how close he was to collecting the other weapons, and now Bellamy was bringing one directly to him. This was a disaster.

The others slowly awakened around me.

Driscoll clutched his head.

Aron's jaw locked when he saw Bellamy had left, and Maverick immediately locked eyes with me, then looked at his sister. Annalee lay on the ground, unmoving. Maverick scrambled to her side.

"Annalee." He shook her gently.

"I'm sure she's just still sleeping." I crawled to them while Aron helped Driscoll to a stand.

"Bellamy came to me in my dream," Aron said. "She's gone."

There was a sadness I'd never heard in Aron's voice.

"I know she was your friend." I looked up from Annalee's still form, "And I'm sorry she used you like that, manipulated you to bring that bolt to her."

Aron's impassive face betrayed nothing. "She did a lot of good. Not just for me, but for everyone. If I were to compare her actions, the good would far outweigh the bad."

Ever the logical one.

Annalee groaned, and Maverick sucked in a sharp breath. "Hey," he said as she blinked her eyes open. "Are you okay?"

"Why are you hovering over me?" She sat up and gave him a light shove.

He clapped a hand on her shoulder and hoisted her up. "Because I'm your older brother. That's what older brothers do."

"I'm fine." She rubbed her eyes. "I'm guessing Bellamy is gone?"

All of us came together in a circle, and I nodded.

"There's something you all should know," I said. "Bellamy visited me as well. She's the one who infiltrated Annalee's dreams, brought her here. When she saw her future, it was Annalee whom she saw helping her escape from the Wilds. She found Annalee and infiltrated her dreams to make her obsess over this place until she'd have no choice but to come."

"I have a confession to make too." Annalee bit her lip.

Maverick's gaze swung to her, and he planted his hands on his hips. "What did you do?"

Annalee winced. "I knew she wanted to escape without you. She told me. She didn't force me or kidnap me. She was upfront about her plans, and I agreed."

Driscoll sucked in a sharp breath while Aron stayed silent, patient, waiting for an explanation.

Maverick closed his eyes, his fists balling tight, and I lay a hand on his arm, hopefully a reminder to not lose his temper.

"Why would you do that?" he asked through clenched teeth.

"Because I don't want to leave here, and you wouldn't listen. You kept making plans for me. I like the Wilds."

"Because you were manipulated into it," Maverick shot back. "You heard Emory. It was Bellamy who did all of this." He gestured to her. "I don't know how she did it, how she could summon that kind of power to infiltrate your dreams from so far away, but she did."

That would be another conversation we'd have to have at a later time.

"I don't think that's it," I said, and Maverick's sharp gaze landed on me. "Your sister knows this place better than anyone. Yes, Bellamy sent her those visions, but she didn't teach Annalee how to make blood beetles sing."

"Technically, they weren't singing," Driscoll said.

I shot him a pointed look. "Bellamy didn't teach her how to host tea parties for the Mad Hatter or talk to caterpillars. Annalee did that all on her own. She has a special gift, and I don't think we should discount that."

Maverick's gaze softened, and he looked up at the twilight sky. "Okay, then."

Annalee mouthed "thank you," and I smiled in return.

"So what do we do?" Driscoll spread his arms wide. "This was our only way out."

"Maybe not," I said. "We could find another way. There has to be other openings like this."

Aron made a strangled sound, and all of our heads snapped in his direction. He hunched over. He shot up, ramrod straight, his head bending backward, veins popping in his throat.

We all stepped back, except Driscoll, who put a hand on his shoulder. "Aron? What's going on? Why are you so veiny all of a sudden?"

He didn't answer, face turning a dark shade of red, all his muscles straining.

"Is he sick?" Annalee said with wide eyes.

"I don't think so," I said slowly.

His teeth lengthened to sharp canines that poked from his mouth. "Step away from me," he said through clenched teeth. "I can't control myself. Don't. Want. To. Hurt. You."

Driscoll's eyes widened in understanding.

Maverick pushed me and Annalee behind him. "He's transforming."

Bloody fucking frost. That was all we needed right now.

But Driscoll didn't move, keeping his hand on Aron's arm as fur began to sprout across his body. "I know that you won't hurt us. You might say you have no control, but you're like the most controlled person I've ever met. You're too in control of every emotion. I think it's time you actually let loose."

"Driscoll," I warned. "Step back. Please."

"Listen to her," Aron gritted out as he violently hunched over again, his clothes and skin ripping open as a furry back sprouted up.

Driscoll stayed planted to his spot. "No. I think you all are wrong and being kind of close-minded right now."

My mouth dropped open. "Driscoll, he tried to kill us in his wolf form. Multiple times."

"But he didn't!" Driscoll shot back as Aron's hands and feet transformed to large paws with razor sharp claws.

"She's. Right," Aron screamed as his nose turned into a long snout.

There was almost nothing left of his human self, save for his eyes, which were rapidly changing from their ice blue to a dark red. He finished transforming, and now the white wolf towered over Driscoll, who stood firm, though I could see the slight tremble in his hands. The wolf threw his head back and let out a howl that split the air.

"Wow," Annalee breathed.

"Do you know how to calm him down?" I asked, Maverick still standing in front of us, fire flickering from both of his outstretched hands, even though we knew it was useless against the white wolf.

Annalee raised an eyebrow. "I don't think I need to."

The wolf looked down at Driscoll, teeth bared, but he didn't attack.

"Hey, Hot Wolf Man," Driscoll said weakly. "I know you're in there somewhere."

Something slipped around my waist. At first, I thought maybe it was Annalee's arm. But it squeezed tight enough to hurt.

I looked down, realizing it was a vine from the wall. We'd gotten too close while trying to stay away from the white wolf. Fuck.

The vine wrenched me backward, and Maverick whirled. "No!" he ran toward me, but I shoved out a hand.

"Stay back," I warned. "We don't need it getting you too!"

Driscoll's head snapped up, his eyes filled with horror while Annalee's face twisted in fear.

"What do we do?" Driscoll yelled.

Maverick threw a ball of fire at the vine, but it dissipated, just like it had when it encountered the white wolf, ever a reminder that our magic didn't work well here, not against these foes.

The vine reeled me closer to the wall, and I squirmed, fighting against it and trying to lunge forward. The wall hissed and spit out all the different types of elemental magic. If I got too close, the impact of the magic alone would kill me.

"Let loose," Driscoll murmured, then looked at the white wolf. "Okay, Hot Wolf Man, it's time to let loose. I need you to save my friend, okay? So go do your wolf thing. I know you're in there, Aron, and if you were here instead of the wolf, you'd know what to do. You'd help us save her."

The white wolf didn't move, just stayed in that crouched position, eyes assessing the situation.

Panic stretched across my chest, making it hard to draw a breath. If something didn't happen in the next few seconds, I was going to die.

"Emory!" Maverick lunged toward me again, but Annalee caught him around the waist, and Driscoll grabbed his arm. "Let me go!" He thrashed against them. "I'm going after my wife!"

A roar shook the ground, a blur of white streaking through the air as the white wolf charged straight for the wall. Vines shot out at him that he snapped with his massive jaws. Fire, ice, and wind bounced off of him like he was a shield himself. The vine that was reeling me back toward the wall froze, and I hung midair. Pops of fire grazed my cheeks while wind barreled past me. Ice shards cut at my clothes, tearing the sleeves of my tunic.

Everyone else stayed completely still, watching the white wolf leap toward the wall, his roar echoing around us. A vine punched him in between the ribs, and he landed with a deafening thud. I stared in horror, convinced this would be the white wolf's end. He bounced back up and snapped the vine in two. Then he leapt off the ground, launching straight past me and right into the wall.

Everything exploded at once. Fire, ice, wind, plant, shadows, and some kind of haze that made my eyes grow heavy again. It felt like the magic Bellamy had used on us. Star magic. It must've only got released when the wall was hit. The vine slipped from my waist, and I fell to the ground, trying my best to lift my head amongst all the magic raining down over me, but I couldn't fight the urge to close my heavy, heavy eyes.

With a final glance at the blurry figure of the white wolf laying on the ground next to me, I fell into complete darkness.

Chapter Fifty-Nine

EMORY

"Well, this is certainly not what I expected," a voice said from above. One I faintly recognized but couldn't quite place in my mind-muddled state.

A blast of wintry wind swirled around me, and the cold jolted me from my stupor. I shot to my feet, already seeing Driscoll, Maverick, Annalee chained to trees nearby. I tried to lift my hand and realized I was chained to a tree as well, and so was the white wolf. Except his head was slumped over, his chest not moving.

"Aron," Driscoll pleaded. "Please wake up!"

Oh, not Aron.

"Unfortunately, I don't think he'll be waking."

My gaze snapped to the voice, and I stiffened. The queen of the frost court stood before me, wearing a gold gown with thick long sleeves, embroidered with flowers and vines. A white cloak was draped over her shoulders. And in her hand, she held . . . an axe.

One that shimmered with blue dust. I tilted my head. I'd seen that axe in drawings. In ancient texts. Spirit Frost's axe.

My mouth dropped open. "How do you have that? How did you

find us?" I shot a glance at Maverick, who shoved against the iron chains wrapped around his chest.

"You're asking all the wrong questions, White Rabbit." She used an inflection on my name like it was an inquiry.

"How did you find out?"

She twirled a finger in the air. "Your little chest of trinkets that you left in Mr. Von Lucas's office. That and quite a few of your servants coming forward detailing your strange outings."

She tsked. "Thank you for delivering her, Maverick," she said to my husband.

His jaw went slack and his wild eyes found me. "No, no, I would never betray you, Emory. I swear, I was going to tell you, but then so much was happening, and—"

I shook my head. "Maverick, it's okay. I trust you. I know you wouldn't betray me like that." I turned my glare on the frost queen as she sent an amused look Maverick's way.

"You and the white rabbit? Really? And you had so much potential."

"She's my wife," he growled. "And if you so much as lay a hand on her . . ."

"You know you're going to prison for this," the frost queen said with a bored sigh. "For harboring a criminal. Marrying one. My goodness." The queen put a frail hand to her chest. "I don't even know if we have a punishment for such a thing." She shot him a smile. "But we'll come up with one."

She heaved the axe into the snowy ground. "Or maybe I should reward you for delivering the white rabbit and the white wolf to me. Both have been a thorn in my side." She tapped her chin. "No, actually, I think I'm going to have to kill you all because of the secrets you've discovered. We can't have any of them getting out."

"Secrets?" I echoed.

The wind whistled an eerie tune.

She leaned forward, a conspiratorial gleam in her hard blue eyes. "It's been difficult keeping them to myself all these years. Achieving such greatness when I had absolutely no chance of inheriting the throne prior to the Shadow War. Not when I was the king's lowly sister."

"What did you do?" Maverick asked.

Annalee and Driscoll watched with matching expressions of horror on their faces.

"Not much, really." A gust of wind lifted her white cloak. "It was very unfortunate that the king and queen of the frost court were killed fighting in the war. I wasn't next in line, of course. No, that would've been the king's younger brother." She tsked. "Then he died in an unfortunate accident. Poison," she whispered with a conspiratorial wink. "Truly tragic. Then his wife died, trampled by my unruly horse, then his daughter, and well, that left only one more obstacle before I could take over."

She lifted the axe and pointed it directly at the white wolf. All of our gazes turned to his lifeless form.

"Aronark. He was the youngest brother of the king. Next in line for the throne, but he was off fighting in the Shadow War. I'd hoped the war would kill him, but I heard reports that he lived. I felt hopeless after all my hard work killing everyone else off. I wasn't sure what I could do until I found this axe. Hidden in the depths of the frost castle itself, which I was exploring one day, hoping to get some answers to my problem. Embedded in a block of ice that only a wielder of royal frost blood could break. I fit that description, so I took it."

My blood ran cold. "And what did you do with the axe?"

"You just came from it." A cruel smile spread across her face as she pointed behind us, where the wall between the star and frost court had been blasted apart by the white wolf, a gaping hole in it. "I brought the axe to the border between the frost court and the star court, and I knew that I could solve everyone's problems while also solving my own. I could create a border that trapped all that wreckage and horror left from the Shadow War, while also trapping the one person who still stood between me and the crown."

"A prince?" Driscoll echoed, gaze bouncing between the frost queen and the white wolf. "Aron is a prince?"

Maverick and I locked gazes, my mind reeling.

"Why didn't you just kill him with the axe?" Driscoll asked.

"That would've meant I had to actually find him. It would've taken time. It would've meant entering the destroyed star court." The frost queen put a hand to her chest. "I think not. Not when the solution was so much simpler."

Maverick's jaw locked. "So you used the magic of the axe to create a border, then what? How did you explain that to the other rulers?"

"I told them I took care of it for them. Gained me so much favor with those idiots. They practically fell at my feet in gratitude, and all of them approved my ascension to the throne." She raised her chin. "They didn't ask any questions. Why would they?"

She was right. Everything got swept under the rug. That was what they did. What we all spent years doing. Spirits below.

"I didn't anticipate the magic of the axe being so strong. I swung that axe straight into the ground, right where I wanted it to break apart and create a chasm, one so far and wide, so deep, nothing would be able to cross it. It was meant to spread all the way around the star court. That's what I told the magic to do." Her eyes grew distant. "Then I saw the most wondrous thing unfold. The axe didn't just create a border. It created an entire new world right before my eyes. It transformed all the carnage, turned survivors into creatures I'd never seen before. Trees shrank; they grew eyes. Flowers shot up into the sky. Plants grew mouths. And instead of a chasm, an actual border grew from the ground. Taller and taller until I could no longer see anything at all." She shrugged. "Truth be told, I figured either that magic would kill everyone or they would kill each other." She pointed a finger at the white wolf. "Imagine my surprise when sixty years later, he appeared. In a village near the Glacier Mountains. A huntsman saw the wolf shift to a man, a man that looked suspiciously like Prince Aronark, before changing back to his wolf form. The huntsman came straight to me, thank the spirits."

So Aron had shifted while he was in Fyriad. It must've been so quick that he didn't remember.

"That's why you wanted me to hunt him." Maverick's eyes widened.

"You're simply the best when it comes to finding unfindable things." She tipped her head. "Except for her. But I wouldn't work with the white rabbit." She pointed at Maverick. "You I could control." She shook her head in my direction. "Her? She was too unpredictable. Too good at finding objects meant to stay buried. Unearthing secrets that I was afraid she'd start sharing. I keep a tight rein on the academy for a reason. I can control the narrative."

"All of this for power?" I asked, voice shaking.

"Well, now you know." She tapped her chin. "Though I do wonder what would happen if I used the axe again?" She smacked her lips. "The white wolf destroyed this part of the border, and that won't do."

"But you don't know the consequences," I said. "Look at what using the axe did the first time. All you meant to do was create a chasm, but the magic did so much more. It had lasting consequences."

The queen didn't seem remotely bothered by my words. "Sounds like a little adventure, hm? What'll the magic do this time? As long as I keep my crown, I don't give a damn."

"You're, like, really old," Driscoll said, and the queen shot him a scathing look. "Regal but old. I'm just saying, maybe your time would be better spent knitting or, you know, dying . . ." He mumbled the last word.

"Driscoll," I hissed.

"She hurt Aron," he snapped, voice hard in a way I'd never heard from him.

Hopefully all she'd done was hurt Aron. I chanced a glance at the white wolf, still not moving. He should've moved by now. Something. Anything.

The queen shoved the axe in my direction, and Maverick struggled against the iron chaining him to a tree. "Don't hurt her, Your Majesty. We can figure this out."

She waved her hand. "I had hope for you. But you're too far gone, Bone Collector."

His eyes widened at that.

She scoffed. "I figured it out recently. Thought maybe you were moonlighting as him to catch the white rabbit. Clever, really. Except you never caught her, did you?"

Annalee whimpered from beside her brother.

"Enough talking," the frost queen said. "Time to see what the axe will do." She raised it high, ready to cleave it down into the earth when a buzzing sound hit the air.

The queen stiffened, axe hovering above her head. "What is that?"

Before any of us could answer, the blood beetles raced through the opened border, past us, and swarmed the frost queen. She screamed over the sounds of flesh tearing, blood squelching, and bones crunching. The axe dropped to the ground with a resounding thud, a crackle of blue light and shimmers spreading from its sharpened edge.

"We have to get the axe before the magic spreads!" I yelled. "Iron. We need iron to stop it."

Did iron even stop divine magic? I had no idea. Also, we were all still chained to trees. The beetles continued to eat the queen as her screams filled the air. I looked away, unable to watch, until the squelching sounds finally died down and the beetles lifted in the air. Bile rose in my throat at the sight they left behind: the frost queen's dress was torn to shreds, nothing but organs, bones, and blood painting the ground.

The axe's magic sizzled in a zigzag line, icy blue with shimmering blue dust flying up in the air in big swaths. The ground cracked in two, a thunderous fissure splitting the air between us so that I was on one side with the white wolf and the axe, while Annalee, Maverick, and Driscoll were on the other side, all of us getting farther and farther apart as the chasm in the ground grew.

"What do we do?" I screamed over the noise.

By now, the beetles had lowered to the ground, feasting on the bloody remains of the frost queen. My stomach twisted as I struggled against the chains, watching the magic continuing on its war path toward the Wilds, the blue light continuing to cleave the ground in half. I had no idea what the frost queen had intended with this magic, what she instructed it to do. Maybe this time it wouldn't just be the star court that got destroyed. Maybe the magic wouldn't stop until the entire world was broken in half by it, everything in its path destroyed.

"Annalee!' I screamed as loud as I could over the sound of the earth cracking between us. "The beetles! Can you get the beetles to eat through my chains?"

Her eyes widened, but she must've been able to read my lips because she nodded, a fierce determination settling in her drawn brows and raised chin.

She clucked her tongue, and the beetles stopped their feasting as they turned and saw her. She mouthed something. Maybe she was speaking, but I couldn't hear her over the crunching and splitting and roaring. Whatever she said, the beetles must've heard, because they flew straight toward me.

Maverick shouted over the hum of their buzzing, probably telling Annalee to call them off, and I prayed to Spirit Frost that the beetles didn't devour me like they had the queen. I just needed to get loose and get to that axe and somehow undo whatever the frost queen had done. Clearly this magic was beyond powerful, beyond unpredictable. None of us had the capacity to wield it.

The beetles surrounded me, and now all I could see were their blue and black bodies, feel their sticky small feet on me, the flutter of their paper-thin wings against my skin. Oh, this was a bad idea. Bad, bad, bad. I faintly heard a crunching sound, but the world was literally busting open, so I couldn't be sure where it was coming from.

All of a sudden, the beetles flew backward, and the chains fell from my chest. I stared in disbelief. They'd done it. They'd listened to Annalee and freed me. The swarm returned to their feast.

I didn't waste any time, grabbing a piece of the iron chain and running with it toward the axe. I reached out to lift the axe from the ground, but blue dust swirled up and formed a mighty jaw that snapped at me.

I jumped back, and the blue dust dropped to the axe. The magic continued on its warpath behind me, sawing the ground in half. So many innocent creatures would die if we didn't stop this soon. The entire star court would be beyond saving.

The white wolf stirred, and my heart skipped a beat. I ran to him, snow kicking up behind me. I didn't know what my plan was, but maybe the wolf could help in some way.

I grabbed a fistful of his fur, falling to my knees, and the wolf reacted immediately, red eyes snapping open, canines bared, a low growl rumbling from his throat. He gnashed his teeth at me, but I didn't back away. The wolf looked down as if just realizing he was chained to a tree. He growled again, this time, shoving forward. The iron blasted into pieces that flew in every direction as the white wolf freed himself. I ducked to avoid getting hit, shielding my face.

"Run!"

I didn't know who yelled it, but I was guessing it was my husband.

"Run!" the voice boomed again.

I looked across what was now a canyon at Driscoll, still chained to the tree. He gave a firm nod, and I nodded back.

"Listen, Aron," I said, turning and staring the wolf in its red eyes. "I know you're in there somewhere, and I know you can come back to us because we need you right now. I think you might be the only one who can pick up that axe and stop this."

He'd been immune to all our magic. Immune to that wall. Maybe he was immune to this magic as well.

The wolf growled again, backing me toward the edge of the canyon. I fell onto my butt, looking up at him as saliva dripped down onto my cheek.

"I know what it's like to feel trapped," I said, voice trembling. "I know what it's like to feel like there's no way out. But when I was at my lowest, you know what I did? I persisted. I couldn't leave my marriage. Just like you can't leave the wolf behind. But I could still be me. I could still carve out the life I wanted for myself, even if it wasn't what I imagined. And by doing that, it led to me being fully free."

The wolf's red eyes flashed, and he lowered his head, mouth inches from my neck. His warm breath puffed onto my face.

"Emory!" Maverick screamed.

"Driscoll believes in you," I said, ignoring Maverick. "And that's good enough for me."

The white wolf's eyes dimmed. My heart hammered as the magic continued to split the ground far ahead. Something had to happen, and soon.

The white wolf blinked, and when his eyelids lifted, his eyes had changed . . . to blue.

Relief flooded me, and I collapsed onto the edge of the cliff while Driscoll, Annalee, and Maverick cheered from the other side. I dug my hands into the snow, trying to ground myself, to remind myself that this fight was far from over. We still had to stop the damage this weapon could do. I glanced behind me at the canyon, wondering how far the magic would stretch. Right now I could still see the land cracking and splitting in the distance, trees, mushrooms, entire hills disappearing in its wake.

"Emory?" a voice asked.

My head snapped forward, the white wolf gone and Aron standing over me, completely naked.

"The axe!" I pointed to it. "Can you grab it? Can you tell it stop or . . . something?"

It sounded so stupid when I said it out loud, but Aron turned his head, a slight frown to his lips. He marched over to the axe and pulled it from the ground. The blue dust didn't fight him, didn't attack. Instead it swirled around Aron like it was part of him.

He stared at the axe, then looked at the canyon separating us from the others, down to the splitting land far ahead. His gaze moved to the chain I held, the iron chain, and he ran to me, grabbing it from my hand and wrapping it around the axe with swift, tight loops.

The rumbling came to a stop, and the ground quit shaking beneath me. In the distance, the land gave a final quake, then stilled. The magic had been stopped. Everything had stopped. But the damage was done, and Bellamy had an equally dangerous weapon that she was taking to the shadow court.

We'd stopped the threat for now. But I feared at this point it no longer mattered.

Chapter Sixty

MAVERICK

A fire crackled in the middle of the small hut we'd found nearby. Abandoned and likely built in the Old World if the triangular shape was any indication. Driscoll had used his magic to make a tree fall over the large canyon. We'd taken a painstakingly long time to cross the tree and get to the other side to reunite with Emory and Aron.

Now we sat around the fire, the logs of the structure peaking over us so that the little dwelling resembled a cone. Old mattresses lay around the edges, full of dust and who knew what else. But none of that mattered. We'd needed a space where we could process everything that just happened.

Aron was now dressed. Thank the spirits because Driscoll had a hard time functioning when the wolf man was naked.

"So the frost queen was responsible for the Wilds?" Aron asked, blond brows pinched together.

"Yes and no," I said, bobbing my head back and forth while Annalee sat next to me, chewing on some of the rabbit meat Aron had caught and cooked for us. "She intended to trap you in there. That was it. That was what she commanded Spirit Frost's axe to do—create a canyon around the court. But the magic warped. It did something far greater, far more unpredictable." Emory sat on my other side, leaning her head on my shoulder.

When I'd thought she was going to die, nothing else had mattered. Not my job. Not my future. Not the world literally splitting in two. I'd just wanted to get to her and make sure she was safe. It had been the most terrifying experience of my life and made me want to hold her tight and never let go.

Driscoll frowned across the fire. "But I've seen another spirit's weapon in use, and it didn't do that."

We all looked at him.

"Spirit Water's trident. The seafolk used it right in front of me." He waved a hand. "Okay, well, technically not right in front of me since I was hiding out in the pirate lord's cabin—" He stopped. "It's a long story. The point is, they used it and it didn't do what that axe did. It did what they wanted it to. The magic worked."

Aron grabbed a chunk of rabbit off the spit that now lay on the ground, popping it in his mouth and chewing while he mulled over Driscoll's words. "The seafolk are said to have been created by Spirit Water's magic. I'm a product of Spirit Frost's magic. Maybe you cannot wield those weapons or use their magic unless you are somehow tied to the spirits who made them."

I stroked my jaw, now bearded more than stubbled. "That makes sense, actually."

Emory lifted her head from my shoulder. "And that means Bellamy won't be able to use the lightning bolt to kill Spirit Shadow. She's going to unleash dangerous magic just like the frost queen did. She's going to get herself and her brothers killed."

"Unless Spirit Shadow gets the bolt from her," Annalee said.

I felt the shiver that rolled through Emory at my sister's words. I didn't actually know which of those scenarios would be worse.

"Speaking of the frost queen, what are we going to do?" Aron folded his hands together in front of him. "From what I saw, she was nothing but a pile of blood and guts."

I still couldn't believe how those beetles had devoured her. The same beetles who played at our wedding, for spirits' sake.

Emory sent a curious look at Aron. "How much do you remember from that whole encounter?"

He sighed. "If you're asking if I know I'm the prince of the frost court, then yes, I do."

Driscoll gaped at him. "You knew this whole time? And you didn't tell us?"

Aron shrugged. "I didn't see how it was relevant."

"What?" Driscoll shrieked. "It is very, very relevant. You're not just Hot Wolf Man. You're Hot Wolf Prince. King, really. That crown belongs to you."

"I never thought it did," Aron said. "Or should. I thought because of what I'd become I wouldn't make a good king. That I was too dangerous with my unpredictable shifting." He met Driscoll's gaze. "Then I met you. And for whatever reason, you believed in me. Not even El trusted me in my wolf form. Whenever I started to shift, we'd had a plan where she would put me to sleep until I shifted back. You didn't fear the beast."

Driscoll looked away, twiddling his hands. It was fun watching him squirm.

"There's the frost queen's husband," Emory said. "And their son. But with you alive, you have true claim to that crown. Though it's going to be hard explaining what happened to everyone."

"We have proof." I pointed to Spirit Frost's axe. "There is a huge canyon in between the star and frost court now."

"What if they think we did it?" Driscoll asked. "Then killed the frost queen?"

"What would be our motive?" Emory asked. "To get some random man onto the throne whom we have no allegiance to?" She shook her head. "It makes sense that the frost queen did it. It aligns with all her actions over the years. She clearly wanted to keep things from changing. It'll be easier than you think to convince everyone."

"Creatures will start coming over from the Wilds," Aron said. "And they're not adapted to this world. They might be dangerous. Misunderstood."

Another huge problem. I rubbed my temples, and Emory pressed a light kiss to my cheek. A reminder that she was here, by my side, no matter what.

"I can help," Annalee piped up. "Let's do what you and Bellamy did so many years ago. Invite them to stay in the frost castle, and I can help them assimilate into society. I can show them how to survive. I can teach elementals how to interact with them."

I looked over at her, my smile growing wide. "You know, that might just be perfect for you."

"Then you're hired," Aron said. "My first official act as the unofficial king."

Annalee was glowing. The irony of all of this was that our father would delight in knowing his daughter was working for the king of the frost court. Yet Annalee couldn't care less. She never had cared about impressing him. She was staying true to herself like she always had. I looked over at Emory. Same as my wife. These two women on either side of me were the most inspiring I knew.

"What about you?" Aron said, looking at me. "You were the frost queen's historical advisor. If I become king, would you be mine as well?"

I glanced over at Emory, and she smiled. "If that's what you want, then you should do it."

I sighed. I was tired of work ruling my life. "I think I might take a step back. Do a little treasure hunting instead." That was when I felt most alive. When I was outside of the classroom, outside of the castle walls. "But I can think of someone who would be a much better fit." I nodded toward Emory.

Aron's blue eyes snapped to her. "I would be honored to have you."

"I'll think about it," she said, then looked at me. "We have a lot to figure out right now."

Branches cracked outside our little abode, and all of us stiffened as boots crunched in the snow. Emory summoned ice daggers while Annalee and I summoned our fire magic, the flames hovering over our palms.

None of us moved as a shadow stretched into the space. No one even breathed. Then a woman burst through. I tilted my head. I recognized her from before we'd fallen into the Wilds.

"Leoni!" Driscoll said, standing.

The short woman barreled into him, wrapping her arms tight around his waist. "You're alive. Oh, thank the Seven Spirits. You're alive." She sobbed.

Driscoll patted her on the back. "Yep, I'm here. In the flesh."

"I'm so sorry." She looked up at him through teary eyes. "About what I said right before you fell into that hole. I was just upset because I thought we were becoming friends. Really good friends. Best friends, actually. And it seemed like it was so easy for you to just leave me, leave our mission. I've been scouring these mountains for you for weeks, and then I stumbled upon this area and saw the firelight, and I hoped—" She stopped, her chest heaving. "I think you're my soulmate," she burst out.

Driscoll's eyes darted to Aron. He scratched his head. "Uh, well this is awkward. I thought you knew I was really into, um, well . . . penises."

Leoni rolled her eyes. "Platonic soulmate, you idiot. Like my best friend in soulmate form, if that makes sense."

"Oh!" Driscoll's eyes widened. "Yes, totally. I love that for us."

"So you forgive me?" Leoni asked. "For being completely awful and a terrible friend?"

"You weren't either of those things," Driscoll said, "but yes, I forgive you."

I leaned over to Emory. "Are they always like this?"

"From what I can tell?" She pursed her lips. "Yes."

"We really got lucky that she didn't fall with us," I whispered. I wasn't sure I could handle all the drama between these two.

Leoni pushed Driscoll at arm's length, then her gaze swept around to the rest of us.

"And you made some friends." She raised a brow at Annalee and Aron. Then her gaze landed on Emory and me as she took in how close we sat, the way my arm was wrapped around my wife. "Are you two a thing? Because I thought you hated each other."

"Oh, they're definitely a thing," Driscoll said. "Like an obsessed-with-each-other, totally-nerdy-together, married thing."

"Married?" Leoni 's eyes widened. "What happened?" Then she saw the axe propped up against the wall, and her face paled. "Is that . . . ?"

"Spirit Frost's axe?" Driscoll asked. "Yes, yes, it is. We have a lot to catch up on. Might as well sit down and get comfy."

Leoni sat in a stunned silence after we finished telling her everything that had happened since she got separated from us.

"Just let her process," Driscoll said as we waited for her to say something. Anything. "She'll say something." He gave a nervous laugh. "I think."

He squinted at Leoni, who sat next to him, then he waved a hand in front of her face.

She swatted it away. "Stop that."

"And she's back," Driscoll said cheerfully.

"Well, it's clear what has to happen," Leoni said finally.

It didn't seem that clear, but I was interested in what she had to say. Leoni seemed practical, a woman who took charge. I respected that.

"What?" Driscoll asked.

"I'm interested to know as well." Aron leaned forward, the shadows from the fire dancing across his pale skin.

She pointed at Aron. "Well, you have to become king and fix the mess the frost queen made by storming out of the conclave and refusing to work with the other courts to defeat Spirit Shadow." She pointed at Annalee. "You need to corral all the creatures from the Wilds and bring them to the castle." She pointed to Emory and Maverick. "You both need to start piecing together what in the bloody water happened so many years ago to the Seven Spirits." She glanced over at Driscoll and smirked. "And you need to go live happily ever after with your king."

Driscoll squirmed, while Aron, as usual, looked completely unabashed.

"I would like that," Aron said.

Driscoll cleared his throat, nudging Leoni. "And what about you?"

She looked at him like it was obvious. "I have to go after Bellamy and stop her from using that lightning bolt."

"I'm coming with you," Driscoll said quickly. He shot an apologetic look at Aron. "We started this journey together, shorty, and now we're going to end it together."

"How do you know this is the end?" Annalee asked.

Driscoll shrugged. "Just a feeling." He grabbed Leoni's hand. "I have to finish this. Plus, I can't let you go back to the shadow court by yourself."

Leoni's gaze softened. "You don't have to do that. It's really okay."

"He should go," Aron said. "Bellamy knows him. She'll be more receptive to listening to someone familiar. She doesn't trust easily."

Driscoll let out a long breath, and I wondered if he was more relieved than he was letting on that he was going on yet another adventure. He might've griped about all this, but I suspected he liked it.

"We should leave now." Leoni stood. "It sounds like Bellamy has quite the head start."

"I was afraid you'd say that." Driscoll groaned dramatically. "I guess a warm bed tonight was too much to ask for."

"You really think you need to leave right now?" Emory asked, coming to a stand. The rest of us followed suit.

"We can't wait," Leoni said. "Not when the fate of the literal world hangs in the balance. We have to get to Bellamy before she makes a huge mistake."

"I mean, I'd take a warm bed tonight, but she's the boss." Driscoll jabbed a thumb at Leoni.

Emory surged forward and hugged Driscoll tight, then gave Leoni a hug. "Come back to us, okay?"

He nodded, swallowing.

"Go save Bellamy." Aron stepped up to Driscoll, putting his hands on his shoulders. "And when you do come back, I'd like to court you. If you want."

"Yes," Driscoll squeaked. "Totally."

Leoni smirked and crossed her arms. "Okay, loverboy. Let's go."

We waved our final goodbyes as she pulled him from the dwelling and they disappeared from sight.

Chapter Sixty-One

EMORY

"It's so quiet," I said as Maverick packed up the final items from his office. "Why is it so quiet?"

"Because Driscoll's not here." My husband stood in front of the bookshelves, back to me as he plucked each book off the shelves and placed them in wooden crates on the floor.

My husband. It would never get old.

"Oh, right." I leaned against his desk. "That does make sense."

He turned, giving me a view of his handsome face, his tight grey trousers and black button-up, tucked in and showcasing his muscled chest and arms. And the sleeves rolled up to his elbows, a sight that always made my knees go weak.

His eyes glinted, and he stepped forward, lifting me up onto his desk as he wedged himself between my legs.

"Professor Von Lucas," I said. "Are you trying to seduce me?"

"Maybe." He tilted his head down, his lips teasingly close. "Is it working?"

I gave him a playful shove, then looked over my shoulder. "It would be if there weren't students in the hallway gawking at us."

I wiggled my fingers at a few of the students who peeked through the little window in his door. They quickly stood at attention and scurried away. "Are you sure you want to quit your job?" I asked, turning back to him. "It's been your entire life for years."

He pressed a kiss to my forehead, still pinning me to the desk, his arm wrapped behind my back. "That's the whole point, little rabbit. I don't want it to be my whole life." His lips skimmed down my jawline. "Not when there are so many other things I'd rather be doing."

I threw my head back. Screw it. If students wanted to watch, they could go ahead. Get a nice show.

"Like what?" I asked breathlessly.

He moved his hand under my long skirt and to my inner thigh. He palmed my already wet panties, pupils now black orbs. "I could show you." I kissed him, and he lay me down on his desk, leaning with me, his body sinking into mine.

He withdrew his hand and all that delicious heat with it. He glanced down and frowned, straightening as he stared at his palm.

"What?" I sat up. "What's wrong?"

"We're going to find this dust on us for the rest of our lives, aren't we?" He faced his palm toward me, covered in black shimmers.

We'd just arrived back from our trek across Fyriad yesterday, and Maverick had wasted no time coming straight here to quit his job and collect his belongings.

Today we'd have to face so much. The entire court. We'd have to reveal Aron, rightful king of Fyriad, the frost queen's deception. We'd have to reveal the truth about the Wilds.

Maverick would speak to the queen's council later, made up of all her advisers. Hopefully they'd be receptive to what he had to say. I was going to reach out to Princess Poppy, whom I trusted more than any of the other leaders. I needed her on my side before Aron called yet another conclave to discuss everything that had happened. If the people accepted him as king, that was.

I stared at the dust on Maverick's hand, then my gaze caught on that scarf, the one I'd used so long ago to bind his wound, peeking out of one of the crates.

"Maverick," I said slowly.

"Ah." He stepped back. "I know that look. The moment's over, isn't it?"

"Do you think it's possible the dust is connected to the Seven Spirits? I know we've talked about it before. But I'm starting to think that each dust color might represent a different spirit?" I nodded toward his hand. "Black for Spirit Shadow. Blue for Spirit Frost." I thought of The Book of Yaraho, the red dust that we'd blown off it. "Red for Spirit Fire."

Maverick took another step back, and I straightened my skirt, still perched on the edge of his desk. "That would explain why the entire star court was covered in that black dust. Spirit Shadow ripped through it, left remnants of it. You think that dust was from him."

"Every time I've found an artifact connected to the spirits, there's been that peculiar shimmery dust on it." I shook my head. "I can't believe I didn't realize it before." I thought back to when I'd first really taken notice of it. In the crypt. "It was coating the walls and the floor of that crypt Spirit Shadow had been freed from." I wrinkled my nose. "But, Mav, there was something else."

"What?" he asked.

"I could've sworn there was another color of dust mixed in with the black in that crypt where Spirit Shadow escaped from. I didn't think much of it at the time, but now . . ."

"Okay . . ." he said, then crossed his arms. "Do you think another spirit got set free along with Spirit Shadow? That there were two spirits trapped in one tomb?"

I bit the inside of my cheek, mulling over the theory. "I think that's a possibility. But which spirit? And why wouldn't they have shown themselves by now?"

Maverick swore.

I hopped off the desk. "I'll have to tell Aron about this, and we'll have to do more digging. I could be wrong about all of it."

He raised his eyebrows. "An extended honeymoon, maybe?'

"We never had our first honeymoon." I rolled my eyes.

"Oh, I seem to remember our first honeymoon vividly, Mrs. Von Lucas. It involved a lightning bolt and a disturbed older man."

"Well, this one will be a little different. More romantic." I trailed a finger down his chest. "Camping under the stars. Visiting all seven courts and collecting any evidence we can to support our theory. Making love every single night. And some mornings. And some afternoons."

"When do we leave?" His eyes flashed with heated desire.

I laughed as he drew me from the desk and into him. "As soon as possible. I'm sure Aron will agree that, as his historical advisor, this is of the utmost importance for me to focus on."

"Oh I'm sure he will." Maverick pressed his lips to mine, a deep kiss that made my toes curl. "Maybe just leave out the making love part."

I swatted his arm, but he only held me tighter. The future was uncertain. It was scary. But with this man by my side, it was also full of hope. And that was all I needed for now.

Epilogue

EMORY

"**M**averick, where are you taking me?"

A blindfold was fastened around my eyes, blocking any view I might have of the space we stood in. I sniffed the air. Must and mold and a hint of snow.

"Are you ready?" he whispered into my ear.

"Yes," I said, exasperated.

He'd woken me up this morning, blindfolded me, and very sternly told me that I was not to peek or ask any questions. We were supposed to leave soon, back to the Wilds to investigate those crypts where Spirit Shadow—and possibly another spirit—had escaped.

Annalee was going to travel with us and corral any creatures who might want to voluntarily come back to the frost court with her, while Maverick and I would travel on to wherever our investigation led us. But first, he'd said we needed to make a stop.

At this mystery place that I still had yet to see. It had only taken a few minutes to walk here from Maverick's apartment in Karstad, but I was brimming with curiosity.

He untied the blindfold, revealing a dim, dank space filled with cobwebs, dust, and quite a few rodents scurrying across the scratched wooden floorboards.

I glanced over at Maverick, who looked uncharacteristically nervous. "What is this?" I asked, running my finger along broken shelves that lined the walls. The wood was splintered, some of the shelves hanging diagonally, others broken clean in half.

"Right now?" Maverick asked. "It's a wreck. But one day? I hope it can be our museum."

I froze, finger pressed into the shelf.

"I hope it's okay that I bought this place." He swore under his breath. "I should've asked first, shouldn't I? This is one of those marriage things where I definitely needed to check with you before doing something so big. I just thought—"

I whirled, throwing my arms around his neck. "I love it. So much."

He pushed me at arm's length, studying my face. "Are you just saying that? Because if you don't love it, we can sell it."

I walked to the middle of the room and lifted my arms. "Right here can be a display case full of all the texts we've found over the years and translated versions." I walked to the opposite wall. "Right here? We could have an exhibit." I spread out my hands. "Royals from the Old World. I'd love to do a comparison between the royals of then and the royals of now."

His lips quirked.

I ran to the back of the room. "And here is where we can display everything we have connected to the Seven Spirits." I gasped. "We could even collect some of the dust that we suspect is tied to each of them, keep it in little jars." I spun around. "We can have workshops for those who are interested in learning more about being a historian. We can have story time for children." I squealed. "There's so much potential here."

Maverick stared at me, his copper eyes following my every move.

"What?" I asked. "Too much?"

"Never," he said fiercely. "I'm just glad you love it. I know this was your dream. I wanted to help you fulfill it."

No one had ever cared about my dreams. No one had ever encouraged them or even entertained them. But here was this man, not just caring about my dreams. But actually willing to help me achieve them.

"It's amazing, Maverick." Tears welled in my eyes. "As soon as we get back from our journey, we'll get to work on it." I leaned against a shelf. "Do you think Aron will be okay without us?"

Maverick frowned. He'd spoken to the council just yesterday, all of them with mixed reactions. Neither the queen's husband or son were fit to rule. She'd married a man with no spine, someone who would just follow along with no ambition for power—and she'd raised a son in the same vein. She hadn't wanted anyone to succeed her. I was starting to think she thought she'd find a way to live and rule forever. It was truly bizarre. Demented. Still, the council hadn't been completely sold on Aron. They believed he was Aronark. He met with them and told them his entire story, and he knew things about the former king, the royal family, that no one could have known other than him.

He was also a shapeshifting wolf. That was hard for them to wrap their minds around. Overall, the meeting had been positive but not decisive.

We needed the other rulers on board to get Aron on the throne. He'd be an amazing king. Exactly what this court needed as we sped toward an uncertain future.

"I know that look," Maverick said. "What's going on in your head right now?"

I bit my lip. "I think before we go to the Wilds, we have to go see Princess Poppy."

His eyebrows shot up.

"We have to tell her where Leoni and Driscoll went. We have to tell her about Aron. She'll believe me. She'll be on our side. And she can call another conclave so the other rulers can ratify Aron's position as king. If all the rulers agree, they can bypass the council."

Maverick nodded slowly. "You're right."

"I know," I said. "I think that's our priority right now. The frost court needs a strong leader. Before we go to the Wilds, I want to make sure Aron gets that chance. He grew up in the castle. He grew up watching his own father lead as king, then his brother. He was the one who ran the Wilds, for spirits' sake."

Maverick let out a quiet laugh.

"You know it's true. He kept El in line. He was the one who guided her. She might have been the queen of hearts. But he was the king. He just didn't want to admit it. Was in denial."

Maverick tucked a strand of hair behind my ear. "Okay, then. To Valoris we go. We'll meet with Princess Poppy. We can talk to the council, let them know we're bringing Aron with us. The council can rule temporarily until we figure this situation out."

I sighed heavily. "Not a very quiet start to our marriage, huh?"

"Is that really what you want, Mrs. Von Lucas? A quiet, calm life?"

I peered at him. "Would you give it to me if I did?"

"Haven't you figured it out by now, little rabbit?"

He pressed a kiss to my lips.

"I'd give you anything."

My heart stuttered. Those were words I never thought I'd hear from anyone. Not after a lifetime of pushing people away, hoarding my secrets like stolen treasure. But I didn't have to do that with Maverick. It was the most free I'd ever felt in my life.

"No." I began walking toward him. "I don't want a quiet life. I want adventure. I want passion. I want excitement."

In the end, the life I'd always wanted was the life I'd gotten. Maverick reached out his hand and we threaded our fingers together, walking out of our museum and onto the snowy streets of Fyriad toward our next adventure.

***

BONUS SCENE: If you want more of Maverick and Emory's epic love story, then click here to get this spicy bonus scene or visit www.teeharlowe.com/subscribe-for-scbc!

NEXT IN SERIES: Click here to read Beasts of Briar now or get it on Amazon!

About the Author

Tee Harlowe writes fantasy romance focused on strong and determined women. After years spent traveling, Tee settled down to start writing her own adventures and is now living out her dream. When not writing, Tee can be found wrangling her children, attempting to bake, and losing to her husband at pretty much every game they play.